A Thin Witchline Between Love & Hate

T.L. Brown

Copyright © 2022 Tracy Brown-Simmons

All rights reserved.

The characters and events portrayed in this book are fictitious. Any similarity to real persons, living or dead, business establishments, events, or locales is coincidental and not intended by the author.

No part of this book may be reproduced, or stored in a retrieval system, or transmitted in any form or by any means, electronic, mechanical, photocopying, recording, or otherwise, without express written permission of the publisher.

ISBN: 979-8-9859503-1-1

First Edition: March 2022

Book Cover Design by ebooklaunch.com
Created / printed in the United States of America

Praise for *A Thin Witchline Between Love & Hate*

"T.L. Brown's best writing yet! *A Thin Witchline Between Love & Hate* is sexy, suspenseful, and scary AF! I'm holding my breath for the next installment."

- Jennifer Brasington-Crowley, author of the Raven Song Series and the Stillwaters Series

"*A Thin Witchline Between Love & Hate* doesn't shy away from difficult subjects, graphic scenes, or mature content, but nothing in the book feels gratuitous. Everything is dealt with in completely believable ways, and the characters are complex and feel true to life. I can't wait for the next instalment!"

- Saffron Amatti, author of the Lucas Rathbone Mysteries

Thank you!

Books in the Bellerose Witchline Series

A Thin Witchline Between Love & Hate (Book 1)
Crossing the Witchline (Book 2, Coming in 2022)

Contents

Title Page

Copyright

Praise for A Thin Witchline Between Love & Hate

Books in the Bellerose Witchline Series

Dedication

Prologue	1
Chapter 1	8
Chapter 2	33
Chapter 3	52
Chapter 4	75
Chapter 5	91
Chapter 6	109
Chapter 7	124
Chapter 8	151
Chapter 9	168

Chapter 10	197
Chapter 11	219
Chapter 12	240
Chapter 13	265
Chapter 14	287
Chapter 15	318
Chapter 16	343
Chapter 17	368
Chapter 18	391
Chapter 19	418
Chapter 20	442
Chapter 21	462
Chapter 22	482
Chapter 23	503
Chapter 24	528
Chapter 25	550
Epilogue	578
Acknowledgements	585
Find the Author Online	587
Other Books by the Author	589
About the Author	595

Prologue

The end of Emily's story.

... I turned to see Rabbit and his men trading punches with the three gunmen. From the inside of the tent, Lucie clutched the Crimson Stone in her left hand. The blackening blood-red glow she wore on her skin rolled over her body as Templeton and Sebastian circled each other at the opening of the tent. Templeton's eyes were colorless; his body tensed as Sebastian went in for another strike.

As Sebastian attacked, I heard glass breaking throughout the complex as warehouse windows shattered and floodlights sizzled out. The air smelled like burnt matches. At first, I thought the Rabbits set off another explosion, then I realized it wasn't a bomb that blew.

It was Lucie.

Gripping the Crimson Stone with both hands, Lucie kept pouring her own energy into it. She crouched; her lips pulled back as she bared her teeth. Something was building and I was afraid.

The firepower in her hands mushroomed and a new shockwave rolled from the witch and across the entire complex. Everyone was knocked to the ground – everyone except for Lucie.

Ears faintly ringing, I placed a hand on my knee and pushed myself back to my feet. Rabbit rose from the ground at my left. His eyes now a solid black, his beat-up hands flexed as he zeroed in on Sebastian. Climbing to his feet on the other side of Rabbit, Templeton warily assessed Lucie.

Sebastian staggered to his feet by the fifth door, battered but laughing. "Lucie, baby, in a different time and place, we were meant for each other."

"I will kill you, Basha," Lucie whispered. She rose from her crouched position, lifting the Stone again and tapping into the power effortlessly. The space inside the tent filled with its crimson glow.

Rabbit's focus flipped to our friend. "Lucie,

that's not who you are. That's not what you do."

She didn't reply.

The energy in the Above door by Sebastian swirled.

"You know what's in the Above?" he taunted her, his hand stroking the energy radiating out of the fifth door. "I do. I've seen it. It's filled with fierce beings, Lucie. They're beautiful beasts. But watch your step. If you anger them, if you break their laws, they'll turn into monsters and rip apart everything in their path. Everything." Sebastian sucked in a deep breath, his eyes rolling up as he quivered. His fingertips continued to dance across the opening of the fifth door. "They'll make powerful allies – or enemies." He suddenly focused on Templeton. "You'll be no match for them."

"Do you know what's in the Below?" Lucie's voice cut into the air. She didn't give Sebastian a chance to answer. "No? Maybe we should find out." Lucie steadily lowered her hand and directed the Crimson Stone's energy toward the bottom of the door. Templeton swiftly crossed to Lucie, anticipating her intention as he slipped behind her. His hand drifted toward her left hip. As his fingers made contact, sparks erupted. His right hand locked onto her other hip and he braced himself. He enveloped Lucie in his powerful blue door travel energy.

"As Above moreso Below," Lucie chanted. A long shadow stretched out from the bottom of the fifth door. The magic sizzled on the ground and the black energy popped upward. As she concentrated, aided by Templeton, the ground split open. A hint of something decaying past the opening wafted up.

"Holy hell, it's the sixth door," I murmured, covering my nose and resisting the impulse to draw away from the gaping hole.

Shocked, Sebastian instead leaned toward the sixth door, gawking into the darkness. He licked his lips. "You opened the Below door," he marveled.

The fury expanded inside my chest as I watched Sebastian. I wanted him to be punished – I wanted him to feel real pain. More than that, he needed to be defeated.

If there were beings who could turn themselves into monsters in the Above, did that mean there were always monsters in the Below? Because 'moreso Below'?

Sebastian was a monster. That's where he belonged. If he remained in the Empire, even if he were to be arrested, there was no guarantee he'd ever pay for what he'd done. The violence may not have always come directly from his own hands, but the blood belonged on him. His hands were dripping with it.

Sebastian needed to be thrown through the door Lucie opened. I edged forward, avoiding Rabbit's touch as he stretched for my arm. I raised energy from the same well I'd developed over the last few days, holding out my right hand palm-first toward Sebastian. My fingers splayed, I pressed my energy out at the depraved Salesman, and he stumbled. Still, he avoided falling.

"You little –" he snarled, spinning around to face me. Hatred rolled off him in thick waves.

"You monster," I shot back, straightening my arm and pressing my energy as hard and fast as I could against his body. It nailed him right in the chest and he floundered backward. I realized he was trying to raise his own door travel energy – a smoky gray swirled around his waist as he reached for the Above door. "Oh, no you don't."

Lucie and Templeton held the sixth door open

as I blasted a third and final surge of my energy at Sebastian. It ripped through his chest, and he screamed as the door travel energy from the Below door snagged his and forcibly yanked him through...

> - Source: *Chapter 24, Doors Wide Open*, by T.L. Brown

∞∞∞

And now... the beginning of Lucie's story.

And the prophecy said:

> *A traveler is born.*
> *The knight protects the light.*
> *Their successor sets fire to the stone.*
> *A shadow is cast out.*

Emily Swift is the traveler. John Templeton is the knight.

And I, Lucie Bellerose, am the light.

I put the Stone to sleep. It's too powerful to remain awake.

The successor has not appeared.
A shadow was cast across my heart.

∞∞∞

And the book of fairy tales revealed:

North, East, West, South.
So as Above, moreso Below.

I closed the fifth and sixth directional doors, the Above and the Below.

I closed the sixth door after my lover was thrown out of this world and into the Below with the other monsters.

There he would die.

Chapter 1

A brownout – that's what I came home to on a bitter night in February. Matar was under a thick blanket of snow and a giant moon hung over the sleepy city in a starless sky. The train from Anwat ran late. As we rumbled into the station, word spread through the passenger cars. To combat the strain on the power grid, the city decided to lower the voltage. Most of us would be returning to frosty homes.

A lot of grumbling followed me off the train as I retrieved my suitcase. I swung the second travel bag over my shoulder and pushed through the crush of people searching for taxis. The moonlight lit up the street with its ghostly glow. Pulling my suitcase behind me, I hurried over the salted sidewalk, lifting my hand high as I neared the edge of the curb. A car rolled up, its tires crunching through the ice-covered slop.

The driver jumped out and stored my luggage as I crawled into the back seat. A trace of halitosis hung in the air inside.

"Where are we heading?" the man asked over his shoulder as he lifted the mic of his radio.

"Clover District. 1106 Autumn Avenue." Pulling my coat tightly around my shivering body, I stared out the window at the unlit buildings while the man prepared to take me home.

The driver repeated the address into the mic, then gestured at the windshield. "Get comfortable. The brownout's making it difficult to get through the city. A lot of the stoplights are emergency blinkers now. Jackass drivers don't know the rules. More than one accident has held me up tonight."

I nodded, knowing the man couldn't see me. I rested my head against the door's dirty window, letting the frosty glass numb my skin. I was sort of glad to be home. It had been well over three months since I up and left everything.

The decision to leave Matar last fall was an abrupt one. One morning I stood in my kitchen staring at the pantry door and thought: I can't do this.

Ironically, I'd only returned to Matar last

spring after studying with a powerful witch in France. Time spent under Guillaume's hand was... *difficult*. He was an extraordinary teacher – his lessons yielded remarkable results. But he was brutal. The choice to learn at his feet was my own. In fact, I had to petition the Congress of Empire Witches for their recommendation of support to even be considered for the opportunity.

Within the Congress I knew few witches personally, but I was fortunate to have a friend in Loren Heatherworth. He and his wife generously advocated for me from the inside, and I earned the chance to present my case. The Congress only agreed to recommend me because of what I believed Guillaume could help me do: Strengthen my thinning witchline.

The idea intrigued some witches, gave others hope, and frightened the remaining few. If it could be done, there was a chance to not only restore the power of the witch community in the Empire, but it would also help some families regain the control they'd lost over time within the witch community itself.

The result was a majority support from witches with conflicting desires.

And it worked. My witchline indeed strengthened under Guillaume's training. I continued to hone my craft, but the vein of power from which I drew – my witchline – was stronger. I could feel the regeneration when I tapped into it.

But I will come back to this. First, I need to explain what happened last year after I returned from France.

After a bright summer where I finally felt as though the Empire was my home again, the fall brought uninvited darkness into my life.

The Empire is governed by the Salesman Court. Salesmen are unique beings. They're human but they also can travel from place to place simply by stepping through a door. That is their power. Traditionally Salesmen are transporters of magical objects, but they are not magical creatures – with the exception of two special people.

Salesmen have run the Empire throughout its written history. Eventually they suffered from an internal festering of competing values. A rogue group of Salesmen eventually emerged, developing into a terrorist group known as the Fringe. The whole Empire suffered as a result of their violence – Salesmen, witches, other magical beings. Everyone.

As much as I wanted peace in the Empire, my first concern has always been my thinning witchline. And yet, I found myself in a battle against the Fringe shoulder to shoulder with Salesman Emily Swift and Salesman John Templeton.

These are the two special Salesmen who can perform magic in addition to their door traveling abilities. Emily is my friend, the younger sister I never had. Templeton is the knight to my light, according to the prophecy set in motion when Emily was born over three decades ago. I chose to be Emily's friend. I did not choose Templeton to be my anything.

My adventure with Emily and Templeton also brought the Crimson Stone into my possession. I was able to use it on that wild autumn night in the Walled Zone before putting the magical gemstone to sleep. It's now back with its rightful owner, but he cannot use it unless I wake the Stone up.

In the days following our victory, the relief I felt over winning the battle against the Fringe faded. People died. Some of them deserved it.

The man we cast into the Below I'd made love to only two days before.

As the dust settled, I realized I needed to go far away – to clear my head and to empty my heart. It was too heavy in my chest.

I'd packed my bags, secured a one-way train ticket out of the Empire, and reinforced the wards I'd set up to protect the townhouse in which I lived. The wards would prevent anyone – or anything – from entering my home while I was gone. I didn't tell anybody I was leaving except for the owner of *Coffee Cove*, a coffee shop where I read Tarot cards in my own private room.

I wasn't sure how long I'd be gone when I left, but I knew the first step to feeling better was getting out of the Empire and away from everything I'd lost. And now I was back.

I didn't feel much better, but I was glad to be home.

Sort of.

∞ ∞ ∞

The taxi driver double-parked in front of my brownstone, switched on his blinkers, and climbed from the car to unload my suitcase. He peered up at my gloomy home. "It's going to be cold in there."

I handed him a few bills for the fare. "It's cold out here."

"Do you need me to take this up the stairs for you?" He motioned to the front of the building. At least a foot of snow covered each step.

"That's okay," I said, pulling the suitcase to my side. "I'll consider the snow traction."

He shook his head but left me to my task. I carried my smaller travel bag to the door before laboring up the stairs a second time, gripping the ice-covered wrought iron railing and dragging the large suitcase through the snow. The bottoms of my jeans were pulled over my ankle boots, but I could feel the snow pushing under the denim. It felt sharp against my tender skin as it crested the top of my boots and bit at my ankles.

I rested on the stoop, looking over my shoulder at the shadowy street. Another car crept by, packing the slush into ice as the temperature continued to drop, but otherwise, the neighborhood was silent.

Breathing in the frigid air through my nose, I

hovered my hand over the black door with its celestial brass door knocker. My palm assessed the ward I'd set up before I left – it was still strong, but it took a lot of hits while I was gone. Almost all of them came from one source. The signature of this intense force was familiar to me. His last attempt to breach my wards was several weeks prior. There were several other minor tests to the protective energy I'd raised, but from nothing I recognized.

Centering my own energy and pressing it out against my wards, I whispered to the invisible walls guarding my home. *"Permitto me."* I felt the energy shudder, recognizing me alongside the words slicing softly through the crisp air. A tiny pop reached my ears. I paused, the noise startling me. That was unexpected. I warily watched the door. Nothing happened.

I sighed. Whatever it was, I'd deal with it later if it became an issue. In the meantime, I had to figure out how to get warm. I fished my keys out of my purse and let myself inside. As expected, the temperature in the townhouse had plummeted without a running furnace. Stamping my feet to shake off the excess snow, I left my luggage at the door and turned into the living room. The moonlight flowed in through the window, lighting up a path. I followed it to the mantel where I fumbled for the candlestick I knew I'd find. Three of my fingertips touched the candle, my pinky and thumb arched away from the surface. I stroked the candle from base to tip. *"Ignis sursum."* The wick sparked, then the flame grew.

With light to guide me, I returned to the entryway, passing through before taking the stairs. I needed to put on dry clothes, then I'd pour myself some wine and burrow under the blankets on my bed. I'd make sure the thermostat was set for a high temperature. Maybe I'd wake up to a warm home tomorrow.

Everything was as I'd left it. I breathed easier when water burst from the bathroom faucet after being turned on. Thankfully the pipes weren't frozen. I left the water running at a constant dribble and flushed the toilet twice.

I broke a land speed record changing my clothes, crying out when I put on my bone-cold pajamas. A pair of thick socks went on next before I pushed my feet into pink furry slippers. I skipped my robe and opted for a bulky wool sweater instead. Maybe I'd grab a knit hat and gloves from the hall closet downstairs before I headed to bed. Dressed for the elements – and bed – it was time for my preferred vasodilator: wine.

Downstairs I passed my luggage. *It can wait until tomorrow,* I thought as I carried the candle into the kitchen. I picked out a bottle of red from the rack and treated myself to a healthy pour. I sipped it, checking the sink's faucet. Again, the water ran. Fortunately, these pipes were fine, too.

My appetite was still light these days, but I opened a box of crackers and nibbled on a couple while I drank my wine. The candlelight flickered over my kitchen cupboards. My mind wandered through my memories as my meditation landed on the pantry door. My heart tightened when I thought about the many times it'd been used for door travel only a few short months ago. What did Emily call it? Oh, right: The Pantry Express.

Since there wasn't much to be done until the power came back on, I hugged the wine bottle to my chest and carried the candle and my wine glass out of the kitchen. As I walked to the front of my home, I heard a brushing against my front door, followed by a light tapping.

It was close to midnight. The knock came again. I could see a shadow moving on the other side of the small window by the door. Surely whoever it was could see me and my candle.

"Lucie?" I heard a man call through the door.

I set my wine down on the hall table and stepped forward. "Rabbit?"

"Lucie, it's me," he called again. I could tell he was trying to keep his voice low.

"*Permitto, Rabbit,*" I chanted as I held up my hand. The wards dropped for him right before I opened the front door.

Standing on the stoop, Rabbit peered out sheepishly from under a gray knit hat, his black curls pressed against his forehead and his temples. "Hey."

I laughed, the sound catching me off guard. It'd been a while and he was a sight for sore eyes. I waved him in. "Come out of the cold."

"Balmy," he joked when he stepped inside, a bright smile lighting up his entire face. "You're back."

"You got lucky. I only got in a while ago." I gestured toward the kitchen. "It's no warmer back there, but do you want something to drink?"

"Sure." He followed me. "It was more than

good luck."

I set the candle down on the counter and grabbed a new glass. "Oh, the network?"

He had the good graces to look at the floor. His already rosy-cold cheeks grew darker. "I got a text when you came home. I was in Matar so..."

"You had someone watching my house?" I lifted my eyebrows as I poured his wine.

"Not exactly." He rubbed the back of his neck with a chapped hand. "We hacked into the camera on the corner and trained it on your front door. Whenever there's movement, I get a text and a screenshot."

I realized my mouth was hanging open. I shut it and slid his wine across the counter toward him. "I don't know what to say to that."

He ignored the glass and reached for me instead. I let him pull me into a hug and relaxed against his chest. Rabbit kissed the top of my head. "We were so worried about you. We couldn't find you." He squeezed me tightly. "I couldn't find you."

"I'm sorry," I said. This was one of the reunions I was dreading. At least Rabbit was kind and wouldn't try to make me feel bad. My guilty feelings were truly my own.

He loosened his grip, his thick fingers tucking under my chin. Rabbit's glittering brown eyes searched my face. "We thought you went back to France at first. We didn't want to alert anyone in case you hadn't. I checked and saw you left your car in the parking garage, and the network tracked down a train ticket from Matar to Anwat. We figured you went to Kincaid. Emily confirmed you visited her. She couldn't tell us much. She said you needed some space, but she didn't think you were going back to Guillaume."

I hadn't told Emily where I was going. I didn't want to put her on the spot when she was asked about what she knew – and I knew they'd go to her for answers. "I didn't tell anyone. And no, I'm in no hurry to see Guillaume. He's certainly not someone I'd go to for comfort."

Rabbit dropped his hand, his expression serious. "You could've told me, Lucie. I would've kept your secret. And then I wouldn't have worried for months."

A pit in my stomach opened and I pulled away. I circled around to the other side of the counter and climbed onto one of the barstools. Even through my long sweater and pajama bottoms the surface of the stool was cold. I winced. "I'm sorry, Rabbit. I never wanted anyone to worry. I figured once you talked to Emily you wouldn't."

Rabbit pulled a deep breath in through his nose and stared at me. "Seriously?"

I lifted a hand. "I couldn't be in my life anymore."

"That's pretty selfish," Rabbit answered, surprising me.

Those words were a direct hit – and unlike him. But I wasn't going to fight. I was freezing and tired. "Maybe it was."

"It was." He pulled off his knit cap and ran a hand over the top of his head, his fingers combing through his thick curls. His hair had grown long. "But you're home now. And you seem to be okay. Thinner, but okay."

He was right. I'd lost a little over 15 pounds. Well, maybe more like 20. But it wasn't like I was gaunt or anything. I patted the stool next to me. "Sit by me?"

"I should let you get to sleep," he said.

"Yeah, but let's finish our wine first," I replied. I patted the seat again. "And you can reassure me you aren't angry anymore. Then I can get to sleep in this refrigerator."

Rabbit caved and sat beside me, his forearms

resting on the counter. "We've got a generator where I'm staying, plus heaters. It's not an environment I'd typically bring a lady to, but it might be better than freezing to death."

I bumped my shoulder against his. "I'll pass. I'll be fine."

"Well, I want you to have this." He fished a compact device out of his pocket. It was a phone. "I should've given you this a long time ago."

"Is this like the one you gave to Emily?" I asked, examining it. Rabbits never passed out phones for their network, but he gave one to her when we were preparing to sneak into the Walled Zone.

"This *is* Emily's," he said, digging into his coat pocket and producing a cord and charger. "I had to take it away from her. She was abusing the privilege."

"How?"

"She kept sending me memes with rabbits in them." He wasn't amused.

I stifled a laugh. "That is so like her."

"Anyhow," he continued, "you can only text me and get texts from me. You won't be able to access anything else on the network. But don't tell anyone I gave this to you."

"Got it." I decided to test if our friendship was still intact. "But the occasional bunny meme is okay, right?"

"No. Behave yourself." His kind eyes sparkled. "Anyhow, let me show you how to use it." Rabbit helped me program one of my fingerprints into the device and then directed me on how to open the text app.

"Thank you." I searched his face. "Is this for me to be able to reach you? Or for you to be able to reach me?"

Rabbit shifted on his stool. "Both."

"Fair enough." At least he was honest.

"And it won't ding or buzz when you get a text," he explained. "Instead, it'll grow warm for a moment."

"Got it." I yawned, then covered my mouth. "Sorry."

Before he could answer, the power clicked on. The clock on my stove beeped and a second later I heard my furnace kick on. I hopped off the barstool and turned on the kitchen light. We both flinched under the glare.

"And on that note." Rabbit emptied his wine glass in one last swallow. "I'll let you get to bed."

"Now that I have power, do you want to stay here?" It wouldn't be the first time Rabbit slept over. Usually, he rode the couch. "For once the spare bedroom upstairs isn't being used when you're here. Why don't you take it?"

Rabbit didn't answer right away, and I expected him to say yes. Eventually though, he shook his head. "Nah. I gotta go. But let's catch up in a day or two, okay? Maybe do something this weekend?"

"Yeah, let's." I followed him out of the kitchen to the front door and flicked on two lights: one for inside the entryway and one over the stoop. "You can text me."

He nodded. "I will."

"Hey, before you go, one more thing." I hated even bringing the subject up, but it would be better to know in advance.

"What is it?"

"You kept saying 'we.' *We* were worried. *We* couldn't find you." I pulled the end of my sweater over my hand and focused on it for a moment. I picked a piece of lint off the cuff. "You meant, 'we' as in the network, right?"

When Rabbit didn't immediately answer, I looked up. He shrugged. "Sure, the network was concerned."

He was being evasive. I pushed on. "But was that the 'we' you meant?"

Rabbit leaned his head back and studied my ceiling. "No."

I needed to hear him say it. "Then you and who?"

He met my gaze. "Templeton won't understand why you left, Lucie. He'll never admit it, but he took it personally. He thinks you left because of him."

"I figured that." I blew out a breath. Templeton was partially right. "I'll deal with it when the time comes."

Rabbit laughed, but it wasn't a friendly sound. "You think he doesn't know you're back in the Empire?"

"Already? No, not unless you sent him a message." I lifted a shoulder. "I mean, I won't hide from him, but I'm not exactly going to send up a smoke signal."

"Funny you should put it that way," Rabbit began. "What makes you think Templeton wouldn't have set something up here to let him know when you came back?"

I sucked in a breath. The little popping sound.

"Son of a bitch."

"What?"

"The ward. I dropped it when I got home and heard a tiny noise – nothing I'd normally expect." My lips flattened into a thin line.

"He spelled your ward?" A hint of a smile appeared.

"He must have. Dammit!" I waved my hands uselessly. "I recognized his energy trail all over the ward. He's tried to door travel into my home while I've been gone."

"I haven't seen him in over a month, but I know he was worried. Not that he said as much," Rabbit told me. "He probably hoped to find a clue to your whereabouts here in your house."

"It was none of his business," I argued. I did not need this drama. This is why I left.

"Good luck with that. I guarantee Templeton thinks you *are* his business – especially after all we learned from the Tortoise." Rabbit referred to a wise, older Rabbit his network called the Tortoise. He was the man who explained the prophecy tying me in some way to Templeton.

My friend pulled his hat on over his curls and continued. "Listen. Keep the phone on you. Remember, don't use it in public and don't tell anyone about it. The network won't be happy if they find out I gave it to you. They'll shut it down."

"Got it." I touched his arm when he put his hand on the doorknob. "I'm sorry I made you worry, Rabbit."

"You're home safe and sound," he answered, but he failed to make eye contact. "That's all I care about now." I watched as he left, trudging through the snow toward the sidewalk below. Halfway down the stairs he turned, waving his thick finger back and forth at the buried steps. "I'll get someone over here in the morning to shovel."

"No, Rabbit, don't worry about it," I called down to him as he pulled out his phone and texted the network. A blast of winter wind kicked up a handful of flakes and I shivered as they pelted my face and neck.

"Done." He pocketed his phone as he hit the sidewalk. I watched as his solid frame hoofed it down my block. He disappeared back into the night.

∞∞∞

The power returning was a lucky break, and I cranked the heat. There was a chance the Empire would induce another brownout, so I left a tiny stream of water running in the kitchen and bathroom sinks. It was probably overkill, but everyone knew the plumbing was old in these beautiful brownstones. I wasn't going to risk pipes bursting.

Truthfully, I was glad to see Rabbit. Before my life took a nosedive we hung out, occasionally going to a summer festival and listening to music. He came over for dinner a handful of times and we watched one or two movies together. Then I met someone, and Rabbit and I spent less time together. Before I could make sense of my love life, I joined Rabbit, Emily, and Templeton in their final battle with the Fringe. After that, I was emptied out.

I ditched the wool sweater and slippers, climbing gratefully into bed. Clicking off the bedside lamp, I snuggled under the covers. My mind wandered back to those fall days.

The four of us tried to wrap everything up after the fifth and sixth doors were closed. Templeton wanted to know what was on the other side – and I truly understood his desire –

but we couldn't afford to let whatever was there get into the Empire. We were told there were 'beasts' and 'monsters' past the two doors. I had the power to make sure the key to open both doors – the Crimson Stone – stayed dormant. After I put the Stone to sleep, I let Templeton take it. It belonged to his family. But he couldn't use the Stone unless I lifted the spell. I had no plans to do that anytime soon.

I saw Templeton a few days after I gave the Stone to him. We planned to meet in the library at the Congress of Empire Witches to begin our research into the book of fairy tales he'd acquired. I was curious as to why Templeton had permission to use the library – he was not a witch. I reasoned he *could* practice magic, and he probably had a few influential connections in the witch community who could help him gain access to what he needed. Then I learned he *was* in fact a member of the Congress, but he refused to elaborate on how that was possible. It was my understanding very few non-witches were ever accepted as members. This was unusual.

When we made plans to begin our research, Templeton also invited me to have dinner with him after our library session. This was a surprise. Well, that's not entirely true. There was an unmistakable chemistry stirring between us. Unfortunately, we can't seem to be in the same room with each other peacefully for more than 10 minutes.

He pushes all my buttons.

Still, we were brought together by the prophecy – something I've yet to wrap my head around – and the Crimson Stone. We were brought together by the fifth and sixth directional doors and what I'd done. I could still feel Templeton's strong door travel energy enveloping me as he stood close on that hellish night. Over the past several months the phantom pressure of his hands rested on my hips, his fingers splayed over my curves as I directed my magic into the Stone and projected it against the directional doors.

And then last October, after a fruitless afternoon of research in the Congress' library, Templeton brought me to the supper club he frequented. He secured a private dining room for us. The view of the city was outstanding – as was the menu. I relaxed and for the first time, I started to enjoy his company once the discussion switched from our research to more everyday topics like books, music, and travel.

Because Templeton is a Salesman, he can travel to most anywhere simply by stepping through a door. The only thing he needs is a door on both ends: the one he enters and the one he exits. Since my mode of transportation is limited to the average person's methods, he hired a car to take us from the library to the dining club, and then to my brownstone. From there he dismissed the service. He could simply door travel to his home in the countryside or to his penthouse in downtown Matar.

I remembered the autumn night clearly. The air was cool, and a brisk breeze blew through my hair as we walked to my front door. I invited him inside for a last glass of wine. It wasn't the first time he'd been in my house, so I didn't think twice about it. He seemed uncomfortable as I poured us each a glass of red. We stood in my kitchen, watching each other.

Drawing in a shaky breath, I rolled to my side and pulled the pillow over my head. I didn't want to think about what happened next. I didn't want to think about how he moved closer.

How he set his wine glass on the counter behind me, the inside of his arm brushing my shoulder.

How I could smell the woodsy soap he used.

How he lifted his hand and caressed my cheek with his fingertips.

How I thought he was going to kiss me.

How he didn't.

How instead he yanked his hand away, mumbled an abrupt goodnight, and bolted out of my home through my pantry door.

How the next morning I stood in my kitchen staring at the same pantry door thinking: I can't do this.

I didn't want to think about any of that.

Chapter 2

Why bother setting the alarm when you have nowhere to go? But I was a victim of my own internal clock. I was wide awake at six.

At least the power stayed on through the night. I swung my legs over the side of the bed and danced across the chilly floor searching for my slippers. I pulled my hair up into a messy bun and studied the shadows under my eyes. I looked even paler after a poor night's sleep.

I hated brushing my teeth before coffee, so I put the task on hold and fired up my coffee pot. It was still dusky outside, but soon the sun would be up. I switched on the outside light and checked my back yard. It was buried under a lot of snow.

While I waited for the coffee to perk, I checked the Empire service phone for messages. I picked up the tan handset and bopped the cradle up and down twice.

The sound of ticking and chimes was followed by a recording. "This is the Empire's award-winning messaging system. You have 47 messages."

I hung up. Later I'd have an operator delete them all. I assumed most weren't even relevant at this point. I paused. I'd need to send a few messages to let some people know I was back in Matar. My eyes cut to the pantry. Rabbit would get a message to Emily. She'd probably come walking through the door within a day or two. I crossed to it and held up my hand. *"Permitto, Emily Swift."* I felt the wards shudder. I stared accusingly at the door, feeling the double-edged blade of hurt and anger twist in my gut. Damn. *"Permitto, John Templeton."* The wards shook again.

I'd probably regret that.

∞∞∞

Bundled up in my winter jacket, I picked my way down the sidewalk. The city kept up with the ice by drowning the sidewalks in rock salt. The slush, however, was miserable and slick. I wrapped my red scarf around my neck, pulling it up and over my nose when one of Matar's notorious winter winds lashed against my face. I had one more block to go before reaching *Coffee Cove*. I hoped Rick would be in his office even though I was also embarrassed to face him. The last thing I told my landlord was something unexpected came up and I'd be gone for a while. I'd negotiated an updated rental agreement and paid to hold my room at the coffee shop. I set up an autopay from my bank account before I fled Matar. I noted a withdrawal from my account on the first of the month and hoped it meant my room was how I'd left it.

Rick Manning was a pleasant man in his mid-50s. Often you'd hear him cheerfully whistling in his office while he worked. According to his staff he was a good employer. The shop hardly had any turnover, and I suspected it was because of fair wages and the happy working environment. Rick owned several coffee shops around Matar. His wife managed one and a brother managed the other.

When I moved back to Matar last year, I bought a townhouse with the money I'd received as compensation for my yearlong study with Guillaume. The Congress was generous to its witches if they completed a full year of training with the man. I still had a large reserve in my account on top of a monthly stipend. I wasn't rich, but I was set for a while.

When searching for a home, I strolled many a trendy neighborhood in Matar. The Clover District, as it's called, is one of the more popular parts of the city. It's a four-block section of brownstones on the north side with a 'stem' of townhouses trailing southward on a slightly curved avenue. The four blocks are laid out in a square pattern. When the 'stem' was considered, the position of the brownstones supposedly resembled a four-leaf clover.

Before I put in an offer on the townhouse that would become my home, I stopped into *Coffee Cove* for some French press coffee. A sign in the back of the welcoming space advertised the room as available for rent. Rick's plan was to provide his customers with the opportunity to sign-up for Tarot card readings with an experienced reader. If the reader brought in more customers, he'd lower the rent. Before I left for my year in France, I had a long list of regulars. I encouraged them to dine at the coffee shop before or after a reading. Rick traced a significant uptick in business to my services. He lowered my rent to the point where a week of readings would cover the amount I paid him every month.

Clients pay well for my services.

I pushed the thick wooden door open and stepped up into *Coffee Cove*. The seductive aroma of fresh-brewed coffee enveloped me. I'd get a cup to go before I left. But first, Rick. The barista recognized me immediately and said yes, Rick held onto my reading room, and yes, he was in his office. A few minutes later he met me in the seating area.

"Lucie! It's so good to see you! When did you get back? Your customers miss you. I had one lady offer me an obscene amount of money to get a message to you," he laughed over the busy din of his shop.

"Roberta?" I groaned.

"I think that was her name," he nodded. "I told her I didn't know where you'd gone, but I knew you'd come back." He opened his arms wide. A customer next to him ducked. "This is your work home, after all."

Even though I lacked Rick's enthusiasm, I chuckled. He was forever cheerful. "Indeed, it is.

But I'm sorry, Rick. There were things I had to deal with."

He looked at me closely. "It was a man, wasn't it?"

"Wow," I shook my head. Rick's accuracy was unexpected. The uneasy feeling returned to my stomach. "Um, it was a lot of things."

"He doesn't come in here anymore if that's what you're worried about," Rick said as he took my elbow and led me through the maze of tables to the door leading into my reading room.

I swallowed. "Who are you talking about?"

"The man in the black leather jacket who used to flirt with you." Rick unlocked the door and flipped on the light. It was cool inside, and there was a film of dust on a few surfaces, but otherwise the room was untouched. "I think I saw you two having coffee together. All the girls at the counter had a crush on him, but he was only ever interested in seeing if you were in." Rick rose the window shade to let in the morning light. He shrugged. "When one of the girls realized she hadn't seen him in here since you left, we joked the two of you had eloped."

The taste in my mouth soured to the point where I was nauseous. "No."

He grimaced. "Sorry, Lucie. Hey, forget him, right? You're here now, and everyone is going to be happy to see you!" He motioned to the room before tapping his chest. "I knew in my heart you'd be back. I said we had to keep everything as you left it. I knew it was only a matter of time."

I floated around my room, running my fingertips over the smooth wooden boxes sitting on my bookshelves. Each held a different deck of Tarot cards. I eyeballed the round table in the center of the room, my gaze sliding to the empty chair where the man in the black leather jacket had sat and asked me out to dinner. My eyes shut against the memory and I turned away. When I opened them again, I reached for a bottle of rosemary oil sitting on one of my shelves. I pulled off the stopper and sniffed. I needed to clear my head.

"I cannot thank you enough for keeping all this safe," I said, turning back to Rick. "My plan is to start reading again in the next couple of weeks. I need to clean up some loose ends first, but soon I'll hang up 'the witch is in' sign."

"Should I take out an announcement in the *Matar Daily*?" Rick asked, touching his chin with a fingertip. "We could run a nice half-page ad."

"Let's hold off." I put up a hand. "I don't want a bunch of people descending on me all at once. Word of mouth spreads quickly in my circle. If business starts out too slow, then we can talk about an ad."

"Perfect," Rick answered. "Listen, I've got to get back to my paperwork, but Lucie, seeing you here has made my whole day – no, my whole month!" He beamed at me as he opened the door to leave. "You let me know if you need anything at all. Anything."

"Thanks, Rick." I gave him a lopsided smile and sunk into a chair as soon as he was gone.

I stared at the shadow wearing the black leather jacket sitting in the seat across from me. His mouth split into that wicked smirk I knew so well. "I believe people create their own fates," he told me, leaning back in the chair and lacing his fingers behind his head. He pursed his lips and watched me with those devilish dark eyes, his eyelids dipping.

"They do," I whispered back.

I sat there until the memory faded. I drew a circle on the tabletop with a finger.

I wasn't completely honest with my friends last fall. Basha – *I mean, Sebastian* – and I'd been intimate for a lot longer than I'd admitted. I don't know why I'd lied. Maybe it was because I was embarrassed by the fool I'd allowed myself to become. He deceived me from the beginning.

The pain inside my chest grew sharp, then subsided when I finished burning the circle into the table with my fingertip. I learned a lot of ways to live with my broken heart during the past few months.

"Okay, then." I said aloud as I stood up and rubbed my hands together. "Time to go."

∞∞∞

Before I went home, I stopped at the corner grocery store to pick up milk. I kept a folding shopping cart in the closet of the reading room at *Coffee Cove*, so I was prepared. I added crackers and cereal to my cart. I also picked up several bottles of wine before starting for home.

As I trundled the cart over the sidewalk and up to my townhouse, I saw Rabbit came through on his promise. Someone had shoveled the snow from my stairs and sprinkled deicer on every step. I'd have to find out which Rabbit did it and make sure I packed them up a good to-go lunch at some point. Rabbits are very resourceful but tend to run low on cash. I've never seen one pass up a free meal.

Back inside my warm home – *thankfully the power grid was still at full force* – I clicked on the radio and dug into my few bags. The beat lifted my spirits and I bopped around the kitchen while I put my groceries away. During a particularly saucy rhythm I lifted my hands high, swinging my hips and twirling. I spun around and came face-to-face with a tall, scowling man standing in front of my pantry door. His arms were crossed and his light blue eyes grew paler as he glared at me. My arms fell to my sides as I stopped dancing.

Ever since he supported me when I used the Crimson Stone, I could see the trails and tendrils of his door travel energy. The waves were a royal blue. I never told him I could see this remarkable display, and even now I marveled at the brilliant color swirling around his legs. His travel into my home was silent and I didn't hear anything when he entered my kitchen.

Well, I *did* drop the wards for him.

∞ ∞ ∞

"Advance notice of your plans to visit would be appreciated." I crossed my arms, too.

"Really?" Templeton's upper lip curled. "Advance notice of *my* plans? Why in the world would I offer you the courtesy? You weren't exactly forthcoming with *your* plans."

I knew this confrontation was coming, but I'd hoped to be home for more than 12 hours before we stood in the same room. I lifted a hand. "There's nothing I can say that's going to make any difference here, so why don't you just go ahead with your rant and get it over with?"

He snorted, dropping his arms, his hands landing on his hips. He glanced around the kitchen before making eye contact again. "You are a piece of work."

"Me? Good god, Templeton. You think you're a pleasure to deal with? You're barely tolerable!" I leaned over and shut the radio off. "Listen, I'm sorry I left without telling anyone. I know people worried and I knew a couple would be mad at me. But you of all people should've cut me some slack."

Templeton didn't respond. I searched for something to do on the counter. I rearranged a tray of flavored oils. Out of the corner of my eye I could see he watched me. Suddenly he spoke. "What do you mean 'me of all people'?"

I turned my head and met his gaze. "All that happened with..." I licked my lower lip and reconsidered my answer before I spoke. "After everything that happened in the Walled Zone. And then the night here." I gestured to the kitchen, then to him. "With you."

He knew exactly what I meant, and I waited to see if he'd acknowledge what happened – or what didn't happen – before he turned tail and ran.

Templeton looked past me, fixating on some imaginary spot. "I'd like to set up a time for us to meet at the library. I think we should resume the research on the book of fairy tales. I think the key is determining what are truly symbols and then aligning them with what we know about the Stone and the doors. There are books I cannot gain access to, and I need your assistance. In your *absence* I've asked Ms. Parker-Jones to review the book of fairy tales – under the Empire's radar, of course."

Tara Parker-Jones served as one of the Record Keepers for the Empire. She replaced a man who was murdered by the Fringe. She lived outside the Empire in the same small city as Emily. The two were friends. Tara was a bunch of bawdy fun. A well-connected bibliophile, she was a great resource when it came to rare books.

A part of me was disappointed Templeton switched the subject, but in all honesty, it was probably for the best. After all, we were only linked by the prophecy and the Stone. Well, that and our interest in the fifth and sixth directional doors. Granted, we had different goals for them. He wanted to know what was on the other side and I wanted those doors kept firmly shut.

Academically, I admitted it: I wanted to know what was on the other side of both doors. But my gut instinct warred against my brain. I didn't need another lesson to teach me why it was a bad idea to ignore your own internal voice when it warned something was wrong.

"Tara is a good idea," I replied lamely. "Does she have the book?"

"No."

I rubbed my forehead. "Okay. Let me... Let me

get my calendar and we can pick a date. I need to reconnect with a few people and –"

"Tomorrow," he interrupted. "You'll meet me at the library tomorrow. We've already lost time because of your extended *vacation*. I don't want to waste any more. Once we have a better understanding of what's beyond each door you can open the one to the Above. I'll be able to do my own exploration. I won't need you."

"No way." I shook my head. The nerve of him! I pointed my finger at Templeton. "I'm not here at your beck and call."

"Clearly," he sneered.

"Enough!" I slapped my hand on the counter. "I don't need to put up with this. Get the hell out of my house, Templeton."

Templeton didn't move, but the remaining color in his faded irises drained, leaving only black rings surrounding where they would normally be. I felt my skin growing hot, the air around my body sparking. A rushing wind sounded in my ears and I snapped my fingers. The pantry door behind him slammed open, banging solidly against the shelves beyond it.

"I said: Get. Out."

He evaluated me, his gaze roaming over my

arms seeing what I could only feel. "I would've thought Guillaume required more control in his witches."

"Templeton," I said evenly, my stomach rolling as I felt the anger burning inside. "Out now before I set you on fire."

He gave me a cold smile. "You haven't yet." His eyes flicked down the rest of my body and I hated him. "But save it for another time, Ms. Bellerose." I saw his door travel energy rising, the deep blue floating in the air around him effortlessly. "In fact, save it for the next man who comes along. Maybe he'll appreciate your charms," he said meanly.

And with that, he was gone.

∞∞∞

It was all I could do to keep from tossing a ball of fire after Templeton when he door traveled away through my pantry. I knew better, however. I'd only end up setting fire to my own house.

The unsent energy coursed through my body. Unless I released it, I'd make myself sick. I took the easy way out. I stormed through my pantry and wrenched open the back door leading into my yard. The snow was at least a foot deep in some places. I whirled around and let my body fall backward into the white stuff like I was a child. I hissed against the frigid cushion and flapped my arms and legs as I made a snow angel.

How dare he speak to me like that?

My arms and legs stopped waving. My breath misted into the air above and I started to quake from the cold. I picked myself up and shook off the loose snow. I'd cooled down, but at a price. I looked at my stocking feet.

I stomped back into my kitchen, peeled my socks off, and threw them across the room.

Briiing! The Empire service phone rang in its cupboard. Now what? I yanked open the cupboard door and jammed the handset to my ear.

"Yes?" I barked into the phone.

"This is the Empire messaging service. I have a message for one Ms. Lucie Bellerose." The operator's voice was borderline mechanical.

"Yes, this is Ms. Bellerose," I twisted the cord around my finger, watching the wintry red skin change to white as I cut off the blood supply.

"Ms. Bellerose, I have a message from Mr. Loren

Heatherworth. Mr. Heatherworth requests that you meet with him tomorrow at noon at the Congress of Empire Witches building. He expects you to join him for lunch. This is the end of the message, Ms. Bellerose," the operator concluded.

I cringed. Great. "Thank you."

"You are welcome, Ms. Bellerose. Have a pleasant day. Goodbye." The operator disconnected.

I pulled the cord off my finger and returned the handset to its phone cradle. I checked the clock on my stove. Seriously, 24 hours hadn't even passed since I arrived in Matar. Was there writing in the sky announcing my return? God help me if Rick decided to run a newspaper ad without waiting for my go ahead.

The snow clinging to my clothes was melting and I surveyed the pools of water dotting my floor. Everything was moving too fast. I took a deep breath and reminded myself I'd made the decision to come back home now. I could deal with whatever fallout came my way.

Upstairs I changed my clothes and wondered what Loren wanted. I liked the man. He was an old family friend. There was some connection between Loren and my late aunt. He and his wife were in their 70s and lived in a wealthy, gated community outside Matar. Inside was a sizable witch population, with the oddball non-magical family home nestled into neighborhoods here and there. I'd visited the couple over the years and attended a few holiday gatherings. I think Loren and his wife Michelle thought it was their responsibility to make sure I had some sort of 'family' – especially around the holidays. My parents died in separate accidents when I was a child, and my aunt, Colette Bellerose, raised me. Aunt Lettie was my father's sister and she passed away seven years ago. She'd never married or had children.

Loren and Michelle were part of the old guard in the Empire's order of witches. When I needed a champion in the Congress to secure support for going to France, Michelle took to lunching with ladies while Loren shared his best Scotch with Congress influencers. I deserved to study with Guillaume but being a 'nobody' in the witch community was a hurdle. I never would've had a shot without the Heatherworths. I was in their debt.

Still, I wondered how Loren knew I was back in Matar. And was this invitation to join him for lunch at the Congress a good thing? I'd find out tomorrow. In the meantime, I had to start putting my house back in order. I picked my wet clothes off my bedroom floor.

I'd start with the laundry.

Chapter 3

The building belonging to the Congress of Empire Witches took up an entire city block in Matar. Its size rivaled the Salesman Courthouse in the center of the city. This building, however, was housed in the northeastern part of Matar where the witch community consolidated its interests. The imposing granite and marble structure towered beyond a wide but ultimately narrow courtyard behind an ornate security gate. The taxi brought me to the curb, and I gave my name to the expressionless man who appeared on the other side of the barrier. Loren had provided my name as a lunch guest on the day's register, so I didn't have to go through the hassle of explaining my business to the bored man greeting me. I'd still need to pass the ritual of recognition before I was allowed to move past the lobby.

The gate swung open and the man waved me through.

The sidewalk leading to the double doors had been scraped dry and I hurried. I'd dressed casually for my lunch with Loren, and my heeled brown leather boots tapped on the concrete beneath my feet. I wore a fitted denim pencil skirt over my black tights, the hem coming to right below my knees. The long-sleeved black cashmere sweater dressed up my outfit and helped keep me warm under a camel-colored pea coat. I'd wrapped a green and red plaid knitted mohair scarf loosely around my neck. I liked to think it added a touch of sophistication to my ensemble.

I detected a vibration in the wards the Congress raised for protection but passed through them without issue. The third approval of my visit would happen with the blind being at the next set of doors. Her appearance was that of a woman, but she was not human. She was not a witch either, but one of the 'lesser creatures' serving in the Congress. The disparagement developed on the lips of old witches who didn't accept anyone other than a witch as worthy. I pulled off my winter gloves and pocketed them as I approached her. I pushed up the sleeve of my coat, baring my wrist. "Good afternoon," I said, my hand extending as I turned my palm upward.

"Hmm." She easily found my outstretched hand and pulled me near, her gnarled fingers rubbing over my tender skin. Briefly, a black tattoo flickered under her firm touch on my wrist. The being gave me a toothless grin, her cloudy eyes meeting mine. "You may enter, witch."

"Thank you," I answered, pulling my hand from hers. It was uncanny how she always knew where to look, but I knew better. She didn't see me – but she did *know* me. The ritual of recognition completed, I passed through the doors at her side.

∞∞∞

"I'm meeting Loren Heatherworth," I told the host at the desk in front of the entrance to the Congress' private dining room. I passed my wool coat to the young woman who waited to take it to a separate counter where she would check it for me. I pulled my purse strap over my shoulder. "I'm Lucie Bellerose."

"Right this way," the man murmured, turning and leading me into the dining area. The carpet was thick and hushed our footsteps as he threaded a path through the room. Along both sides of the fine space there were alcoves with hidden tables nestled inside. Heavy drapes were pulled over the openings of several of these alcoves indicating they were in use. *Private lunch dates,* I thought. People not wanting to be watched, secret conversations.

Fortunately, Loren didn't reserve one of the private alcoves and I felt whatever he wanted to discuss might not be bad after all. He sat at the table watching us approach, standing as we arrived. He kissed my cheek and shooed away the host. Loren pulled out my chair and rested his hand on my shoulder briefly after I lowered myself onto the seat. Two glasses of Sauvignon Blanc were already poured and he toasted me immediately when he sat down.

"To your return, Lucie." He lifted his glass.

I lifted mine and took a sip. "Thank you. Did someone make an announcement? It seems like I didn't arrive home under the radar."

Loren took another sip of his wine before setting the glass down. "Word travels when a witch who had such success under Guillaume's tutelage disappears. People have been watching. I'm sure you'll be seeing Guillaume soon, too."

I pressed my lips together. *That* I didn't want to hear. Whether we were seated in a private alcove or not, it appeared the conversation might not be as lighthearted as I'd hoped. I tamped down the urge to get defensive with Loren. None of this was his fault and frankly, he was doing me a favor by warning me. "I had a personal matter I needed to attend to, Loren. I couldn't do it here in the Empire."

"And how is Colette's cottage?" Loren raised an eyebrow. The soft folds of his face supported a smug expression.

"I should've guessed you'd figure it out." I spun the wine glass in a circle on the table. I stopped myself when I realized what I was doing. Even an accidental spell cast without permission inside the Congress' building could get a witch into a lot of trouble.

"Well, I was worried. I hired someone to check, and he reported a woman fitting your description living there. According to him you seemed fine and not under duress. I let it be. I engaged him several more times for updates. He didn't relay anything concerning." Loren paused when a waiter approached. I browsed the menu, but nothing appealed to me. Loren ordered the salmon en croute for both of us. He requested it be served at room temperature.

"And how did you know I was back?" I asked.

"Pure luck. Roberta."

"Oh, that one." I snorted. "She's a witch, for crying out loud. She should practice her own divination."

Loren raised a hand and shrugged. "You're the best. Roberta likes the best."

"Yeah." I reached for my wine again. I thought about the messages I brushed aside in the fall. Even 'the best' makes bad decisions. "Well, anyhow. I'm back and that's about it." I studied Loren wondering what else he knew. He was put together so precisely in his gray flannel suit with its matching vest. His tie was solid navy, topping a dove-colored dress shirt with pinstripes. A snow-white handkerchief poked up out of the left breast pocket of his suit coat.

"Tell me about last year after you returned from France," he prodded. I'd conveniently forgotten how extensive reaches could be in the witch community.

"Okay," I began. "Um, I came back, bought a townhouse in the Clover District, and started readings at a coffee shop."

Loren made a moue. "About that. Lucie, a coffee shop?"

"Oh, it's not quite what you think. I leave my headscarves and costume jewelry at home." I tried for levity. I rested my elbow on the table and my chin landed on my palm. "I rent a room there. Almost all my old clients are making their weekly appointments. I didn't want to do it out of my home like I had in the past. I always felt vulnerable allowing a lot of strangers into my house – especially those who also practiced magic."

"Understandable, but you could rent space in one of the buildings near here. There are wonderful studios with rooms that would be ideal. Most of your clients are from our community. It would be convenient for them. I could speak to some associates."

"But it wouldn't be convenient for me," I answered. I tried to be gracious. "I appreciate your offer to help, but I'm happy where I am right now. I can't wait to get back to doing readings." Even as I said it, I realized I wasn't telling the truth. I was dreading returning to *Coffee Cove*. I knew the feeling would pass. I *hoped* it would pass.

"Alright, we'll leave it for now. But if you change your mind, I am here to help you, Lucie." He sipped his wine.

"And I appreciate it." I took a breath and prepared to change the subject to something safer, like updates on his family.

"Tell me about the friends you made last year." Loren was faster.

I delayed answering by putting my wine glass to my lips. I glanced around the dining area hoping for a return visit from our waiter. When he didn't come, I was forced to give a careful reply. Loren's requests proved there was something he knew. Something concerned him.

"A lot changed after the year I spent in France," I admitted. "Some friends moved out of Matar, but I contacted one of the local method covens and met new people." A method coven emphasized improving technique and routine practice. Both natural and self-taught witches participated in the group. Many traditional witches rebuffed such collaborations, but Loren was a smart man. He recognized the value of learning from other witches regardless of their witchlines – or even if they didn't come from one. Of course, Loren would never join a method coven, but he didn't necessarily judge others who participated in them.

Loren offered a patient smile. "Lucie, you are being evasive."

"And you are asking me questions about things I think you might already know." I squinted at the man, lifting my chin. "I'm right, aren't I?"

He nodded. "Some information made it to my ears."

"Such as? I'm happy to answer your questions if you'd like to be specific," I said. "I'm not hiding anything." I immediately clenched my teeth. *Damn.* I shouldn't have said that. Loren would sense the lie. Before he could respond, I held up a hand, conceding. "That's not entirely true and I don't want you to think I'm lying to you."

His expression indicated he had indeed sensed my white lie but was waiting for me to go on. He gestured toward me with his wine glass. "Continue."

"I don't want to go into details, but yes, I met someone last year and we had a relationship.

It didn't end well." *Understatement.* In all my secrets, alluding to my involvement with Sebastian was, sadly, the safest conversation topic in light of everything else that happened. "This man was not the person he pretended to be, so I'm reluctant to discuss it. I'm sure you understand."

Loren's calm features morphed into a deep frown. "Was this a Salesman?"

I faltered. Sebastian *was* a Salesman like Templeton. I didn't know this until I found out he was also a member of the Fringe.

Only, it turned out he wasn't just a member. He was one of the top leaders of the terrorist group. He was a violent man who hurt a lot of people. When angered, Sebastian became unhinged. I witnessed it firsthand when his true identity was revealed in a lonely pub in the Walled Zone.

I wasn't sure how Loren knew about Sebastian, but if the staff at *Coffee Cove* had suspicions about my relationship with the man, I supposed anything was possible. I opened my mouth to give Loren the 'family-friendly' version of the story, but he spoke first.

"I ask because you were seen here in the library last fall with John Templeton," Loren said.

Oh. Loren thought Templeton was the man in the failed relationship. I looked down at my napkin while I considered my response.

Witches and Salesmen are two classes that traditionally don't mix well. Part of the reason is because Salesmen have been able to retain top control of the Empire for centuries. They were the wealthiest class overall and held many influential positions inside and outside of the government. Of course, there were affluent and powerful witches in the Empire, too. But the truth was Salesmen outnumbered witches and all the witchlines were thinning. To add insult to injury, the birthrate of natural witches had plummeted in the last four decades.

Moreover, Templeton was not well-liked in the magical community – *period*. Some of the animosity was well-earned, but if the truth were to be told, many practitioners were jealous of his seemingly effortless abilities. I'd witnessed his magic firsthand. While I'm sure he studied diligently to learn many of the spells and skills he displayed, it was clear Templeton's natural talent was off the charts.

There had to be someone or something in his family tree with a massive amount of magical power. I understood his late father was a practitioner of black magic, but I didn't know much about him. It was certainly something Templeton hid from others. This father was not a witch, but Templeton never shared what kind of being he was – if anything other than human.

Oddly enough, Templeton *was* a member of the Congress of Empire Witches – not one with full rights because he was not a witch – but he was indeed a recognized constituent. When I learned this tidbit, he wouldn't explain how it came to be. He simply gave me a thin smile and changed the subject.

"Lucie?" Loren prompted. "Were you involved with Templeton?"

I shook my head, fiddling with my napkin. "No, he was not the man I was seeing last year. It was someone else. He, ah, left the Empire. He's gone."

Loren reached across the table and patted my hand. "I'm sorry you got hurt. Some men have no honor."

"I'm fine," I assured him. My heart twisted as it thumped miserably against my breastbone. "There were a few bombshells at the end, and I needed to get away." I returned to sipping my wine. I couldn't wait until our food arrived and interrupted us.

"But you were seen with Templeton in the library." Loren fixed a beady little eye on me. "I was unaware you two knew each other. I wouldn't think you traveled in the same circles."

"You know, we don't," I said. "But we do share a mutual friend – another Salesman, actually. Emily Swift."

"Swift?" The wheels turned in Loren's brain as he searched his memory for the name. "Ah, this must be the daughter of the late Salesman who sat on the Court? I heard she got herself into trouble when she came of age."

"That would be Emily." I gave a tiny laugh. Emily fell ass-over-tin-cup into trouble wherever she went. She was also one of the biggest reasons the Fringe took a solid hit and started to collapse. Not many people knew this, however. There were a lot of secrets we all kept.

"And you are friends?" Loren mused. "Interesting. Well, there are good Salesmen. Her father was well-respected. I didn't agree with all his policies, but he was honorable."

"And so is Emily," I replied.

"Templeton, however, doesn't have the best

reputation," Loren added. "He doesn't even play well with other Salesmen, much less witches."

"This is also true," I agreed. "But he's been helpful once or twice. And he's a powerful practitioner of magic. You never know what I might learn." I tried to shrug off Loren's questioning.

The waiter chose that moment to bring our lunch. He retrieved the wine from the tabletop chiller and refilled our glasses.

I'd hoped the arrival of our food would signal a good time to change the subject.

No such luck.

"I've personally never had an issue with Templeton." Loren returned to the conversation as he dug into the puff pastry. "He's a tad standoffish as a rule, but probably because of his lower status here in the Congress."

"I'm sure that's it." I took a big swig of my wine and eyeballed the bottle on the table. At this rate, we'd need a second one before lunch was over.

"In fact," Loren began as he lifted a fork of fish and flakes, "you could do worse."

I was surprised. "I could?"

He finished his bite. "Weren't you also running around with a bunch of Rabbits?"

I took in a deep breath through my nose. "Yes. Yes, I was. I have a very good friend who is a Rabbit. We have similar interests."

"Such as?"

"Kindness." I focused on my own plate and used the side of my fork to cut into the food while Loren chuckled.

"Point taken, Lucie," he said. "I only want for you to be happy."

"I am happy." I met his eyes. "Truly. I've got good friends, and there's the..." I waved my hand, searching my brain for another positive item I could talk about. "Um... *Ah!* The success with strengthening my witchline."

Loren nodded. "Guillaume reported to the Congress your training went exceptionally well. He was pleased with your results. He said you were one of the most dedicated students he's ever had. That's high praise, Lucie."

I knew what Loren said was true. I might hate Guillaume, but I knew he was impressed with what we accomplished. It came at a price, but I could justify the experience when I tapped into my witchline and felt how much stronger it'd become. I continued to work on it and I was able to keep increasing its power bit by bit. All these things pulled together were good signs.

"Guillaume contacted the Congress shortly before the end of last year and a demonstration in front of a select group of elders was discussed. However, he was told you were not 'readily available.' Naturally he was not satisfied. Since I was your chief advocate here in the Congress, I was asked to relay how you were traveling out of the Empire for an extended period." Loren speared a piece of asparagus.

I fought to control the instinctive fear churning up from my belly and into my chest. I couldn't afford to carry both a hurt heart and terror in the same spot, so I pushed down the latter. "And?"

"He demanded to know where you were, as you would expect." Loren took a moment to wave at another witch as he passed through the dining room and signaled a greeting to my lunch date. Loren returned his attention to me, an unpleasant smile gracing his lips. "While I respect Guillaume's expertise immensely, I do not answer to him. I assured him you were continuing your self-studies and we'd be in touch when you were back in Matar."

"And now I am. Have you been in touch with

him?" I had to know.

"My concern was he'd learn of your return before I could send an official message – which yes, I have sent." Loren drank from his wine glass. "I explained you had some immediate duties to attend to as required by a Congress elder and would be available afterward, stressing your obligations to the Congress supersede everything else. *Everything.*"

"Let me guess," I said, a wave of relief washing over me. "You are that Congress elder?"

Loren winked.

"Thank you." It was a small reprieve, but a welcome one. It was enough to allow me to comfortably take a bite of my lunch. "But he's not in Matar now, right?"

"I'm not sure. I haven't heard he's come into the Empire." Loren's eagle eye landed on something behind me. He blinked rapidly several times. "On a separate note, I expect you to attend the Witches Gala this weekend. In fact, I daresay you cannot avoid attending. There are witches who wanted to see you fail under Guillaume's tutelage. Since you didn't, they'll content themselves with the story you did succeed and are now failing to serve the Congress.

Not only is it social suicide, it's dangerous to upset certain factions in the Congress."

"The Witches Gala? God, Loren. It's not really my speed," I protested.

"I can see if my nephew is available to escort you," he said as he continued to study something over my left shoulder.

"No! I mean, thank you, but I'd rather find my own date – or even attend by myself. That's preferable," I prattled on as Loren donned his polite meet-and-greet visage. What, or who, had captured his interest?

"Miss Waverton, a pleasure," said Loren as he stood, placing his napkin on his chair. "I hope you enjoyed your lunch."

I peeked up at the striking blond woman who appeared beside me. A pair of sharp green eyes glanced down to see who Loren dined with, barely delivering an acknowledging nod. I raised my eyebrows and went back to my plate, pushing the pieces around. I didn't have time for Congress snobs.

"Good afternoon, Loren," she sniffed. "Yes. We dined in one of the private alcoves. I can't imagine sitting out in the center of the room like this. Can you, Templeton?"

At the name my head jerked up, my mouth popping open. Templeton stepped around the woman and looked down his nose at me. His ice-blue eyes grew even colder. I snapped my mouth shut.

Loren inclined his head. "Templeton. I believe you know Lucie."

"Miss Bellerose." Templeton briefly scanned my face as he rested his hand on the small of the woman's back. He greeted the older man. "Loren."

"We'll be seeing you and Michelle at the gala this weekend?" The Waverton woman spoke to Loren.

"Of course," he answered. "And you two are attending?"

Together? I thought. *You might as well have asked it, Loren.*

"My father assigned a suitable escort to me for the event," she pouted. "I've encouraged Templeton to attend, but he insists he has another commitment."

My mouth was dry, and I reached for my wine. My hand shook and I returned it to my lap. I looked up and realized Templeton witnessed my aborted beverage mission.

"You should come," Loren encouraged Templeton. He gestured to me. "Lucie will be attending without an escort. Michelle and I will serve as her chaperones."

"Oh, hell," I muttered. Shaking hand be damned. I swiped the wine glass and drained it.

Templeton smirked.

"Forgive me," the blonde began, giving me the once over. "Do I know your family?"

"Lucie is of the Bellerose Witchline," Loren informed her. "She studied with Guillaume and recently returned from an extended holiday."

The woman dangled her pale hand in my direction. "Elaine Waverton."

I wiggled the limp offering. "Nice to meet you."

She evaluated me, her upper lip tightening. "There's been talk about you, hasn't there?"

"Wouldn't be the first time." I wished I wasn't sitting. I felt like I was at a disadvantage.

"You supposedly went to France to fix your witchline. Some witches are claiming you made it stronger." She glared at me. "I can't imagine how that would be possible."

"Guillaume has colorful teaching methods." I stole a peek at Templeton. He was paying close attention to this conversation. Time to shut it down. "Anyhow, I'm sure the details wouldn't interest you." I motioned to Templeton. "And you don't want to keep your lunch *date* waiting while we discuss boring witch politics. I doubt he'd be interested in anything I had to say."

Templeton's nostrils flared once.

"I do have to go," Elaine said turning to Loren. "I look forward to seeing you at the gala." She leaned over and presented a cheek. Loren gave her a peck before wishing her a good day.

Templeton seemed to be amused by the woman's display. He nodded his goodbye to Loren before ignoring me and guiding Elaine away from the table. I was glad I didn't have to watch them walk out of the dining room.

Loren sat back down in his chair. He shrugged. "That was unexpected."

"What do you mean?" I asked.

"I wouldn't think Templeton would be interested in Elaine Waverton as a lunch date."

"Why is that?" I was tired. This was turning into a long lunch.

"She's spoiled. Rather unpleasant. Shallow. He doesn't seem to be the type of man who would put up with that." Loren nodded once in the direction Templeton and his date had disappeared.

"And I wonder what she's up to? I wouldn't think she'd spend time with a Salesman here at Congress. It would upset her father." Loren rubbed his chin.

"How old is she?" The woman was certainly old enough to pick and choose who she dated.

"Hmm. Probably in her early thirties, I'd guess," Loren replied thoughtfully. "But her father still wields a heavy hand over his children."

"Like picking her event escorts?" I shook my head.

"Probably someone being courted for a sizeable donation."

"That's even worse."

Loren nodded. "It would not be a role I'd want my daughter to play."

"And what's this about you and Michelle being my chaperones?" I pinched the bridge of my nose between my thumb and index finger. I shook my head a second time and dropped my hand. "Seriously, Loren? I'm turning 38 in a couple of months."

"Appearances and tradition, dear." Loren picked up the wine bottle. Disappointed, he realized it was empty. "I think I should like to order another bottle. Do you need a refill?"

Chapter 4

After lunch, I walked into the Congress of Empire Witches' library, my gaze skimming the first set of tables. I knew Templeton wouldn't be sitting front and center but pausing gave me another moment to compose myself before dealing with him. One of the assistant librarians lifted her head, registered my presence, and returned to her paperwork.

Elaine Waverton, hmm? Was this a first lunch date? His hand seemed comfortable on her lower back. It was so damn *intimate*. I felt the temperature over my skin tingle and I reigned in my agitation.

Why did I care? I blew out a breath, earning a stern headshake from the assistant librarian. She put a finger to her lips.

I knew where to find Templeton. He'd choose to sit in the back near the Historical Meaning section. This is where we first explored, and my sense was it was still the right trail to follow. I weaved through the polished library tables and turned into the stone passageway on the right.

My footsteps were silent – a function of the spell cast over the library to keep patron visits quiet. I could've put on a pair of tap shoes and danced my way through the stacks and you wouldn't hear a thing. I turned again to the right, rounding the tall shelves. The air felt like it hadn't been touched in ages. Dust, old books, and ancient magic flooded my senses. It was comforting. There was a point in my life when I spent half my time in libraries studying.

I paused at the end of a row where it opened into a secluded area consisting of half a dozen empty tables. Templeton sat at one toward the back. He was the only person studying in this section. Books were sprawled out across the table in front of him. I took a moment to observe him as he took notes, his head bent over a book, a hand gliding across his notepad. He concentrated on his work. Sunlight poured in from one of the high windows above where he sat, bathing him in the afternoon light. He wasn't exactly the golden child, but he was certainly something unique within these book-lined walls. I pushed the unbidden smile away from my lips before choosing the center aisle and crossing the space to his table.

"Good. You're finally here." He didn't bother to look up as I approached.

"Nice to see you again, too." Placing my purse on the table, I pulled out a chair to sit. I intended to put my irritation aside, but he'd better drop the snotty act. I wasn't going to have it.

"Don't get comfortable. I need you to request this book." Templeton slid a piece of paper across the table. He remained focused on the open tome in front of him.

I read the title. *Poems from the Black Sky*. "I'm not your gofer."

"My request was denied because I am not a witch." He scribbled another sentence on his notepad. "Therefore, I need you to ask for the book." His chin lifted. "I've been waiting to examine it for weeks."

I almost asked why he didn't have Elaine Waverton get it for him, but one, that was childish, and two, I was certain our research – his research – was still being conducted privately.

I swiped the slip of paper from the table and

turned away. His stare stamped into my back. I stalked off, disappearing around the stacks to work my way back to the front of the library.

The assistant librarian said it was available for me to view – but there was a catch. I couldn't take it back to the table. I could only look at it in a private room. The room would be locked by a spelled key from the outside the entire time I had the book. All this for a book of poetry? Maybe Templeton was onto something.

The assistant librarian explained there was a secluded room upstairs in the back of the library used for these private viewings. Did I still want to request it?

I drummed my fingers on top of her elevated desk. "Yes, but I need to get someone first. I'll meet you upstairs."

"That Salesman?" The woman's face contorted. It was ugly.

"Yes." I lifted my chin, tilting my head to the side. "Is there a problem?"

"Not exactly, but only witches are allowed to request certain books, and that's one of them." She raised her pointed nose.

"I don't see the problem. A witch *has* requested it. Me." I waited.

"Well..." Her head swiveled back and forth as if some solution might be written into the air on how to deal with requests she didn't want to fulfill.

"Well, what?" I pressed on. "A witch made the request, the book was confirmed as available, and I agreed to view it in the private room as required. Unless there's a rule stating I'm not allowed to be joined in this viewing by a non-witch, then I don't understand the issue."

"Alright." She gave her head a frustrated shake. "But it's a terribly confined space. There is one chair and a table. Quarters will be tight."

"I'll sit on his lap then," I sneered. This was an example of the bigotry you'd find within the Congress walls. Templeton was a full-fledged member and yet because he wasn't a witch, he was not seen as an equal. Ironic since he was probably more skilled than most people studying within these walls, and his knowledge was likely greater than many of the witches wielding control in the Congress.

Templeton was unlikeable, for sure, but at least narrow-minded witches such as this one should dislike him for the right reasons: He was a jerk.

My words flustered the assistant librarian, but she directed me – and 'the Salesman' – to meet her upstairs in 10 minutes and she would have the book of poems. I thanked her for her efficiency.

When I returned to Templeton's table, I explained the situation. He didn't comment, but I'm sure he was annoyed. He gathered up his notes, sliding them into a manila envelope. Next, he placed the books he'd been studying on the returns cart. I watched as he completed these basic tasks. He moved gracefully. I assumed his coat and Salesman top hat were left at the coat check. Door traveling in and out of the Congress building was considered magic and therefore not permitted. He'd removed his suit jacket and I admired his build. The tailored burgundy shirt Templeton wore fit him well. His body was the type of firm muscle won through exercise and restraint. He was trim. I judged him to be about six feet tall. Templeton caught me studying him and paused. Embarrassed, I turned my head.

I waited for him to finish before leading him through the tall rows of books to the spiral staircase connecting to the second floor. I was very aware of his proximity as we climbed the stairs, our bodies circling upward. I wish I would've retrieved my coat before coming to the library. My skirt fit snugly over my curves, and I was conscious of it tightening across my backside with every step. At the top of the stairs, I eased to the side – noting and ignoring the smug expression on Templeton's face.

"This way," I directed, turning my back to him.

The assistant librarian met us at the door of the private viewing room. She cast a sideways glance at Templeton before speaking directly to me. "The book is inside. You have one hour and you will be locked in. If you need to be let out sooner than the allotted time, pull the cord hanging in the corner. I'll return at my earliest convenience to unlock the door. But again, you only have one hour with the book."

"I doubt we'll need the whole time," I said to her, stepping inside with Templeton following behind me. The windowless door clicked shut and I heard the spelled key rotating in the lock. "Talk about overkill," I breathed.

"What do you expect from witches?" Templeton said over my shoulder. He leaned toward the table. He wasn't touching me, but he was close.

I caught a hint of his soap. Overwhelmed by the memories called up by the fresh scent, I closed my eyes and thought about the night in my kitchen.

I felt his steady breath against my ear. He was no longer looking at the book. Goosebumps cascaded down my neck and over my chest.

"Okay, wait a minute." I pushed the vision away. Remaining mindful of our cramped space, I pivoted carefully to face him. I startled slightly at the bitterness I found hardening his features and dropped my gaze to his collar. "I'm going to sit on the table – there's enough room. You take the chair." I shifted sideways, my backside resting against the table's edge. Reaching back, I placed my palms on the tabletop and hopped up. I crossed my ankles and gestured to the book on the table. "You wanted it; here you go."

He cocked his head to the side, contemplating me. His lips parted, and for a moment I thought he was going to say something. Instead, he huffed and yanked the chair away from the table. Before sitting down, he thrust the envelope with his notes toward me. "You should catch up."

"Sure," I replied, reaching into the envelope as he sat down and opened *Poems from the Black Sky*. I took out the papers and read through his slanted handwriting. He'd included dates. Templeton had been coming to the Congress' library steadily since our first meeting last October. My attention wandered to the man beside me. I watched his elegant fingers turn the book's pages and skate over the lines of text as he searched.

His hand stilled. "Yes?"

"I felt so broken by everything that happened in the Walled Zone – by everything leading up to that night last fall." The words were out of my mouth before I had time to stop them. "I left the Empire because I was hurting."

He looked up, puzzled. "It's not my job to fix you."

I swallowed. "You're right. It's not. And I never expected it. But I'm not here to serve you either, Templeton. Hell, I'm not even here to help you unless I want to. Like now. I want to help. I want..." My eyes were glued to the floor. Being near him was harder than I'd anticipated. I thought I'd allowed enough time pass.

His frown was curious. "What do you want,

Lucie?"

I lifted a shoulder. "I don't know."

"Then that's a problem for you," he said, returning to the book.

I don't know what I expected. We needed to get past whatever didn't happen between us. It wasn't in the cards. I winced. *Poor choice of words,* I thought. I rubbed my forehead and prepared a different approach. "Alright. How about this? Tell me what you're searching for in this book of poems. Maybe there's something I'll recognize."

He sat back in the chair. "In *Empire Tales for Children* there's a story called *Black Sky*. The child appearing in *Six Doors* is the same girl appearing in all the tales. In *Black Sky* she meets a poet. He tells her about wondrous beings of light who crawl over the stars in a nighttime sky. These beasts are majestic, but if angered, they're dangerous."

I waited a moment before I spoke. "This sounds familiar."

"Sebastian described 'beautiful beasts' you didn't want to anger on the other side of the fifth door. I believe the creatures described in *Black Sky* are the same as what he saw." Templeton said Sebastian's name so casually, it took my breath away. I forced myself to not react. "It's taken me some time, but through my research, I learned of this book of poetry. I'm hoping what's inside will give me more information on what I'll find beyond the fifth door."

"Going there, Templeton, I mean..." I shook my head. "It's too dangerous to go by yourself. No, we need to do something different."

He scowled down at the book. "Your concern for me is touching."

"That's it." He'd stepped on my last nerve. I hopped off the table and reached for the cord. I was done with him. I was trying to do the right thing and he wasn't giving me an inch. I wouldn't spend my days being his verbal punching bag because his ego was bruised. I'd been punished enough and for a long time.

"What are you doing?" Templeton stood up quickly, pushing the chair backward and slamming it into the locked door. He grabbed my wrist as my fingertips grazed the hanging braid, twisting my arm and putting his body in front of the cord used to call the assistant librarian. I drew hard and fast from my witchline, automatically raising my magic so he'd get a taste of my fire. The temperature hovering over my skin increased dramatically and he released me to avoid being burnt. We glared at each other.

"You better start playing nice with me," I warned, holding the heat tight to my body while maintaining the power.

The menacing smile crawling across his face reminded me of who I was dealing with. "Lucie." Templeton leaned in close, ignoring the magic coasting over my body. This time I felt his breath on my mouth. His irises lost all color, leaving only angry black circles surrounding his pinprick pupils. "Don't make the mistake of thinking I won't strike you back when you pull stunts like that with me, witch. This is your one warning."

The moment lingered. Neither one of us was willing to back down.

"I don't think you want to be this close to me." I wrinkled my nose. "After all, what would your precious Elaine think?"

Templeton flinched as if I'd slapped him. He struck back. "Jealous?"

I'd touched a nerve. "Not in the least. I don't care who you fuck, Templeton."

"Well, she's hardly a murderous psychopath,

but we all can't have your discriminating taste in lovers." Disgust crawled across his face.

My magic dropped immediately as his words slammed into their target. My face softened under the verbal blow. I shook my head at him but refused to look away. "Wow. Okay, then." I cleared my throat. "Now that we got that out of the way."

Templeton said nothing, but the muted color rushed back into his eyes as his anger fell away. He blinked several times.

I heard the slight intake of breath as he prepared to speak, but I couldn't keep doing this. I motioned to the book of poetry. "Get what you need. You have the rest of the allotted hour. Use it well because I'm not meeting you here again. This is your one shot."

I picked up the notes he'd handed me earlier and turned my back to him. I pressed my hip against the table and began to read, forcing myself to focus.

"Lucie."

I lifted my hand but didn't face him. "Please just get what you need. I'm done talking to you."

He waited a full minute. When I didn't turn around, he gave up. I heard the chair scrape over the floor and sensed his body lowering back to the seat.

The rest of the hour passed at a snail's pace.

∞∞∞

The assistant librarian unlocked the door precisely one hour after she'd shut us in. I stuffed the notes I'd been reading back into the manila envelope and left it on the table. I didn't know if Templeton had gathered the information he'd hoped to find, but I didn't care. I wanted out of there.

I mumbled a 'thanks' to the assistant librarian and hustled to the spiral stairs. I descended as fast as I could. Templeton was only a few steps behind me.

I assumed he'd return to the Historical Meaning section, but apparently, he was ready to leave the library as well.

My heeled boots beat into the marbled floor as I hurried toward the coat check. I gave the young woman my name and she slipped behind a rack to retrieve my coat. Templeton appeared at my side. He leaned both hands against the counter but turned his head to stare at my profile.

"I want to talk to you," he said.

I shook my head. "No."

He gritted his teeth. "We need to talk."

"No."

"I want to dis—"

"Lucie Bellerose?" A man interrupted us from behind.

I glanced over my shoulder. "Yes?"

"This is for you." He held out a narrow envelope.

I turned and accepted it. My name was printed on the front. "What is this?"

"A copy of your citation. You used magic in the building approximately —" he looked at his watch "— 54 minutes ago. Information is included on when you are to appear at the Oversight Office to defend your actions and receive your penalty."

"What? I didn't... *Oh.*" Dammit. I resisted the urge to ball up the paper in my hand. I took a deep breath, giving the man a forced smile. "Is there someone I can meet with now to discuss this?"

"I'm afraid not," he answered. "Fortunately for you it's only a level four violation. You will not need to be arrested today."

"Fine," I capitulated. I'd had my fill of the Congress and wanted to leave before the day became even worse. The coat check employee stood waiting, my wool coat in her hand. I shoved the envelope into my purse and took the garment.

Templeton held his dress coat over his arm, a finely made Salesman top hat dangling from his fingertips. He tried to make eye contact with me. "Lucie."

"Dammit, Templeton, no. Leave me alone!" I slipped my coat on and rushed off, hauling my purse strap over my shoulder.

I was spared. He didn't follow me.

Chapter 5

It was such a relief to be home. I stripped off my boots in the entryway and tossed my purse on the table. What a hellish day. Which god did I piss off? I opened the door to the hall closet and draped my coat over a hanger. As I shut the closet door, I felt the wards protecting my home give and heard the pantry door in the kitchen open.

"I will kill him," I seethed as I stormed toward the kitchen.

"Lucie?" A female voice called out.

I found a smiling Emily Swift swinging her top hat back and forth while she waited to learn if I was home. I crossed to my friend and we hugged.

"I'm so glad it's you," I told her.

"I bet." She grinned, her eyes twinkling. "Is The Pantry Express getting a lot of use these days?"

"Some," I shrugged. "But seeing you is exactly what I needed. Come in, grab a stool. Are you thirsty? Coffee? Water? Wine?"

"Wine," she replied, choosing a barstool. She tossed her top hat onto the counter. "Let's do happy hour and celebrate your return."

"Works for me," I said. "Although, this isn't my first glass today. If I abruptly fall asleep, don't hold it against me."

"Yeah? What's the occasion – outside of the fact you are back and we're all happy to see you? Oh, wait!" She reached into her jacket pocket and brought out a fistful of confetti. She threw it into the air. "Welcome home!"

I watched the pieces of colored paper drift over my counter and floor. "Gee, thanks."

Emily laughed. "I couldn't resist. We had a bunch left after Tara's birthday party last year. It was a spur-of-the-moment grab."

I retrieved the broom from the closet and handed it to her. "Your celebration was much appreciated. Cleanup is a bitch."

Ever the good sport, Emily took the broom. She brushed the confetti off the counter and proceeded to sweep the floor. "Rabbit said you got in late Tuesday night. I didn't want to overwhelm you, so I decided to give you a day to yourself. I figured you'd need a little space at least for 24 hours before everyone descended on you."

"Thanks, but you were the only one who waited," I said. I placed two glasses of Pinot Noir on the counter. "Rabbit was here within – god, maybe an hour? An hour and a half?"

"Of you getting home?" Emily stopped sweeping. "You're kidding?"

"He was watching with the great aid of Rabbit technology," I answered. "Dustpan is in the closet."

"Thanks." Emily finished cleaning up the confetti and dumped the paper bits into the trash bin. She returned everything to the closet. I handed her the wine and we clinked glasses. "To coming home to all of us. We missed you, Lucie."

To *us*. Her words made me tear up. I set my glass down and wiped my eyes. "Sorry."

"No, hey!" Emily gave me another hug, splashing some wine onto the floor. "Oops. Sorry."

"It's okay." I let out a tiny chuckle and wiped up the spill with a paper towel. "It's great to have you here. I need a friend." I let out a shuddering breath.

Emily rubbed my arm. "So, tell me everything."

"That would be a long story," I said.

Emily waved her arms, catching herself in time before she spilled more wine. "I've got time."

"I don't even know where to start," I said, circling the counter and climbing onto one of the barstools.

She joined me. "You could start with where you've been. Rabbit couldn't find you. We figured you were outside of the Empire since you'd stopped at my house first, but he couldn't pick up your trail. It drove him nuts, by the way."

"It was intentional," I admitted. "I didn't want people to worry, but I didn't want to talk to anyone, either. I'd hoped touching base with you before I left would've been good enough."

Emily took a drink of her wine. "Did you really think so? Or were you hoping it would pan out that way?"

"The latter," I sighed. "I suppose it was sort of a cover-my-ass move."

"Yeah, how'd it work out for you?" Emily smiled wryly.

"About as good as you'd expect." I craned my head back and forth and rolled my shoulders. I was getting a headache.

"Have you seen *him*?" Emily wasn't talking about Rabbit now.

"Twice." I hesitated. "Well, maybe three times if you count the two separate experiences I had today."

"He was upset when you left." Emily's face grew serious. "He came to my house more than once – and you know how Jack loves it when Templeton shows up out of nowhere."

"I could teach you how to block him with wards," I offered.

"Do you have wards up now to block him?"

"No." I fiddled with my wine glass.

"Then why would I?" Emily touched my knee. "What exactly happened between you two?"

"When?" I flinched. Did she know about the aborted kiss?

Emily raised her eyebrows and lifted a finger. She wiggled it at me. "Whenever *that* was."

"Oh, god." I groaned, pushing my wine glass away and burying my face in my hands. I shook my head.

"Right. Definitely start there."

"Fine." I caved, straightening back up. "Last fall when I came to your house and said I was going away for a while…"

"Go on."

"The night before, Templeton and I had a date." I shook my head. "We even had a good time. I mean, not right away, but eventually."

"Well, yeah, this is Templeton we're talking about." Emily pursed her lips. "He's not mister merry sunshine on his best day."

I continued. "We'd met at the Congress of Empire Witches library and were doing research on the fifth and sixth doors."

Emily's face grew serious. "Did you find anything about them?"

"Only enough to convince us we'd have to keep digging." I studied my friend. I may have been the one who opened and closed the directional doors, but Emily was the one who blasted Sebastian through the sixth door – and into the Below. I didn't blame her. Sebastian attacked her only days before that violent night in the Walled Zone. She used her magic to escape. "Anyhow, after we spent time in the library, we dined at his supper club. And Emily, eventually it was okay. It was almost like a real date. Templeton was –"

"Like a real person?" Emily interrupted.

I grimaced, but I knew what she meant. "Yes. Like a real person."

"Then what happened?"

"We came back here. I offered him wine, and then..." I waved a hand.

"Oh, my god – you slept with him!" Emily covered her mouth with both hands.

"No." I took a sizable swig of my wine. I was feeling dizzy, but I didn't think it was the alcohol. "I thought he was going to kiss me, though. He leaned in, and then at the last minute, he turned on his heel and left. I felt like an idiot."

"He's such an ass." Emily's gaze moved to the pantry door. We both stared at it for a beat. "Then what?"

"Then nothing. The next day I decided I needed to get away and get some perspective." I lifted a shoulder.

"Hmm. And you've seen him since you've been back – what, three times?"

"He spelled my ward. He knew when I came home."

Emily wasn't surprised. "I can totally see him doing that. And he showed up then?"

"He generously waited until the next day." I rubbed a spot over my left eye with a fingertip. I was definitely getting a headache. "Anyhow, we argued. Then he demanded I meet him at the library to do more research. Words were said. I almost set him on fire."

Emily nodded understandingly. "I once tried to set his study on fire. He stopped me." My friend pouted into her wine. "That's probably a good thing."

"Anyhow, I didn't intend to meet up with him, but I was summoned to a lunch date with my benefactor at the Congress of Empire Witches – which is where I was today. Loren is one of the witches who supported my bid to study in France. I couldn't say no to him," I finished.

"I want to know more about that," Emily said.

"Maybe someday. There's nothing to tell," I lied.

She didn't believe me but didn't pursue it. "How did the lunch with this Loren person go?"

"It was fine," I assured her. "He's an old family friend and he wanted to check in and make sure I was doing okay." I glossed over the details, but most of it didn't concern Emily anyway. I took a deep breath. "During lunch I saw Templeton. He was with another woman – another witch – and they seemed quite comfortable together."

"Ugh." Emily wrinkled her nose. "A date? I'm sorry."

I thought about what I'd seen and what Loren had said. "I guess. Loren knows who Templeton is and he didn't expect to see him with this woman. But who knows what was going on? It doesn't matter."

"Are you sure about that?" Emily gave me the eye over her wine glass.

"I caught up with him later in the library and again, it didn't go well. We ended up in a locked room saying hurtful things." I wondered if he was wounded by anything I'd said, or if it was a one-way street.

"Locked room? How'd that happen?"

"We were only allowed to view a certain book in a private room. Library policy. They locked us in."

"And you fought again?" Emily prompted.

"Things got out of hand. I called up some magic and we threatened each other." I ran both of my hands through my hair. "I've been losing control of myself since I've been back in the Empire."

"Now that's interesting," Emily replied. "But only with Templeton I'm betting."

I nodded.

"I think I know why he didn't kiss you before you left." Emily heaved a sigh.

"I don't understand." What was she talking about? "Did he tell you something?"

"Yes and no." Emily set her wine glass down and took my hands in hers. "Remember last year when all of us were here? And I mean all of us. All the freakin' Rabbits. You, me, Rabbit, Templeton – everyone. We were getting ready to head into the Walled Zone. I was asking Templeton questions about Sebastian. I let it slip you were hurting after finding out Sebastian and Basha were one and the same."

My hands clenched and Emily rubbed her thumbs over the backs of both to soothe me. "Go on."

"We were talking, and I wondered what information Sebastian might've gotten out of you without you even realizing it." She gripped my hands when I tried to pull away. "No! Don't. Listen to me. We weren't angry at you. Templeton was the one who said we'd need to give you time. He recognized you'd need to get over Sebastian first. Templeton, for all his self-centeredness, could see you were hurting. I think he cared."

I watched Emily's thumbs as they brushed over my skin. "If this is true, then why did he ask me out to dinner and then run off when things were getting..."

"Intimate?" Emily released my hands. "After what I told you, are you honestly still wondering why? Can't you see he wanted to give you some space?"

"You think that's what happened?" I wasn't sure I agreed.

"I think Templeton got in over his head. Suddenly you two were alone and sort of relaxed in each other's company. And everyone can see it. He likes you. You like him." She hesitated. "You liked him regardless of what you were feeling for *Basha*." Emily used Sebastian's nickname and pulled a face. "I'm sorry, but I'm trying to make a point. Before you knew Basha was Sebastian, you had chemistry going with Templeton. You just weren't acting on it because you were kind of getting involved with someone else."

Kind of getting involved.

This day kept getting better and better.

Oh, hell.

"I need to tell you something, Emily, but I don't want... Damn. I'm not ready for anyone else to know this, but I need to come clean with you." The words stuck in my throat, but I found the courage to admit I'd lied. "I was sleeping with Sebastian for a lot longer than I said. It wasn't only that one night. We were more involved than I let on."

Emily's lips formed a little 'O' and her eyes widened. Then she nodded. "Okay."

"In the beginning, I was simply trying to keep my relationship private. Then there were times I felt something was off and I didn't want to parade it in front of my friends – like you or Rabbit. After I learned the truth, I didn't admit to how long things had been going on with Sebastian because I was worried everyone would judge me even worse than they were."

Emily's finger was back in the air. "No one judged you. He was using you."

"Templeton did." I thought about the hateful words he said earlier at the library.

"He didn't last fall," Emily said. "But now might be different. He's had months to be angry with you for leaving."

"You said he came to your house looking for me?" I asked.

"The day after you left. From what I've pieced together, you raised your wards against him before leaving home because he couldn't door travel into your house anymore. Then he and Rabbit must've connected pretty fast and he learned you weren't in the Empire. He came to me next. I told him you needed to get away, but I didn't know where you went. He was livid."

Emily continued. "He demanded I tell him immediately if I heard from you. And you know, usually I would've told him to shove it, but he was beside himself. I told him I would. He came back to check in several times, but there was nothing I could give him."

"I'm sorry I put you in that spot." I rubbed my forehead.

"Don't worry about it. I knew it was beyond your control. You also know Rabbit came to my house looking for you, too, right?"

"What?" This was unexpected.

"He did. Same week."

"He left the Empire? I had no idea." Ugh, what a mess I'd made.

"I knew he was coming. He sent me a message

and took the train into Kincaid." Emily tilted her head, remembering. "He told me what he knew, and I confirmed you'd come to my house. I think Rabbit was way more understanding, but he was still sad."

"He told me I was selfish for leaving." The words from such a good man still smarted.

"I don't think you're selfish, Lucie. I think you were more overwhelmed than any of us realized – and I'm sorry we didn't see it. First you found out you were tied to a prophecy, then about Basha being Sebastian. And then everything that happened in front of the directional doors – it must've been so hard." Emily dropped her gaze to the countertop. "And if you were more involved with him than we knew, did you love Sebastian?"

"It was complicated," I whispered. "But I was getting there."

"I'm sorry none of us could be there for you." Emily lifted her head, concern creating faint vertical lines between her eyebrows. "But I'm here now. And we're all still on the same side."

∞∞∞

The conversation with Emily had been difficult, but it was done. We talked about the night in the Walled Zone – especially our fears of what was still to come. One thing was clear, both of us worried Templeton might try to cross over into the fifth door all alone.

"Does Rabbit know about this?" Emily asked. We'd abandoned the kitchen and opted to relax in front of the gas fireplace in my cozy living room.

"I have no idea, but we're going to get together. I'm going to text him." I cringed.

"You have a phone?" Emily's mouth popped open. "He gave you a phone?"

"He gave me the phone he took back from you." I fake ducked as if I expected her to hit me.

"Figures." She blew out breath and the hair sweeping across her forehead moved. She pointed a finger at me. "You'd think Rabbit, of all people, would have a sense of humor, but he doesn't. And I sent him funny stuff."

"I'm sure you did," I laughed before growing serious again. "I want to know what Rabbit knows. He must've kept some sort of monitor on the Fringe's compound and the directional doors."

"Well, the Empire confiscated the property. As far as I know, nothing happened after that. You locked away the two directional doors. You can't even see where they were." Emily stared at the flames dancing over the gas vent. "And Templeton needs you to wake up the Crimson Stone if he wants the doors opened. He's not going anywhere without your help."

I nodded. "But I don't underestimate him."

"Neither do I." Emily yawned and sat up. "Alright, I gotta go. I'm meeting the Maid of Honorzilla tonight."

"Is that a thing?"

"Yes, and she's horrible! The wedding's not until spring and Tara's already made the person designing the wedding invitations cry. Twice."

"You're kidding?" I snickered, shaking my head.

"Then she ripped Rabbit a new one when he was late for his suit fitting." Rabbit was escorting Emily down the aisle along with her mother.

"In a way, that's kind of funny," I said.

"Oh, no it's not." Emily's mouth slipped into an evil smile. "But I'm not planning on bearing the burden of the wedding party monster on my own for much longer."

"What do you mean?" I picked up the bottle of wine and squinted. Damn. Empty.

"Lucie Bellerose, will you be my bridesmaid?"

∞ ∞ ∞

I was touched Emily invited me to be in her wedding. I said yes. It was only short notice because I'd been away. She'd been waiting to ask me.

I was thrilled Rabbit would walk her down the aisle. In a way, he was somewhat of a surrogate father to Emily when she needed it. Rabbit was friends with the late Daniel Swift, and he loved Emily very much.

A tipsy Emily gave me one last hug in the kitchen before donning her top hat and door traveling back to her house in Kincaid. We promised to get together soon.

A bellyful of wine and no dinner muddled my mind. I checked my fridge, then looked in the cupboards. My appetite still came and went. I seemed to be able to eat if I had something – or someone – to distract me. I bit my lip.

I pulled the phone Rabbit gave me from my purse and pressed my finger against the reader.

The phone lit up and I called up the app like Rabbit had showed me.

Hey, I texted.
Hey back. What's up?
Are you in Matar?
Yup.
Hungry?
I could eat.
Want to come over?
Give me 30.

Chapter 6

I decided on takeout. I liked to cook, but I didn't have the energy for it these days. Plus, when I stuck my head in my sparsely stocked refrigerator, nothing sounded good. I remembered a local Thai restaurant a block from my house and dug around for an old menu. The Empire service operator transferred me to the restaurant's order line, and I requested Tofu Pad Krapow for Rabbit and Chicken Gai Krob for myself. I added jasmine rice, papaya salad, and spring rolls for both of us. I figured Rabbit would eat whatever I didn't – with the exception of the meat dish.

About 30 minutes after texting, Rabbit tapped on my front door. His hands were thrust into his pockets and his shoulders were pulled up to his ears. He bounced while he puffed warm breath into the frigid air.

"Get in here," I said, standing to the side so he

could enter. His knit cap was pulled down but as usual, his big hands were bare. He blew into them to warm them up.

"We're hitting the February freeze season." He pulled off his hat, his jet-black curls spilling out around his head.

"Why don't you ever wear gloves?" I admonished. "I'm going to get you some."

"What? Nah. It's all good." He flexed his fingers and I noticed the split knuckles.

"I ordered us Thai food. It'll be here in the next half hour. Let me get you some wine." I spun around to head to the kitchen and stumbled slightly to the left. Rabbit grabbed my right arm, steadying me.

"Looks like you started the party without me," he said, dropping his hand. He eyeballed me.

I laughed off his comment. "Emily was here earlier. We cracked open a bottle. I'm fine. Come on." I waved for him to follow me into the kitchen.

"I figured she'd be coming by. I got a message to her yesterday." He watched me pour a glass of wine for him. "How many bottles did you guys share?"

I sulked under his scrutiny. "I might've had a

teensy bit more after she left. Here." I slid a glass across the counter to him. I held up mine in a toast and waited.

Rabbit evaluated me as he removed his coat and slipped it over the barstool. I sized up the black concert tee shirt he wore – some death metal group called *Bile Muffins*. Their 'mascot' retched out their band logo. Good god. The tee was worn over a long-sleeved shirt in another shade of black. Both were left untucked over a tight pair of jeans. A thick, silver chain ran from his belt to his wallet. On his feet, a beat-up pair of Doc Martens. Rabbit climbed up onto the barstool, sitting on his coat. He didn't lift his glass. "What happened today?"

I shrugged and instead took a gulp of my wine. "Emily came over."

"For the entire day?"

"No. Later in the afternoon." I circled the counter and sat beside him. "It was good to see her."

Rabbit picked up his glass of wine and peered into it thoughtfully. "What else?"

"I had lunch at the Congress of Empire Witches." I stuck out my tongue and crossed my eyes. "That was fun."

"Yeah? Summoned?"

"Sort of," I replied. "How did you know?"

He shook his head. "Just a guess. Are you in trouble for something?"

"No, not so much. I mean..." I lifted a shoulder. "I have obligations to meet. I have a lot of loose ends to tidy up. Things I should've taken care of last year."

"We ended up keeping you busy." Rabbit smiled faintly and sipped his wine.

"Long before that whole mess," I admitted. "I'm not a fan of answering to the Congress – even though I understand what's expected of me."

"And that is?"

"I need to show their support of me spending a year in France was a good investment." I swirled the wine in my glass. A fruit fly floated on the surface. I pulled it out with a fingertip and flicked it away.

Rabbit's eyebrows went up another notch. "Why don't you tell me about that?"

"You mean you don't know everything by now?" I teased. "The network's slipping."

"Witches are a crafty bunch."

"That's a horrible pun," I groaned.

Rabbit grinned. "It was unintentional. But I

am serious. The Empire is easy to crack into. Witch secrets are a different story."

"Yeah." I sobered up for a moment. "A lot of secrets."

Rabbit spun our barstools and we faced each other. "I could tell you what I do know, and you could fill in the blanks. What gets said in this room goes nowhere."

I knew he was being honest. I nodded. "Go on."

"I know you spent a year in France training under a witch called Guillaume. From what I was able to pick up, witches need to apply in order to study with him. He never accepts more than one student per year, and he doesn't even agree to teach every year. But he only takes the best witches as students." Rabbit paused to see if I'd add anything.

"All of that is accurate." I reached for my wine. Rabbit pushed it beyond my stretch.

"Wait until the food comes," he said.

"Fine." I rolled my wrist, waving my hand. "You were saying?"

"This Guillaume, he's not nice to his students. His methods are questionable." Rabbit watched my face carefully. "At least two students died as a result of torture."

"That's not entirely true," I said. "They died as a result of trying to escape."

"You knew this before agreeing to go study with him?" Rabbit frowned.

"I didn't agree to go study with him. I requested to study with him," I clarified. "And I petitioned the Congress for support."

Rabbit was clearly bewildered. "You weren't forced to go?"

I shook my head. "I was not."

"Lucie, look. I'm trying to be delicate here, but what I heard… What he supposedly does to students…"

"Is probably true." I crossed my arms over my chest. "Guillaume employs some brutal methods to achieve the desired result. I knew this going in."

"Did he hurt you?" Rabbit's shoulders stiffened.

"I needed to strengthen my witchline – I still need to increase it. I don't want it to die out. I don't want any of the witchlines to die out. We're a disappearing breed, like the Rabbits." I watched him shift uncomfortably. "It's no secret your numbers are going down no matter how many kids your women pop out."

Rabbit twitched at my words. "You're a bit of a mean drunk."

"I'm sorry." My eyes pressed shut. "That came out the wrong way."

"Whatever," he replied. "Keep going. Tell me about this witchline."

I opened my eyes. His normally friendly face developed an edge, but his hand landed on my knee, and he squeezed it gently. I took a deep breath. "All natural witches are born with access to a vein of power – something unique to their own biological family. The witchline isn't magic, but it consists of a raw power fueling the magic we do. The witchline automatically knows its own witches and who to feed. It's never drained, and in fact, it thrives when it's used. Um, I'm not sure how to explain this feeling, but if I tap into my own witchline, it feels more alive inside me. I always know it's there, but when I use it, it feels more energetic."

"The witchline is inside you?"

"In and around me. It's outside of me, but I feel it running through me, too."

"Right, that doesn't sound complicated. Witches," Rabbit joked. He no longer appeared to be upset with me. I was grateful.

"It doesn't feel weird if you're born with it. It's a part of you," I explained.

"I think I've got it. As much as I can understand anyway. But you said it's getting thin? Is it because there are fewer natural witches being born?"

"Probably to some extent," I said. "But it was long before that. Most of us believe it's because the witchlines weren't being used by their natural witches. Magic became less important – or maybe even less necessary – to witches. Also, as time went on, witches left the Empire, choosing a non-magical world for their homes. Perhaps they never rejected being a witch, but they didn't use their magic as much. They tapped into their witchlines less because they didn't 'need' it. Plus, they were living in a world where magic wasn't believed to be real. They chose other routes to accomplish what they needed to do instead of practicing magic. This affected the familial witchlines."

"It atrophied," Rabbit realized.

"Exactly." I looked at my wine glass wistfully before continuing. "And no matter what anyone did, they couldn't recover their witchlines. It was as though they became sick and could not return to their original strength. It was too late. And some families really did try. Directives were issued to pull large numbers of witches back into the Empire. It didn't make a difference."

"Then this is a problem all witchlines have?"

"Almost all. A few haven't significantly experienced the issue, but they are very old witchlines and tend to keep to themselves." I twisted my lips to the side and thought about it. "They're not incestuous, but they tend to carefully plan out who is marrying whom and who is breeding. They eschew a lot of technologies and practice magic in the most mundane of activities. Living in the Empire serves them well. One of the families is extremely powerful. The Actons. Wealthy, too. The current matriarch in the family holds a high position in the Congress. She fought against my studying in France."

"Because you're not part of the old money upper crust?" Rabbit gave a half nod.

"To some extent. How dare the rabble muddy the floors of Congress with their common feet? But it was also because if it worked, then maybe other witches could go and do the same thing – witches who could challenge a family like the Actons for power in the witch community."

"I can see it. Plays out in even the friendliest Empire groups," Rabbit observed.

"In the Rabbits? I wouldn't think your brethren would be like that."

"You'd be surprised," he said. "But you did go to France, and you did have success, right?"

"I did. I had a theory about what we might try from what I've studied over the years. And I believed Guillaume was the right witch to help me." I didn't want to tell Rabbit the details, but I knew he'd ask what my theory was. He didn't disappoint.

"Your theory must've been right if it worked."

"That appears to be the case." I licked my lips.

"What was it, Lucie?"

I chose my words carefully. "Feeding the witchline back my own raw energy. Sacrificing pieces of me back into it. Think of it like adding stem cells to a body to help replace cells damaged by disease – that's the only way I know to describe it succinctly."

"How did you do it?" Rabbit searched my face. "And why did you need Guillaume?"

We sat for a long minute staring at each other. The loud banging of my door knocker echoed from the front of the house. My savior came in the form of Thai food delivery.

"Food's here," I said, hopping off the barstool. "I'll get the takeout. You grab the plates and silverware."

"Lucie, you never answered my earlier question," Rabbit said as I reached the kitchen door.

I paused. "Which one?"

"Guillaume. Did he hurt you as part of this witchline healing? I mean, physically?" His eyes took on a glossy appearance as they darkened.

"How do you think I fed my witchline?" I turned my back to him and left to answer the front door.

∞∞∞

After paying and tipping the delivery guy, I brought the sacks into the kitchen. Rabbit stood by my kitchen sink knocking back a shot of vodka.

"I had vodka?" I asked, setting the bags on the counter.

"Yup. In the pantry." Rabbit put the cap back on the bottle and returned it to its home.

"I don't get a shot?" I called after him.

"Nope." He shut the pantry door behind him.

He grabbed two plates from a cupboard and passed them to me before fishing out a few forks and knives. "You need to eat."

"Honestly, I'm not drunk," I objected. "Well, not horribly so."

"Have you been eating?" Rabbit grabbed a couple of paper towels. "You're too skinny."

"Ha! I'm not skinny." I pointed to the containers as I opened them. "Pad Krapow with tofu for you, papaya salad here – it's vegetarian. I got us a bunch of spring rolls." I spooned a big portion of the jasmine rice onto both plates.

"You lost weight," he argued.

"Didn't we cover this?" I shook my head at him. "Eat, Rabbit."

He piled Pad Krapow onto his plate. "So whatever Guillaume did, it worked?"

"We're still talking about this, huh?" I meticulously arranged the crispy chicken on its bed of rice before drizzling the sweet chili sauce over it. "I ordered medium spicy for both of us."

"It worked, though? You accomplished what you hoped?" He bit into a crunchy spring roll.

My fork hovered over the food on my plate before I chose a small piece of chicken. "It did. I want to keep strengthening it."

He was thoughtful as he concentrated on his food. "What about the other witches in your family? Can they tell?"

I finished chewing my bite, swallowing and running my tongue across the front of my teeth before speaking. "My parents died when I was young. Accidents, remember?"

"Right, I remember you mentioning they'd passed away." He forked a piece of tofu. "What about cousins? Or aunts and uncles?"

"Last of the Bellerose line right here," I told him. "My mother was an only child and my father's sister Collette never married. She died seven years ago. No children there."

Rabbit stopped eating. "You're the last one?"

"I am." I gave him a tight smile.

"If you have children?"

"Well, yes, they'd have access to the witchline." I dipped a spring roll into the leftover chili sauce.

"Do you want children, Lucie?" Rabbit's voice turned tender.

The question was innocent enough, but it left me feeling vulnerable and I couldn't look at him. "Never has come up. Did you get enough rice?"

"Help me understand. You did this 'studying' with Guillaume. And you might, I mean, when you're gone, the witchline is gone?"

I nodded. "Unless I can find a way to let in another witch to draw from it. Then it will live on."

"Has it been done before?" Rabbit still wasn't eating. Instead, he watched me push the food around on my plate.

"No. But neither had strengthening a witchline, and Guillaume helped me do that." I met his gaze. "I don't want my witchline to die out, Rabbit. But even if I can't continue mine, maybe what I've learned and accomplished can help the other witchlines and we won't die out."

He nodded. "I understand."

I took a deep breath. "Enough of this serious talk. Tell me what's been going on in your world. What's the network up to?"

∞∞∞

I knew Rabbit had more questions, but he gave me a break. Instead, I ate the most I had in months while I laughed at the stories he told me – from dealing with Tara the Maid of Honor-zilla, to our friend Big Rabbit's disastrous attempts at dating a female Rabbit he'd been crushing on for months. I managed to get my wine glass back and filled it up more than once.

We left the containers on the counter and moved into the living room. He kicked off his boots and chose the sofa. I plopped down beside him, snuggling into his side. I reached up and ruffled the unruly locks he was growing.

"What's up with the hair?" I asked, running my fingers through his curls.

"Stop that!" He shivered, then grabbed my wrist and pushed me away. He grinned. "I haven't had time for a cut."

"You look like Big Rabbit," I smirked.

"I'll take your wine away again," he threatened.

I laughed and settled back into the sofa. Propping my feet up on my coffee table, I watched the tongues of fire wave across the vent in the fireplace as I gripped my wine glass. The heat inside my body rested. "Grab the throw. It's cold."

Rabbit pulled the blanket from the back of the sofa and covered our legs. "Better?"

I leaned my head against his shoulder as my eyes floated shut. "Yes, finally."

Chapter 7

"Oh, hell." My temples throbbed and the inside of my mouth felt like I'd sucked on a lint trap. I tried to moisten my lips with a parched tongue. I could tell it was bright on the other side of my eyelids. There was no way I was prying my eyes open.

I was on my back, and I sensed I was in my bed. *Let's see,* I thought. *The last thing I remember?* Right, Rabbit and I had dinner, then we were on the couch talking. I might have had some more wine. The thought of fermented anything made my stomach somersault. Then... What then? The fireplace was lit, but I was still cold. Rabbit covered us with the blanket. But then what?

I allowed my hand to drift slowly to the left of my body, my fingers seeking to learn if I was alone in my bed. Cautiously, I reached farther. The spot was empty. Was it warm, though? Was it *recently occupied?*

I let my head roll to the left over my pillow, opening one squinted eye.

Did the pillow next to me look like someone had rested on it, or was it only my imagination?

"Rabbit?" I called softly.

No answer. My skin felt uncomfortable. I gathered the courage to peek under the blankets at my body. I was wearing the clothes I put on yesterday. Relief washed over me. Thank god. I pulled down the covers and swung my legs over the edge of the bed as I slowly pushed myself into a seated position. Concentrating on taking deep, steady breaths, I noted my bare knees poking out from under my denim skirt. I must've taken my tights off. I hesitated and sat stone still as I mentally evaluated myself. My underwear was still in place. Good sign. Standing, I shuffled my bare feet into my slippers and headed downstairs to see if Rabbit had crashed on my sofa.

The living room was empty and so was the kitchen. Rabbit's coat was gone. I ran my hand across my mouth as I tried to recall the end of our evening. Nothing.

The clock on the stove indicated it was after

9 o'clock. My phone sat on the counter, a cord running from it to a charger sticking out of the outlet. Rabbit must've taken care of it before leaving. I picked up the phone and checked the screen. A message sent earlier said: *Text me when you're up.*

"Yeah, but not yet," I said to the phone, placing it behind my radio so I didn't have to see it. I needed coffee but decided it was preferable to sit on a barstool with the side of my face resting on the kitchen countertop, my arms folded on my lap. The surface was cool against my cheek. My hair draped over my face.

I heard Templeton come in through the pantry door only because the house was silent and I was still. The door shut behind him, and I waited, but he said nothing. Sighing, I lifted my head, pushing my hair back.

He stood in front of the pantry door, his hands resting on his hips. I watched as his gaze roamed over the countertops – the dirty wine glasses and the empty bottles sitting by the sink. His eyes slid to mine.

"If you've ever had one ounce of compassion in your body, Templeton," I began, my voice hoarse even to my ears. "Then please don't say anything. In fact, please go away. This is me begging you."

Templeton didn't answer. Instead, he walked to my refrigerator. He scanned the few staples dotting the mostly empty shelves inside. Pressing his lips into a thin line, he closed the door and retrieved a glass from the cupboard. He filled it with cool water from the refrigerator dispenser and set it in front of me. He said nothing as he studied me.

"Thanks." I reached for the glass with a trembling hand. How nice. I hit bottom in front of Templeton.

He waited until the edge of the glass touched my lower lip before turning back toward the pantry. A second later he'd door traveled out of the house.

"I suppose I should be grateful," I said aloud. I sipped some more water and contemplated the whole damn mess I'd managed to create. What made me the angriest was this was not like me. I was not like *this*. I'd become a person I was not. I didn't like feeling out of control.

Before going to study with Guillaume, I would've described myself as self-possessed. I worked hard for the life I'd created. When I submitted to Guillaume's lessons, I willingly gave up control over my own life. Everything was to his precise instruction. Obedience was expected.

And then, as I readied to leave France, my new power seemed to simmer constantly below the surface of my skin. As proud as he was with what we'd accomplished with my witchline, this incessant coursing through my veins perplexed my teacher. It was not this way with previous students. He was concerned I wouldn't be able to harness it, regardless of my skills.

I had a choice: Stay with Guillaume and focus on controlling this live wire we'd opened together, or move forward on my own, shouldering the responsibility – and the consequences – without his guidance.

At last, I had a say in something. After a year under Guillaume's tutelage, the latter was preferable.

And at first, I *was* getting a handle on it. I was back in Matar and made new friends – like Emily and Rabbit. Then I met someone who made all the feverish energy sparking through me hum. In retrospect, I suppose I understood why I'd been attracted to Sebastian. Through him raced a similar seductive current – although I never understood how dangerous it was until it was too late. It felt good to be with him. His own power stroked the restlessness agitating right below my skin. I felt reborn after the difficult year with Guillaume. But I didn't realize what I was sensing inside Sebastian was really the edge of a depraved man, not the magnetism of a charismatic bad boy.

And then everything fell apart. The firepower coursing through my veins exploded that night in the Walled Zone. What no one knows is I could barely keep control of myself when it happened. My friends could've been hurt.

Although, when I allowed myself to remember the night in detail, I think Templeton picked up on my tenuous grasp on the power.

I took another drink of water. Rolling this over in my brain for the thousandth time wasn't going to change what happened.

Reaching behind the radio for my phone, I re-read Rabbit's text and winced. Once he checked his phone, he'd know I'd seen the message he sent earlier.

I typed back: *I just got up. Give me a while, okay?*
Sure. Need anything?

I'm good. I hit 'send' and put the phone out of sight – and out of mind – a second time.

Okay, coffee. I started to slide off the barstool when my pantry door opened for a second time. Templeton returned with a brown paper sack. He ignored me and unloaded the bag by the stove: a carton of eggs, an avocado, a loaf of bread, a stick of butter, and a half gallon of orange juice. I watched as he rolled up his sleeves and set about going through my kitchen drawers and cupboards, pulling out several items.

I opened my mouth to ask him what he was doing, and he shot me a dirty look.

"Drink the water. You're dehydrated." He reached up and plucked a short glass from the cupboard. He filled it with juice.

I coughed. "Um, I'm not big on orange juice."

He inclined his head to the side and gave it a tiny shake before taking a drink from the glass. "I am."

"What are you doing here?" I asked, resettling myself on the barstool.

"What does it look like?" Templeton set a non-stick pan on my stove. He pulled the cutting board from its resting place against the backsplash, sliced a couple of pieces of bread from the loaf, and popped them into the toaster. Next, he ran a sharp knife through the avocado lengthwise, before spinning the two halves of the fruit and pulling them apart to reveal the large pit. Whacking it with the edge of the knife, he twisted and removed it. Discarding the pit, he set about meticulously slicing the flesh. The toast popped up and was put on a small plate. The avocado was soft, and he spread it evenly across both pieces. He tapped salt and pepper over the dish.

"You don't have to eat all of it, but I expect you to eat at least one slice." He set the toast in front of me.

"Thank you." Somewhat humbled, I nibbled on a corner of toast.

As Templeton moved to the sink, he froze. I realized Rabbit had probably left our dinner dishes in it.

His jaw tightened. "Should I make breakfast for your guest as well?"

"We're the only two people here," I told him.

He nodded, a muscle twitching in his cheek once.

I watched Templeton whisk three eggs in a

bowl with some cold water. He paused to cut a thick tablespoon of butter into the pan, eyeballing the flame under it as he set it to medium. He went back to whisking.

"I'm assuming you have white pepper?" he asked. He poured the eggs into the pan, using a spatula to lift and scramble the eggs. Occasionally he'd shake it to keep the eggs level, running the spatula along its sides. His technique was good. Templeton knew what he was doing.

"In the pantry, second shelf on the right. There's a row of seasonings. I'm pretty sure I still have white pepper," I told him. The avocado toast was simple, but good. I was feeling more human.

Templeton reduced the heat and continued to fuss over the eggs. While they were still wet, he removed the pan from the burner. He deftly rolled the egg mixture into the beginnings of a French omelet with the spatula. When he was satisfied, he added another pat of butter and nudged it around the cooked egg. He slid the omelet to the pan's edge and with a practiced hand, flipped the omelet seam side down onto the plate. He swiped another line of butter over the top before retrieving the white pepper and giving it a light sprinkle, along with a dash of salt. He shaped the ends of the omelet between the spatula and a fork.

He raised his head. "Do you want me to cut it for you?" The knife hovered over the middle of the omelet while he waited.

"Please." I watched as he sliced it and separated the two halves at an angle. The inside was slightly wet. It was flawlessly prepared.

Templeton set the dish in front of me along with a clean fork. He hesitated, but then nudged the plate toward me before spinning around and starting to clean up. "Don't let it get cold."

"Thank you." I speared a piece of the omelet and brought it to my lips. It was heavenly. Figures, he could cook. I gave him a smile. "It's perfect."

"Eat. I'll take care of this." Templeton turned the faucet on and resumed cleaning up the modest mess he made while cooking breakfast. He washed the dishes left over from my dinner with Rabbit the night before.

I marveled at him. I knew what this was. It was his apology – a surprising one, for sure, and nothing I would've expected. But I'd accept it.

He finished his chore before I finished the

omelet. When my water glass was half empty, he filled it back up without asking if I wanted more. He wiped the last speck from the stove and looked around the kitchen.

I waited.

"I assume you feel better, but we should probably table any discussion until you're not hungover," he said.

"That's a good decision." *Don't screw this moment up*, I warned him from inside my head.

He stood awkwardly in the middle of the kitchen staring at the floor. Eventually, he raised his head, the corners of his mouth turning down. *Great, here it comes*, I thought.

"I don't like how you've lost weight, Lucie. Start taking better care of yourself." And with that, he grabbed the half gallon of orange juice and door traveled out of my house via the pantry.

I couldn't help it; I grinned the whole time I ate the rest of my omelet.

I even finished the avocado toast.

∞∞∞

I had two new problems: I was stuck going to

the Witches Gala and I had one day to find an appropriate dress. Any suitable clothing I had in my closet no longer fit me well.

After eating breakfast, I felt much better. With a full belly, my hangover lessened. Templeton's unusual act of kindness made a difference. At least I wouldn't be at my worst when I went searching for a new dress. There was a string of shops and boutiques near *Coffee Cove*. I decided I should get it over with.

I hated to shop.

Before I left home, I texted Rabbit. I couldn't remember if I told him about the gala. He texted a thumbs up and asked me again if I needed anything. I told him I was all set, but I wanted to connect with him later. Now that I'd sobered up, it was probably a good time to learn what became of the space in the Walled Zone where the fifth and sixth directional doors were hidden. My discussion with Emily reminded me we'd left a few loose ends. There were still two unknown worlds to think about and both were probably dangerous. I also wanted to know what Rabbit knew about Templeton's plans. Rabbit would be on my side – Templeton should not attempt to get past those doors alone.

I retrieved my RAV4 from the garage and risked finding parking near the clothing shops I planned to visit. I caught a lucky break, shimmying my little SUV into a slot within a short walking distance of my destination. This was good as I dressed light, wearing jeans and a long-sleeved tee shirt under my pea coat. I wanted to keep trying on dresses as simple as possible. I did forego sneakers for a pair of heelless red suede ankle boots.

The first two boutiques I tried offered nothing I'd ever consider wearing, but as they say, the third time's the charm. Between the crowded racks of floor-length prom gowns and mother-of-the-bride dresses, I found a vintage sleeveless swing dress in royal blue.

The neckline was a V-neck, but it didn't display too much of my cleavage. The soft material was covered by a layer of lace in the same color. The garment narrowed at the waistline and was free of silly bows and dangling ribbons. The skirt allowed for a natural draping over my hips versus an abominable belle-of-the-ball flare. The length of the skirt – with its asymmetrical hemline – ended at mid-calf. Because Matar was still deep in the clutches of winter, the woman helping me try on the dress suggested I add a simple black wrap trimmed with lace to cover my shoulders and bare arms. After I checked my coat, it would be more than enough for the evening. I knew the ballroom in the Congress building would be well-heated to keep guests at the gala and making donations in support of the Congress' agenda.

The staff seamstress made an adjustment to the bustline and fussed over me as I watched her in the mirror.

"This was made for your shape," she declared. "Let me put in a few stitches and you'll be all set to go. Your date's going to love this."

I simply said 'thank you.'

Impulsively, I decided to purchase a new pair of silk stockings to wear underneath the dress. Sometimes it feels good to have a secret for your own pleasure – even if you know it won't be discovered by anyone else. The shop carried a name I recognized from my year in France. I had several garter belt sets at home, although it'd been over a year since I'd worn any of them. I didn't allow the attentive shopkeeper to talk me into the stockings with seams but chose a pair in black.

With a closet full of heels, I could skip shoe shopping. My purchases boxed, I carried everything out to my car. While it warmed up, I fished the phone from my purse. It was mid-afternoon on a Friday, but I figured I should talk to Rabbit sooner rather than later. It was probably better to fill in the holes in my memory and move on. I squirmed in my seat. Hopefully I didn't make too much of a fool of myself before going to bed.

I tapped in a short message: *So, I'm upright and out in the world.*

Barely 30 seconds passed before he replied: *An improvement.*

I pulled a face before firing off another text: *Was I that bad?*

I've seen worse. Been worse.

Okay, I'd comfort myself with that. *I want to make it up to you. Where are you?*

Nowhere you should be. How about I meet you?

Where? My gaze drifted up from my phone and I did a double take through the windshield. A tall man with tousled, dark hair wearing a black leather jacket passed by on the sidewalk. He turned his head before I could see his face, disappearing around the corner. I shook my head at myself. The phone in my hand grew warm and

Rabbit's next text appeared.

I see you're near Coffee Cove. I'll meet you there in 15.

I laughed at the device in my hand. Of course. Rabbit had applied a setting to track the phone. I wouldn't expect anything less.

See you there, I texted.

∞∞∞

Scoring a table near the barista's counter, I asked for a to-go cup of the strongest roast available when Rabbit arrived. I figured he'd eat no matter what, so I ordered him a mock chicken salad wrap and veggie chips. I picked at a banana muffin while I sipped a café au lait. A couple of *Coffee Cove* employees came out and chatted, asking me where I'd been and telling me they were glad I was back.

I managed to sidestep some of their more pointed questions. Before I knew it, Rabbit was coming through the door, the collar of his bulky work coat pulled up against the cold wind. He slid into the seat across from me, his rich brown eyes twinkling as he pulled off his knit cap.

"You look a lot better than you did the last

time I saw you." He popped a veggie chip into his mouth.

"Yeah," I began. "About that, I'm sorry." The legitimate need to apologize was becoming way too frequent for my tastes. "It won't happen again."

Rabbit wasn't convinced. "Shit happens. Don't worry about it. But I'm surprised to see you out today."

"I guess it was a good night's sleep," I said. "And I had a visitor this morning. He cooked me breakfast."

Rabbit's eyebrows shot up. "This the first time you've seen him?"

"Nope."

"Let me guess – he was the reason for getting your drunk on?"

"Oh, not completely." I shrugged. I took a deep breath. "It was a bunch of things at once. But I feel more centered. Present. And I want to talk to you about last fall."

"Sure." Rabbit paused. "Here?"

I glanced around. He had a point. The barista appeared with Rabbit's to-go cup. "I ordered you a black coffee," I told him.

"Thanks." He gestured toward the lunch plate.

"You don't always have to buy, you know."

"I know," I replied. "How do you feel about eating in my car? We can talk privately."

"Sure." He bundled up his wrap while I slipped on my coat.

At the curb, I unlocked the RAV4 with my fob and started the engine. I flipped on the heat before moving my seat back so I could sit sideways.

For a moment he was silent, chewing a bite of his lunch. He dropped his attention to his lap, retrieving a napkin. "Last fall. What about it?"

If anything, my experience with Rabbit taught me once something serious happened, revisiting the topic was not something he'd often do. But this time might be different. "I want to talk about the directional doors and the Empire."

He motioned with his wrap, encouraging me to continue after he swallowed. "Go on."

"Has the network been monitoring the area?" The Rabbits were the ones who helped Templeton, Emily, and me into the compound held by the Fringe where the doors were hidden.

Rabbit wiped his mouth with the napkin. "Off and on. In the beginning we kept an eye on the region – mostly through tech. We didn't want to continue a physical presence, especially after the Empire seized the compound."

"Do you think the Empire leadership has any idea about the two directional doors hidden there?" I asked.

He took his time in answering, pawing instead through the bag of veggie chips. "No, I don't think so. In fact, I bet they had no clue as to what they were sitting on."

"Were?" I cocked my head to the side. "Aren't they still there?"

"Nope, not like before." He tilted his head back and tapped the last bit of chip crumbs into his mouth.

"But they are still there?" I pressed him again.

"It's still restricted, but no, there isn't an active contingent of Empire guards patrolling the place. When the Empire first took the asset from Ivanov Transport, they spent time removing stored merchandise out of the warehouses, but they left a lot of equipment behind. Most of it wasn't usable. They probably didn't think it was worth the effort to move it. I'm sure they were also looking for evidence of Ivanov's involvement with the Fringe." Rabbit shrugged. "As predicted, Ivanov got a slap on the hand and mostly walked away from the loss."

Ivanov Transport climbed into bed with the Fringe every now and then, but the company with ties to organized crime in the Empire seemed to come away unscathed from most situations when they ran afoul of the law. Still, the Rabbits discovered a lot of Fringe money running through Ivanov. I hoped the latest charges would stick.

"Yeah, speaking of Ivanov, what about the fact Fringe members and their families were sending money through them into the pockets of corrupt officials?" I remained calm on the outside as I asked these questions. Sebastian's family was one of the worst offenders. They also owned one of the biggest private banks in the Empire.

"Trials are ongoing for most of the families involved." Rabbit eyed me. "You asking about the St. Michel family?"

I nodded.

"Trial is still coming up." He finished his wrap and crumpled the paper. "We'll see what happens. Empire leadership is nervous about setting off an economic shitstorm if the St. Michels are found guilty. Some of the other families are trying to plea bargain their way out of this. Same with several influential Salesmen. They're requesting banishment from the Empire instead of going to trial and risking imprisonment or worse."

"I can't see how banishment is a punishment for any of these people. They'll have their freedom outside the Empire. And there's no guarantee they won't pick right back up." I skimmed my hand back and forth over the steering wheel. "What about Fringe activity?"

"Nothing. They took a hard hit between the network turning over the financial records we found to the Salesman Court, and you and Emily decapitating the Fringe leadership – figuratively, of course. Any remaining members turned tail and ran. They went underground. There were families who split to try and save themselves, claiming not to know what other members were up to and disavowing any connection to the Fringe." Rabbit looked out the windshield, squinting as the sun cut through the glass and into his face. "The Salesman Court has strong, new leadership, but that's part of the problem. They lack experience. What they accomplish will be limited." He sighed. "But right now, it's quiet."

That was at least some good news. My next question turned us back to the fifth and sixth doors. "So, I've seen Templeton more than once since I've been back."

His thick eyebrows hopped back up. "Yeah?"

"Yeah." Now it was my turn to stare into the sunlight. "Like I said, he's been to my house. He was also at the Congress of Empire Witches. He needed me to request a book of poetry for him from the library there."

"Hmm." Rabbit took a moment. "And all's well between you two?"

I barked out a laugh. "What do you think? I've wanted to throttle him at least twice since I've been home."

Rabbit grinned and shook his head. "Well, some things don't change."

"But what I want to know is, are you aware Templeton plans to travel through the directional doors? Alone?" The two men might not share much with each other, but I knew they came together every so often – mostly because one wanted something from the other. Mostly because Templeton wanted information from Rabbit.

"I could see that," Rabbit answered. "It's not like he'd expect to take Emily with him."

"But you know as well as I do, Rabbit, these doors – hell, any of the Empire's directional doors – might be able to transport beings other than Salesmen." I bounced my palm off the steering wheel and gave my head a shake. "We can't let him take off by himself."

"We can't stop him," Rabbit argued.

"I can. I won't open the doors. I won't wake the Crimson Stone. No one will be able to open anything." Even as I said the words, a niggling worry whispered in my mind that something opened the fifth door without me and without the Crimson Stone. It was open when we found it.

"Templeton had the Stone the whole time you were gone. I bet he's been trying to find a way to wake it without you," Rabbit told me.

"That's probably true." I thought about the spell I placed on the Stone when I put it to sleep. Templeton was powerful, but I was, too. It would take a lot to undo what I had done.

"Lucie," Rabbit took my hand. "While I'm in no hurry for more trouble, Templeton does have a point. We should learn what's on the other side.

Sebastian admitted he went through the fifth door. He said he saw dangerous things there. We can try to fight Templeton on this, or we can work with him to keep him from doing something stupid."

I let Rabbit hold my hand and stroke his thumb over my skin. His hands were rough, but his touch was always gentle. "I'm afraid of what we'll find."

He nodded. "Me, too. And so is Templeton – although he'll never admit it. Listen, why don't I have the network tap into the Walled Zone and see if they notice anything. I'll have them focus on the location of the old compound. Okay? It can be the first step."

"I'd appreciate it," I replied. "And I'll try to keep Templeton from jumping the gun." I stopped. "Wait, do you think he's already gone back to see if the fifth and sixth doors have reappeared?"

Rabbit released my hand. "I'd count on it. That's why he's still doing research in your witch library. He hasn't found a way to wake the Stone or open the doors without you."

I knew Rabbit was right. "We should all meet. All three of us."

"What about Emily?" Rabbit asked.

"No. She's planning a wedding. She's got a good life and doesn't need to come back to this chaos." Emily had already given so much of herself. She deserved to be spared this time around.

"I don't disagree. She's earned her peace." Rabbit pulled his phone out of his pocket and scanned a new text. "I should get going. Do you want me to get a message to Templeton? Tell him to meet up with us, maybe tomorrow?"

"Sure – no! Wait, not tomorrow." I leaned my head against the seat. "I have to go to a gala at the Congress. Black tie fundraiser."

Rabbit scowled. "Fun."

"Please be my date?"

"Not for all the money in the Empire – and that's no reflection on you."

"I get it, trust me." I smiled at my friend. "I bet you clean up nice. I'm picturing you in a tux right now."

"I do clean up nice," he winked. "But it'll be the last day of the Empire before a Rabbit walks into the Congress on a witch's arm."

"You could be the first," I teased, poking at him with a finger.

He regarded me for an extra beat. "Nah. You've got enough trouble, Lucie."

"Sadly, you are correct." I sat up. "Hey, before you go, I really am sorry about last night. I didn't mean to be so –"

"Shitfaced."

"Right." I cringed. "I don't remember anything after we hit the couch and..." My voice trailed off and I waited.

Rabbit's expression became guarded. "Nothing to remember." His gaze momentarily slipped down my face before he met my eyes once more. He shrugged. "You fell asleep. Then I carried you upstairs and put you to bed. That's it."

There was something Rabbit left out, but I knew there was no use in pushing it. He wouldn't tell me, and frankly, I had a feeling I didn't want to know. Like a dream you don't remember upon waking, but flashes come to you throughout the day, I caught a glimpse of pressing my mouth against his. "Okay," I answered, shaking the image from my head. "I'm glad I wasn't any worse than I thought. It won't happen again."

It was barely perceptible, but I noted Rabbit's brown irises had grown a shade darker. "No worries. No big deal. Anyhow, maybe we can shoot for Sunday. I'll get a message to Templeton and tell him noon."

I was relieved we'd changed the subject. "Noon should be fine."

"I'm on it." Rabbit opened the car door and climbed out.

"Hey, wait," I called after him.

"Yeah?" He ducked his head back in.

"I'm totally dreading this gala. I'm hoping to get out of there early. If you're in the neighborhood tomorrow night and my stoop light is on, stop by? In fact, I'm assuming there's still a camera on my front door?" I raised an eyebrow.

Rabbit's cheeks colored. "I haven't had time to turn off the camera access."

"Uh-huh." I rolled my eyes. "But seriously, I promise I'll be much better company."

"Maybe." He turned his head and looked down the street before peering back inside. "I gotta run. I'll talk to you later. Text me if you need anything."

"Thanks, Rabbit." I bobbed my head once, waving at his back as he hustled away, his hands buried deep in his coat pockets.

Chapter 8

Dress shopping finished, I decided to hit the grocery store and restock my larder since I was driving. Honestly, it's much easier to get around Matar on foot or by public transit. The intercity trains are usually reliable. What's not convenient is hauling many bags of groceries back home on foot or by train.

And yes, I stopped at the liquor store to fill my wine rack. While I certainly was not planning a repeat of the night before, it was time to act like I was home for good and replenish the kitchen bar. I picked up a 'top shelf' bottle of vodka for Rabbit.

By the time I arrived home, daylight was fading into evening. After putting away the groceries I realized I had an appetite. In fact, I felt much better overall. There was still a lot I had to deal with, and tomorrow night's gala would bring its own set of unpleasantries. But it wasn't anything I could avoid, so there was no sense dwelling on my reluctance to attend. I thought about the Congress and wondered what Guillaume had in mind for a demonstration to prove how my witchline was strengthened by our work together. We never discussed this when I was in France. I'd thought his official assurance to the Congress would be enough. No one would dare question Guillaume's word.

I unpacked my new dress and hung it from a hook on my bedroom wall. I smoothed out the skirt as I examined the intricate lace. Most of the other witches would wear full-length gowns, but a few would opt for shorter dresses. I wouldn't be too out of place. I traced my fingers over the neckline. The style suited me, and the color complimented my eyes. Usually, I went for red or emerald green, but I was drawn to this bright blue.

The silk stockings were also boxed, and I flattened them out along the top of my dresser. They were intimate by design, but this pair was understated with a thick black band at the top of each leg where the garter would attach. They were a luxury I craved, even in their simplicity.

I rummaged through my underwear drawer and found what in France I called *un porte-jarretelles*. This one was plain black satin with four elastic straps – two in the front and two in the back. The edges of the belt were trimmed in a strip of mesh as narrow as a pinky nail's width. An unadorned pair of black satin underwear would be pulled over the straps, the waistline resting just below the belt, leaving a strip of flesh between the two garments.

I placed the garter belt next to the stockings. A pair of pointy black and blinged-out pumps with a three-inch heel matched everything perfectly. The 'bling' was a thin layer of tiny black rhinestones dotting the suede shoe from heel to toe.

I examined the ensemble before me and laughed. No one else would see any of the more private pieces, but they would help me feel... Feel what? I frowned at the accoutrement.

Powerful.

I'd need that tomorrow night.

∞ ∞ ∞

The Witches Gala was an important event.

Held every February, it was an excuse to add more color to life during the long cold days of winter as it marched toward spring. It was also important for the Congress coffers. Wealthy witches prepared for the shakedown. There would be a contingent of non-witches attending – some as escorts on the arms of witches, others as invited guests. Those 'guests' sported healthy bank accounts or a sizable amount of influence in witch interests in the Empire – or both. I wondered into what camp Elaine Waverton's date fell? I'd need to learn more about her family. Elaine's comment about not believing claims I'd strengthened my witchline tipped me off to some of the pushback I'd get from certain groups in the Congress.

But no matter what they did to me, they couldn't take away what I'd learned and gained. And Guillaume wouldn't tolerate any doubt over his abilities.

Friday night came and went without much more than a book by my fireplace and a cup of soup. Saturday morning was uneventful as well. I did check with the Empire's messaging service and requested they delete any communication older than three weeks. That left only a couple of messages, and both were from members of the method coven I worked with last year. They were simply checking in to see if I'd returned from my 'vacation.' It was nice to be remembered. It was not lost on me these messages came from self-taught witches and not natural-born ones. In fairness, there were not many witches like me in the method coven who came from traditional witchlines. I sent my own messages back through the service and suggested we get together soon. The moon would be full in a few days, but I didn't feel up to attending a group event yet. Still, it would be nice to see the women who reached out to me. I needed more friends.

The official messaging system was a free service provided to all residents of the Empire and to all its citizens whether they lived inside the Empire or not. Additionally, all Salesmen had access to it regardless of where they lived even if they were *not* official citizens. The messaging system was put into place by the Empire's governing body of Salesmen. Empire residents do not have their own phones.

There are no cell towers in the Empire – it's pointless. The system the Salesman Court developed to monitor the door traveling of its Salesmen interrupts the same technologies cell phones use. Everything is hardwired in the Empire. The Empire permits a few radio stations and those operate normally as they use a longer wavelength than cell phones. They are not affected by the Empire's monitoring system.

Rabbits – and specifically the Rabbit network – have figured out a way around this. They do not share their technologies with the Empire leadership. It's no secret Rabbits are treated poorly overall. It's the old story of the 'haves' suppressing the 'have-nots.' But the Rabbit community is remarkable and resourceful. Spending time with Rabbit last year taught me a lot about their often-hidden world. On some level I question whether they want to change their position in the Empire. They've created their own domain and frequently follow their own rules and community laws. And they know they have power because they are technologically superior to everyone in the Empire.

As a rule, Rabbits and Salesmen do not get along. I was surprised to witness how deep the relationship between Emily and Rabbit ran. Rabbit, although he looks like he's 25, is probably closer to 55 or 56. He was a friend of Emily's late father, Daniel Swift – a Salesman who sat on the Salesman Court in a significant position of power. I wonder how those two men became friends? Rabbit was usually tight-lipped about his past, so I didn't press.

The Rabbit network helped us last year because of Rabbit's advocacy and Emily's relentless fight against the Fringe. The Fringe also targeted the technologies the Rabbit network developed. Even worse, more than one Rabbit has died during a Fringe attack. Emily, like her father, built a good name for herself in the Rabbit community. They know she's a good person. She's also not a bigot.

Rabbits and witches aren't typically friends either. In short, Rabbits don't trust witches, and many witches are snobs. They treat Rabbits much the same as Salesmen treat Rabbits.

And, of course, witches and Salesmen do not get along well. Salesmen tend to think they're better than everyone. Like the Rabbits, they distrust us, viewing our community with suspicion.

At the end of the day, the Empire is full of intolerant groups who do their best to not like each other. There's no great movement to change either. It comes down to individual friendships, like mine with Rabbit and Emily, or even with Templeton – although he and I were far from friends.

I spent time thinking about all these strange relationships I'd built as I got ready for the gala. Dinner would be served at 8 o'clock, and I planned to miss as much as I could of that awkward portion of the evening. I sent a message to Loren explaining I'd arrive in time for dessert. He'd fuss some, but otherwise be fine. Much of the earlier small talk would've been conducted over pre-dinner cocktails. I'd smile my way through dessert, dance with Loren and a few of the older witches he would introduce me to, and then I'd enjoy a little wandering around the Congress halls with a glass of champagne. I'd return to the ballroom when I suspected Loren's wife was resting her feet where I'd enjoy a cup of coffee and her entertaining witch gossip. Then I'd request a taxi be hailed and *voilà!* I'd head home and put my own feet up. And maybe Rabbit would stop by. I'd leave the stoop light on. It'd be nice to end the night on a cheerful note.

This is the routine I promised myself as I

brushed out my hair and twisted spiral curls through my long locks with a flat iron. My bangs had grown to chin length, and I pulled back the longer sections, securing them at the back of my head with a silver clip. I angled a thin wire band from my crown to the clip, creating an illusion of an intricate metal halo over my auburn tresses. My jewelry was simple: a pair of delicate silver hoops. I decided to forgo a necklace but chose a ring from my armoire. I slid the white gold band over the index finger on my right hand and admired the sapphire stone. I'd purchased it for myself before I left France.

A sweep of the black eyeliner brush along the edge of my upper eyelid was followed by mascara of the same color. I assessed the shades of lipstick in front of me. I usually kept things pretty natural, but I glanced across the room at my dress, popping my lips. Sometimes it's a no-brainer. *Red it is,* I thought. But first I'd slip on my dress.

I'd already donned the silk stockings and garter, as well as the black panties and matching bra. I stood in front of the cheval mirror in my bedroom. My curves were smaller than they were four months ago, but they weren't gone. I ran my hand across my torso. I had butterflies spinning in my stomach.

The lace dress slid softly over my head and shoulders. Living alone, I'd invested in a zipper helper making dressing easier. After lifting the chain and zipping the dress up, I lowered my chin to my chest and reached back to remove the hook from the puller before tossing it on the bed. I appraised myself in the mirror while I adjusted my clothing. The dress was beautiful. It was a good choice. I draped the black stole with its lace trim over my shoulders. I certainly wouldn't need it all night at the gala, but it would be handy to have for wandering without a coat.

My feet slid into the pair of heels I'd decided to wear. The asymmetrical hemline allowed the dress to fall longer on the sides. The heels lifted me by three inches and showcased my stocking-clad calves. I paused to paint my lips red and daub some perfume on the sides of my neck and on the insides of my elbows. A sensual mix of spice and vanilla complemented the natural oil in my skin.

I was ready to go. *Sort of.*

Retrieving the stylish black clutch I'd be carrying for the evening, I moved downstairs and checked the clock. There'd be plenty of time to call for a taxi and ride to the Congress building.

As I was adding my house keys and phone from Rabbit to my purse, the phone grew warm. I read the text from Rabbit.

Have fun tonight.

Kill me now, I typed back. I added a smiley face.

You'll have a good time.

It's an evening making small talk with a bunch of witches, I replied.

Some witches are okay.

I chuckled and tapped in another smiley face before adding: *Stopping by tonight?*

He didn't reply immediately, but eventually I saw the answer come through: *Maybe. Need to take care of something.*

I nodded at the phone. *Okay. If the light's on, I'm awake.*

He sent a thumbs up.

∞∞∞

Traffic wasn't nearly as heavy as I expected, and I asked the driver to take an extra spin around the block where the Congress of Empire

Witches building was housed. I'd planned on arriving later, but a second circle around the block would've been overkill.

I provided my name at the security gate as a private car with tinted windows passed through without a second look. As I sauntered up the perfectly dry and snow-free sidewalk, I watched a younger couple exit the car, the driver handing off his keys to the valet. His date's hand on his arm, they disappeared into the building.

The wards shuddered as I passed through and an unusual pull tugged on me. I paused to interpret the sensation. Something else must've been added to the wards, but I couldn't get a firm grip on what it was. I didn't dare poke at it with my own energy. Curiosity in the Congress building could get me into trouble. I picked up my pace and walked toward the blind being sitting to the side of the next set of doors. She examined my wrist, stroking a shadowed fingertip over the black tattoo that surfaced for a brief second.

"You may enter, witch." She held my hand for a moment longer, her unseeing eyes staring up into mine. "But be aware, witch. He is here tonight."

I startled. She never spoke more than her approval when I came to the Congress. "Who? Who is here?"

Her empty mouth stretched into an eerie grin. "The one who seeks you. He is here."

To my left, a throat cleared and I jumped. The being released me and gestured toward the two witches behind me. She began the ritual of recognition and I drifted forward. What did she mean?

∞∞∞

My coat checked, I wandered in the direction of the ballroom. I pulled my wrap snugly around my shoulders and pondered the being's warning. I wasn't sure what to make of her words. Unfortunately, she wasn't someone I could question further. Instead, I'd have to watch for whatever – or whomever – she alluded to through her strange words. I shivered as an errant prickle ran down the back of my neck. It wasn't unusual to feel like you were being watched in the Congress – you were – but this observation didn't have the same flavor. It felt dangerous.

My heels echoed in the empty corridor and

eventually I reached the grand staircase leading up to the second floor where I'd find the ballroom. I followed the distant buzzing emanating from the end of the long hallway. I was no longer alone and let out a breath. Witches roamed in and out of the busy ballroom. Every time the door opened the noise grew louder. I adjusted my wrap, lowering it from my shoulders and allowing it to dip down the center of my back and loop over my bent arms. I held one end in my right hand and rubbed it between my fingertips as if it had become a security blanket. I gripped the black clutch in my other hand.

My heart raced as I stepped into the room.

The ballroom was bright and decorated in a riot of springlike colors – daffodil yellows, spritely greens, delicate pinks, and sky blues. One of the evening's gala hosts greeted me and asked if he could assist. I asked for Loren Heatherworth's table. The man escorted me to the right, following a path around large circular tables. Occasionally I felt a pair of eyes land on me – some witches immediately knew who I was. Others were only curious. A few gazes lingered, appraising me more intimately for reasons other than who I was and where I'd been.

Natural witches know one another. It's instinctual. Drop me on an island in the middle of nowhere in a crowd of people I don't know and if I cross paths with another natural witch, we'll both know it. Not all magical or 'special' beings have this recognition. To my knowledge, Salesmen don't have this built-in sense. Rabbits have a sort of familiarity among themselves that doubles as recognition of belonging to each other. Other beings you might find in the Empire – like shapeshifters – are able to fool even their brethren. They can conceal their identity from their own kind as well as others.

To be polite, I nodded to two older witches I recognized as elders. They certainly knew who I was. Conversations stopped as I passed their tables. I hoped my deference would afford me some grace later.

Loren saw me approaching with the host and rose from his chair, his lips moving. The others at the table turned and the men stood as I joined the group.

"Lucie," Loren stepped to my side, his hand resting on my arm. He kissed my cheek before hovering his mouth over my ear. "He's here."

Before I could ask him who, Loren's wife called my name and motioned to the empty seat beside her. Loren escorted me to his wife's side where Michelle gracefully rose to her feet and hugged me.

"He's here tonight," she said low as she slowly pulled back to study my face.

"Who?" I asked quietly.

"Everyone, please sit. Our Lucie's here now," Loren interrupted, taking his wife's elbow and directing her back into her chair. He held mine for me as I sat, sliding it in gently.

My gaze skittered around the table. The Heatherworths dined with their peers. This was a welcome arrangement. The conversation would stay light and polite with the older witches. I nodded and said hello. Before I could discreetly ask Michelle *who* was here, a deep baritone cascaded over me from behind.

"Lucie."

The gooseflesh rose on my shoulders and upper arms. A pit opened in my stomach as I connected the voice with its owner. My mouth suddenly dry, I turned and looked up into the face of the man who helped me strengthen my witchline.

Guillaume.

Chapter 9

"Guillaume, Lucie just arrived," Loren stated, standing again and moving to my side. His hand landed on my shoulder and stayed.

"I am aware. She was never late when she studied with me." Guillaume's eyes snapped back to mine. "I'm disappointed in you, Lucie."

That simple phrase forced a shudder through me as memories of my time in France with Guillaume surfaced. I struggled to press down the heat threatening to erupt over my skin. I hadn't anticipated such a panicked reaction. Before I could reply, Loren squeezed my shoulder and answered for me.

"I did not expect her until now." Loren delivered one of his faint smiles to my onetime teacher. "She respects her Congress elders and arrived when she indicated she'd be joining us. I've promised my wife she'd be able to enjoy Lucie's company during dessert – which I see has only begun to be distributed. I invite you to speak with Lucie later in the evening when her obligations to this table have been met."

I held my breath. Loren couched his challenge to Guillaume's wishes in polite language, but no one was fooled. Certainly not Guillaume. I saw the dangerous glint in his eye. His sensual mouth slid into a mocking sneer, but he did not argue. Instead, his menacing gaze shifted to me before his hand drifted forward, cupping my chin. His gentle gesture fooled no one.

"I look forward to the first dance with you."

∞ ∞ ∞

After Guillaume's departure, the table eased from tense hushed tones to a more upbeat conversation about the evening. Dessert has a way of lightening the mood.

I jabbed my fork into a lemony confection while Michelle shared updates on her family. Her cheeriness helped steady my nerves. Witches can develop many different talents and powers, but some are present from birth. Michelle's family came from a healing branch in her witchline. Her innate power was the ability to create a balm of calm. In fact, I'd wager Michelle risked the Congress' ire by casting a tiny spell to help me settle down after Guillaume's appearance. Loren's influence would convince the Congress to overlook the transgression.

And yet, I continued to feel Guillaume's scrutiny. Regardless of Loren's wishes – and mine – Guillaume was not patiently waiting. As soon as I left the safety of the table, I'd be fair game. As Michelle answered a question from the octogenarian sitting across from us, I surveyed the room. I found Guillaume sipping a glass of champagne. He glowered at me while he leaned against one of the large pillars dotting the ballroom. *You no longer belong to him,* I reminded myself. *You completed your year. You do not need to cower before him. He's not allowed to touch you anymore.*

Defiantly, I lifted my chin, my gaze unwavering. That earned an amused smirk and a raised glass. He turned and disappeared behind the pillar.

"I wouldn't tempt fate," Michelle admonished.

"If I don't stand up to him now, who knows what he'll think he can do?" I said to the older woman.

Michelle's head toggled from side to side as she mulled over my words. "Perhaps. But don't do it in front of others. He won't tolerate it and it might land you in more trouble."

"Ironically, I'm not even trying to get into trouble," I told her. "At all."

"Loren said he enjoyed lunching with you." Michelle's soft face dimpled. "We've missed you. We're glad you're back."

"I'm glad, too," I said, meaning it. "And I'm starting to feel more at home."

"Because you're back with your kind, dear." Michelle patted my hand. She meant well.

"It's been good seeing my friends," I said cautiously.

"Your Rabbits and Salesmen?" Michelle's eyes lit up. "After that tidbit of information surfaced, Loren was ready to begin a campaign to get you married off to a witch."

"Oh, you've got to be kidding, Michelle?" I shook my head in disbelief. "No way!"

She wrinkled her nose. "I could not agree more, but he was on a tear for a few days. I finally convinced him if he put your name before the Congress for an official marriage arrangement, Guillaume might step forward to be considered."

I sucked in a breath, my head swiveling to check Guillaume's abandoned spot by the pillar. "He wouldn't. No, he wouldn't do that."

"I think he would, dear. Which is why I warned Loren. The thought stopped him in his tracks and there was no more mention of it." She sipped her champagne. "Problem solved."

The seesawing of my emotions was exhausting. Fear swam back to the surface and took a big breath, leaving me without one. "Could someone else put my name before the Congress for the same purpose?"

She contemplated her glass. "Yes. But I can't imagine who would. Although..." She paused again while she put her thoughts together. "By strengthening your witchline, there might be families interested in bringing you into their branches. Some because they think you would be able to help them, others might want you close so they could keep you under control."

I hadn't thought of any of these possibilities. "But I could refuse."

Again, she wobbled her head. "Perhaps."

The music playing lightly in the background

grew louder. A partition at the end of the room slid to the side and a group of musicians played a big band version of *Come Dancing*. Those milling about in the center of the ballroom either moved with the music or moved to the side. Couples rose from tables and meandered onto the dance floor. Loren swept in to pick up 'his bride' – the words causing me to wince in light of my conversation with Michelle – and the two blended into the throng of dancers.

If I stayed at the table, I'd be easy pickings for Guillaume, or any other dance partner for that matter. I wasn't in the mood for either. Scooping up my wine glass and evening purse, I risked being caught and put some distance between me and the dance floor. It might be preferable to wander those Congress halls now. Earlier I'd been troubled over the blind being's warning of someone 'here' looking for me. Knowing Guillaume was at the gala, I didn't give her words another thought. Somehow the woman knew and tried to alert me.

I'd almost reached a set of side doors leading out of the ballroom when I heard Guillaume's deep voice say my name. I hesitated. There was no way to avoid him. Remembering the earlier words of comfort I'd given myself, I squared my shoulders and turned to face my pitiless mentor.

"Guillaume." Standing before him and saying his name out loud gave me an unexpected jolt. I hadn't spoken to him directly in almost a year.

Without the other witches around us – in particular, Loren – Guillaume took his time as he casually appraised me with those penetrating caramel-colored eyes. He'd changed little since I last saw him. His ash brown hair had a touch of additional gray, but it was still thick and combed back from his face in gentle waves. His eyebrows retained their full color, and the right one remained raised while he regarded my dress. The laugh lines at the corners of his eyes implied a sense of humor – a misleading facial feature. Guillaume's square chin was covered with its perpetual stubble where the majority of gray made its appearance. The lips of his wide mouth were pressed together. I heard him breathe in through his aquiline nose as he prepared to speak.

"I prefer you in red."

"I know." I waited.

"I'll forgive you." His generous mouth split

into a broad smile. "You didn't know I'd be here tonight."

"I did not. Why *are* you here?" I maintained my composure by fidgeting with my black wrap.

"To see you. To discuss what the Congress expects of us – of you." He reached for my hand as the music changed to a slower tune. "Come, Lucie."

Reluctantly, I allowed him to lead me back through the ballroom. As we passed Loren's table, he paused to take the clutch from my hand. When he put it on the chair I'd sat in earlier, I detected a barely perceptible burst of power roll off him as he cast a spell of protection over my purse.

"Flaunting Congress rules?" I asked softly.

"They dare not sanction me." His eyes tracked back to my purse. "A working electronic device in the Empire? How interesting. What have you been up to?"

I balked. How Guillaume sensed the phone Rabbit gave to me I'd never know. Did other witches pick up on it, too? Damn. I should have left it at home.

Instead of answering, I raised one shoulder and turned my head. I felt Guillaume pull the stole from my shoulders, his fingertips grazing my skin. I stiffened. He draped the garment over the back of the chair.

His right hand came to rest on the small of my back and he directed me onto the dance floor. We circled toward the center of the other dancers, and he pulled me around to face him. His left hand caught my right and he lifted it as we swayed to the music, his right hand settling comfortably on my hip. Even in my heels, Guillaume had several inches on me. I turned my head to the right, lowering my eyes. I could smell his cologne – exotic and complex.

Guillaume cut a nice shape in his tux. At 56, he was more fit than many men half his age. He maintained his body with a control only mastered by such a strict disciplinarian. He earned his share of appreciative glances from the witches around us.

"Lucie, look at me. I want your attention," he commanded in a low tone.

I gave in, raising my head. "You have it. What do you want to discuss?"

His lips pursed briefly. "I can feel you've lost weight. I'd judge..." He paused, his right hand rubbing along the side of my body with a familiarity I'd rather he not display to those around us. "I'd judge over 10 kilograms."

"It's barely 20 pounds." The discussion of my weight was becoming tiresome.

"Your scale is wrong, then." Guillaume pressed his fingers into the side of my waist. "But I'm pleased you're still choosing stockings over the ridiculous hosiery some women insist on using to cover their more intimate parts."

"About the Congress." I attempted to switch the subject. "Loren says they want a demonstration. We never discussed this. What does this mean?"

Guillaume stroked my back. "I think this means they want to see for themselves the methods used to accomplish what we did together."

"No." I gave my head a shake. "I appreciate what you helped me do and what I learned from you, Guillaume, but our *practices* are complete. There is nothing for us to show the Congress. Your word alone is more than good enough. You could make them accept your assurances."

This time it was his shoulder hopping up in a shrug. He turned us in time to the music. "I think they question whether you can continue to strengthen your witchline alone. They'll want a demonstration proving you can do it on your own."

"Trust me, it's possible," I muttered. I stared at his shirt.

"Psychological suffering can be quite powerful," he acknowledged. An edge crept into his voice and his breath caressed my temple. "Care to tell your teacher what you've employed?"

"I do not." I remained focused on his shirt.

"Lucie, I'm not going to ask you again to look at me when you are answering my questions." His voice developed a threatening tone. His fingers curled into my dress.

I glared up at him. "Obeying you is no longer something I'm required to do."

His laughter resonated around us, belying the true tenor of our conversation. He shook me almost fondly. "Obedience was never your strong suit."

"Loren indicated this 'demonstration' would only need to be in front of a few Congress elders." I ignored his attempt at playfulness. "If this is unavoidable – which I don't believe is the case – then let him set up a meeting and we'll be done with it. We'll give a sample of what we did.

Something simple. Something light. We don't need to go overboard."

Guillaume leaned in, his words trickling into my ear. "You disappoint me. I thought you'd want to show them how much you could take – how *powerful* you're becoming."

"There are other ways to display power." I was working on keeping mine under control. I felt it rising inside, bucking against Guillaume's close proximity and his attempts to force me back into the role I once played. I wondered if I could smack him with a touch of my firepower and give him a taste of the heat I was capable of delivering. It would be more than he'd expect. I felt my lips curling as I let some of my control go. I saw the ripple of realization run over his face as my skin grew warm. *Control it, control it,* I chanted silently. *Just a sample for the revered witch.*

"Pardon." The word came from somewhere to my left, breaking my concentration. Templeton stood beside us, his eyes growing lighter. He scanned my naked arms before shooting me a dour look.

Guillaume furrowed his brow at the intrusion. "Yes?"

Templeton cut his eyes to the other man. "Ms. Bellerose promised a dance with me this evening."

"Oh." The sound passed through my lips unnoticed. The relief washing over me was far greater than the shock I felt at Templeton's sudden appearance.

"I'm afraid Lucie is unavailable tonight," Guillaume replied. He regarded Templeton curiously.

"I prefer Ms. Bellerose to speak for herself." The last bit of color slid out of Templeton's irises, leaving a ring of black around his pupils.

"Lucie will only be dancing with witches this evening," Guillaume stated. Our movement had halted at Templeton's arrival, but he still held me firmly in his grip. I resisted the urge to twist away. "And you are not a witch."

"I am a member of Congress and I've requested a dance with Ms. Bellerose. She agreed." He extended his left hand toward me, his palm facing upward, his fingers curved in invitation. "Ms. Bellerose?"

"Guillaume!" Michelle exclaimed to my right. "Perfect timing!" Loren spun his wife in a circle and she laughed, bumping sweetly into

Guillaume and causing him to release his grasp. "Let the young ones have a dance or two. You can take me for a twirl while Loren retrieves poor Marlena and steps all over her feet during the next song."

Loren held his wife's hand out to Guillaume, fixing him with an uncompromising stare. "Please. I insist."

Guillaume's eyes shifted back to me, and I read the promise in them. At my left, Templeton's hand waited. Ignoring Guillaume's silent threat, I placed my hand in Templeton's and his graceful fingers pulled me toward him. I locked my gaze with his and he smoothly spun me away as his right hand found its home on the top of my hip. His touch was light, but confident.

"Lower your energy, Lucie," he directed. "You can't afford two citations from the Congress in one week. Unfriendly witches will use it as proof you're not able to control yourself."

"You saw it?" I grimaced.

"I can *still* see it. It's lingering." His irises were regaining their color. "Take a moment. I'll lead."

I automatically relaxed at his words, my body listing toward his for the slightest of beats. The rage threatening to race unchecked through my body lessened as Templeton floated us farther away from Guillaume and his new dance partner.

"I feel better, thank you." I let myself fall into Templeton's rhythm. He didn't reply. A few minutes later, I broke the silence. "Let's see. You can cook a perfect French omelet and you know how to dance. What other talents are you hiding?"

"Dance was required in prep school. I could not avoid it." His expression remained neutral. "But I excel at many things."

Had I not been watching I might've missed the corners of his mouth momentarily quirking up.

"Are you flirting with me?" I wasn't as skilled as Templeton when it came to keeping a straight face. The grin stretching across mine was impossible to suppress.

"I don't flirt," he told me.

"That's probably true." I nodded and felt the coiled energy inside me finish the last of its unwinding.

"Good," he said.

"Good?"

"You stopped giving into it."

"You see when I...?" My voice trailed off. I

wasn't sure what I wanted to ask.

"This I could feel." He flexed the hand resting on my hip. "You only now stopped putting your feelings into the power you're tapping into."

"How do you know this?" I examined his face.

He shook his head. "I only know it's what I could feel last fall when we were in the Walled Zone together."

My heart skipped a beat, but I forced myself not to react to bad memories. "I see. Do you think others can detect this?"

He thought about it for a moment. "I'm not sure. Maybe Guillaume."

I blew out a breath, my cheeks puffing up. "I hope not."

"What did he want from you?" Templeton's question seemed innocent enough, but the slight tensing I felt in his body signaled differently.

"He said the Congress is demanding a demonstration of our work together. He's telling the truth. Loren told me the same." I shuddered, inadvertently tightening my grip on Templeton's hand.

"When?"

"Nothing is scheduled. Loren said he could arrange it so the demonstration would only be in front of a handful of Congress elders." The band began to play a new song, and I recognized the melody as *Beautiful Night*. I wished our discussion matched the lovely music.

Templeton nodded, again surveying the room over my head. "We'll figure out how to deal with the Congress demands." He dropped his attention to the lacy fabric of my dress, his eyes moving from shoulder to shoulder. He cleared his throat. "I like the color of your dress. I like how you look in royal blue."

∞∞∞

As Templeton and I danced, we neared Loren's table. I paused to retrieve my wrap and clutch, observing the soft note of Guillaume's protection spell falling away when I picked up the purse.

"Would you like to go for a walk? Get away from all this noise?" I gestured to the room.

He nodded and we made our way past chatting witches and drink-delivering servers to another set of side doors exiting out into an empty hallway. Dimly lit, it was not as grand as the one leading into the ballroom. Perhaps it was used as a shortcut to the back of the ballroom by those running the evening event.

The corridor widened with concealed alcoves to our left and the occasional window on our right. Sounds of rustling and low murmurs could be heard coming from one of the shadowed nooks. A simultaneous moan and gasp penetrated the relative quiet and I bumped into Templeton's side. I put my hand on my chest and snuck a peek at him. Amused, he raised an eyebrow.

"This way." I pointed, eager to leave the lovers behind. The carpeted passageway sloped downward suggesting we were descending to the first floor of the Congress. Eventually it connected us to a wider hall. "I know where we are."

"We're not far from the library," he noted. We turned in a familiar direction, my heels tapping lightly against the marbled floor. Templeton loosened the collar of his tuxedo shirt as we strolled through the empty halls, leaving his black bow tie dangling.

"I'm sure they've limited where we can go because of the gala," I said. "But at least we're less likely to have traffic down there." As we approached, I could see the library wasn't locked as we assumed it would be. Instead, one of the doors was left ajar and a faint light stretched toward us from the inside.

Templeton hesitated, pulling the door open. "I'm surprised they haven't assigned someone to monitor this space."

"Maybe they aren't as strict as I thought they'd be tonight." I slid under his arm and into the library.

"I doubt it," he muttered. "There are probably several spells in place this evening to make sure nothing walks out of here."

"That you can count on." We stopped in the middle of the library's first room and listened to the silence. We appeared to be alone. A few lamps were left on and the light cast what it could touch in a gold glow. I took a deep breath in through my nose, letting my eyelids drift shut. The library was the best part of the Congress as far as I was concerned. When I reopened my eyes, I realized Templeton watched me, a ghost of a smile tugging at the corners of his mouth.

Unapologetic, I lifted a shoulder. "I like the smell of libraries."

He turned and looked up toward the indistinct balcony of the second floor. "So do I."

I moved through the low light toward the spiral staircase leading to the upstairs. "I lived in libraries when I was a child. When I was a teenager, too."

Templeton was on my heels. I paused at the bottom of the stairs as he stepped forward. "I spent most of my free time in libraries as soon as I could read. It was preferable to everything else," he said.

"You didn't live in the city then. Where did you go?" I started up the stairs. He followed.

"The school's library. I also had access to a private college's library from a young age." His voice flowed up from behind me.

"That would've been wonderful," I replied as we circled upward. "You used the college's library as a child?"

"Yes."

I shook my head as I climbed. Even when he wasn't trying to be difficult, he was. His answers only ever hinted at the full story. "Why did they let you?"

"My mother was a professor there."

His words caused me to stop and turn. He

never casually offered up information about his family. "Oh?"

Templeton hadn't anticipated my stopping and gripped the handrail as he found himself suddenly shortening the space between us. His tall frame swayed, but he took another step. "You're surprised?"

"No. Well, yes. She's a Salesman, correct?" Whereas Guillaume's cologne created a wave of nervousness inside me, the woodsy scent of Templeton's soap was very appealing. I didn't want to move.

So I didn't.

"She is, but she doesn't work for the Empire." Templeton didn't move away either.

"What does she teach?" I set my clutch on the stair behind me.

Templeton gave a quiet laugh. "You're interested in my mother?"

"Well, yes. I mean, I'm interested in knowing more about you – more than what I know now. The basics." I searched his handsome face and squeezed the handrails on either side of me. "I don't even know the basic stuff about you, Templeton."

"Ask away."

It was my turn to laugh, and I shook my head. "It's never going to be that easy with you."

"True," he agreed. I could see his pale eyes shimmer in the delicate space we inhabited between the first and second floors. "But I'd take this opportunity if I were you."

"Okay." I touched the tip of my tongue to my upper lip, mentally choosing my first question. "When is your birthday?"

"April."

"Mine, too."

"I know."

"It drives me crazy how you know more about me than I know about you," I complained.

"I make it my business to know things about the people around me."

"I'm assuming you went to college if your mother teaches at one," I pressed on. "What did you study since you like libraries so much?"

"History and Theology. It was a double major. My concentration in Theology was Witchcraft."

"You'll have to tell me more about it sometime," I said. "You have your bachelor's degree in both History and Theology then?"

"No," he answered. I detected another hint of a smile.

"I can't believe you wouldn't finish," I told him.

"I finished. I earned my Ph.D. in each discipline."

"Of course, you did." Dr. Templeton. *Figures*.

"Anything else you want to ask me before we go upstairs?" He was an inch closer.

"I want to ask you a million questions." My heart pounded in my chest. If he could see when I raised my power, could he hear my heartbeat now?

"One more then." His hand slid up the railing, his fingers covering mine.

"Do you want to kiss me?" I whispered. I strained to see his expression in the half-light.

"Yes."

Templeton dipped his head forward and allowed his lips to skim over mine. I felt the first contact all the way down to the soles of my feet. My legs quivered. I didn't dare let go of the handrail lest I fall, knocking us both down the stairs. The tip of his nose bumped mine lightly as his left hand slipped under my hair and his fingers curled around the back of my neck. His head tilted to the side, seeking my lips a second time. I opened my mouth under his, inviting his tongue to touch mine.

The kiss was slow and tender. Templeton gingerly pulled on my lower lip with his teeth, before easing his tongue forward. He didn't press his body against me, nor did I release my grip on the handrails. I gave in to the singular thrill of his tongue chasing mine deep into my mouth and the resulting tingles sent scurrying over my skin.

The fingers at the nape of my neck threaded themselves through my hair. Templeton gently twisted a handful of it as he pulled my head back. He nipped a teasing trail with his teeth from my jawbone down to the hollow of my neck.

"Please," I hummed.

His mouth was at my ear in an instant. "Please what?" he breathed.

"Please don't stop."

Templeton's hand abandoned my hair, tracing a path down the center of my back. He tightened his grasp, gliding his arm around my waist as my breasts crushed against his chest. He kissed me hard, soft lips demanding more as he pushed me backward onto the stairs. A faint moan sounded from his throat.

Our risky position forced me to let go of

the handrail as the metal edge of the stair bit through my dress into the back of my thighs. I reached behind me to steady myself, my hand knocking my clutch through the opening at the other end of the step. It clattered to the floor below, spilling its contents.

Templeton pulled away confused as he tried to make out what caused the noise.

"My purse," I groaned. "It fell."

Neither one of us moved for the next few seconds. Templeton's breath was ragged, and my body trembled under his with an intensity I hadn't experienced in a long time.

He broke the silence. "This is dangerous." He reluctantly disentangled himself from our precarious position on the stairs, pulling me to my feet. Templeton guided my hand back to the railing. "We should get your purse."

I nodded and trailed him on shaky legs as we spiraled back down the staircase. At the bottom, he recovered the clutch that failed to keep its contents inside when it tumbled from the stairs. Handing it to me, he continued to pick up the few items scattered across the floor.

I retrieved a tube of lipstick and scanned the floor in the poor light looking for the other pieces of flotsam and jetsam. Templeton bent to pick up another purse escapee. He rose, his eyes fixed on the object in his hand. His relaxed posture tensed and he gave his head an aggravated shake.

"What's wrong?" I asked, crossing to him.

He held up the phone Rabbit gave to me. "What's this about?"

"It's one of the network's phones," I answered.

Templeton clenched his teeth. "I know what it is. Why do you have it?"

I didn't like the sudden change in his demeanor, and I certainly didn't care for the flinty edge in his tone. "I have it because Rabbit gave it to me." I held out my hand.

He snorted, slapping the device into my palm.

"What just happened?" I asked, my own temper starting to flare. I shoved the phone into my purse before waving a finger upwards toward the stairs. "What happened between there –" I redirected my finger so that it was pointed to the floor where we stood "– and here?"

"I'm not interested in competing for you, Lucie." Templeton turned his back to me and took off toward the front of the library.

"What in the hell are you talking about?" I

exploded. "Dammit, Templeton! Wait!" I gave the floor another quick scan before chasing after him. I caught him at the library door and grabbed the sleeve of his tuxedo jacket.

Templeton shook off my grasp and grabbed me by the upper arms, spinning us around. He shoved me up against the wall by the library door, squeezing my bare arms. "I'm not interested in sharing with Rabbit, either."

Fury flitted through my chest. "Rabbit is my friend, Templeton! And I certainly don't need to explain myself to you." My hands pushed against his chest as an angry flame inside me charged my skin in warning. "Get off me."

He released me immediately, flicking his fingers dismissively before dropping his hands to his sides as he stepped back. We stared at each other, the library the only witness to what had happened between us – and what continued to happen between us no matter our best efforts to avoid it.

Templeton spared one last look for me, his cold eyes raking over me bitterly. He gritted his teeth and stormed out of the library, shutting the door behind him.

"Yeah, that seems about right," I mumbled. I

pushed off the wall and checked the contents of my purse. We'd collected everything but my house keys. Damn.

Returning to the spiral staircase, I searched the floor for my keyring. It couldn't have gone far. I kept hunting until I heard a soft *Click!* behind me. A chill ran up my spine as I looked over my shoulder. A desk lamp had been switched on and my keys sat in its beam of light. My gaze roamed the room, my heart beating double-time in my chest. It appeared I was alone, but I knew better. I was being watched.

I wasn't foolish enough to call out to whoever was hidden in the murkiness surrounding me. With deliberate composure, I claimed my set of keys and slipped them into my purse. I straightened my shoulders, pulling my black wrap over them as I walked away from the desk, head held high.

My gut instinct told me whoever – or whatever – watched me wanted me to be anxious. I wasn't going to reveal how uneasy I felt. Calmly, I returned to the front of the library, exiting by the same door Templeton had disappeared through.

Closing the door behind me, I picked up the pace, hurrying down the hall away from the library entrance. I'd had enough of the gala. I'd retrieve my coat from the coat check counter and head straight home. I'd make my apologies to Loren and Michelle later.

Chapter 10

The steps leading up to my front door were brushed clean of snow while I was gone. We didn't get much more than a dusting during the day, but the Rabbits laid down a fresh layer of rock salt anyway. I sighed as I turned, studying the steps. I wasn't sure how I felt about this service I was getting. My focus shifted to the corner at the end of my block. Did Rabbit know I was home earlier than I'd planned?

I let myself into the townhouse, pausing with my fingers on the switch controlling the light over my front stoop. I stewed, thinking about what Templeton had said in the library about Rabbit. It made me angry.

I left the light on.

It wasn't yet 11 o'clock. The evening certainly didn't go well. I kicked off my heels and hung my winter coat in the closet. What a horrible night.

I didn't know what was worse – the danger Guillaume brought, the demands of the Congress, or the mess with Templeton. How did it even happen? I dug a glass out of a cupboard and poured myself some wine before pulling out a chunk of cheese from the refrigerator and slicing off a few thin slabs. Templeton left the loaf of bread he'd brought me for breakfast, and I nibbled a day-old slice with the mild cheese.

The worst part? I wanted him to kiss me with every fiber of my being tonight. Wanted it more than anything. Wanted more than a kiss from him. And then... *Dammit.*

I've dealt with my share of jealous men. Even the nicest guys have their moments. A perfectly rational person can spin on a dime when their ego is at risk. Most get past the moment and whatever perceived infraction set them off.

Templeton's lack of self-control was unusual for him. I was even more bothered by it because Rabbit was no stranger. The two knew each other better than I knew either of them. They were on the same side. And Rabbit was about as close to a friend as Templeton could get.

Although, there were instances last year when the two of them almost came to blows. When

Emily was in danger, and Templeton seemed unwilling to help, Rabbit blew sky-high and slammed Templeton into the side of my car. That's when we learned Templeton had lost his ability to door travel and couldn't go after Emily. He'd kept it a secret and it cost us. Rabbit went ballistic at the news and repeatedly punched the side of my RAV4. But it was better than pummeling Templeton.

Later that same night they were back in each other's faces after I made a trade with a frightening magical being. The woman, called Nisha, agreed to return Templeton's door traveling abilities to him after I gave her something of significant value. Rabbit wasn't happy with my deal and Templeton was even angrier. And because Rabbit took me to Nisha, Templeton blamed Rabbit.

I carried my wine to the living room and lit the fireplace, still thinking about the two men as I wrapped the black evening stole around my shoulders in lieu of a blanket. But no matter what, Rabbit and Templeton worked together when we fought the Fringe. They counted on each other like I counted on both of them.

I stewed over Templeton's words. He said he

wouldn't compete for me. Was there a competition? I didn't see one. As for 'sharing me' with Rabbit, I wasn't a prize bone to be pulled back and forth between the two. I resented what he said. Besides, Rabbit and I were friends. We spent time together, sure, but that's what close friends do.

Templeton would need to get over it. The three of us needed to make sure whatever was behind the two directional doors in the Walled Zone stayed there. And Rabbit and I needed to make sure Templeton didn't try to get on the other side of those doors by himself.

I knew in my heart it would be a bad thing if he did. If he door traveled through either, he might not be able to get back.

And I didn't want to lose him.

"Argh!" I put my fingertips to my temples and lowered my head. Just thinking about him gave me a headache. I reached for my wine. The irony was the argument with Templeton in the library earlier was the least of my problems.

If I didn't have to answer to the Congress and their demands for a demonstration with Guillaume, I'd refuse to see my old teacher. My commitment had been met. He'd been well-compensated by the Congress – and by me. I paid him in pounds of flesh many times in our year together. Still, because I was stuck with him while the Congress exercised their interest, it would probably serve me well to decide how we would present our process. Leaving it up to Guillaume would be dangerous – it would hurt.

I held my breath while I imagined what could happen. It *was* going to hurt, but if I chose exactly what we did, I could control the level of pain inflicted on me. I'd learned to tolerate a lot, but it was not something I'd seek out if I didn't have to.

I set the wine glass on the table and leaned back into the couch cushions. Templeton knew exactly who Guillaume was this evening, but Guillaume had no clue as to Templeton's identity. Tonight on the dance floor, Guillaume was at a rare disadvantage. I could imagine the intensity of his fury inside. On one hand, I relished the upper hand Templeton had, if only for now. On the other, I knew it would cost me.

By now Guillaume knew exactly who Templeton was. Oddly enough, Guillaume didn't express the same level of bigotry toward Salesmen as most witches did. He simply looked down on everyone equally, even other witches.

Guillaume also lived in the Empire only briefly, choosing to spend most of his life in France – although I believed he was still recognized as a citizen of the Empire. His interactions with Salesmen were limited.

But his observation tonight of Templeton not being a witch revealed a willingness to sink to class-level prejudices if it would serve him.

Templeton would interest him because of his magical abilities and reputation. Templeton would draw his ire because of his connection to me. I pulled on my lip. It occurred to me as the taxi ferried me home from the gala that it might've been Guillaume in the library leaving my house keys under the lamplight. How long he'd been watching – if it was him – I could only guess. It's possible he saw Templeton kiss me. Either way, I planned on receiving a thorough questioning the next time I faced Guillaume.

My history with Templeton, whatever it was or wasn't, would be pulled apart. It would get worse when he learned what I gave up to Nisha when I traded with the priestess to get Templeton's door traveling powers back.

I gave to her what Guillaume had presented to

me on the day I left his home after I completed a year as his student: a blank page from his personal book of magic.

I didn't know of another student who'd received such a gift. If Guillaume found out I no longer had it, that I gave it away as payment to Nisha – a non-witch – I'd be punished. I had no doubt. And the Congress would back him completely. I'd given a potent piece of witch magic to an outsider.

I knew what I was doing when I went to Nisha and told her what I wanted. We needed Templeton to be at full capacity and I couldn't stand to see him helpless. He hid it as long as he could, but once I knew what had happened, I decided I'd do whatever it took to help him. Why the compulsion drove me so furiously, I wasn't sure. Maybe it was because of the prophecy linking us, maybe it was the undeniable chemistry between us, or maybe it was because I had feelings for him. I covered my face with a throw pillow.

Tap-tap-tap. I heard Rabbit's knuckles rapping lightly against my front door. I abandoned the couch, dropping my wrap on it before greeting him. He grinned, his whole face lighting up.

"Hey," I said, sliding to the side. "You decided

to come by after all."

He shrugged as he stepped into the entryway. "It was either you or squeezing into a sweaty club downtown. *Rhino Vomit's* playing."

I faked shock. "What? You picked me over *Rhino Vomit*? Are you feverish?" I reached for his forehead.

"Stop that! You haven't been drinking again, have you?" he asked, dodging my waving hand.

"Yes, but this time I truly am sober. It was not a fun night and I didn't stay at the gala. I had a miserable time." I watched as he squatted and untied his boots. "I haven't been home long."

He peered up at me while his fingers worked the laces. "I can see that." He checked out my dress before sneaking a peek at my discarded heels. "You look really nice, Lucie."

I laughed, slipping my shoes back onto my feet and giving a twirl. "And this is the last time I'm getting dressed up until Emily's wedding, so get an eyeful, Rabbit."

He paused and nodded. "I like it." He dropped his head and finished untying his boots.

"What do you want to drink?" I kicked off my heels for a second time and headed for the kitchen.

"Water's fine," he answered.

"Lightweight!" I called over my shoulder.

Rounding the corner, I found Templeton in my kitchen. He leaned back against the counter, his palms resting on the edge. His shirt was still unbuttoned at the top, but the black tie was long gone. His head was lowered and he stared at the floor.

My body stopped in its tracks, but my stomach flip-flopped forward. "I didn't hear you come in," I heard myself saying.

He lifted his head. "I figured as much." His angry gaze moved over my shoulder.

"Hey, Templeton," Rabbit acknowledged as he came into the kitchen behind me. "I didn't know you were here."

"All kinds of surprises this evening," Templeton replied coolly.

"I've been trying to get ahold of you," Rabbit continued, undeterred. "We thought it was a good time for us to meet and discuss the directional doors now that Lucie's home." Rabbit picked out a tall glass from the cupboard and filled it with water from the refrigerator dispenser.

"Is that so?" Templeton sneered. He still hadn't

moved from his position at the counter, but the tensing of his body was obvious.

Rabbit cocked his head to the side and evaluated the other man as he took a drink of water. "Yeah."

"First thing in the morning after you roll out of bed? Maybe over breakfast?" Templeton's tone was mocking.

Rabbit bristled as he set his glass of water down on the counter by the barstools. "Is there a problem I don't know about here?" Rabbit turned to me. "What's going on?"

"It's been a long night of misunderstandings." I held up both of my hands in surrender, my palms facing out. "I need both of you to listen to me."

Concerned, Rabbit placed a hand on my shoulder, giving it a tender squeeze. "What's wrong?"

Templeton ran a hand through his short hair and swore.

Rabbit turned on Templeton before I could intervene. "And what the hell is your problem?"

Templeton straightened, his faded irises losing more color. "Stop touching her."

"Enough!" I stepped between the two men. "Both of you. Both of you knock it off!"

"I don't think you want to start something with me," Rabbit warned Templeton. His eyes hadn't grown fully black, but they glittered with a savage brightness I'd seen before.

I'd had about all I could take. My hands balled into fists and my temperature rose. "If you two cared about me, you wouldn't be pulling this shit in *my* home. I have enough problems without either of you adding your testosterone-driven pettiness onto my shoulders. You have no idea what hell I'm going to be facing at the Congress. It's going to be bad – probably even worse than I'm already imagining. And yet I'm willing to do my part as 'the light' in the prophecy to help you deal with the doors in the Walled Zone – and whatever might happen if they're breached. I'd think you'd both have the decency to not piss all over my kitchen in some ridiculous attempt to mark your territory here tonight." I was disgusted with both men. I turned my back to them and stormed out of the kitchen. "I can't stand the sight of either one of you. I want both of you to leave. *Now*."

∞ ∞ ∞

Upstairs, I fumed. How dare they behave that way in my home? I paced back and forth over the hardwood floor in my bedroom. And Templeton? What was his problem?

I threw my hands up into the air. He was impossible. I grew weary of trying to understand his behavior and my feelings for him no matter how frustrated I became with the man.

I stopped. But he didn't immediately turn tail and leave when he realized Rabbit was here tonight. In fact, he held his ground. I might not be happy with what happened, but for once he didn't run away from me.

But then I kicked him out – for the second time in a week.

I stood in front of my mirror, unhooking the silver clip and pulling it and the matching band from my hair. Next, I removed my earrings and pulled the sapphire ring from my finger. I contemplated my tired face. Another evening that went from bad, to better, to worse. These low spots were becoming a trend.

A door opening and closing downstairs startled me, but I realized it was only the front door. Rabbit must've left. Templeton would, of course, leave through The Pantry Express and door travel out of my kitchen to wherever it was he went to lick his wounds.

Before I shed my stockings and dress, I decided to do a run-through downstairs. I trusted Rabbit to lock the front door, but I wanted to make sure the lights were off and the stove – which I hadn't turned on anyway – wasn't left on. It was a compulsion. Once it reared its ugly head, I had to touch all the knobs to make sure they were off.

As I descended the stairs, I could see a soft light shining. They'd left one on in the kitchen after all. I turned the corner at the bottom of my stairs and halted. At the other end of the hall, I could see into my kitchen. Templeton sat on a barstool, his hands clasped in front of him and resting on the counter. His head turned in my direction as I walked toward him, emerging from the shadowy hallway. I stood in the doorway and glanced around the kitchen. We were alone.

Before I could say anything, he spoke. "Rabbit left."

I didn't go into the kitchen, preferring to stay where I was. "I thought I told you both to leave."

"I decided not to," he replied.

"Why?" I crossed my arms.

He blew out an exasperated breath and swiveled the barstool toward me. Sliding off, he took a step. "Because of tonight in the library. Because I didn't want to leave. I don't believe you wanted me to go either."

"Now you think you know what *I* want?" I scoffed. "Templeton, admit it. Half the time you can't decide what *you* want. This 'push me, pull me' habit of yours is getting old."

"Every time I make a move, I come face-to-face with one of your wannabe lovers or some ghost from your past. So, no. I don't know what you want." He stood directly in front of me but left a narrow buffer of space between us. "But I'm not going to compete with anyone or any memory you can't let go."

His comment about my memories stung. My arms dropped to my sides, my fingers flinching. I took a deep breath. "I'm not asking you to compete. We've already had this conversation tonight. I'm not going through this again," I said evenly.

Templeton advanced and I reacted by taking a step back into the hall. His eyes shimmered in the lightest shade of blue as I retreated.

"What do you want, Lucie?" His voice grew

husky. "I'm not going to keep playing these games with you."

"I'm not playing games, Templeton." I was angry, but I forced the uneasy fury roiling inside me down. I wasn't going to lose control this time. I started to turn away, but he matched my movement, his body seeming to use up all the space in my hall as he circled me and prevented my getaway. My shoulder blades came in firm contact with the wall behind me when I shifted to avoid him.

Templeton was close; only a few inches separated us now. The powerful energy he carried inside rolled off him in hot waves, enveloping me. Placing his hands on the wall on either side of my shoulders, he leaned in, examining my face. "Then tell me what you want." He enunciated each word deliberately.

My arms at my sides, I pressed my own palms back against the wall. With our bodies almost touching for a second time that night, I knew exactly what I wanted. Templeton knew, too. He wanted the same thing. But there was no way I was going to admit it after the evening we'd had. Instead, I said nothing.

He bent closer, his mouth hovering at my ear.

I felt his wet breath first, then his lips as he brushed them over my ear as he spoke. "Tell me."

I shut my eyes, berating myself silently for wanting this while I also willed him *not* to stop. I swallowed my words before they could escape and betray me.

He smelled so good.

Templeton kissed me softly under my ear. His nose nuzzled against the same spot as his lips moved lower and grazed the side of my neck. He licked my charged skin.

Refusing to respond, I held my ground, but the tiny gasp slipping past my lips gave me away. Gooseflesh spread over my shoulders and down my chest, my nipples tightening under my dress. My fingers splayed against the wall as I kept my palms flat against the wood. Pleasure tingled over my skin as he kissed my neck. My toes curled.

Oh, god.

Templeton molded his body against mine. His mouth was greedy now – all traces of tenderness were gone. He covered mine with his, thrusting his tongue as one hand wrapped possessively around the back of my neck. The other hand he dropped to my hip, digging his fingers into the lace covering my dress, pulling the material into a fist.

He rocked forward, bending his knees slightly and rolling his hips into mine. I could feel him through our clothes – he was already hard. He ripped his mouth from our kiss and returned to my ear.

"I need to know what you want, Lucie," he rasped.

I didn't answer, my fingertips attempting to push into the wood of my hallway's wall. The air around us felt hot – smelled hot. I responded by turning my head and seeking his lips. He obliged, burying his tongue into my mouth again.

The hand at the back of my neck slid down, catching my dress' zipper and lowering it bit by bit. Templeton abandoned our kiss, sliding both of his hands up my naked arms before peeling my clothing down over my shoulders. His eyes followed the material, skittering across the top of my breasts before the black satin bra appeared. Bowing his head, his warm lips skimmed over my rounded flesh before he continued lower, kneeling before me. I stared down at him, my dress hanging around my waist, its armholes now surrounding my wrists. Unless I freed my palms from the wall, the dress wasn't going any farther.

Templeton traced my waistline with his fingertips, dipping his fingers under the material of the dress. They met the top of my garter. He froze, his tongue sweeping over his lower lip when he realized what I wore under my evening dress. The light from the kitchen tossed a pale-yellow beam across his face and I focused on the wet sheen glistening on his bottom lip.

His left hand slid under my dress, exploring up the side of my leg. As his fingers found the top of the silk stocking, he moaned, pitching forward and pressing his forehead against my stomach. His right hand tugged impatiently at my dress. When I didn't voluntarily remove my hand from the wall, he straightened, his fingers wrapping around my wrist as he wrenched it free. His other hand gripped the bottom of my clothing, yanking my dress lower. He repeated the action on my left side. With my dress puddled around my ankles, he remained on his knees, but sat back on his ankles.

To hide my shaking hands, I again glued my palms to the wall behind me. I still wore my undergarments, but I'd never felt so exposed – *so bared.* Templeton raked his gaze over my body, from the soft curve of my belly, over my hips, to the top of my silk stockings. He stroked the skin between the stockings and my panty line, his fingertips barely making contact.

I felt like he could see all of me. I felt naked.

After what seemed like an eternity, he lifted his head. The cool flame in his strange eyes flashed.

The intensity I saw there, the longing I found, stole my breath.

"Tell me what you want from me," he whispered.

When I still didn't answer, Templeton bent forward, pressing hot kisses along the top of each stocking, running the tip of his nose up the right suspender before tilting his head and brushing his face over the thin fabric of my satin panties. He kissed me through them... *there.* He gently pulled at the material with his teeth, before again rubbing his nose and mouth over the front of the undergarment.

I gasped as his hands unexpectedly squeezed the front of both my thighs before they crept upward, stopping at the waistband of my underwear. His fingertips teased along the material's edge, but he didn't pull them down.

I didn't want him to stop. I could feel the heat building inside, spreading up my back as my hips twitched. A deep ripple rocketed through my lower belly.

My skin glowed, brightening the hallway and bathing both of us in its unusual light. But the rage I usually felt churning under my skin was absent. Instead, my body felt languid and wonderfully warm. Just outside the blissful haze, I could smell something burning, something scorched.

Templeton sat back again on his haunches. He paused to survey my bare skin and its glow but said nothing. His eyes, brighter than usual, lifted to mine. I couldn't look away.

His right hand drifted to the hard shape pressing through the fabric at the front of his trousers. He idly rubbed himself for a moment before rising to his feet. Again, he pressed into me, his lips over mine while his tongue fucked slowly in and out of my mouth.

Templeton stroked the curve of my left breast, his deft fingers teasing just under the fabric at the top of my bra. My anticipation of what was coming next made my stomach ache. I finally allowed my hands to abandon the wall behind me and ran them up his arms and over his chest, searching for his shirt buttons. I was eager to feel his bare skin against mine.

He broke our kiss, raising his hand and stroking my cheek lovingly with the back of his fingers. The pad of a fingertip eventually found its way to my bottom lip. He pulled on it gently. My impulse was to flick it with the point of my tongue.

Templeton flashed a rare smile at me – it was unexpected and sexy. "When you can tell me exactly what you want, Lucie," he began softly. "I'll give everything to you."

He suddenly pushed away from me, his hand straying to the front of his trousers briefly before a satisfied smirk slid over his face. He turned away, leaving me mostly naked and starving for what he could do to me.

Aghast, I watched as he disappeared into the kitchen. I heard the pantry door open and shut as he door traveled out of my home.

I slid down the wall to the floor, groaning and pulling my crumpled dress over my body. I buried my face in my hands as the glowing subsided.

I simply could not decide whether I hated Templeton or wanted him more than ever.

But what was that hot smell? I lifted my head and sniffed. It reminded me of... *burnt vanilla.* I twisted my head to the side and looked up at the wall.

My handprint was burnt into the wood.

Chapter 11

The next morning, I stood in the hall, sipping my coffee and contemplating the *two matching handprints* scorched into the wood.

My hands themselves were unscathed. I had no burn marks, and I certainly didn't feel the fire – or at least the intense power – that burnt reflections of my palms and splayed fingers into the wall. Obviously, this all happened when my hands were pressed against it – and when Templeton was pressed against *me*.

"I'm going to end up burning this place down if this continues," I muttered to myself.

Earlier I'd crawled from bed after a frustrating night of tossing and turning. Templeton had lit me up in ways I'd never expected.

I wrinkled my nose at the handprints. Literally lit me up.

In the kitchen I'd found a note Rabbit left the

night before. He'd written:

> *L.*
> *We'll be here at noon on Sunday to discuss the directional doors.*
> *R.*

Apparently the two men put aside their egos after I left them to it last night. This afternoon's meeting would be interesting on many levels.

I inspected my handprints. Their location on the wall would make it difficult to hide the evidence. I decided I could move the small hall table over and cover one of them. The handprint closer to the kitchen entrance would be more difficult.

While I was sliding said table to the right, I heard a rapping at my front door. I groaned. Now what? Peeking out the window I saw Loren standing on my doorstep, dusting the snow off his sleeve. Damn. I hadn't expected him to show up at my home.

"Loren," I acknowledged as I held the door for him, allowing him to enter. "I'm sorry I left the gala without saying goodbye last night. Once I saw Guillaume, the idea of staying and facing off with him all evening was overwhelming. I trusted I could count on you to understand." I shut the door on the cold.

"I certainly understand," he said. "Guillaume's attendance was a surprise to all of us. I do hope he'll respect your wishes and give you space. However, I fear after what we witnessed last night that won't be the case."

"You're probably right," I said. "But I'm hoping you can offer some sort of buffer for me while he's in the Empire. I know the Congress wants a demonstration, but I'd like to control what we do. I want to limit Guillaume's level of participation."

"I'll see what I can do." Loren glanced down the hallway. He inclined his head toward the kitchen. "I hope you don't mind the unexpected visit, but something happened last night during the gala. It's quite concerning and one of the reasons why I'm here today."

"Let me take your coat," I said, holding out my hand. I hung his fine dress coat in my hall closet before leading him into my kitchen. "Would you like coffee?"

"That would be nice. Thank you," Loren said, pausing by the unconcealed handprint before following me.

I set about pouring him a cup of black coffee. "Would you be more comfortable sitting in the dining room?" I gestured to the rarely used room.

"Oh, no. This is fine." He hoisted himself up onto a barstool and I set the coffee in front of him.

I tidied up as I poked gently at Loren with the same sort of energy I used when reading cards for my clients. I could feel the worry and reluctance he held inside. "You said something happened during the gala?"

"Yes." He blew over the surface of his coffee before taking a cautious sip. "There was an intrusion last night into the Congress building. Something unwelcome managed to get by the wards."

"What do you mean?" I hung the damp dishrag over my sink faucet and faced the older witch.

"We believe it was a demon."

"A demon?" Demons were all too real, but not common in the Empire. They weren't welcome creatures. "How could a demon get into the Congress building?"

"That's exactly what we hope to find out. At

first we thought it'd been conjured, but that would require a level of experience not many witches come by easily. Even then, conjuring a demon within the Congress walls would be next to impossible." Loren shook his head. "Of course, one of the most powerful witches inside or outside the Empire was there last night."

I refreshed my own coffee and added a dollop of milk. "Guillaume."

"Yes." Loren's shrewd eyes peered over his cup. "While I have no direct knowledge of Guillaume ever performing such an act, it's not unreasonable to assume he's experimented with less acceptable practices over the years as part of his extensive research. He could've learned such a skill."

"But bringing a demon into the Congress building? To what end? No. This is not how Guillaume operates," I defended my former teacher. "Certainly, there must be other witches who could pull off calling for a demon? The conjuring isn't the hard part, Loren. Containment, however, is a different story." *Which is one of the many reasons to not ever summon a demon*, I thought. "Was it named?"

Loren pulled a face. "We've found no evidence

of the demon's name. Some would argue invoking a demon within the building wouldn't ever be feasible with the wards and other protections set up by the Congress. But this hasn't quieted speculation from other corners."

I wasn't sure how to reply, so I waited.

Loren chose his next words carefully. "John Templeton was an unexpected guest as well last night. His name was included in this morning's discussion amongst the elders."

"Templeton was not at the gala to whip up a demon." This was even more absurd than accusing Guillaume.

"I don't believe he'd do anything of the sort either," Loren agreed. "But a contingent of witches would be happy to accuse him of performing such a dreadful act. You know the Salesman is not well-liked. And he went missing about the same time you did. Were you with him the whole night?"

"Yes. Well, for the most part." I felt my cheeks flush. "We both left the ballroom at the same time and we... We walked the Congress halls, chatting." I looked at my coffee cup and realized I was spinning it between my fingertips. I stopped as soon as I noticed my fidgeting.

Loren smiled. "I'm not going to ask for details of your personal interactions with Templeton, Lucie. That's not why I'm here."

"He was with me the whole time after leaving the ballroom," I told Loren. "We separated briefly at the end of our conversation. But I believe we both left the building at about the same time. In fact, he may have left before me by a few minutes."

"I see. You didn't leave together then?"

"No."

"Well, talk about Templeton's attendance coinciding with the demon gaining entrance to the Congress won't stop anytime soon." Loren shrugged. "It's unfortunate, but some will use it as an excuse to cast aspersions on the validity of his membership in the Congress."

"Jealous witches," I muttered.

Loren continued. "There is an additional concern that another powerful witch was in attendance last night. This is being gossiped about in some of the pettier camps in Congress and fueled by certain prominent families."

I gritted my teeth and waited.

"This witch has pulled the spotlight in her direction through her successes but also through several perceived transgressions." Loren tapped his finger against his cup's handle. "And she slipped away without anyone noticing she'd left the ballroom. You should know your name was mentioned during early morning conversations, too."

"I can't stop people from gossiping."

"You know as well as I do your power has grown exponentially," Loren said. "And in fact, Guillaume has described you privately to certain elders in the Congress as one of the most powerful witches he's taught. This is high praise."

"Is it possible the demon managed to get into the Congress building by itself without any magical help from someone on the inside?" I didn't want to discuss my abilities alongside the demon's appearance.

"Yes, in that anything is possible," Loren replied. "But it's also unlikely. A demon would have to pass through the wards. It's not as though it would seek to complete the ritual of recognition. If it entered the Congress without being summoned, it would not have waltzed in through the main entrance. There are less than a handful of other entrances into the building, and they were guarded. As such, the Congress continues to revisit the idea it was conjured from within even while they contend it's not possible."

I knew I couldn't argue with Loren, and I definitely couldn't convince Congress elders otherwise. I puzzled over what the being said to me as I completed the ritual of recognition. What did she say? *'Be aware. The one who seeks you, he is here.'* Or something like that.

Last night I assumed she meant Guillaume, but now I wondered if she meant something more sinister was afoot. Was she referring to the demon? I didn't meet Loren's eyes. I thought about kissing Templeton in the library and how after he left, the desk lamp was switched on and my keys had been placed under its light. I remembered the feeling of being watched. Was there a demon in the library? Had it seen us on the stairs?

I needed to tell Templeton about this when I saw him later. I'd let Rabbit know about the demon's presence as well. It didn't have anything to do with our discussion of the fifth and sixth doors in the Walled Zone, but it'd be of interest to the Rabbit network. They'd be curious about a demon managing to breach the walls of the Congress of Empire Witches.

Sharing these thoughts with Loren was a bad idea. Again, I didn't want my name – or Templeton's – to be associated with the demon's invasion. Besides, all my thoughts were conjecture. There was enough speculation going on.

"I know Guillaume is eager to provide a demonstration at the Congress," I said, switching to the other unpleasant subject. "When do you think the elders will want this to happen?"

"I'm not sure how long Guillaume plans to remain in the Empire, but I think this is something the Congress expects to see in the next several days. Are you ready?"

"I'm not entirely prepared," I admitted. "I had no idea this would be something the Congress would require of me. But I'll be ready when the time comes."

"I know you will be," Loren nodded. "I know I can count on you. Michelle and I are proud of the woman you've become – of the witch you've become. Your family would've been proud of you, too. Your ancestors are surely grateful for what you've done to strengthen your witchline. They understand the sacrifices you've made. Your heirs will be grateful to you, as well."

Loren saw me shift uncomfortably in response to his words.

He soldiered on as I squirmed. "Do you have someone in mind to... I mean, I would be willing to go to the Congress on your behalf and inquire as to a suitable partner for you. Someone for you to, ah, couple with and produce an heir if need be."

His words left me stunned. This was worse than Michelle telling me Loren was ready to go before the Congress and lobby for them to find me a husband. I adored Loren, but I had to stop this crazy train before it pulled out of the station. "I'm not looking for a sperm donor. I'm sorry to be crude, Loren, but that's not something I'm interested in – ever."

"I understand," he replied. "But we both know your witchline dies with you as it stands today."

"Yes, it does. But if Guillaume could help me learn how to strengthen my witchline – something no one thought could be done – then why couldn't I learn to open it up to another witch? Why couldn't I choose my heir – whether it's a child or even another adult – to take on my legacy? To graft them onto my family tree and plug them right into my witchline? This is what I want to do. I made it clear when I started down this road," I reminded him.

Loren held up his hand. "I know and I do support you. But if it cannot be done and you want to continue your witchline – which is important not only for you, but for all witches here in the Empire – you need to think about other avenues. If you're unable to open your witchline to someone who is not born from your body, you might need to make a difficult decision."

The direction our conversation turned floored me. But Loren was no misogynist. True, he swung toward the more traditional conservative camp, but he never treated women as less than equal. At worst, he tended to be overprotective. This was why his words troubled me. I worried he might be getting pressure from inside the Congress.

"If the time comes when I'm in a position to have a child of my own, I will do it with someone I love – someone I want to raise a child with," I told him gently. I leaned across the counter and put my hand on his.

Loren turned his hand over to give mine a loving squeeze. "Of course, Lucie. I don't want you to do anything you don't want to do. And no one can force you to make those decisions now, but it's something I want you to think about. Be aware others are thinking about you and your legacy, especially those who have a significantly thinning witchline. Some families have much to gain by bringing you into their fold and uniting you with an eligible witch to produce children."

Knowing there were people thinking about these things shook me up. I kept getting hit with scenarios, ideas, and expectations I never anticipated. After I returned from France, I never thought about any of these subjects. I'd had other things to worry about, other parts of myself and my spirit to heal without worrying about trying to please other people – other witches – who would make demands upon my body.

"Well," Loren interrupted my thoughts. "I must be going. I'm sorry last night at the gala did not go well for you. I wanted the event to be a happy occasion."

"I know," I said. "I'm grateful to you and Michelle for your kindness. I don't know what I'd do without you."

The man nodded once, acknowledging my

thanks as he reached into the inside pocket of his suit jacket. He attempted to squash a satisfied look as he placed a white envelope on the counter and pushed it toward me. "A copy of the citation you received the other day."

I grimaced. "Yeah, about that. After our lunch I was in the library and I might've let a little magic slip – not to do any damage, but to, um, slap back some attitude I was getting."

Loren laughed. "You were seen with Templeton in the library after we dined. And I've observed the interaction between you two. I'm assuming your unplanned magic happened in Templeton's company."

"I didn't purposely set out to break any rules," I defended myself.

"I don't believe you intended to run afoul, but mistakes like that will trouble some witches, which is why it's important for you to remain available in the Congress – especially to the elders. Tend to your reputation in such a way that they can only speak of the generous and trustworthy witch you are. They already know you're powerful. Now let them see the kind witch I know and love. Let them observe the witch who is a part of their community – *who is a vital part of their community* – and who will support the Congress above all."

I balked at his language. "That last part is hard for me to guarantee, but I understand what you're saying. I will do my best."

Loren accepted my assurance and nodded toward the envelope I held in my hand. "It has been dealt with. You won't need to appear at the Oversight Office and no penalty will be imposed. You will see the citation has been rescinded and any demerits assigned have been removed."

"Demerits? Are we all in boarding school now?"

"Think of receiving a demerit as the same thing as losing a poker chip," Loren said. "Whether you like it or not, Lucie, you are deeply ensconced in Congress games now – and you want to keep all your chips. Avoid demerits. Citations are forgotten; demerits are constantly being considered."

Loren prepared to leave, standing and taking his cup to the sink where he rinsed it out. Michelle trained him well. I listened to the water splashing in the sink. "Thank you for the coffee. I'm sorry Michelle didn't get to say goodnight to you after the gala, but she does send her best. She wants you to know if you need anything to call upon her. She will be at your side in a heartbeat – as will I."

"Thank you." We embraced. In my heart I was thankful for such a kind friend. I needed someone like Loren who could understand what I was going through as a witch – and as someone who managed to cause a stir in the Congress.

I had good people in my life I could talk to, friends like Rabbit, Emily, and even some of my non-traditional witch friends, but no one could understand what I was facing and what was in store for me. But Loren could and he was on my side.

After retrieving his coat from my closet, I walked him to the front door.

"I'm off to brunch," he said, buttoning up his coat. "I hope you're getting to relax today."

"I have company coming over at noon," I said.

He paused. "Your Rabbit?"

I nodded. "You would like Rabbit. He has great integrity."

"I'm not here to tell you who to spend your time with but be careful. Rabbits are unpredictable creatures."

"That hasn't been my experience," I said. This was a battle for another day. "Thank you for coming here to check on me, Loren. And for everything else. You'll let me know if you hear anything about when the demonstration has been scheduled?"

"I will," Loren confirmed. "It will most likely be this week, so be ready. And be prepared to see Guillaume prior to the demonstration. I would not be shocked if he sought you out in the next day or two. He was quite frustrated when he couldn't find you last night after he finished dancing with Michelle."

"I was afraid of that," I said.

"And he is very concerned about you spending time with a Salesman – one who, as he put it late last night – comes to the Congress with a shadowy lineage like Templeton's."

I startled. "What do you mean?"

"How much do you know about Templeton's line?" Loren asked.

I shook my head. "Not a lot. But his mother is the Salesman and that's where he inherited his ability to door travel. I don't know much about his father, but I believe he's deceased. He practiced magic and I assume he's the one Templeton inherited his own magical powers from."

Loren pursed his lips and nodded. "I think you should have a conversation with Templeton. You should know more about his lineage and how it might impact you."

"Impact me?" I wasn't sure where Loren was headed.

"I don't give much credibility to rumors I've heard, but often there's a thread of truth in them. If that is the case, then you would do well to learn what kind of magical line Templeton comes from – and what it means for any relationship you have with him."

"I didn't say I had a relationship with him," I protested warily.

Loren chuckled. "It was written all over your face when the two of you were dancing last night. There is definitely an attraction between the two of you. I looked at my Michelle the same way Templeton looks at you. Right now it's desire, but I could see more in the way he attended to you. If you have the same feelings for him, then yes, I do have a concern. Whatever it is, ultimately, it's between the two of you. But you do need to know more about him, and you should make it a priority to find out."

"Is there something in particular you're referring to?" I wavered between irritation and interest.

"I know Templeton's father was banished from the Empire – that he was a practitioner of magic. If the Salesman Court banished him, they had a reason." Loren pressed his lips together and had the good graces to seem embarrassed. "I have a friend who works within the Salesman Court's system and documents about the senior John Templeton are sealed. They cannot access them. There is a secret in Templeton's family history, and you should learn what it is and how it could affect you."

I blew out a breath. "We're all entitled to our secrets. But I'll talk to Templeton eventually. He's shared a little about his family history in the past." I thought back to our fall visit to the Tortoise when we learned Templeton's father was a practitioner of black magic. The Tortoise revealed the secret, but Templeton didn't deny it. "I will talk to him. But don't worry about me, and don't worry about Templeton. Besides, at the rate he and I keep going, the moon and stars are never going to align for us. It's been a battle. This conversation is probably a moot point."

"Sounds like a perfect storm for a grand affair." Loren's small eyes sparkled. "At the end of the day, I want you to be happy regardless of who you're with – although I'd like you to be cautious with the Rabbits."

I shook my head. "Loren, you're going to be late for your brunch."

"I will be in touch within a day or two." He leaned over and kissed my forehead. "Be ready. It could be short notice as to when the Congress will see you."

"I will. Be careful on the steps," I told him as he shuffled outside and descended to the sidewalk. I watched as a waiting car pulled to the curb. Of course Loren wouldn't be about driving in the city. He waved goodbye before climbing into the back seat.

Closing the door, I thought about our conversation. There were so many moving parts and more than a handful bothered me. Most worrying was the fact a demon broke into the Congress. My intuition told me it was the demon watching in the library before I left last night.

I wondered if Templeton had sensed anything off. Still, as much as he casually broke the laws of the Empire – and certainly the rules governing him as a Salesman – letting loose with any magic while inside Congress might strip him of membership. As a non-witch, he might not get a second chance.

But I'd ask. I checked the clock. I had two frustrating men coming to my house and had yet to prepare. I'd make a fresh pot of coffee. If they were hungry, I'd make sandwiches. Well, Rabbit would eat, but Templeton probably wouldn't. I frowned at Rabbit's note. He said they'd arrive at noon. I ran my tongue over my front teeth. Guess he neglected to include an apology when he penned the note.

Not that I was expecting one, but it would've been nice.

Maybe I wouldn't bother making sandwiches.

Chapter 12

At approximately seven minutes before noon, I was aware of the pantry door opening silently behind me. I'd caved and stood at the stove grilling half a dozen portabella mushroom and Swiss cheese sandwiches on pumpernickel rye bread. I flipped a sizzling sandwich before peeking over my shoulder. Templeton stood just inside the door in a pair of tailored black trousers and a long-sleeved, gray button-down shirt. His black leather shoes were polished to a high shine. One hand rested casually on a hip. In his other hand he held the book of fairy tales. I noted he didn't bother to wear his 'official' Salesman top hat. This was one of the rules he broke often. The Salesman Court *required* all their Salesmen to door travel with their top hats so they could be monitored by the Empire. He rarely wore his when door traveling into my home. I doubted he wore it many places.

I turned and motioned to the coffee pot. "Coffee?"

"No, thank you." He crossed the kitchen and set the book on the counter by the barstools. "I thought you might want to refamiliarize yourself with the stories."

"I probably should." I cut the flame below the frying pan. "Will you leave the book here with me?"

Templeton nodded, the corners of his mouth quirking up once as he glanced toward the hallway beyond the kitchen. "Did you sleep well?"

I shot him a withering look. "Of course. You?"

"Like a baby," he replied smoothly.

"You have some lint on your sleeve." I pointed my spatula at him before turning away, a grin plastered across my face. I transferred the toasted sandwiches from the frying pan onto an oval platter. They'd be fine at room temperature. I snuck a peek at Templeton. He was scowling. Ha! The lint comment poked the right nerve.

I topped off my coffee. "Would you like something other than coffee then? Water, maybe? Orange juice?"

His eyes narrowed. "You don't like orange juice."

"I don't. But you do." I decided to pour him a glass even though he hadn't said yes. I opened the refrigerator and retrieved the half gallon I'd purchased while shopping. I poured the drink and set it beside him. Taking a moment to think about the right way to address what happened the night before, I rested my palms on the countertop. "I'd like to talk about…"

The rim of the juice glass was at his lips. "No." He took a sip.

"Ah, yes," I huffed. He was impossible.

He took a breath in through his nose. "We don't have time to get into a discussion about anything personal before Rabbit arrives. He'll be here any minute."

Templeton had a point. I fluttered my fingers against the countertop. "I suppose it's nothing that can't wait. But I do want to discuss several things with you sooner rather than later."

He took another drink while he contemplated my words. "Is there something new I should know about?"

"Not really," I said. "It's much of the same. I've been wanting to talk to you about the prophecy and what this means between the two of us. But it's not a discussion Rabbit needs to join."

"Agreed." Templeton set the glass on the counter and opened the book of fairy tales. For him the subject was closed.

I rubbed the tips of my fingers together, remembering Loren's prodding to learn more about Templeton's family. "There's more."

"Oh?" He looked up.

"I'd like to know about your family – especially in light of the prophecy."

He crossed his arms. "Anything in particular you want to know?"

I checked the time. "Yes. Specifically, I want to talk about your father."

At my words his face turned to stone. "There's not much to discuss."

"I'm not so sure," I answered. "He practiced magic, and I believe your own magical abilities come through his line. I don't think this is something you inherited from your mother."

Templeton's jaw worked while he regarded me. "Where is this coming from?"

"This is not a new curiosity," I told him. "And, well, we were observed at the Congress by Loren – and others at the gala, of course. Loren had a few questions about how we came to know one another."

Templeton didn't blink. "Go on."

I rubbed the back of my neck. Suddenly I couldn't believe I was having this conversation and dreaded the words as they came out of my mouth. "Loren comes from a more traditional branch of witches and was wondering about your intentions. He wants to make sure I understand where you come from and who you are."

Templeton's eyes wandered around the kitchen as I spoke. "I think you know me better than most, Lucie."

"Do I?" I asked before continuing. "But there's more. Loren came here this morning. He wanted to know if I was okay since he didn't see me at the gala after you and I danced. I told him we left the ballroom to put some space between Guillaume and me, that you and I walked the Congress halls and talked. I explained we left the building shortly after that." I waved a hand and shook my head. "I assumed you left the Congress right after you left the library."

Templeton was in no hurry to answer, but eventually he spoke. "Are you questioning where I went after the library?"

"I'm not."

"But Loren wanted to know where I went?" Templeton lifted his chin and looked down his aristocratic nose. "What's this about?"

"Loren also came by to tell me about an uninvited visitor breaching the wards and making it into the Congress building."

"What kind of visitor?"

"Apparently a demon managed to sneak in." I pressed my lips together, reflecting on the strange occurrence. "Anything unwelcome getting through is pretty extraordinary, but a demon sliding under the radar of an entire set of safeguards put in place by witches is unbelievable."

"Was the demon named?" Templeton asked. He'd moved to a barstool and sat down.

"No. But it's possible if it wasn't conjured inside the Congress building it was able to hide its name." I shrugged. "This is speculation, of course. I've never worked with demons – and I never want to."

Templeton didn't answer immediately. He tapped his fingertip on the countertop. "They've found no evidence of a conjuring inside the Congress?"

"None. But the Congress leadership is having a hard time accepting a demon getting in on its own." I sighed, leaning my hip against the counter. "They're investigating several different possibilities."

"Like if the demon was summoned by a practitioner other than a witch?" A hint of amusement danced across his face.

"That's one of them," I replied. "You'll probably be questioned. As will I. Apparently, they count us as possible offenders."

"Not surprising." He shrugged. "But to answer your earlier question as to whether I left the Congress building after I left the library, I did. There was nothing more for me at the gala."

Rabbit chose that moment to knock on my front door.

∞∞∞

Rabbit followed me into the kitchen. I pointed to the barstool next to Templeton and retrieved the platter of sandwiches. The two men briefly acknowledged each other – Rabbit delivering a curt nod and Templeton flaring his nostrils. It was a start. Rabbit didn't take a seat, but he grabbed a sandwich after I handed him a plate and stood by the stove. I sat another plate by Templeton, but I didn't anticipate him eating with us.

As I poured Rabbit a cup of coffee, I brought him up to speed about the demon. I left out the portion about the Congress casting suspicions toward Templeton and me with regards to manifesting the creature.

Rabbit was amazed to learn a demon got past the Congress wards. He also understood the gravity of the situation. No reasonable person blew off a demon's presence – especially one who seemed to move freely without constraints.

"What's the CEW doing about this?" Rabbit asked. He licked the side of the sandwich where the Dijon mustard oozed out.

"They're at the investigation stage," I told him.

"They're not out searching for the demon?"

"I don't think they are. I mean, we're assuming it's no longer in the Congress building." I twisted my mouth to the side. I assumed the demon was no longer there, but did Loren say that was the case? Surely they'd know if it were still in the building?

"But there is a demon on the loose in the city," he argued.

"It's hardly the only demon in Matar," Templeton muttered.

I helped myself to a sandwich, cutting it in half. "I'm sure it's crossed someone's mind, but I know the Congress. It will be a slow process. First, they'll fixate on the fact a demon got inside – either on its own or by a conjuring. Obviously if they determine it was summoned the next step will be to punish the guilty party and find out the purpose behind it."

Rabbit chewed a bite of his lunch thoughtfully. He swallowed, his Adam's apple bobbing up and down. He turned to Templeton. "What's your take on this?"

"Whether it was conjured or broke in on its own, I'd be searching to see if anything was missing from the Congress," he answered. "I'd want to know what parts of the building it visited."

I circled around Templeton and sat on the barstool beside his. Annoyed, I realized even sitting next to the irritating man during lunch was enough to wake up my skin. I pressed my thighs together and I focused on my sandwich for a moment. When I raised my head, I noticed Rabbit's curious inspection. His nose twitched – an involuntary reaction all Rabbits seemed to experience when they suspected information was forthcoming or being kept secret.

"I think it was in the library." I took a bite of my sandwich.

Templeton turned his head toward me. "Why do you say that?"

I finished chewing before I spoke. "I didn't get a chance to tell you earlier." I wiped a napkin over my mouth and addressed Rabbit instead. "I visited the Congress library last night during the gala. Guillaume was there and I wanted to put some distance between us." I could feel Templeton tensing beside me.

"Guillaume was there?" Rabbit's eyebrows dipped.

"Unfortunately, yes." I peeked at Templeton. His expression – or lack of one – revealed nothing. He crossed his arms over his chest and angled the barstool toward me. I kept my eyes on Rabbit. "Anyhow, I was in the library before I left the Congress building last night. I ended up dropping my purse and everything spilled out. The space wasn't well-lit and I had difficulty finding all my stuff. Before I left, I realized I was still missing my house keys, so I went back to where I'd dumped my purse."

"And you were in the library alone?" Rabbit finished his first sandwich. He snagged a second one from the platter.

"Mm-hmm." I dipped a corner of my sandwich into a blob of Dijon mustard that had bubbled out onto the plate. I took a bite and methodically chewed as I concentrated on my napkin. When I looked up, Rabbit's sharp eyes flitted back and forth between Templeton and me.

"Go on," Rabbit said.

"I walked all the way back where I'd dropped my purse. While I searched, I heard a lamp behind me click on. My keys were sitting on top of the desk under the lamplight." I leaned over the counter to grab my coffee cup. Rabbit stepped forward and pushed it into my grasp. "Thanks."

"But your keys wouldn't have landed on a desk," Rabbit said. "I don't understand."

"Someone put them there." Templeton studied the side of my face as I took a sip of my lukewarm coffee.

I turned, meeting his gaze. "That's what I'm assuming, yes. Someone picked my keys up off the floor and put them on the desk. Someone was watching me from the shadows while I was in the library last night. I felt it when I found my keys. As for how long I was being watched, I don't know."

He nodded, understanding what I left unsaid. "Why didn't you mention this before?"

I lifted a hand. "This is my first chance."

Templeton raised an eyebrow.

"And you think it was the demon?" Rabbit interrupted.

"Well, now I wonder if it was the demon, yes." I rubbed my forehead. "But last night I worried it was Guillaume. I didn't know about a demon in the Congress building until this morning."

"But why would Guillaume spy on you?" Rabbit drank from his cup. His inquisitiveness shifted between Templeton and me. "What's going on?"

"Nothing," I stressed. "But Guillaume wasn't too happy with the way our 'reunion' went last night. He was the first person who came to mind."

"Hmm." Rabbit wasn't convinced, but he let it go in favor of asking a new question. "Let's say it was the demon watching you in the library. Do you think it was a random crossing of paths or were you being targeted?"

"I don't see why I'd be targeted," I said. "But maybe it was looking for something in the library and then I showed up." I nodded toward Templeton. "You know we're not the only ones who do research in the library. You also know there are people who'd love to have access to the Congress' books, but never will. Maybe someone sent the demon to retrieve something?"

"Certainly possible," he agreed. "But without the demon – or without being able to determine if something is missing – there's not much of a trail to follow."

"There's one more thing." I winced. I had a feeling in light of the demon story I was not going to get a lot of slack.

Templeton gave me his long-suffering *'now what?'* look. "Continue."

"When I went through the ritual of recognition last night, something unexpected was said to me." I gestured to Rabbit. "It's one of the gatekeeping measures the Congress set up to monitor witches coming into the building. It also alerts the Congress when non-witches have moved past the wards. A being is positioned to evaluate you before you enter the main hall. She usually simply recognizes you and you pass. But last night she held onto my hand and said something like, *'be aware, he is here seeking you.'* She has never said more than *'you may enter, witch'* to me." I turned to Templeton. "By the way, how do you get by the being?"

Templeton didn't answer my question, but I could hear the frustration in his voice when he spoke. "Why didn't you tell me this before? It was clearly a warning."

"Because I didn't think there was a reason to be concerned once I saw Guillaume," I defended myself. "I thought she was referring to *him*. I had no reason to think otherwise. I mean, she could have been referring to *you*." I rolled my eyes before realizing what I'd said. I pulled a face.

"Oh, I get it," Rabbit interjected. "Templeton was at the gala, too." His eyes cut to the other man. "You were alone in the library with Lucie?"

"Briefly," Templeton snapped. He continued to glower in my direction.

"He was long gone by the time I had the odd experience with the keys." I ran both hands through my hair. "I don't have proof the demon was in the library, but my gut instinct is saying it was. I will tell you – both of you – if something else strange happens." I looked from one man to the other. "Good enough?"

Rabbit nodded, his face unreadable as he pulled his phone from his jeans pocket. Templeton snorted, grabbing a sandwich from the platter. He took my knife and cut it in half before taking a bite and shaking his head at his plate. In spite of myself, I smiled. He infuriated me but he'd come such a long way from the non-participatory, awkward man who stood in my kitchen four months ago, standing out like a sore thumb.

Rabbit lifted his head, his fingers instinctively completing the text. "I put out an all-points bulletin to the network about the demon. We'll see if anything was reported at any other place in the city, or if there was something unusual. I didn't mention one was in the CEW, but I said I heard of a report of one in the northern part of the city."

"Thanks. Last thing I need is the Congress yelling at me for leaking the news," I said. "I'm already on their shit list."

"Understood." Rabbit paused. "Templeton?

Anything else?"

"Ultimately the demon is of no concern to me."

"Really?" I didn't see that coming.

"If a demon was at the Congress, he was there because of a witch – or witches." Templeton nodded at his sandwich. "I'm not sure I'd like this without the Dijon."

"Oh, seriously." I picked up my empty plate and took it to the sink. Just when I was having warm fuzzies for the man. When would I learn?

"What if the demon was there because of *our* witch?" Rabbit's features darkened.

"Then I will make sure she is kept safe," Templeton sniffed.

"Okay, we're not doing this again." I finished drying my hands on the dish towel. "Like I said – I'll keep you both in the loop if I find anything out. And as far as needing any protection, I can certainly take care of myself with a demon. Next subject."

Templeton sneered. "Lucie, if you think –"

"Next. Subject." I turned my shoulder to him. "Rabbit? We need to talk about the directional doors in the Walled Zone. Did you have your guys check out the area around the compound? Is there any activity?"

The compound was formerly used by the Fringe when they gained access to the fifth door. We didn't know how they found it, but it was open when we showed up on the scene. We didn't know if it was already open when it was discovered, or if they'd managed to trigger the portal's appearance. Either way, Sebastian claimed to have door traveled through the fifth door to the other side. I believed him.

The sixth door was opened when I used the Crimson Stone that fateful night. Its shadow rolled out from under the fifth door and cracked the ground open. It was into the gaping hole we'd pushed Sebastian.

Then I sealed it over him and shut the fifth door. It shrank until it collapsed on itself and disappeared into thin air.

"I do have news. The network uncovered static coming out of the Walled Zone – specifically in the area where the Fringe's old compound is located." Rabbit refilled his coffee cup.

After our battle with the Fringe, the Empire seized the compound. We never told anyone about the directional doors. As far as we knew, the Empire leadership had no idea the fifth and sixth doors were located there. This was one of our secrets.

"What do you mean, static?" I asked.

"A couple of Rabbits have loosely monitored the area since the Empire removed its presence. Turns out everything's been quiet until this past week," Rabbit said. "In the beginning, no one could get a handle on what was being heard. The network thought it might be the result of equipment malfunction. But it's clear now. It's static, but there's a low pulse underneath it. We don't know if the static is there to camouflage the pulse, if it's part of it, or if it's completely unrelated."

"Why are we only hearing about this now?" Templeton asked Rabbit.

"Because the network didn't report any of this to me until this morning. They needed to complete their investigation," Rabbit replied smoothly. He wasn't bullied by Templeton. Rabbit pointed a thick finger at me. "Turns out the static coincides with your return to the Empire this past Tuesday night."

"There was a brownout here when I got into the city," I said. "Could it be related to that?"

"Typically, we know right off if it's something caused by the Empire. They can't do anything without stamping their fingerprints all over it," Rabbit said. "But to your point, we did wonder if it might be something the Empire set up to monitor the region. They haven't done anything in the Walled Zone since they occupied the compound."

"And?"

"And we're confident it's not related to something the Empire did."

I pulled out a roll of tin foil and set it by the sandwich platter. "This isn't good. I don't like it. What about the Crimson Stone?" I lifted my gaze. "Templeton?"

He chose his words carefully. "The Stone has not awakened since you put it to sleep."

"Have you tried to wake it?" I knew the answer.

"Yes." He showed no remorse. "I want to know what's on the other side of the fifth door. You left the Empire. I didn't know if you'd return." The last bit was said in a quiet voice.

I nodded, pulling off a sheet of foil and wrapping the last two sandwiches for Rabbit to take when he left. "If the Stone hasn't reacted, perhaps this anomaly the network picked up doesn't have anything to do with the fifth or sixth doors."

Templeton pressed his lips together. Finally, he replied. "I don't leave a lot of room for coincidence. I wonder if you somehow pulled part of the directional doors' energies into you. Maybe the doors are responding to your return to the Empire. They might not be open, but perhaps they're reaching out to you."

As much as I didn't want to believe the static was somehow related to my return, his words worried me. Was the demon's appearance also related? "Do you think it's possible the static is a signal something has come through one of those doors?"

Rabbit was glum. "Anything's possible."

"The demon." Templeton confirmed my thoughts aloud.

"I think it's worth considering," I said. "We don't know what's on the other side of either of them."

"Sebastian reported 'beasts and monsters' on the other side. And if there are beasts and monsters, I bet demons aren't far behind," Rabbit replied.

I saw Templeton's scrutiny flip to me to gauge my reaction to Sebastian's name. I remained indifferent. "If Sebastian went to the other side of the fifth door, that tells me the door can be opened without the Crimson Stone. Whether it means it was opened from our side or their side, who knows? But there's more than one way to open the door. We know this."

A peculiar expression flashed across Templeton's face. Rabbit caught it at the same time as I did. Rabbit spoke first. "Have you tried to open the fifth door, Templeton?"

"Yes." Templeton raised a shoulder. "But I haven't had any success."

"But you've tried more than once?" This is what I was afraid of him doing.

"Yes."

We were back to dragging information out of the exasperating man. "What have you used?"

Templeton paused. "I tested several portal commands from my research at the Congress library, but the words are difficult to decipher. The language is archaic and it's one of the few I'm not familiar with. I assume the lack of precision works against me."

Learning more about the doors was the purpose of using the Congress' library, but we risked Templeton running off on his own afterward. The fact he'd already tried some of the spells he'd found was troubling. "What's our next step?" I asked Rabbit.

"I've assigned three Rabbits to investigate on the ground. They're doing a perimeter check now. If it appears to be free and clear of Empire guards, I've directed them to check the quad in the center of the compound. They know to be careful and what to look for when they get there. If there are any abnormalities, they'll let me know right away," Rabbit finished.

"Let me know as soon as you hear anything," I told him.

"I'm also hoping they'll find out more about the static. They'll set up equipment to better monitor it. We have a few guys who are good at sussing out if there are any messages being communicated," Rabbit added. "But first things first. We need to determine the source."

I trusted Rabbit to handle the static issue, but there was one person in the room I didn't have complete faith in. I turned to Templeton. "The thing I'm most concerned about right now is you. I don't want you to go by yourself and try to crash on through to the other side of either door if they're opening on their own. It's dangerous. If you go alone, you might not come back."

Templeton raised an eyebrow. "Who do you propose I take with me?"

"If you insist on going, me. I will go with you," I said.

"Absolutely not," he replied.

At the same time Rabbit laughed and shook his head.

"What?" I glared at him.

"I'm with Templeton on this one, Lucie." Rabbit's shoulders hopped up once. "Going with him is not an option for you."

Flabbergasted, I stared at both men. "Are you kidding me? All of a sudden it's too dangerous for me? I seem to remember being toted merrily along when Emily was on her 'bring down the Fringe' crusade. What was I told? Oh, right. 'Lucie, we can use all the help we can get.' Now it's too risky for me? When did you two become such sexists?"

"Rabbit's always been sexist," Templeton noted. I ignored him.

Rabbit folded his arms over his chest. "It's not about sexism, Lucie. It's about *you*. We knew we were going into a big battle last fall. And we did need all the help we could get. Help from a witch with your power and your abilities was welcome. We didn't know you'd be able to do what you did, but we know now – especially after you mushroomed." Rabbit referred to the sonic wave I sent out across the compound when I connected to the Crimson Stone.

"Then I don't understand. Why wouldn't you want me to go with you?" I gestured toward Templeton.

"Because I believe you'd be at risk," he said. "I think your relationship with the Crimson Stone complicates things. We don't know what that will look like on the other side of the door."

"I do not want you to go alone, Templeton," I repeated.

"Alright, we're going in circles here," Rabbit interrupted. "First, we're going to wait to hear back from the network and find out what they've learned. Then we can decide. Agreed? Templeton?"

Templeton gave a reluctant nod. "Fine."

"Lucie?" Rabbit lifted a hand, his palm pointing up.

"We'll wait for the network," I answered. Hopefully Templeton would stick to the agreement. "It'll give me time to go through the book of fairy tales."

Briiing! The Empire service phone sounded from its cupboard. "Now what?" I complained, opening the cupboard door and lifting the handset.

"Yes?" I tracked Rabbit as he wandered from the kitchen toward the hallway.

"This is the Empire messaging service with a Level 1 message from Mr. Loren Heatherworth for Ms. Lucie Bellerose," the operator announced.

"This is Lucie." I cringed as I saw Rabbit's head turn. He moved into the hall and squatted. His hand reached out to the handprint burned into the wall. He touched it with a fingertip. My eyes flicked to Templeton.

The bastard smiled wickedly.

I realized the operator was speaking again. "I'm sorry. Can you repeat that?"

"Mr. Heatherworth asked the service to deliver the following message: *Guillaume has arranged for the demonstration to be scheduled on Tuesday at 1 o'clock in the afternoon at the Congress of Empire Witches. The elders have agreed to allow you to choose the method to present your work with Guillaume. He is aware of the elders' decision.* This concludes the message. Thank you."

Chapter 13

And there you have it. I had two days to prepare. But I'd be able to exercise some control. Thank you, dearest Loren.

I returned the handset to the cupboard. I stood there, my fingers resting on the phone as I contemplated the best way to handle the Congress' expectations.

"What's wrong?" Templeton interrupted my thoughts.

I raised my head. "It was a message from Loren. The demonstration at the Congress is scheduled for Tuesday."

"When?"

"At 1 o'clock. I'll get there early." I shut the cupboard door. "But Loren managed to convince the elders to allow me to choose how we demonstrate the success we've had."

"Do you know who will be present?" Templeton asked. Rabbit returned to the kitchen. He'd been listening to our conversation.

"I'm not sure. I'd expect a representative from each of the more important houses. Loren will be present, of course. The Acton matriarch, I'm sure." I lifted a shoulder. "I won't know most of them by name, only their faces."

"I'd count on the Waverton patriarch," Templeton told me. "Rumor is their witchline is thinning rapidly. They still hold a lot of power in Congress, however. They'd rather not see an upstart like the Bellerose witch strengthening hers." One of his rare genuine smiles swept across Templeton's face, catching me off guard. For a moment, he appeared almost boyish. I wanted to reach across the counter and touch his face.

I shook the thought from my head. "I don't get it. One of my reasons for studying under Guillaume was for all of us – all the witchlines. If I could do it, then others could, too. Guillaume would be available to other families, other witches. He wants to see all the witchlines strengthened as well."

Rabbit spoke to Templeton. "She's wrong, isn't she?"

Templeton nodded.

"What do you mean I'm wrong? Guillaume is not a nice person," I said. That was an understatement. "But I do know he wants to see each individual family's witchline strengthened."

"Oh, no doubt," Templeton replied. He left the barstool and rinsed out his juice glass in the sink. He set it on the counter and turned to me. "Guillaume is not stupid. As the witchlines thin, so will the overall power of witches in the Empire. Not sharing the knowledge of how to do what you have done, Lucie, is suicide for your kind. And this further elevates his standing in the witch community – being the teacher who helped you learn to do what you've done."

"But Rabbit said I was wrong," I argued.

"You're wrong in the sense you believe other witches can do what you've done," Rabbit cut in. He gestured to Templeton. "It takes a really special witch, right?"

"It does." Templeton reached down to adjust his cuff. He hesitated, awkwardly removing an invisible piece of lint.

I snuck a look at Rabbit. He grinned, shaking his head.

"I don't believe that," I responded.

"I bet Guillaume didn't think it was possible either," Templeton continued. "But it probably sounded like an interesting experiment, so he agreed to take you on as a pupil. And then you did the impossible. No wonder you're valuable to Guillaume."

I winced. "I'd prefer you not use that language. It makes me feel like I've been stamped with a price tag."

"You have," Templeton sighed. "But what's done is done. You must address the place you find yourself in now. You'll have to own it, Lucie. Your battles in Congress are just beginning."

His melancholy troubled me, but I shrugged. "Well, I can only handle one ball at a time."

Rabbit saw the question on Templeton's face. "Juggling reference. She only needs to catch the first one falling before worrying about the next. Right now she only needs to concentrate on Tuesday's demonstration. Future Congress fights aren't dropping into her hands yet."

"Exactly. Which means I'd better get ready for Tuesday." I put my hands on my hips and sighed. The book of fairy tales caught my eye. I nodded toward it. "I'd also like to read through the book Templeton brought over."

"We should leave you to it. I gotta go anyway," Rabbit said as his phone buzzed and he checked it. He took the foil packet I passed to him as he texted a reply one-handed.

"But you will let me know what the network finds out about the static and the pulsing as soon as you hear anything?" I asked.

"I will. I'll also let you know if I get news about a demon." He'd retrieved his coat from the hall when I was on the phone with the Empire service. He tucked the sandwiches into an inside pocket and gave Templeton the once over. "Leaving?"

I saw Templeton's shoulders stiffen. "Yes."

"See you around then," Rabbit said. "I'll get a message to you when I have something to say."

"Of course, it would be easier to reach me if I had a network phone," Templeton replied.

Rabbit snorted and turned. He didn't leave, but instead dug back into his coat. He fumbled with something in his hand, then walked over to Templeton. "Finger."

Templeton held up a graceful hand, a satisfied expression stretching across his face. Rabbit grabbed a finger, pressing it against the small phone, then proceeded to tap a line of code into the device. When he finished, he shoved it into Templeton's chest. "This time you won't be able to abuse the privilege. You'll only get texts *from me* and you can only send texts *to me*. No other network access."

"It's all I ask for," Templeton purred.

"And it's only for a short time. I'll shut it off when I decide you don't need it anymore," Rabbit finished. He ran his hand over his head, nodding at me. "Alright, now I'm leaving."

"Bye, Rabbit." I watched him disappear around the corner and a moment later my front door opened and closed. I blew out a breath and looked at Templeton.

He spoke first. "I have some things I need to address, and you need to get ready for your demonstration."

"Yeah," I agreed. "I can't put this off. But at least I know Loren will be there, so I'll have one friend in the audience."

"You'll have two."

I tilted my head. "What do you mean?"

"I'll be there."

I laughed. "Okay, Templeton, I will give it to you. You never cease to amaze me with what you pull off. But getting the elders to agree to let a non-witch – especially *you* – sit in on anything they do will be nothing short of a miracle."

"I'll be there, Lucie," he promised as he reached for the pantry door. "You'd be amazed at what I can do."

"I'll believe it when I see it." I shook my head, but this relaxed atmosphere between us was welcome.

I saw his door travel energy growing, the royal blue waves rising and falling around his legs. His mouth split into an unexpected grin and he motioned to the hall with his chin. "I know a woodworker who could buff those burn marks out of your wall. Unless you'd like to keep them as a reminder of what I can do when I want something?"

My cheeks grew hot and I pointed to the pantry door behind him. "Goodbye, Templeton."

The sound was new to my ears but thrilled me nonetheless: Templeton's laugh echoed behind him as he door traveled out of my home.

∞∞∞

I had two tasks on my plate: I needed to prepare for the demonstration before Congress and

I needed to refamiliarize myself with the book of fairy tales. Admittedly I was more enthused about the book.

I'd gotten a peek at it when we headed into the Walled Zone the first time. Templeton and Emily found it when they broke into Sebastian's cabin. Before joining Rabbit and his crew to sneak into the Fringe's compound, I spent time paging through the book.

Somehow it'd made it outside the Empire before landing in the possession of an Empire Record Keeper, the late Rene Blackstone. He'd stolen it from the Cooper-Hewitt Library in New York City when he'd realized what they had. It was a handwritten book of fairy tales, labeled as a children's book. Blackstone recognized its value and took it, hoping to locate the Crimson Stone by finding a clue in the book. It was too late to ask him if he knew the book contained other messages, but we assumed he knew there were secrets hidden in all the tales.

After Blackstone's personal library was ransacked, the book of fairy tales disappeared again. We were astonished to learn Sebastian ended up with it, but then again, we knew the Fringe had stolen it from Blackstone. I believe

Sebastian knew what he'd acquired. I wondered if he'd figured out more than we had.

And now the book of fairy tales was sitting in my kitchen. My fingertips skimmed the handwritten table of contents. If I had to guess, the handwriting was from an aged person. The cursive letters were slender but slanted heavily to the right. My intuition told me the pages were written by a woman.

I thought about the speculation Templeton and I engaged in previously. The book was older than the Crimson Stone and we theorized the author was a seer, either providing information or a warning – or both.

On the first page, the author listed the tales in the order they appeared in the book:

Three Pieces
Beams of Light from Above
Six Doors
Beasties from Below
Black Sky
The Man with the Red Eyes
Dancing Shadows
The Blending
The Ending

We believed *Three Pieces* was about the Crimson Stone. It was likely *Six Doors* was about the six directional doors leading into the Empire – the North, East, West, and South doors already counted amongst the Empire's official doors. We assumed we'd find the fifth door in the Walled Zone – specifically in the region where the Fringe built their compound. We did. We had no idea we'd find the sixth door there, too.

I hadn't seen the book since that dreadful night. As I read the titles, I thought about what Sebastian said before we sent him through the sixth door.

There were beautiful beasts on the other side of the fifth door who would turn into monsters if they were angered, if their laws were broken.

But what about the *Beasties from Below*?

I turned to the first tale. I'd start there.

∞∞∞

Three Pieces

This is a tale about a clever young girl who caught a shooting star in her hands as it tumbled from a

Black Sky.

The girl cradled the glowing rock in her palms, admiring its fire and promising it she would keep it safe. She liked to play with pretty stones, placing them in long rows as she decorated her altar with drops of sunshine falling from her fingertips. This newest stone she placed in the center of her altar, telling it stories about her heart and listening as it whispered its magic back to her.

But soon the girl realized the stone's magic tasted of a tremendous power, one that would be coveted by the blackest hearts. She decided to break the stone into three pieces and hide it in plain sight. There it would be safe.

Before the stone was broken, it told her one last secret. There were portals to many other realities and imaginings across the universe. If she carried fire in her hand, she could open and close these doors as she wished. She could cross through them. All the knowledge in the universe could be hers.

The child's hands held the stone to her chest as she listened. It beat alongside her heart, a pulsing promise of power. But it was too much for her young body and all that power in one pair of hands could turn the truth into lies. She squeezed and broke the stone into three pieces while she also chanted the spell to unite it.

She would hide the stone so the ones with the blackest hearts would not find it.

But first she would search the Empire for the doors leading to other places in the universe.

∞∞∞

Beams of Light from Above

As the child prepared to journey across the Empire, a new sound touched the inside of her ear. She pressed the pieces of the stone into her pocket and left her altar to seek out the source. The sharp whine grew in its intensity.

The girl climbed the tallest hill and peered into the sky. A featureless being of the whitest white vibrated in the air. Tall and narrow, it stretched its body to the land below. A tear appeared where its mouth should be, allowing a band of blinding light to shoot out. The shriek pouring from the gap sang into her brain.

The child widened her eyes and covered her ears. She listened closely to the terrifying creature.

Its song told her about its life as a Beam of Light from Above, how it guarded the doors used to travel to other places across the universe. How imaginations birthed new worlds and how the One Truth threaded the entire universe together. Creatures moved back and forth through these doors to ensure the One Truth was spread to the edge of the universe. But the One Truth was as fragile as it was powerful and could be torn apart by the untruths. It needed to be protected.

The tenor of the Beam of Light from Above grew foreboding as its song shrieked of the Beasties from Below, how they hungered for the One Truth, but they spit it out when they were fed.

More Beams descended onto the hilltop, their singing crashing around the child as her mouth opened and she drank in their songs by the mouthful. She listened and promised to protect the One Truth. Only then did the song retreat along with the Beams of Light from Above.

When only the last Beam remained, it told her she must find the portals leading into her world and sew them shut with fire. It was the only way to keep the Beasties from Below from soiling the land with their untruths. They were hungry and refused to eat. Her world was in danger.

The child's fingers touched the broken stone in her pocket, and she vowed to keep the Beasties from

Below out of the Empire. She watched as the last Beam shrunk and winked out in the air in front of her.

∞ ∞ ∞

Six Doors

The next morning, the girl set out traveling across the land to learn what she would find at each of the four corners of the Empire. After singing with the Beams of Light from Above, the child understood there were portals to many other realities and imaginings across the universe. The Beams sang of creatures passing through these doors, easily moving between worlds and imaginations, celebrating the One Truth and sharing it with those who made their ears listen.

But the Beams of Light from Above warned of the Beasties from Below and how they would consume her land if they escaped through their locked door. She would need to make sure they could not cross into her world.

She searched under the mountains. She rode the sea into the artist's painting and looked under the canvas. The child climbed across the trees of the forest and peered into the icy desert. She listened for footprints and watched the wind. She began to discover the doors.

Whenever she found one, she pulled magic from her pocket, weaving a tapestry of energy from the fire in her hands. She placed it over the openings separating the planes to make sure nothing unwanted could slip into the Empire. She named the six doors she found, calling them North, East, West, South, the Above, and the Below.

When she finished, she laid her head on the ground and slept.

∞∞∞

Beasties from Below

The Beasties from Below were starving. Their mouths were empty of the truth and they gnashed their teeth in anger, their tongues slippery with lies as they hungered for Light. The door to the Above was locked to them, and they howled their frustrations against the walls and ceilings of their endless prison.

The thin shadows leaked into the Below, their pitiful cries adding to the bleak wailing of the

Beasties. Light. Light. Light.

None of them could see as they searched the Below. But if they could bring the Light to the Below, they could see the food and eat the truth.

Then they would know the way to open the door to the Above. They would feast on the truth guarded by the Beams of Light from Above.

They would eat the One Truth. They would control knowledge.

But first they needed the Light.

∞∞∞

Black Sky

Days later, the clever girl sat on a rock, her chin resting upon her knees as she stared out over the Empire. She missed the Beams of Light from Above. They made her heart happy with their One Truth. They showed her the truth through their singing.

The moon rose and a man stepped off a comet as it floated by. He bowed, introducing himself as a Magician and a Poet. She asked him for a tale and he told her of the wondrous beings of light who crawled over the stars in the night sky. These beasts are majestic, he said, but if angered, they are dan-

gerous.

She should watch out for the beings of light, he warned.

The child grew afraid and told the man about the Beams of Light from Above who sang to her about the One Truth.

The man turned upside down and revealed a secret. He told the curious girl there were many truths, and not just one.

He told her she would need to visit the Darkness to know where the Light lived.

He kissed her in the center of her forehead and fluttered back up into the night sky.

∞∞∞

I closed the book, staring across my kitchen and seeing nothing. The author of these fairy tales certainly weaved messages into the stories, but like any book of this sort, the reader would need to determine what was the secret and what was simply lines of silly words. The ridiculous was there to hide the real messages.

The reference to the 'one truth' stuck out. I wondered what Templeton's take was after all this time and his research. I realized I never learned what he found in the book of poetry he had me request from the Congress' library. Assuming the two were related, what was the connection between the book of fairy tales and *Poems from the Black Sky*? We'd have much to discuss.

I'd spent time going through *Empire Tales for Children* and taking my own notes, but I needed to address the more pressing issue.

The demonstration with Guillaume was in less than… I looked at the clock. In less than 48 hours. I rubbed the back of my neck.

Guillaume would want to use physical pain, and it was effective. Yes, the crude act of inflicting pain on another person could produce wondrous results. The promise of stopping horrendous pain will help you find a way to pull off the impossible. Thoughts of what I'd experienced when I studied with Guillaume assaulted me. Until this demonstration was required, I'd managed to push away humiliating memories of begging him to stop hurting me, to promising I'd do *things* if only he'd stop. I swallowed the bile rising up into the back of my throat.

Congress elders were aware Guillaume slept with his students. I'm sure they suspected some of the despicable things he did when teaching. The degradation produced a set of rituals you learned quickly. He broke you so you'd obey without thinking. This emptied you of any thoughts other than what you were there to learn. In some ways, it made you a better student. I'd like to say it wasn't true, but I'd be lying.

Guillaume flirted with inflicting emotional and psychological pain as well – and it was effective, but I guarded my most horrifying memories from him. He couldn't use them against me.

I could use them, however, and I did. But they were my secrets.

Months ago, when I left the Empire to heal my heart, I eventually dragged myself back to the critical task of regularly feeding my witchline. I had new heartbreak to use, and I did. It wasn't as strong as my worst memory, but it worked.

Truthfully it was about as much as I could handle then.

That was the vein of pain I planned to open during the demonstration at Congress after Guillaume helped me force my witchline open. The elders wouldn't be able to see it as much as feel it: the energy leaving my body and the witchline feeding on it.

As much as I knew Guillaume wanted the opportunity to inflict pain for his own pleasure, he also wanted to show off what he'd accomplished as the teacher who worked with me. I understood that. He earned it.

But I was going to be the one in control. It would be on my terms. We only needed to give the elders an example, a taste.

I would not let anyone feast on my pain.

Usually I practiced my magic in my back yard or in my kitchen, but when it came to feeding my witchline, I wanted a darker space. It made it easier to tap into the things that hurt.

I retrieved a set of keys from a kitchen drawer and unlocked the rarely used door to my windowless basement. Shedding my clothes, I slipped into the inky space below and prepared for Tuesday's demonstration.

∞∞∞

The wind whipped outside my home as I finished drying my dinner dish and placed it into a cupboard. My brain was filled with too many worries and I was tired. The melancholy clouding the latter part of my day sucked any productivity out of me. Turning in early was probably the smartest idea. If I could bring myself to do it again, I'd spend time tomorrow with another run-through in preparation for the demonstration.

I tossed the towel onto the counter and thought about making tea.

I'd spent most of my life alone, and I liked my company. Tonight, however, I felt a longing inside. I couldn't quite name it – the feeling wore many faces. People I'd lost, new friends I'd made who weren't nearby... One new pain-in-the-ass man I wanted to get to know more – even though he drove me nuts.

I walked into the hall just beyond the kitchen. I studied the handprint burned into the wall, remembering his hands and mouth on my skin.

Really get to know more.

The thought made me smile.

The network phone in my jeans pocket grew warm. I fished it out, expecting an update from Rabbit about the Walled Zone, or maybe even a friendly *'how's it going?'* Instead, I read:

Rabbit was wrong.

He's not the only one I can text.

Goodnight, Lucie.

T.

I laughed, texting back a smirking emoji and my own *'goodnight.'*

What do you know? Sometimes he gets it right.

It was time to go to bed.

Chapter 14

Despite the late winter storm blowing outside, I skipped the flannel pajamas. Even if no one could see me, I wanted to wear something to make me feel special. It was a weakness of mine when I felt like things were out of my control.

I pulled *une nuisette* from my dresser drawer and slid it over my head. The satin garment was the palest shade of pink, slightly fitted and simple with thin straps traveling over my shoulders. The hemline landed at mid-thigh with a thick band of scalloped lace. Matching lace ran along the top of the V-neckline, and a swatch of the same trailed down the front on top of the satin material. Running a hand over the little nightgown, I appraised myself in the cheval mirror, turning to examine my figure from the side and questioning if the gown fit better since I'd lost weight. I've always had a love-hate relationship with my curves. In college, a well-meaning friend once described my shape as 'healthy' – I wasn't sure how I felt about that.

At 5'6" I think I carried my proportions well, but there's a mean little voice in the back of my brain that tells me if only I were a couple of inches taller, or if my waistline was an inch or two less, or my bust a bit smaller, my hips slender instead of full, my stomach flatter... *then* I'd be sexy... or pretty... or desirable. I didn't *need* to be wanted, but I *wanted* to be wanted.

I left my self-indulgent thoughts in front of the mirror as I pulled back the bedcovers, smoothing the wrinkles out of the cotton sheets. I'd set the phone on my nightstand and I picked it up, shaking my head at Templeton's message. Things had taken an interesting turn, but truthfully, it wasn't much easier than when we were coming to verbal blows – or magical ones for that matter. The truth was, I had a hard time trusting Templeton because he would always put his interests first. He'd hold his cards – and his secrets – close to his chest. This was how he always operated. He wasn't going to change.

Was he attracted to me? Yes, that'd certainly been proven. Did I want him? God, yes. But was it only chemistry sparking between us? And was it enough for both of us? Admittedly I cared about him, too, but I didn't trust my feelings to do right by me after how hard I fell the last time.

I set the phone back on the nightstand.

Turning off the lamp, I climbed into bed, rolling onto my side and relaxing into the pillow. The streetlight outside cast a glow into my room and I watched the branches of the bare pear tree wave its shadows across the wall. The wind didn't howl, but every few minutes a solid gust blew tiny pebbles of ice against my window.

My eyes followed the swaying silhouettes, and my mind wandered to dancing with Templeton at the gala. I remembered how his long fingers wrapped around my right hand, raising it as his other hand slid softly along my waist on my left, coming to rest on my hip. It felt natural to have his hands on my body.

I rolled onto my back, yawning and closing my eyes as the music played across the dance floor inside my mind. My eyelids fluttered and I caught a glimpse of the shadowy shapes playing along the ceiling before my thoughts drowsily drifted into the night. The dreamy memories of us dancing morphed into more sensual spaces, and my tired brain conjured our first kiss in the library before my thoughts swirled toward the steamy encounter in my hall. I pressed my thighs together, curling my toes as I remembered how he made my body feel. What would he have done if I answered his question and told him what I really wanted? How I wanted *him*. Was he really ready to hear that from me?

Yes, he was. I could see it in his face, too. I could feel it when he started to undress me. When he rained kisses down my body. When his fingers touched my thigh and I heard him moan. When his mouth pressed intimately against the thin material of my underclothing…

He desired *me*.

My hips instinctively bucked once, and I gasped. My memory of that night was vivid.

Reluctantly, I pushed the sensation away. Taking a deep, centering breath, I willed myself to settle down. I needed to regain control of my thoughts and go to sleep. I couldn't afford to be distracted by Templeton.

But it had been too long since I felt someone's warm skin against mine – too long since someone tongued a path down my belly and up my thighs. Too long since a lover pressed their naked chest against my back, slipping an arm around my body to hold me while I slept. My fingertips bounced gently from my collarbone to the neckline of my nightgown. As I slipped toward sleep, my hand floated to the bed, my fingers relaxing against the sheet.

∞∞∞

A hand swept gently across my cheek and covered my eyes. Startled, I reached up, touching the long fingers doubling as a blindfold. *Templeton?* I thought sleepily. I traced the thumb stroking lightly against my cheek. His touch was so tender it made my body ache.

I hadn't even heard him enter my room – his door travel energy floating under my radar. Was I dreaming? My lips parted as he drew my blankets down and sat on the bed beside me. I stirred, the chilly air driving goosebumps over my skin. "Templeton?"

"Shh." The hand resting over my eyes tightened as he eased my head to the side, pressing me into the pillow. His other hand slipped to my thigh, sliding under my nightgown and tracing a feathery path across my skin. Deft fingers moved upward, smoothing over my hip, squeezing my flesh. Warm lips grazed the curve of my bare shoulder, planting sweet kisses in a circle.

"Yes," I shivered. *Oh, yes.* I abandoned the hand touching my face and blindly reached for him. My fingers touched the collar of his jacket, and I ran them over the supple leather, tugging at it. *When did he get a leather coat?* My face pulled into a frown as I inhaled a familiar cologne – but not a scent like the warm, earthy one I associated with Templeton. This fragrance was heady, sensuous. Notes of bergamot.

I stilled for a beat, my mind belatedly waking up. Something was very wrong. This was no dream.

And this was *not* Templeton.

Nausea swept through my belly as his fingers dug into my hip. At the same time, he bit into my shoulder hard, making me cry out. I tried to pull away.

"No, Lucie." His voice exhaled near my ear. The hand over my face shoved my head deeper into the pillow at a cruel angle.

"Stop it!" I panicked, digging at the viselike grip holding me down. My fingers tried to peel the hand away as I felt him lean into me, swinging a leg over both of mine and dragging the lower half of my body to the edge of the bed. The mattress dipped under us as he pressed his hips against mine, grinding. I lashed out blindly with my left hand, my palm connecting solidly somewhere in the vicinity of his nose.

"Witch!" he snarled. I kicked my legs, arching my back as I tried to force the man off me. He had the advantage of being on top and twisted my head back toward him, his wet mouth smothering mine. A slippery tongue thrust between my lips, filling my mouth with the taste of metal. I stabbed my fingernails into his cheek as I tried to push away the bloody kiss. The hand once covering my eyes now grabbed at my wrist, tearing my fingers from his face and pressing my wrist against the mattress. With one hand still free, I grasped a fistful of his hair and wrenched his head back as hard as I could, ripping his mouth from mine. The faint morning light leaking in through the bedroom window laid a strip across his face. His grin threw terror into the center of my heart.

Sebastian stared down at me, his eyes tinged with a red haze. Blood leaked out of his nose and over his upper lip into his mouth. "Hi, Lucie. Miss me?"

"No!" My whole body contorted, and I bucked upward, calling upon my deepest power hard and fast, raising my temperature to a blistering heat in an instant.

Sebastian laughed, unaffected. "Heating things up for me? I like it."

We struggled, the heat on my skin doing nothing to dissuade Sebastian. I managed to land a second strike, my fist hitting his cheekbone. This time he answered with a slap across my face.

The battle was short. Using his body to hold me down, Sebastian threaded his right arm under mine and over my throat, before reaching around my neck and pulling me securely against him. He squeezed, his forearm pressing against the nape of my neck, forcing my head back as I arched. My right arm waved uselessly above my head. Wide-eyed I gasped, my neck pinned between his bicep and forearm as my left hand pulled uselessly at the sleeve of his jacket.

I couldn't breathe.

Sebastian's lips were against my ear again. "No.

No struggling," he murmured. "Shh. I want you to take a short nap. Go to sleep for me, Lucie."

The chokehold did its job. Within seconds I was unconscious.

∞∞∞

When I awoke, I was on the floor. I rested on my side, my cheek pressed against the hardwood. My arms had been pulled behind me, and I realized my wrists were tied together with fabric. My muscles felt sore after the attack and the side of my face hurt from being struck. I tried to breathe quietly while I listened to the silence around me.

I raised my head and peered cautiously through the curtain of hair covering my face. The window let in more light now. The storm was over and the February sun was up. I faced the bed and could see the dust dragons poking their noses out from under the bed skirt. My legs were free, and I awkwardly scooted myself into an upright position and onto my behind. Bending my knees, I pushed my heels against the floor to steady myself. I froze when I saw Sebastian stretched out on my bed, his back against the headboard and his hands laced behind his head.

He grinned, dropping his arms and swinging his long legs over the side of the bed. He made a show of looking up my nightgown. "I think that's what they call the money shot."

Gritting my teeth, I pressed my legs together and heaved myself up onto my knees, smarting as my kneecaps rolled over the hard floor. My body rocked precariously, and I almost toppled over. I struggled to regain my balance. The top of my nightgown stretched, and I adjusted my posture.

"But I do like it when you're on your knees," he continued to taunt me. "This is a good look for you."

Ignoring him, I shuffled away as I pulled at my restraints.

"Ah, ah, ah!" Sebastian warned. "You don't want to touch that." He pointed to a black line of soot on the floor. I turned my head. A circle of the substance surrounded me.

"What have you done?" I croaked. My chest tightened. I was aware of a pressure moving the air around me, against me.

"Demon ash." Lifting his chin, Sebastian

screwed his head back and forth and cracked his neck. He stretched his arms upward, causing his tee shirt to rise. I could see the hard line of flesh stretching from hip to hip over low-slung jeans. He relaxed, his arms back at his sides, his fingertips roaming along the edge of the bed. His eyelids dipped. "Turns out witches don't like it. You touch it, it'll burn you. Try to cross it, it'll knock you on your ass. Don't even think about trying to cook up a spell inside the circle. You'll get zapped."

I let loose a slip of my energy and cautiously poked at the invisible walls of the circle Sebastian created. I felt a sharp sting zip through me, forcing me to cry out. It felt hot and dangerous.

Sebastian laughed, the sound bouncing obscenely off my bedroom walls. "You never listen, do you? It's cute. I love that about you."

I needed to ignore his attempts at banter – engaging with him would work against me. I needed to stay calm. "Let me out of this circle."

He shook his head deliberately. "No. It took me a long time to get back here. We're going to spend some quality time together, Lucie."

"No, we're not." I pulled at the cloth tying my wrists together. *He must've used one of my scarves,* I thought, my eyes flitting to my dresser where multiple drawers were pulled open. I went through my mental database of spells, searching for one used to untie knots. I chanted the first line under my breath and got shocked again. I grimaced, lifting up on my knees, my back curving.

Sebastian mocked me. "You're still trying to get out of this with magic?" He waved a hand dismissively. "Well, go on if you're into that sort of thing. I can wait until you tire yourself out. I kind of like watching you squirm every time you get blasted."

Magic was not going to be my friend. I sat back on my ankles, warily studying Sebastian. He looked much like the man from last fall. His hair was a little longer, wavy and so dark it was almost black. His eyes, framed by a mass of long eyelashes, were still a deep brown, but I could see a reddish haze coloring the whites and infiltrating his irises. His smirk sat under a straight, narrow nose on provocative lips. A line of facial hair – somewhat thicker than his 5 o'clock shadow – curved under his lower lip. He was tall and lean, hard muscle under olive skin. He was as beautiful as he was brutal.

I noted bruising under his left eye and faint lines stood out on his cheek where I'd scratched him. His upper lip on the same side was slightly swollen – the product of my wild swings when he crawled on top of me. The blood I'd seen on his face had been wiped away. I touched the tip of my tongue to the corner of my mouth. There was a small cut from being hit. I also realized I could still taste his blood on my lips. Some remained on my face.

Sebastian scanned my bedroom, his eyes continuously roving over the space. He sniffed. "It smells like you in here. Like burnt vanilla." He refocused on me, his expression softening, the timbre of his voice suddenly pleading. "We didn't always have to go to my place. Why didn't you ever invite me in, Lucie?"

The idea of discussing the time we spent together before his truth was revealed was absurd. I gave my head a tiny shake. "Don't."

"I get it," he bobbed his head in return, his face lighting up. The pendulum swung again and Sebastian's tone became agreeable in a flash. "You want to leave the past behind. Me, too. We can start over. We don't have to talk about what they made you do in the Walled Zone."

"This needs to stop." I plucked again at my restraints, rolling my wrists. I wondered if the demon ash around me would prevent him from touching me again. Was my prison also my protection?

He ignored me. "I liked that hot shit you called up before. It felt good. I want you to do it again." Sebastian tucked his lip under his teeth and he considered me. "I want to feel your skin against mine."

"That's not happening." I stiffened.

His face hardened.

Sebastian leaned toward me, his forearms resting on his knees. He tilted his head and raked his gaze over my bare arms. "You know what kept me going in the Below, Lucie? When the nightmares wouldn't go away? When it was really loud and sickening and I would've done anything to make it stop?" He rocked forward, growling low.

I watched him uneasily, afraid he'd pounce. "Stop it, Sebastian."

Without warning, he dropped to his knees in front of me, inches from the circle of ash. His brown eyes were swimming with red. Sebastian swung his head back and forth before cocking it sharply to the side and wincing. Those frightful eyes rolled toward me. "You. Even after what you did. You kept me going when it was bad and dark – you and your glowing skin. That night, that last night we were alone together. You were riding me." He quivered. "I opened my eyes and –"

"Stop it!" I didn't want to hear this. I turned my head away as I shifted, trying to add another inch to the space between us.

"Your head was thrown back and your eyes were closed. Your skin was glowing so bright. I'd never seen anything like it, I couldn't stop watching you." His expression softened. "You were my witch. *Mine*. It was for *me*."

His words unnerved me. I didn't know about the glowing, and I didn't want to think about what it meant. "I do not belong to you."

Enraged, he spun on his knees and was on his feet before I could register his actions. His movements had become so fast. Sebastian swung his arm, palm open, smacking the lamp on my nightstand. It flew to the floor. "Because of pencil dick? I saw you two in the library. You let him kiss you."

Talking about Templeton would only fuel Sebastian's anger – we were not going down that road. Before I could speak, Sebastian zeroed in on the phone Rabbit gave me. He snatched it from my nightstand, immediately realizing what he held. He raised his head, the fury skittering across his face driving chills down my spine.

I blinked and Sebastian was back at the circle's edge, squatting and facing me. He waved the device at me. "You fucking a Rabbit, too?" His voice was dangerously low.

"Listen to me." I spoke softly. I was powerless inside the circle – I had to get beyond the demon ash. "You need to stop this. You need to let me out of the circle."

His head dropped and he looked up at me from under a menacing brow. "No."

My fingers picked at the scarves tied around my wrists. There was no way I was getting free on my own. "Sebastian –"

"What happened to you calling me Basha?" He jerked his head up. "Are they making you call me Sebastian?"

"Sebastian is your name." My stomach soured. Images of our time together played across the screen inside my brain. "Basha was not real. You used me. You lied to me."

A firm rapping on my front door startled us both. Sebastian's lips pursed as he sucked in air through his nose. He rose, pocketing my phone and crossing the bedroom to the window overlooking the sidewalk in front of my brownstone. He pulled one of the sheer panels aside, pressing his forehead against the windowpane. His agitation grew, a hand balling into a fist and pounding rhythmically against his upper thigh. "Who the fuck is that?"

I heard more knocking and a muffled voice calling. The circle held me hostage, but I risked placing my mind's eye outside the demon ash and concentrated my thoughts on my front stoop. It wasn't calling upon my magic, it was simply extending the part of my awareness I used when reading for clients. I jammed my eyes shut, letting them roll up under my eyelids. *C'mon, c'mon.* I dug deep inside myself. Who do I see? Who is there? Familiar feelings flitted through my chest. A male. Anticipation, followed by a sharp slash of pain racing over my back, causing my body to convulse. I panted, opening my eyes.

"Guillaume!" I screamed, letting my fear overflow my senses as I pictured my former teacher in sharp detail. "Guillaume!" I prayed the intimate connection I once had with him would revive itself enough to alert him to the danger I was in.

"Shut up!" Sebastian hissed from the window. I heard another yell and then banging on my front door. Sebastian advanced toward me, both hands raking through his hair before he grabbed fistfuls and pulled, screwing his eyes shut. "Shut the fuck up, Lucie!"

"Guillaume, help me!" I shrieked a moment before I felt my entire home shudder, making Sebastian stumble against the side of my bed. Guillaume had forced all my wards to drop at once. The next noise I heard was my front door being blown off its hinges.

"Lucie!" Guillaume called from downstairs.

"Guillaume!" My eyes stayed trained on Sebastian as his arms dropped and the wild look in his eyes made them shimmer with red. Struggling, I climbed from my knees to my feet. I could hear Guillaume pounding up the stairs as he ran. It was enough to make Sebastian start backing up toward my closet door.

Guillaume appeared in the bedroom's doorway. He quickly assessed the scene, his left hand automatically lifting toward Sebastian. He chanted a banishing spell.

"Save it," Sebastian scoffed over the droning of Guillaume's words. He shifted his gaze toward me as his hand reached behind him and he connected with the doorknob. Sebastian's angry face instantly transformed into a playful expression, one I'd recognized from a different time with the man. "We're not done, Lucie. I'll come back for you. I promise."

Guillaume's voice rose and I could feel the power pouring off him as he pushed toward Sebastian. But he was too late. Sebastian's door travel energy had activated, and he whipped out of my house through my closet door in an instant. The door slammed shut behind him, shaking the wall hard enough to cause a picture to fall to the floor.

Hanging my head, I blew out a breath. Guillaume came to the circle's edge and I shook my head at him. "Demon ash. Don't touch it."

Guillaume rubbed his hand over the stubble on his chin, contemplating his next steps. "I need a jar with a secure lid."

"My kitchen pantry," I told him. He nodded

once before disappearing back into the hall outside my bedroom.

While he was gone, I took several full breaths, calming myself. The fear still coursed through my veins like a runaway train roaring off its tracks. Sebastian was alive! Or was he? No, he was no longer human. He was... *a demon*. My teeth sunk into my lower lip.

What had we created when we tossed him into the Below? What monster did Sebastian become?

∞∞∞

Guillaume returned with a jar and used a basic air spell to coerce the demon ash into the container. I watched his effortless work, a reluctant admiration creating angry butterflies in my stomach. I hated him and was grateful to him.

I washed my face in the bathroom sink, using a cloth to dab Sebastian's blood from my lips and the skin surrounding my mouth. I brushed my teeth to rid myself of the copper taste left on my tongue. As I wiped a towel across my lips, my eyes wandered to the waste basket. Bloody tissues filled the bottom.

Sebastian's blood. He must've used my bathroom to take care of the bloody nose I gave him. *That* was a mistake. I picked up the basket and returned to my bedroom. Guillaume waited for me downstairs. I ran my tongue over my teeth. What I held in my hand was valuable. I crossed to my jewelry armoire and pulled out a slim drawer, emptying it into the one below. I shoved the now empty drawer back into its slot, tucking the bloody tissues inside. They were dry, the rainbow of red shades running from crimson to a brown stain. I secured the door to the armoire by casting the smallest protection spell I could get away with while Guillaume was under my roof. If he sensed my magic, he'd want to know what I was up to.

I snagged a sweater from a chair, yanking it over my nightgown before grabbing a pair of jeans from the laundry basket. I hopped into the hall, pulling my pants up. At the top of the stairs, I zipped them, fastening the button as I hustled. Now that the Sebastian-induced adrenalin stopped pumping through me, I was conscious of leaving Guillaume unsupervised in my house.

I stopped in the entryway to gape at my missing front door. Well, it wasn't missing as much as it was unattached. Guillaume had propped it against the door jam.

"I'll deal with it later," I mumbled to myself as I padded across the frigid floor in my bare feet. I'd neglected to put on socks.

Guillaume stood in the kitchen, thumbing through the pages of the book of fairy tales. *Shit.* He looked up, closing the book. Lifting an eyebrow, he crossed his arms as he leaned against the counter. He was dressed casually, in jeans and a heather gray cotton shirt left untucked. A navy blazer dressed up his cool elegance. He had pushed up his sleeves. "Playtime with a lover get out of control?"

His words knocked the breath out of me. I was shocked at how callous he could be. *Let it go,* I told myself. It was better for him to waste energy on deriding me rather than asking questions about the book. I moved to a barstool. "Guillaume..." I faltered as the turmoil of the morning overwhelmed my body. Feelings of panic and relief spun together violently inside. My eyes betrayed me, filling with hot tears. My home had been so easily violated. How could I let that happen?

Guillaume circled the counter, his hand touching my chin as he directed me to face him. He appraised my swollen lip. "You're barely hurt."

I rubbed my lips together, moistening them. "I'm fine. You're right."

"What happened?" He lifted my chin higher, peering at my throat. "You do have some red marks, but nothing I'd be concerned about. I doubt you'll bruise."

"I was attacked."

His eyes flicked to mine. "Do you know him?"

Angry at myself for being weak, I blinked back tears a second time. "His name is Sebastian. Sebastian St. Michel. We knew each other once."

"And he's a Salesman?"

How did he know? Right, Sebastian door traveled in front of Guillaume. "He was. I think he's something else now."

"Let me guess." Guillaume kept his hand on my chin, holding me hostage. A year's worth of training kicked in and I remained still. "He's also a demon. Maybe the one who got into the Congress building?"

"I think so," I answered. I wasn't going to tell him Sebastian admitted to seeing the kiss I shared with Templeton in the Congress library.

My pantry door swung open then, and Templeton burst through, rushing Guillaume. Before I could stop him, he grabbed the older witch's shoulder, pulling him away from me and spinning him around. The two men wrestled, before Templeton slammed Guillaume against the wall. His hands twisted Guillaume's shirt at his neck as he held him. Guillaume lifted his left hand and my toaster flew from the counter, striking Templeton in the side of his head. Staggering backward, Templeton released his grasp.

"Stop it! Templeton, no!" I yelled as I jumped between the two men. I wrapped my arms around his waist, using my body to push him away from Guillaume.

He didn't know what my former teacher could do.

Templeton's eyes were colorless save for his pupils. Even the black rings circling his irises were gone. He targeted Guillaume, spitting out a spell before I could stop him. Guillaume's head whipped to the side as if he'd been punched. As his head cracked into the wall behind him, he retaliated with his own spell, ripping Templeton from my arms and forcing him to his knees. A storm in my kitchen rose around us as the magic Guillaume conjured tore open a cupboard. Dishes flew from their shelves, pelting Templeton as he shielded his head with his arms. The sound of my knife drawer screeching open behind me ripped through my ears.

"Guillaume, mercy!" The words flew from my mouth, and I dove for the floor in front of him, pressing my forehead to his feet. "Please! *Maître, je vous en supplie!*"

The room instantly grew still. I lifted my head, peering up at Guillaume. The vicious smile greeting me was familiar. I turned toward Templeton. He remained on his knees, his body straining against Guillaume's last spell, his back arched, his arms stiff at his sides. Templeton glared at the witch who'd overpowered him.

I knew it could get worse – *oh, so much worse!* Templeton simply couldn't understand. I crawled across the floor and faced him, rising to my knees and placing my hands on either side of his face. "Look at me," I murmured.

For once he listened to me, his eyes shifting in my direction.

"Templeton, you need to hear me. Guillaume didn't hurt me. It wasn't him." I saw a question spark in his eyes. My voice quavered. "It was Sebastian. He was here. Sebastian was here in my home, Templeton."

"Here?" Templeton's voice sounded as though he were far away. I was stunned he managed even one word under Guillaume's spell.

"Yes, here. In my home." I repeated, shuddering. *One hellish moment at a time,* I thought. "Listen to me. I need you to apologize to Guillaume."

Templeton's face pulled into a sneer.

"Please. Just do it." I bowed my head. "I need you to do this for me. Please trust me."

The sneer disappeared and Templeton stared blankly over my shoulder at Guillaume. I let my hands fall away from his face.

Guillaume sauntered in a circle around us, his course bringing him to stand beside me as he looked down at Templeton. At the same time, Guillaume petted my head, running his fingers through my hair.

"Touching, Lucie," Guillaume chuckled. "I've never seen you grovel so eagerly." He waved a hand and Templeton's body relaxed. "You would like to say something to me, Salesman?"

Templeton climbed to his feet. I could sense the energy pouring off him – it wasn't the controlled power I was used to feeling. The rage reverberated in the space around him. I felt it surround me and tighten.

Templeton's eyes remained mostly white. He didn't blink.

"Well, son?" Guillaume needled.

"You have my apologies, Guillaume," Templeton replied evenly. "Now get the fuck out of Lucie's house."

I smacked my forehead with my palm.

Guillaume laughed, the sound jarring. His laughter could scare me as much as his anger. He shook a finger at Templeton before holding the same hand out to me. "You may rise, Lucie."

Setting my pride aside, I put my hand in Guillaume's and let him pull me to my feet. "Thank you," I muttered. I put a hand to my chest, trying to push down the mass of feelings swirling inside me. Anger, fear, and shame flowed uncontrolled out of me in a thick stream. I felt my witchline opening – something I didn't intend to do. It sucked the energy out of me. The feeling of it feeding on me like this left me nauseous. I was going to be sick.

I had to get Guillaume out of my house. I had to tell Templeton what happened upstairs. We needed to find out how Sebastian was able to come back from the Below. I opened my mouth to speak when my front door slammed to the floor in the other room. A flood of Rabbits swarmed into my home, several crossing into the kitchen and catching us all off guard. Rabbit targeted Guillaume, lunging at him. I reacted by throwing up my hand.

"No!" The sonic pulse flowing out of my body and throughout my home knocked everyone to the ground – even Guillaume. With my witchline still open, the course of my energy switched direction and flooded back into my body, charged by the raw power. I stood in the center of the chaos as my kitchen window exploded and Rabbits covered their faces. The pantry door shut with a crash, before opening and banging closed again. The timer on the oven beeped erratically and my refrigerator rocked back and forth. Out of the corner of my eye, I saw Big Rabbit scramble forward on his hands and knees. He leaned his muscular body against the appliance and kept it from tipping. The cupboard doors vibrated while all the drawers shimmied. Beyond the kitchen, something electrical popped and shattered. I covered my ears as the noise reached a fever pitch. "No," I repeated, this time my voice hushed.

An abrupt stillness rang in my ears. I opened my mouth wide to relieve the pressure that had built, hearing the pop inside my head.

"Hunh," I exhaled as my hands drifted to my sides. Helplessly, I looked to Rabbit. He climbed to his feet and nodded. His brethren rose behind him, their eyes solid black and glittering as they waited. I glanced over at Big Rabbit. The giant looked shell-shocked. A burst of laughter escaped my lips, followed by a hiccup and a sob. "My god, you all are going to give me a breakdown – and you're my friends!" I covered my mouth with both hands and suppressed a second sob. I was *not* going to lose it now. I took a deep breath, evaluating how I felt. I realized my witchline had closed and my energy was centering itself. My self-control returned.

Rabbit's nose twitched, his eyes clocking Guillaume as he moved to my side.

"An interesting lot of friends you've made." His hands pushed nonchalantly into his jeans pockets, Guillaume appraised the men and women who'd streamed into my kitchen. "That was also quite the display, Lucie. Your power has grown more than I expected. However, your control needs much work."

Guillaume needed to leave before any more trouble rolled through my door. I squinted at the man. I knew how to make him leave. My voice sounded calm to my own ears when I spoke – I hoped the others were fooled by it. "Loren sent a message yesterday, Guillaume. I know the demonstration is scheduled for tomorrow and I assume that's why you came here this morning. I'm sure you're aware the Congress elders gave me permission to choose the method we will use. I also know I'm in your debt after what you did for me this morning. But if you agree to leave my home and never return, I will repay my debt now and owe you nothing more."

Guillaume laughed, motioning to the mess in my kitchen. "I'm not sure what you can give me that would top this morning's entertainment."

"I will repay my debt to you by giving up the right to choose the demonstration method tomorrow." I stole a look at Templeton. Speechless, he lowered his gaze to the floor. I could see his chest rising and falling as he worked to keep his anger under control. I turned back to Guillaume. "Do you agree?"

"I do." Guillaume reached up and patted my

cheek. I felt everyone in the room tense. The hostile pleasure I saw filling Guillaume's face made the panic bloom inside my chest once more. He shook his head. "My special witch – demons, Salesmen, and Rabbits surround her like she's their queen. You never fail to delight me, Lucie."

His power over me firmly established, Guillaume strode to the counter and picked up the jar holding the demon ash. He inspected its contents before throwing a cold smile in my direction. "I shall take my leave. There is much to prepare for our demonstration tomorrow." He retrieved his wool dress coat from a barstool, ignoring the others as he exited the kitchen without a backward glance, taking the jar with him. Rabbits parted warily, letting him pass. Moments later he was gone.

Chapter 15

As Rabbits worked to repair my kitchen window, fix my front door, and restore the light fixture that exploded in my dining room, I stayed wrapped in a blanket on my sofa.

After installing me on the couch and planting Big Rabbit next to me as guard, Templeton and Rabbit disappeared upstairs to check out my bedroom. I didn't even put up a fight. I let them do whatever they needed to do to feel like they had a measure of control. When they returned, Rabbit silently handed me a pair of socks and I burst into tears.

Big Rabbit rubbed my back as I cried self-consciously into my hands. A female Rabbit with a thin scar on her cheek brought me a glass of water and a handful of napkins, setting them on the end table beside the sofa. When I finished crying, Big Rabbit and his girlfriend left the living room, sliding the pocket door closed behind them. I took a gulp of water and blew my nose.

I told Rabbit and Templeton what happened when I woke to find Sebastian touching me and pulling my blankets down.

Rabbit sat in the chair across from me, leaning forward as he rested his forearms on his knees. His head stayed bowed, his eyes on the rug beneath his booted feet. Templeton stood still as stone by the fireplace, his shoulder pointed toward me as he stared in the direction of the window at the front of the room. Only now was a hint of blue returning to his irises.

They didn't interrupt as I described what happened when Sebastian invaded my room. While I didn't give them a blow-by-blow of the attack, I made it clear certain personal violations had *not* happened before Sebastian rendered me unconscious and put me in his circle of demon ash.

"I've never seen anything like it," I said, adjusting the blanket around my shoulders and sitting up straighter. "He moved unbelievably fast. Whatever changed inside him, speed is now on his side."

Rabbit raised his head. "He can still door travel, so he didn't lose his abilities as a Salesman."

"But that was his only ability before," I replied. "Door traveling was it. He's not like Templeton." I gestured toward the stoic man leaning against the mantel. "Sebastian can't do magic."

"But he must have." Rabbit rubbed the back of his neck. "He contained you in a circle."

"That's true, but you can learn a spell. You don't have to be born with any natural ability," I said.

"Learning to practice magic takes time – especially if you do not come by it naturally." Templeton broke his silence.

"He's had four months to learn all sorts of things," I snapped, before pausing and giving my head a shake. "I'm sorry."

"We understand." Rabbit shot Templeton a cautious look. Templeton's face remained impassive. "Did he tell you anything about where he's been? Where he's going now?"

"He was in the Below. From what he said, I think he's been there the whole time." I pictured Sebastian sitting on my bed, rocking back and forth. "He said it was a nightmare. Loud and sickening."

"Sickening?" Rabbit's brows pulled together. "Interesting way of putting it."

"Yeah, it was." I swallowed, feeling exposed as the emotions played across my face. I felt Templeton's gaze harden. "Do you remember last year when Emily said Sebastian was unhinged?"

Rabbit shrugged. "No, but he's not the poster child for sanity."

"The man I faced this morning is well past unhinged," I told them. "His emotions swung back and forth like a ping-pong ball. One minute he was raging at me, the next he was…"

"What?" Rabbit asked.

I couldn't explain to them what I saw – the vulnerability and fear permeating the rage. The horror I felt as I watched him. The language he used. I pulled on my lower lip. "He thinks I was forced to close the sixth door over him."

"He said that?"

We don't have to talk about what they made you do in the Walled Zone…

I nodded at Rabbit as I recalled Sebastian's ranting. "He said, *'what they made you do in the Walled Zone.'* I think it's safe to assume he means you two and Emily." Oh, Emily! "Holy shit. We have to let Emily know about this." Fear gripped me again. He'd attacked her before.

"I'll get a message to her right now," Rabbit said, running a thumb over his phone.

"No." Templeton pushed off the mantel.

"What do you mean, no?" I stood up, tossing the blanket on the sofa. "She needs to know about this as soon as possible."

"I agree. I'll go tell her. She's going to have questions and someone needs to be there to answer them," Templeton finished.

"Oh," I nodded. "That makes sense. Okay, go. But then come back here so we can –"

"Lucie," Templeton's voice grew softer. "Slow down. Emily's going to want to know what Sebastian said about her."

I shook my head. "But he didn't mention her at all. He was laser-focused on me. He also referred to both of you."

"What did he say?" Templeton asked.

"He called you a name, and well, he alluded to being in the Congress library during the gala." I figured that was all I needed to say. The brief flash of understanding crossing Templeton's face proved I was right. I turned to Rabbit. "He saw the network phone you gave to me and knew what it was. He took it with him when he left."

"He can't access anything without your finger pass," Rabbit replied. He grinned, new lines appearing at the corners of his eyes. "But this might work in our favor."

"You can track him," I said, remembering how Rabbit knew I was near *Coffee Cove*.

"Yup. Let's hope he doesn't dump it once he realizes he can't use it." Rabbit started to tap the screen on his own phone. "Got it."

"Where?" Templeton growled.

Rabbit raised his head. "No. You're not going after him by yourself. Let's track him. See where he leads us. The phone shows it's still in the Empire – I'm going to assume he has it on him for now. I'll watch to see if it moves. When we're ready, we can work together, bring in the network for backup. If we can contain him, we can banish him."

Templeton wasn't as generous. "We're not banishing him. I'm killing him."

His declaration jolted me, and I looked to Rabbit. The other man simply nodded at Templeton and went back to his phone.

"Okay," I breathed. I didn't want to talk about killing Sebastian – *again.* For four months my spirit suffered after we pushed him into the

Below. I was so angry that night. I'd wanted him to pay after learning he'd deceived me. I'd wanted him to die along with my heart. But in the months that followed, I was pulled apart by my conflicting feelings: anger, guilt, sadness, loss. I wasn't ready to rip open old wounds by planning his death now.

Templeton stared at me and I worried he sensed my internal struggle.

"Crimson Stone?" Rabbit's voice cut through the tension.

"What about it?" Templeton scowled.

"Did Sebastian mention the Stone, Lucie?" Rabbit ignored Templeton.

"No, he didn't. Maybe he doesn't need it anymore. I don't know." I flapped my arms. "I was unconscious for some of the time he was here. Most of our 'chat' was limited to his ramblings of what happened between us. But Emily and the Crimson Stone didn't come up at all. Then Guillaume showed up and he took off." I paused. "Wait. How did you two –?"

"Rabbit texted me about Guillaume," Templeton replied, his visage darkening. "Apparently there's a camera trained on your front door. He can watch who comes and goes."

Rabbit let out a slow breath, his cheeks growing pink. "She knows. I set up the connection when she was gone." He motioned to his phone, addressing me. "You know how the camera sends me a screenshot when there's activity at your door? It caught Guillaume. I, ah, didn't get it right away because I was busy." Again, Rabbit was uncharacteristically uneasy. "When I saw it, I texted you but there was no answer. Then I messaged the phone I gave to Templeton. I was too far from here to get to you any sooner than I did. There wasn't one damn Rabbit in the area who could get here fast. I grabbed my crew, but it still took us time to get across Matar."

"And that's why you attacked as soon as you got here," I realized, gesturing toward Templeton. "You thought Guillaume was here to harm me."

"Not a stretch."

"Well, it's not his style to blast his way into a house, but I get where you're coming from," I admitted.

"How could Guillaume get through your wards?" Rabbit asked. "Or aren't they raised against him?"

"He read her signature. He knows her magic,"

Templeton interrupted. "She was his student. He dismantled the spell based on what he knows about her."

Templeton was correct. I studied him. "Do you do that?"

"I have before," he answered. I was rewarded with a brief quirk of his lips.

"Huh. Well, whatever. It worked in your favor today," Rabbit said to me. He pointed at Templeton. "Go get it over with and tell Emily about Sebastian's resurrection. Let her know we're monitoring his movements and we'll keep her in the loop. She might want to get ahold of Anne. The two can add a protection spell to her house." Anne Lace was a mutual friend I'd met through a Matar method coven. She'd relocated to Kincaid and was the person who directed Emily to me for help last year. She was also Templeton's aunt on his mother's side – something she had kept to herself at Templeton's request until last October.

"I'll take care of the spell for her," Templeton grumbled. Emily was a thorn in his side.

"Oh, and good luck with Jack," Rabbit added, suppressing a smile. Emily's fiancé hated Templeton.

Templeton glared at the other man, before turning to face me. "I'm coming back here. I want you to pack a bag. You're coming to the estate with me."

The 'estate' was Templeton's family home – a place I'd never visited. "Um, no. I'm not leaving the city, Templeton, but thank you."

"Fine. I have the penthouse downtown. We'll go there."

Sometimes I forgot Templeton came from a wealthy family. I shook my head. "I'm not being chased out of my home. I'm staying here."

He pressed his lips together, his eyes not leaving mine. "Fine. Rabbit, I have a commitment I cannot miss tonight. Can you stay here with Lucie?"

"Already planned on it," Rabbit answered smoothly. "I'll have Rabbits in the area as well. Big Rabbit's already making arrangements."

"Fine," Templeton said for the third time. He was gritting his teeth more with each sentence. "Lucie, I will come back here after I see Emily. There are a few more things we should go over."

"Great," Rabbit dismissed him, returning to his texting. "See you then."

"I'm glad I have a say in all of this," I huffed.

"You don't." Templeton stepped around me, slamming the sliding door open and door traveling out of my living room, presumedly to Emily's.

"Wow." I ran a hand through my hair. "Sometimes I don't know what to do with him."

"Tell me what it's like after two decades with Mr. Personality," Rabbit snickered. "Spoiler alert: he doesn't change much."

∞∞∞

The Rabbits reattached my front door and replaced my window in no time. The explosion in the dining room had been cleaned up, but the electricity feeding the light I blew was shut off. I literally fried the wiring leading into the fixture that burst. Eventually I'd choose a new light and they'd install it for me.

The last of Rabbit's crew packed up and left, but Rabbit remained. We'd moved into the kitchen. After Templeton left, I'd asked Rabbit where Sebastian had gone – I had to know. Rabbit traced my stolen phone to an address northeast of Matar. He determined Sebastian had run to his family home. It was seized by the Empire following the charges against his family when the Fringe was being dismantled. It was probably empty and boarded shut. Rabbit checked his phone periodically to monitor his whereabouts.

Sebastian's immediate family, as wealthy as Templeton's, was awaiting trial for their involvement with the Fringe. Both of Sebastian's parents were Salesmen. Sebastian had inherited his door traveling ability from his mother *and* his father. Rabbit didn't know offhand if Sebastian's parents were still in the Empire but assumed so. Did they know their son had returned? Did they know he was a demon?

I made a cup of soothing tea. Earlier I'd showered, washing off the feeling of being held captive by Sebastian. I'd cleansed my bedroom as well, smudging the space with a smoldering sage stick before spritzing consecrated water throughout the room. Sebastian had pulled clothes from my dresser looking for something to tie my wrists together. My underwear drawer was clearly rustled through. I refolded the garments as I mentally inventoried my clothes to determine if anything was missing. Across the hall my sheets tumbled in the dryer with a couple of wool dryer balls anointed with frankincense as a purifier.

After I felt my room was free of Sebastian's crazed energy, I spent time raising wards of protection around my home. Guillaume had blasted them apart and it took me time to rebuild the magical barrier. As an extra step, I placed consecrated salt in front of every window as well as along the two separate entrances into my home before remembering Sebastian retained his door travel power. Any door could bring him into my house. I'd have to be vigilant about keeping all entrances protected. I'd need to create something specific to keep him out.

"He's still got the phone on him," Rabbit said all of a sudden. "He's at his cabin in the Walled Zone."

The cabin was more like a private lodge. I remembered the secluded place on the lake. "Didn't the Empire seize it as well?" I asked.

"You'd think. But Sebastian wasn't around to be charged when his family was brought into the Salesman Court. The cabin was owned solely by him. Perhaps it never made it onto the Court's radar." Rabbit shrugged.

"He's carrying the phone with him. I wonder

why?"

"Maybe he's hoping to find someone who can help him get past the finger lock," Rabbit replied. "Whatever the reason, it works to our advantage."

"Templeton's been gone for quite a while," I noted. "You think he's still at Emily's? Can you track his phone?"

"I can, but if he's outside the Empire, I can't." Rabbit paused and fiddled more with his own phone. "Nope. He's not in the Empire."

"Maybe he's still at Emily's," I said. "Or even Anne's."

"Maybe." Rabbit sipped a glass of water. "You doing okay?"

I sighed, leaning against the counter. "Everything feels too close and far away at the same time."

"I get it," Rabbit replied. "Seeing Sebastian messed with your head."

"Yes." I took a breath. "I can't help but feel guilty."

Rabbit didn't answer right away. He continued to study me with his curious eyes. "I know you spent a lot of time with him," he spoke at last. "But you can't beat yourself up over what he is now – he was already halfway there when you were seeing him. You just didn't know it. The face he showed you was false. He was a sadistic man."

"The person I knew was different," I said softly. "And that makes a lot of things difficult for me."

Rabbit struggled to find the right words. He twisted the fingers on his right hand, cracking his knuckles. "Lucie, last year at the Wayside Pub when he showed up out of nowhere and you realized your 'Basha' was really Sebastian, he threatened to hurt Emily. For fuck's sake, he put a gun to your head."

I pulled the tea ball from my cup and set it into the sink. "I know. But it was a knee-jerk reaction and…" My voice faltered. No one knew how my heart split in two at that exact moment.

Rabbit was appalled. "Do you even hear yourself?"

A knot formed in my stomach. I knew what Rabbit was saying. "I'm not defending him – good god, I couldn't begin to defend him! But this morning… There was a quality, something terrible inside his mind I could sense. It was overwhelming him. It was hard for me to watch."

"You have a big heart." Rabbit shook his head. "But don't be a fool. Any hell he's going through he's created for himself. Now's not the time to have compassion."

"Yeah." I wasn't going to confess the whole story of my relationship with Sebastian to Rabbit like I did with Emily. What difference did it make anyway? I sipped my tea. "You're right."

"I'm sorry." Rabbit's face was grim. "We don't always get to choose where our hearts go. Just know you have people around you who love you. Who will do anything for you." We held each other's gaze until I finally looked away.

∞∞∞

I didn't have much of an appetite for lunch, but I ate a peanut butter sandwich at Rabbit's insistence. He checked his phone often. I refrained from asking about Sebastian's whereabouts. Instead, I picked up the book of fairy tales. There was a story I needed to read, the one following *Black Sky*.

∞∞∞

The Man with the Red Eyes.

The young girl was confused by what she'd learned from the Magician who disappeared into the Black Sky above. His story smelled of earth and trees and she wondered if she was supposed to see its color.

She didn't understand how there could be more than the One Truth. The Beams of Light from Above sang about the One Truth threading the universe together. They did not sing about many truths. They warned about untruths.

The child slid down the side of the rock on which she sat, passing by the fields of grain and the seas of fish where the birds swam in shallow pools. At the bottom of the rock, she climbed onto a feather and glided back to her altar. When she arrived, she discovered another man. He was walking in circles and chanting. She watched him from the edge of the clearing, politely waiting until he finished.

When the man noticed her, he held out his hand. "Come see the stones," he said. "They are dancing on your altar."

The girl joined him, watching as the rows of gemstones rolled and jumped.

"Can you hear the music?" the man asked. The

girl looked up into his eyes. They glowed red.

"I only hear the song from the Beams of Light from Above," answered the girl. "They sing of the One Truth, but the Magician from the night sky said there are many truths. I no longer know how to listen."

The Man with the Red Eyes took her hand in his and bit her finger. He lifted it over her head and a river of blood ran down her arm. "Seek the land where the Shadows Dance. There is magic inside the Darkness. It will teach you about the many truths."

The girl watched the blood, surprised by its appearance. "But how do I find the place where the Shadows Dance?"

"Follow the river," said the Man with the Red Eyes. He kissed the inside of her blood-covered wrist before releasing her and hopping up on the altar with the shaking stones. "If you get lost, look under your feet to find where you are."

He bounced off the altar and plucked a white star blooming in the fragrant Clematis growing around her sacred place. The Man with the Red Eyes ate it because he liked the smell of vanilla.

"Remember to follow the river," he said once more before catching the tail of a dragonfly and zipping

away.

The girl waved goodbye, touching the pieces of stone in her pocket.

Maybe after she heard about the many truths, the land where the Shadows Dance would be a good hiding place for the pretty stone. Maybe then she could hide it in plain sight.

She began to search for the river.

∞∞∞

It was disturbing to study a fairy tale called *The Man with the Red Eyes* when only this morning I'd stared into the face of a demon – one with red filling his eyes. Templeton and I needed to sit down and talk about this book.

I grew restless. I felt trapped in my own home, which was ironic since I'd argued to stay in it. But I hated not being able to do what I wanted, so I decided to go get coffee from *Coffee Cove*.

Rabbit was tired – I could see it in his face. "Why can't women ever stay in one place?"

"Listen," I said. "I'm going stir crazy. I need to do something to get my mind off what happened this morning and what I'm facing tomorrow with Guillaume."

"Yeah. I get it." Rabbit passed a hand over his face. "Okay, let's go down and back. But let me do a location check first." He tapped the screen on his phone. "Our demon is still at the cabin – assuming he's traveling with your phone."

"Check to see if Templeton is back in the Empire," I told him as I shrugged into my wool coat. "If he is, let him know where we're going. That way if he comes back while we're gone – god forbid – he won't have a meltdown because we're not here."

Rabbit grinned as he executed a search for Templeton's phone. "You seem to be feeling better. You sound like the Lucie I know." His upper lip rose. "That idiot."

"What?" I leaned closer, puzzling over the lines of numbers on his phone screen.

"Templeton's at Sebastian's family home north of the city." Rabbit texted furiously.

"What are you doing?" My heart dropped when I learned Templeton was back in the Empire but searching for Sebastian.

"Telling him I can see where he is and to get his ass out of there."

"You don't think he'll go to Sebastian's cabin next?" I knew Templeton had door traveled there before with Emily. He knew where the cabin was located.

"I do." Rabbit's lip was curled back again. "So. Much. Work."

"I know how to get him back here." I pulled on my gloves and marched to the front door. "Tell him I took off for the coffee shop and you couldn't stop me."

∞∞∞

Rabbit hustled and caught up with me on the sidewalk. He was laughing. "I should show you the messages he's sending me. Pissed doesn't cover it. Apparently, I need to learn how to deal with you."

I raised an eyebrow. "That so?"

"Yup. Plus I've grown soft. I let you get away with anything – just like Emily." He chuckled, cramming his bare hands into his pockets.

I glanced over at him. Today he wore a red knit hat. It pushed out a bunch of curls around his face. "When we get back home, I could trim your hair for you," I teased.

"You're fixated on my hair."

"It's cute. Maybe if I took a little off the back."

We paused at the corner and waited on traffic.

"I'm happy with my hair," he said. "Why are we talking about it?"

"Because I can hardly tell the difference between you and Big Rabbit," I continued.

"Okay, that's enough out of you," he grumbled. "I don't want to hear anything more about my hair."

I laughed. We finished the rest of the walk in silence. He held the door open for me at *Coffee Cove* and I stepped up into the shop. Templeton was already inside.

I tossed a smug look at Rabbit.

"What are you doing?" Templeton asked through clenched teeth.

"I'm treating Rabbit to some French press. Can I get you a cup to go?" I squinted at the menu. "Oh, thin mint latte. I might try that."

"Lucie, this isn't a game," he snapped.

"I'm well aware." I yanked my purse open and dug out a debit card. "It was my bedroom Sebastian visited this morning. It's my spirit Guillaume will be working to break tomorrow. I needed to take a break from the hell surrounding me before I set myself on fire, Templeton. You running off to chase Sebastian isn't helping.

Now, would you like a fucking French press to go?"

Templeton snorted.

"I'll take that as a yes," I said, stepping up to the counter and placing an order for two French pressed coffees and a thin mint latte. Templeton stormed outside, Rabbit shaking his head as he followed. Through the window I watched as Templeton laid into Rabbit, the other man standing there patiently with his hands still deep in his coat pockets. Rabbit looked bored.

"Lucie!" One of the young baristas realized it was me waiting on the other side of the counter. I recognized her from last year. Sienna something-or-other. She was a student at the university, working at *Coffee Cove* part time. "I can't believe it's you. It's been forever!" She hurried out from behind the counter to give me a hug.

"It's good to see you, too," I said. "How's school?"

"Great! This is my last semester." Sienna pulled me by the arm, bringing me to the end of the counter. "Hey, I heard about what happened from Rick."

I pasted a fake smile on my lips. "Oh?"

"The guy. I'm sorry." She pulled a sad face. "I

saw him, though, and wanted to tell you."

"You... You saw him?" I stammered. She saw Sebastian? "What do you mean?"

"He was here late Friday afternoon. He got a coffee and said he heard you were going to start reading again. Wondered where your appointment book was." Sienna's eyes grew wide. "I knew you used to see him, and Rick said you two broke up. I thought, well, maybe he was interested in patching things up."

This was horrifying. I kept my voice low to help mask the trembling I felt inside. "What did you say?"

"I told him you only put your appointment book out when you were here reading for people." She pointed in the direction of my reading room.

"And?"

"And he asked when you would be here next. I told him I didn't know, but to come back this week." Sienna was hopeful. "Was that okay? He seemed eager to see you. He was all smiles."

"Um... Actually, I'd rather not see him." I saw a to-go carton appear on the counter with three coffees. "And Sienna, he's not a nice guy. Try to avoid him if you can. Tell the other baristas, too."

"I'm sorry, Lucie." Sienna's brow wrinkled.

"Don't worry about it." I stepped away to get the coffee I'd ordered. I paused, turning back to her. "Hey, did you notice anything different about him? Like his eye color?"

Sienna shook her head. "He was wearing sunglasses, which was weird because it was starting to get dark out."

I nodded, balancing the to-go carton as I headed for the exit.

Friday. We could've crossed paths at the coffee shop if I'd met Rabbit later that day. I stepped outside into the misleading sunshine and carried the coffee over to my two brooding attendants.

"Sebastian was here looking for me on Friday," I told them as I gave a to-go cup to each man. I turned away before they could reply and headed for home.

Chapter 16

Rabbit and Templeton followed me but hung back. I knew now Sebastian had been in the Empire for at least four days.

At my front door, I waved a hand to see if I could sense any attempts to gain access while I was gone. There were none. I felt Templeton's energy floating alongside mine. I wondered if he'd be placing his own spell on my home. *Again.*

The three of us went inside and I dropped my keys on the table in the entryway. I turned to the two men. "Now what?"

"I need to go out," Rabbit answered, checking his phone as it buzzed several times in quick succession. "Templeton can stay here. I'll be back later to spend the night. I'll bring you a new phone, Lucie."

Templeton didn't acknowledge Rabbit. He

turned and headed for the kitchen.

I tossed an annoyed look at his disappearing frame before addressing Rabbit. "Thanks. Hey, will I be able to track Sebastian with my phone?"

"No." He shook his head, his curls bouncing. "I do it through the network's connection. It's sort of a pinging system."

"Can you tell me where he is now?" I asked quietly.

Rabbit tapped code into his phone. "Still at his cabin."

"If the phone loses its charge, can you still track it?"

"Once it's dead, no. Do you know how much battery life was left?"

"I don't," I said. "But it wasn't at 100 percent."

"We'll probably lose it by tomorrow then," Rabbit replied. "Alright, I'm out of here. Make sure Templeton's phone is charged. You can use the cord I gave you. I'll text him if I have an update." He reached over and let his knuckles graze the side of my arm. "I'll be back tonight. You'll be safe."

"I know."

With Rabbit gone it was only Templeton and me. I hung up my winter coat in the closet, my attention drawn to the handprints burnt into the wall. I didn't even have the luxury of thinking about Saturday night. Too much had gone down since then.

Templeton sat on a barstool, the book of fairy tales open, his hand slowly turning through the pages. I climbed on the stool next to him. "Do you think it's a coincidence that Sebastian's eyes were red and there's a tale called *The Man with the Red Eyes*?"

"You know how I feel about coincidence," he said. He lifted his head.

"I know we believe the stories about the 'pretty stone' relate to the Crimson Stone, and the door tales are referring to the directional doors here in the Empire, but who is this girl?" I touched the text on the page, my hand brushing Templeton's.

He looked down, his fingers moving and threading through mine unexpectedly.

"Are you prepared to face Guillaume tomorrow?" Templeton shifted in his seat. He pulled my hand, spinning my barstool to face him. We were close and he stretched his legs, placing his feet on the rung of my stool. I found myself sitting between his knees. Our legs brushed against each other. He released my hand and I let it fall to my lap as I crossed my ankles.

I wasn't prepared for the sudden intimacy. I hesitated so I could recall his question. Guillaume, right. "I'm probably about as ready as I can be. I know what he's capable of doing. It will be horrible, but at the very least I know he wants to prove to the Congress what we've said is possible. Our success is for his benefit as well. Any doubts the Congress has will be put to rest. That's what I need to focus on now."

"You gave in to him too easily this morning." Templeton's accusation was more hushed than harsh.

"I was afraid of what might happen if I didn't get him out of my house immediately," I explained. "You saw what he can do."

"I only failed because I reacted out of fear." Templeton's admission caught me off guard. "I was afraid for your safety. I misjudged the power behind his ability this morning, but I won't make such a pitifully amateur mistake again."

As I listened, I wondered how much of what Templeton said was true. Guillaume was the most powerful witch I knew. Strike that, he was the most powerful witch, *period*. Templeton's magical abilities were formidable, but was he as strong as Guillaume? Did he think he was?

"Do you believe you are as adept as Guillaume?"

He smirked. "Moreso."

I laughed, dropping my chin to my chest, my hair sliding forward along my cheek. "Of course."

Templeton reached over and pushed my hair back from my face as I raised my head. The affectionate gesture sent a rush through me. "You don't believe me?"

"I'm still trying to figure out what you are." I lifted a shoulder.

"Are you?" His eyes searched my face. "What does it matter?"

"Curiosity, mostly."

"Not Loren's prodding to know my lineage in light of my intentions?"

I twisted my lips to the side. "What are your intentions?"

A Cheshire cat grin appeared. "To see how many handprints we can add to your wall."

"Oh, good god." I tried to turn my barstool away, but his hands landed on my knees, stilling me.

"Why don't you look?" A serious expression reclaimed his face.

"I don't understand."

"I've seen what you can do with your magic. Why don't you..." His voice trailed off and he raised both eyebrows. "I'll let you look."

I mulled over his words. "I'm not sure I know what you mean."

"Yes, you do. Let it happen. Close your eyes and look at me, Lucie." The sound of his voice bounced around inside my head, tempting me.

My eyelids eased shut and I took a deep breath. Templeton's warm hands still rested on my knees. I covered them with mine. "Okay."

"Relax," he instructed as he flipped his hands over. His palms pressed lightly up against mine. "Relax and let me in." His silky voice was in the center of my mind.

I shivered, but the experience wasn't unpleasant – only unusual. I allowed my thoughts to drift. The well where I kept my energy was full and I dipped into it with my awareness, coating my wonder with a longing to know the man sitting across from me. I abandoned the tools I used for divination and drew instead from a deep desire that had been coursing through me since the first time he stood in my kitchen.

My energy was drawn to his then. It felt brighter when he was near. I understood now he experienced the same.

I was used to pushing my energy outward when seeking to understand something new – to take a taste. My anger and fear drove my energy in violent waves from my body when I wanted to press something away from me. I realized to know Templeton, I had to stop sending my energy away. Instead, I needed to let his flow into me.

My wariness fell away, any resistance I'd nursed with my energy being shed with each breath I took. My mouth opened when I sighed. Simultaneously, my shoulders relaxed, my hands rested trustfully in his, and my ankles unhooked – my legs swaying slightly as my knees parted.

Templeton's own energy – vigorous and masculine, refined and precise – flowed over me. It was warm as bathwater, covering my skin and sinking into me. I felt him pushing it steadily, his actions controlled.

"What do you see?" Templeton was closer. I

felt his breath on my lips.

"I see you," I sighed. In the middle of my mind, Templeton's essence took shape. It shimmered like an illusion, blending through outlines and silhouettes. I tried to catch it. The vision stopped, letting me draw near, before playfully pulling away.

I heard a quiet laugh echo far back in my brain.

I stopped trying to catch the silver shadow I saw in my head. Instead, my mind's eye watched as it morphed into Templeton. His eyes glowed in the most brilliant royal blue as he waited for me to see his actual magical nature – the man who was more than a door traveling Salesman. The man who was so much more than a skilled 'practitioner' of magic. A surge of energy filled me and I understood exactly *what* he was.

"Oh," I exhaled as the Templeton inside my brain stepped forward. "You're a *Magician*."

I could see him in fine detail – the magical heritage running through him, the intensity of the power behind his true nature. In his eyes I saw a whole universe forming. While physically he looked like the Templeton I knew, magically he was more than anyone could imagine. I watched as he raised a hand, palm up, and sent a shower of gold stars upward. As they fell around him, I realized he'd disappeared. A trail of twinkling footprints led away from me. I opened my eyes.

He was still close, his irises completely white, the black ring surrounding his pupils prominent. Templeton gave me a thin smile. "I am. But don't ever request that I pull a Rabbit from my hat. We have enough of them in the Empire."

He started to draw the rest of his energy away from me but hesitated. His brows pulled together as his expression became puzzled.

"What's wrong?" I watched his pupils turn into pinpricks and he gazed upward.

"I can see it." He leaned to the side as if to look around me. "I can see your witchline."

The revelation took my breath away. "You can?"

"I can." Templeton's pale eyes roamed down my body. "It runs like a waterfall of red light, pouring down from above. It enters at the nape of your neck, then comes out through your throat, traveling down your body – through your chest, stomach. It goes lower until it flows from your... From between your legs. It bubbles up in a mist, rising and spinning as it reenters the witchline stream above your head."

I didn't know what to say. No one had ever described such a thing.

I'd never seen my witchline. I could feel it, but it was not visible to me. Even when Guillaume helped me open it, it remained invisible to both of us.

Because witches couldn't see their witchlines.

I could only experience what it was like through the fascination on Templeton's face. I saw the waves of his door travel energy rising. A tendril reached out to me, caressing down the front of my body. Although I couldn't see it, I knew Templeton had dipped his own magic into my witchline. The pleasure I felt was exquisite. I gasped, shutting my eyes and quivering.

"Lucie, we need to stop now." Templeton's voice hitched.

I felt him withdraw from me, shuddering when his energy completely retreated. I wobbled, gripping his hands tightly. Taking a deep breath, I recentered myself. The soothing hum of my witchline continued and the lightheadedness I'd experienced drained away.

Opening my eyes, I met Templeton's gaze. The faded shade of blue had returned to his irises.

"That's never happened to me before," I said.

He gave a small nod. "That's what I thought."

"You could see it?"

"And feel it."

"It was like you were inside it." I pulled my hands from his. "But Templeton, it wasn't even open."

"What do you mean?"

"I mean, the witchline was in its natural state. It wasn't open, like when I pour my energy into it to strengthen it." I didn't know why it was important, but I sensed it was. "How do you feel?"

"Like I want to go deeper when it's the right time."

"Oh."

We sat in the quiet room, unmoving. I stared at the buttons at the top of his shirt while I processed what had happened. His eyes remained on my face and his hands were back on my knees.

Finally, I gained the courage to speak but he grimaced, pulling a hand away and reaching into the front pocket of his trousers. He fished out the network phone and read the message.

"Rabbit says he has news about the noise coming from the Walled Zone. He said the pulses under the static are getting louder. He's going to try to get back here early."

∞∞∞

Rabbit's text broke the tension. I moved away from Templeton and made tea to keep my hands busy. I wasn't energized or drained. But I was confused.

There was so much I wanted to talk about. What started as an exercise to learn what Templeton was – that is, to learn more about the magic lineage he inherited – turned into a revealing experience proving my theory was possible.

A witchline could be accessed by a magical practitioner outside of my family branch.

This suggested I could open my witchline to a non-biological heir.

I didn't ask if Templeton wanted tea. I assumed we both could use something to help us ground. I went with a chamomile blend, adding honey to sweeten it.

Setting the cup in front of him, I remained on the other side of the counter. The intimacy we'd shared left me feeling vulnerable and I needed a barrier between us. Templeton's expression gave away nothing.

"So, a Magician?" I began. "There aren't many of you left."

He shrugged. "We don't recognize each other. I've not met another."

"Which means your magic comes through your father's line."

"Yes." His cheek twitched.

Templeton's father had practiced black magic, and I wanted to respect his troubled feelings toward the man. "I know some about Magician lines, but I admit it's not much. He was also a –?"

"He was an Alchemist." Templeton's voice remained even. "He did not nurture his innate ability and chose a different path."

"Alchemy." It sort of made sense. The senior Templeton had commissioned the Crimson Stone. I could see a line stretching between the two worlds. "And do you know about his father?"

Templeton flexed his hands and I watched his elegant fingers encircle the teacup in front of him. He spun it slowly clockwise. His attention dropped to his cup and he blew across the surface of the tea.

I watched transfixed as the steam twirled in the air and started to take shape. The image of an old man appeared, rising above the cup. Suspended in the wet air, its features sharpened. The steam billowed and the face filled out, turning as if it were looking in my direction. I was struck by how much the aged man resembled... *Templeton*.

"My grandfather," Templeton acknowledged my unasked question. He fluttered his fingers around the cup of tea and the ghost of the older man dissolved into the air. "My paternal grandfather was a Sorcerer."

My mouth popped open. "A Sorcerer," I breathed. Realization washed over me. "Oh, *that's* how you secured membership with the Congress."

He inclined his head, a satisfied expression resting on his face.

"But wait," I hesitated. If Templeton was a close descendent of a Sorcerer and a member of the Congress, I had to assume the elders knew about his grandfather. Even a Magician's membership could be denied – witches weren't altogether sure of what to make of such beings. His membership had to be the result of the

Sorcerer connection. "Who at the Congress knows?"

Templeton raised a shoulder. "My membership was guaranteed at my birth by the late venerated witch Theodosius. His letter of approval was sealed by his own hand in magic before he died. The Congress elders only know I'm an approved member. They don't know why. They also know if I choose, I can legitimately press for recognition as an elder."

"What?" This day was full of surprises.

"I've never felt the need to push the envelope, as it were," he finished smugly. "But yes, if that's a direction I wanted to go, I could. However, I have no desire to take on such a tiresome responsibility. Besides, keeping the company of pretentious old witches doesn't appeal to me. I prefer to spend my time with a different kind of witch."

I felt my face grow warm. "Well, you never cease to amaze me, Templeton." I took a sip of my tea, reflecting on what he'd shared. I met his eyes. "Thank you for trusting me."

He nodded, looking away uneasily.

"Does Rabbit know about… I mean, does Rabbit know about you? About your family line?"

I asked. Rabbit was as shocked as we were last year when we'd learned Templeton's father had commissioned the creation of the Crimson Stone. As plugged in as Rabbit and the network were, they didn't know everything.

Templeton gave his head a little shake. "About your witchline."

"I guess it's my turn." I forced a laugh.

"Have you considered there are better ways to feed it than through pain?"

"It's been the most effective," I told him.

"Because that's what Guillaume likes," Templeton replied.

"It's also what I presented to him – to the Congress elders – when I made my case to study under him. I believed large gains could be achieved quickly by applying pain in the early stages of strengthening my witchline. I was right. When we used pleasure as a comparison, it was not as committed to the job." I wanted to be as open with Templeton as he was with me, but it was difficult. "When you're desperate to stop excruciating pain, you find ways to do what is demanded of you."

"Pain is a strong motivator, but I believe pleasure can be as persuasive. Are you not willing to learn other ways?" he challenged.

"Of course, I am. And I experiment," I said. "But so far what I achieved while studying with Guillaume has produced the most success."

Templeton motioned to the empty barstool next to him. "After what we experienced here, I believe I can help you. I can directly access your witchline."

I rubbed the back of my neck, nodding. "I'd be willing to try new things, but I still need to provide a demonstration of my work with Guillaume tomorrow. I need to show the elders what was accomplished. I can't say no. I don't have time to make the case for anything different."

He nodded. "I will be there tomorrow."

"As much as I want a friend in the audience..." Feeling lightheaded, I searched for the right words. "I don't want you to see what... God, I just don't want you to see." I covered my face, already imagining the indignities Guillaume would inflict upon me.

"Look at me. Please."

I dropped my hands, but balled them into fists, pressing my fingernails into my palms. The discomfort forced me to come back to the present.

"Yes?"

"I will be there tomorrow. The only thing I will see is your strength and your character. Nothing he will do to you can take that away." Templeton allowed himself to gather his thoughts. "And afterward, we'll find a different way to feed your witchline. Guillaume and the Congress be damned."

∞∞∞

While we waited for Rabbit, I returned to *Empire Tales for Children*. I opened the book to the next fairy tale.

∞∞∞

Dancing Shadows

The child walked until her feet were tired and the sun had run past the horizon twice. She could not find the river the Man with the Red Eyes said would lead to the land where the Shadows Dance.

"Perhaps I need to plant my own river?" she thought, looking at the finger the Man with the

Red Eyes had bitten. She picked at the scab on her wound until it bled and seeded the fertile soil below with droplets of blood.

A gush of water burst from the earth. The girl had no tools to weave a raft, so she jumped into the water and floated on her back. The current drew her spinning through the Empire, the river twisting and turning as it narrowed to a trickle where it fed the sea. When she climbed from the water, it was dark again and time to rest.

She laid her cheek against the ground and fell asleep. She dreamt of inky echoes bubbling under her ear: Light. Light. Light.

Instead of waking, the young girl plunged her hands into the earth and traveled into the Below. There she saw the thin shadows. They raced toward her, running up her legs, crawling across her belly, and slipping into her mouth.

Light! Light! Light! they wailed. The girl tasted their hunger and felt sad. She wanted to bring them the Light, but she couldn't see where it was hiding in the dark Below.

"Do you know of the Dancing Shadows?" she asked the thin shadows. "Maybe they can tell us where the Light has gone."

Light! Light! Light! they answered.

The girl felt her way through the murky otherworld. She called out to the Dancing Shadows in hopes they could hear her and would come help.

"Please be quiet," came the reply. "Do not wake the Beasties."

"Who is there?" She watched as the gloom swayed and weaved.

"We are the Dancing Shadows," it said. "Did you come to steal the magic from the Darkness?"

"I'm here to learn about the many truths and to find the Light," the child said. She did not tell the Dancing Shadows about her pretty stone.

"The Light does not come here anymore," it told her. "It stays above in the Between. But the Darkness has magic and can teach you about the many truths."

Secrets flowed into her ear as the Darkness wrapped its arms around her. It told her about the different truths. It said there were no untruths. The Darkness whispered she must let go of the One Truth. It was the only way to understand the other truths.

But the girl had promised to protect the One Truth and decided to leave the Darkness with its magic. She would not hide the pretty stone in the Below. She would need to find another place in plain sight in which to put it. Instead, she followed the thin shadows across the Below until they reached a sealed door.

Light... Light... Light... they whimpered.

The young child touched the three pieces of stone in her pocket. It was time to return to the Empire, so she woke up.

∞∞∞

Reading the book of fairy tales was like smoking a hookah while in the company of a caterpillar. Or drinking some of Anne's special tea. *Hmm.* My eyes strayed to the pantry door. Probably not a good idea to imbibe any natural pharmaceuticals at this point. My gaze next slid to Templeton. Notepad in hand, he stood staring out the new window over my kitchen sink. He absently spun a pencil between his fingers. I wondered if he'd ever tried Anne's tea? Now there was a picture: Templeton on tea. It would either be really amusing – or very annoying.

Probably the latter.

"You'd think these fairy tales would make more sense after what we learned in the Walled Zone," I said.

His eyes scanned my back yard for things we couldn't see. "Some of it is fluff. It hides the real messages."

"What do you think the 'one truth' is?"

He turned, crossing his arms and leaning back against the side of the counter. "You think there's only one truth?"

"You sound like the Magician in the *Black Sky* fairy tale," I replied.

"Do you believe there is only one truth?" He asked again.

I tapped my fingers on the counter. "Ultimately? No. I understand there's a gray area – that there are many lenses to look through. I think the author of the book of fairy tales was referring to something else. Maybe something specific."

"Perhaps." He was thoughtful.

"Did you notice the only beings referencing 'untruths' are the 'Beams of Light from Above' and the 'Darkness' in the Below? I'm assuming these 'untruths' are lies. The Beams said lies can tear apart the one truth. The Darkness simply says there are no lies but to let go of the one truth. The Magician tells her there are many truths, but never speaks of 'untruths' – or lies."

I chewed on my lower lip. "Same with the 'Man with the Red Eyes.' He only references many truths. I think this is important. When you were going through *Poems from the Black Sky*, was anything similar referenced?"

"Regarding the one truth or an untruth? Not explicitly in that language."

"Do you think the Magician-Poet is the same person who wrote *Poems from the Black Sky*?" I asked.

"I do not. In fact, I believe there were at least several authors contributing to the book of poems," he said.

That was interesting. "Why? Did the poems seem to have different voices or styles?"

"The styles ranged from narrative to free verse. There was one acrostic poem I found which might be connected to *The Man with the Red Eyes*." Templeton set his notepad on the counter and wrote:

Covered by vanilla stars
Lovers wrap stems and petals
Each careful breath is
Mouthed against lips
As pure as clouds

> *Trailing across darkened skies*
> *Innocence is bled away*
> *Seduction sows its secret seeds*

I read the poem silently.

"This is the acrostic poem," Templeton reminded me.

My brows knitted together. "Clematis? Like the flower?"

"Like the flowers surrounding the girl's altar in *The Man with the Red Eyes*," he said. "He ate one."

I read the poem a second time. "Are you saying the man deflowered her?"

"I think he took away her innocence." He blinked. "In the fairy tale there are references to the man biting her finger and making her bleed, among other provocative lines."

I returned to *The Man with the Red Eyes*, re-reading the tale. "This definitely has explicit overtones I didn't consider before. The altar he climbs on top of could be her... *womanhood*." I felt sheepish. It was such an archaic word, but I couldn't bring myself to speak clinically. "But I don't think the man literally took her virginity."

"Of course not," Templeton agreed. "But these references reinforce my belief the two books are related."

"That day," I winced, remembering our argument in the locked room at the Congress library. "Were you able to get through the entire book of poetry?"

"I was not." The expression on Templeton's face told me he remembered our unpleasant interaction, too.

"We'll need to go back then." I blew out a breath and saw a narrow lock of hair wisp by my eye. I brushed it away from my face with a finger. "In the meantime, where are you going tonight?" I asked the question as casually as I could.

Templeton smirked and shook his head.

"Fine," I said. "But the timing is odd. It's the only reason I asked."

He still said nothing. I'd have to accept that in spite of any revelations or connections shared between us today, he was still holding many secrets close to his chest.

It was fair. I kept my secrets, too.

I didn't see that changing any time soon.

Chapter 17

Templeton's reputation preceded him. Emily told me some of his backstory. He'd become a Salesman before he turned 30 – that's the age his door traveling powers should've come into play. But he was door traveling as a teenager, maybe even younger. It was no secret he was practicing magic when the Salesman Court agreed to recognize him as a Salesman at age 19. But they didn't understand *why* he was able to practice magic.

Because they didn't know what he was.

The origin of the Magician line in the Empire is murky at best. There are a few legends, but the most popular one claims the first Sorcerer mated with another magical being – its lineage unknown – and produced a male child who grew into what we know as a Magician.

Magicians are always male; the genes being

passed from father to son through the Y chromosome. However, having a Magician for a father did not automatically mean the son was one. It's like a muscle – it must be attended to and developed. The seed is there to be nurtured and grown. And yet, it was an elusive power to build. It came down to the individual man's abilities. It took time plus a lot of study and work. It needed to be an all-consuming obsession – and even then, there was no guarantee. A perfect storm of genetics, talent, fixation, self-awareness, and knowledge had to come together.

But Templeton achieved that mysterious level of mastery. It wasn't a bunch of tools and tricks – although I'm sure he had a hypothetical chest full of those. It was what he'd *become*. Templeton the child, born a door traveling Salesman from his mother's line, had morphed into Templeton the Magician via the genetic mutation provided by his father and his own tenacity and talent.

Becoming a Magician also affected his physiology. He was a changed being.

A Salesman *and* a Magician. *Oh, my god.*

And his grandfather was a Sorcerer.

Sorcerers are the unicorns of the Empire's

magical community. Ascending to such a plane of metaphysical existence is nearly impossible. Even though I knew I *might* cross paths with a Magician during my lifetime, I couldn't begin to imagine coming face-to-face with a Sorcerer – or even knowing someone who could count one in their family tree.

Here's where it gets tricky: Sorcerers are never born, they only evolve. They develop themselves. It's not the same process as a man becoming a Magician. There's no particular gene seeding the pot.

Sorcerers, when they appear, can emerge from any of the magical lines in the Empire. The fact Templeton became a Magician told me his grandfather also carried the gene. The grandfather thus would've been a Magician who further developed his magic – and ultimately his biology – into a Sorcerer. Like Magicians, physical compositions are changed as they become the advanced magical being.

Sorcerers guard their secret status. Only a handful in history have made their abilities known. The most famous one was absolute evil. It took another Sorcerer to defeat him, stepping out from the shadows to challenge him. She sacrificed herself, dying when she destroyed him.

This type of supernatural being could be male or female. The Sorcerer's magical line could be that of a Magician, a necromancer, a seer, or a witch. It's believed Magicians and witches have traditionally made up the majority of Sorcerers, but because of their secretive natures, who really knows?

Templeton's revelations were a lot to process. It didn't change how I felt about him one way or another, but it slipped some important pieces of the puzzle into place. I didn't want to take for granted how he'd shared such deep secrets with me. As I thought about what he'd admitted, more questions brewed inside me.

But I'd give him time to live with the reality of how I now knew what he was and about his family line. Truthfully, I wasn't ready to know all the answers to my questions. The more I knew about Templeton, the more precarious the ground under my feet felt.

∞∞∞

Rabbit arrived around 5 o'clock, stamping the snow off his boots in the entryway before warming up in front of the gas fireplace in the living room. He rubbed his hands together, bobbing his head once in thanks when I brought in a snort of vodka. I figured it'd give him a head start on shaking off the cold. Templeton's expression remained blank when I set the shot glass on the mantel, but I noted the barely perceptible lightening of his eye color.

"Anything on your end?" Rabbit asked.

I glanced at Templeton. "Nothing to share here. We've been going through the book of fairy tales."

"What about Emily?" Rabbit motioned toward Templeton. "How's she handling the news of Sebastian's return?"

"She wasn't too surprised," Templeton answered. "I made it clear he didn't seem to be interested in the Crimson Stone – or her."

"And she didn't question that?" Rabbit frowned.

Templeton crossed his arms. "She accepted what I told her, but she wants to be kept updated. She was curious to learn if the sixth door had been opened."

"She's not going to check for herself, is she?" Rabbit hung his head. "She never stays put."

"I anticipated that. I told her the fifth and sixth doors were not opened," Templeton replied.

"But we don't know that yet." I turned to Rabbit. "Or do we? Everything's been so crazy. The Rabbits you sent to investigate, did they see anything?"

Before Rabbit could respond, Templeton cut in. "I checked the compound before I went to Emily's."

"You did what?" I spun on him. "What were you thinking?"

He scowled. "If the doors had been opened, if that's how Sebastian came back to the Empire, we needed to know right away."

"And you're just telling me this now?" Son of a bitch.

"Okay, you two, enough." Rabbit rubbed his face. He seemed unwell. "The Rabbits I sent into the Walled Zone reported the same thing this afternoon. The doors haven't been opened – there's nothing unexpected in the quad. They also trained their equipment on the static coming from inside the compound and the pulses are getting louder."

Templeton and I still glared at each other. This whole taking off on his own and not telling us what he was doing wasn't going to work for me. We all needed to be on the same page. We all needed to know what the others were doing. Exasperated, I turned my attention to Rabbit.

"Can they pinpoint the static or the pulses?" I asked.

"The static is all over the compound," Rabbit said. He tossed back the vodka before moving to the chair and sitting down. He pulled a red knit cap from his head, running a chapped hand through his curls. "One of my guys thinks the pulsing is coming directly from the center of the quad though."

"Maybe Sebastian opened and closed the doors." I lifted a hand. "Or the doors aren't even involved, and he came back from the Below another way." The simple truth was we didn't know.

"Or was conjured?" Rabbit's brows knitted together.

"You'd have to know his name to conjure him," I replied. "Who'd know it? Who'd know Sebastian became a demon?" I shook my head. "No, he wasn't conjured."

"Unless someone is working with another demon," Templeton mused. "Someone could conjure a demon and if powerful enough, compel it to open their book of names."

I was still angry with him. "And then they conjured Sebastian for what purpose?"

"Whatever domain he has power over."

"And then he escaped?" I huffed. "No. I'm not buying it."

"You don't think we should consider all the possibilities?" Templeton pushed.

Rabbit continued as if Templeton and I weren't in the middle of a disagreement. "My guys are staying in the compound for now. They're going to keep an eye on the quad in case the doors appear while they try to strip away the static and learn more about the pulses."

"Do they know about Sebastian being a demon? They shouldn't approach him if they see him," I told Rabbit. "I know your crew's experienced and well-trained, but a demon is dangerous. Unless it's being controlled with magic, it's a force you don't want to deal with." I blew out a breath. "I mean, I'm a witch and look how easy it was for him to get the upper hand this morning."

Rabbit's expression was grim. "We won't let it happen again. And yeah, my crew knows not to engage without backup." His somber eyes flicked to Templeton. "When are you leaving?"

Templeton was still annoyed following our conversation. "Now."

I bit my tongue.

"Alright. I'll text you if I have any updates," Rabbit told him. "I'll be in touch either way tomorrow first thing."

"I won't be available for most of the night," Templeton replied. "But I'll expect a message in the early morning."

"Yeah, it'll be there." Rabbit sighed, closing his eyes.

My irritation with Templeton waned as I surveyed my friend. I moved to Rabbit's side, squatting by the chair. I studied his face, letting a slip of my power reach out to touch his natural energy. Magical being or not, everyone is surrounded by their own personal vibration and I could sense when it was off.

A sour taste formed on my tongue.

Rabbit was sick.

∞∞∞

Templeton left shortly after I tucked a blanket

over Rabbit's chest. He didn't argue. He asked me to let him rest, saying he only needed a catnap and would be fine afterward. I pushed the ottoman under his feet.

I didn't say much to Templeton. He was back to his reticent self. Before door traveling to wherever he'd planned to go, he'd tersely reminded me he'd be present for the demonstration at the Congress the next day. He hesitated at the pantry door. We stared at each other for a beat. I lifted my hand in question. But instead of adding anything else, he turned and left my home.

Shedding my frustration with Templeton, I concentrated on putting together a healing concoction for Rabbit. I practiced herbal magic alongside my fire magic, but I didn't know the extent of his illness. My plan was to keep the brew to the basics, but as I began, I had an overwhelming urge to use milk thistle, making a potion with ground leaves and seeds. It would infuse while he slept. I'd need to get some answers from him so I could help.

For the first time that day I was alone – *sort of* – and my house was quiet. I was glad. I needed to process everything I'd experienced.

I also had a startling realization: I wanted to do

a reading for myself.

Months had passed since I last looked at my life through my Tarot cards. The thought of doing it now made my heart thump impatiently. I touched my chest, sensing its urgency. I was being drawn to my cards for a reason.

∞∞∞

When I read Tarot, I skip a common practice and only read cards right side up. If I deal a card, or a client pulls a card and it's upside down, I turn it. There are 78 cards in a deck and multiple combinations of cards for a spread. I'm not limiting possible meanings; I'm narrowing down the message I want to offer to the querent.

My Aunt Lettie is the first person who taught me how to read Tarot. My lessons began when I was a teenager. She explained the most common meanings of the cards, then assigned a study of each. I started with the 22 cards in the Major Arcana, then went on to explore the 56 in the Minor Arcana with its court cards. My daily lessons included pulling a card for myself in the morning and then interpreting the mystical connection to my mundane acts during the day.

Aunt Lettie would quiz me: Did my day bend and turn in the ways it did because the card suggested the outcome? Or was my day manipulated by my own acts based upon what I dealt myself from the deck? Did I align with the card, or work to bring about a different result?

I asked her which was the correct answer – and how would I know?

She told me when I could answer the question for myself, I would begin to truly know Tarot.

For me, Tarot is art and art delivers messages. I might look at an image and see one thing while another person sees something completely different. In my experience, if an image comes to represent something to you, that's how you will consistently interpret it. You might change the lens you use to look at it based upon the other images around it. You will also bring your history, your experience, and your current state of mind to the table when you are doing a reading. It's not a precise science; it is an art. To master it, you needed to spend time with it.

Tarot was art I could understand. I had a natural affinity for it. Over time Aunt Lettie allowed me to read for her clients as a bonus when they came for their regular appointments.

While Aunt Lettie excelled at a broader perspective, I could zero in on the specifics surrounding a querent's question. It was then I developed my own habits of card placement and only reading them right side up.

I used my magic to take a peek at a person's energy, tapping against it with mine to understand the motivation driving the question they asked. This was key to helping me find the right interpretation for their query.

A successful reading happens when the querent is honest and willing to be open about what is happening in and around them. I've been fortunate; only a handful of cynics have wasted my time over the years. Ultimately, it was their time lost. I couldn't help them discern the message they sought if they wouldn't come to my table honestly. I wasn't interested in performing some sort of trick and I am not a charlatan. The people who weren't willing to be engaged typically lived outside the Empire. Here in Matar – and throughout the Empire – divination is a respected artform.

Over the years I'd developed an extensive client roster. Some came weekly – my absolute maximum for seeing a particular person.

Most regulars came monthly, with the occasional extra appointment if something important cropped up in their lives. Occasionally I'd pick up a fresh client. Once I started reading at *Coffee Cove*, I met a bunch of people who were more interested in a passing reading than anything long term. These appointments were relatively short and I could offer them at a lower rate. I enjoyed these mostly lighthearted readings. My longtime clients, however, paid me well for longer sessions. We worked together to shape their lives through honest discussion, reflection, and the catalyst created by exploring Tarot together.

I had many decks and clients might try several before finding the right artwork. It needed to resonate with them. With new clients, I tended to guide them to a particular deck based upon what I picked up through casual conversation. Sometimes I offered several choices to see what they were drawn to for a first reading. With my frequent flyers, we'd switch off to a more appropriate deck if the query was a match for a different style or theme.

The deck I kept at home for myself was one I never used when reading for others. It came into my possession nearly two decades ago. I took good care of it, but the deck was beautifully worn – a combination of the natural oil from my skin and the supernatural imprint of my personal energy.

The cards were crafted by an artist I met in college. A friend of mine suggested we serve as subjects for an art class. I agreed, with a caveat being I wasn't willing to sit as a nude model – she'd be the one shaking off her skivvies. Unfortunately for me when I arrived the first evening, I learned my friend had begged off sick. I still was unwilling to pose naked for the assembled group of students, but I compromised. I did shed all my clothes, but I covered up my front with a white sheet. I sat with my bare back to the class, my then waist-length hair pulled over one shoulder.

In the end, it was a wonderful experience. The students were talented and respectful, producing amazing sketches. Afterward I was approached by one of them. Niccolò was my age and it was clear he was a gifted artist. He asked if I'd be willing to sit for him privately, and of course, I said no.

Fate intervened. We found ourselves in a common class and stuck in the same group project. I got to know him over the course of several weeks, and when he asked if I'd come to his studio to see his work, I couldn't say no. He was so eager. After visiting his cozy space, I agreed to sit for a few more poses. I also dropped the sheet for him.

Both of us were scraping by as college students and he couldn't pay me to be his model. Instead, he created a deck of Tarot cards with his sketches and filled them with brilliant colors. He used my likeness on all the Major Arcana cards and most of the Minor Arcana ones, except for the aces and court cards. Niccolò blended a mix of traditional symbols and my own everyday life. He revealed me as a witch in some of the cards, but almost always portrayed me as a student. He managed to create a timeless image of me. When I looked at the cards, the much younger version of me seemed as familiar now as she was all those years ago. I could still perceive the student in the scenes as me.

Niccolò and I were occasional lovers, and I did care about him. But it was nothing more than two young people exploring the convergence of art and passion. Eventually graduation came and it was time to say goodbye. He took pieces and parts of me in his sketches and paintings when he left the Empire.

I retrieved my special deck from upstairs. I carried a cup of tea into my dining room before lighting a pair of white candles. Sandalwood incense burned on the buffet and I brought a lamp into the room since the overhead light wasn't an option after the morning's blowup.

I spread a white scarf across the end of my table and gently shuffled the Tarot cards. The incense and soft light helped me to relax. As I mingled the cards, I focused on the relationship I had with them – with the art – and connected with the energy surrounding the deck. When I was ready to begin, I placed it facedown in the middle of the scarf, hovering my hand over the top card. I listened for the hum.

When the soft vibration grew, I snapped my fingers above the deck. The hop of the stack was barely perceptible, but I saw it. The card representing the querent – me – was ready. I flipped over the top card and chuckled: The Hermit, Major Arcana, card number nine.

On it, Niccolò had drawn an image of me surrounded by books and candles while I studied.

The Hermit served as my querent card most frequently. A part of me wondered if I not-so-subconsciously called it up.

I laid out a nine-card spread I dubbed 'life right now.' I placed the querent card in the center before dealing two cards to the left – what was driving me; two to the space below The Hermit – where I stood; two more cards above it – what I needed to consider; and finally, two to the right – a likely outcome from where I stood at this exact moment.

All cards were dealt facing up. As I placed two cards in each of the four spots, I overlapped them in the order they were pulled: the first card being the situation, the second card alluding to what influenced it.

I surveyed the cards revealed in the spread, noticing a predominance of swords. *No shocker there*, I thought wryly. Many swords in a spread indicated difficulty or suffering.

I pressed my lips into a tight line, picking up the two cards showing what was driving me: the Nine of Swords covered by the Three of Swords.

I'd come to truly hate the Three of Swords. It represented heartbreak. The Nine of Swords revealed a Lucie tossing restlessly in bed, swords pointed at her body. The heartache was not letting go. Or maybe I was not letting go of it.

I skipped ahead to what I needed to consider. The cards placed above The Hermit were more interesting. The Magician covered the Seven of Wands. The Seven of Wands showed me writing in a notebook at a table outside on a sunny day. The scene reminded me of the picnic tables located in a park near my college. I spent many an afternoon studying and writing there. On the card, I held a wand in my free hand. Six other wands pointed at me from the ground. A man stood over me, his hand resting on mine, his fingertips touching the wand I held. He studied the notebook as I wrote.

This same man appeared throughout the deck. His features weren't particularly distinct, and it wasn't anyone I recognized when Niccolò presented the deck to me. When I asked him who the man was, he shook his head. The figure wasn't based on anyone he knew.

The Seven of Wands in my deck represents the querent successfully working through a series of challenges, but it's a reminder there's someone ready to help if I ask. The querent doesn't have to go it alone.

It wasn't lost on me that the card covering the Seven of Wands was The Magician. In its broadest meaning, this card represents using the tools at hand and embracing the path you've chosen. In other words, the querent has the tools she needs and already knows how to use them. She can shape her destiny. Niccolò had drawn me in the role of The Magician. The four suits of the Minor Arcana surrounded me as I held a book to my chest, my eyes cast upwards.

But sometimes the Tarot can be quite literal in its message. After learning about Templeton, I couldn't help but think of him – the Magician he admitted to being. Was the man in the Seven of Wands also a Magician? Was that why The Magician card appeared in this position?

Two more cards from the swords suit appeared below The Hermit in the space 'where I stood.' I groaned, skipping them to review the two cards in the outcome position.

I picked up The Tower and made a face. This was my least favorite Tarot card. My experience with it was never good.

In other decks I've owned, the imagery found on The Tower card typically included a building in an active state of destruction. It might be on fire with people jumping from the windows, or it might sit in the center of a storm, its walls blown apart. It was always something terrifying. If the imagery didn't include an actual tower, it might be a massive tree on the receiving end of a lightning strike. Fortunately, this card rarely appeared when I conducted a reading, but when it did, something very bad was going to happen. The Tower in an outcome position usually meant that whatever it was, it was going to be life-changing and hard to avoid.

In the deck Niccolò created for me, The Tower card was especially different from anything I'd ever seen. An orgy appeared on the card. In the middle of the chaos, I sat naked from the waist up, my arms wrapped around my chest, my hair a mess, my head down. The lower half of my body, except for my bare feet, was wrapped in a white sheet. My eyes were closed and I was alone in the center of the lust surrounding me. The floor in the picture was strewn with clothing, but there was a clear path leading from the bottom of the card to my feet.

I asked Niccolò why he chose to represent The Tower in this way. I remember him taking the card from my hand and studying it, a shadow dropping over his face. He told me to make sure I was always on the right path, or life could turn ugly for me. I'd be forever changed and nothing could undo what had been done. I could only live with the aftermath.

I returned to the spread before me. The Two of Chalices covered The Tower in the outcome position. Two versions of me stood facing each other in this card; the idealized version looked out from a mirror. A harmony between the two was being sought.

Both Lucies held a glass of wine. The one in the mirror smirked at the Lucie peering into it. The Lucie on the outside smiled shyly back, lifting a glass to herself in a toast. A choice needed to be made.

"Choose wisely, Lucie," I muttered. "Make sure you're on the right path. Make sure you're doing the right thing." I touched each card a second time, reflecting on the imagery and applying it to what was happening around me. My thinning witchline, dealing with the demands of the Congress, Guillaume... Not to mention an ex-lover who'd returned as a demon. Then there was the likely danger on the other side of the fifth and sixth doors.

I had to make sure I traveled the right path to deal with all these problems.

My eyes wandered back to the Three of Swords. I worried my bottom lip between my teeth. With so many swords showing up in the reading along with The Tower, it was possible the spread suggested death.

"Lucie?" Rabbit tapped on the open door. He sagged against the door jamb.

"Hey," I startled. I gathered the cards from the table, shuffling them and signaling the end of the reading. Now it was time to let my subconscious work on the imagery. "Are you feeling better?"

"Oh, yeah," Rabbit dismissed me, standing taller and wrinkling his nose. He waved a hand. "It's nothing. A bug."

A card popped out of my hand, landing on the table face up. It was another message from the swords suit.

Deception.

Rabbit was lying to me.

Chapter 18

I fed Rabbit vegetable soup for dinner after convincing him to drink the milk thistle potion. He pulled faces the whole time he sipped at it, eventually deciding to get it over with and chugging it down. I promised to brew some more for him.

I didn't push him about being sick. Rabbit wouldn't tell me anyway. Maybe when we got to the other side of all these nightmares, I'd get him to open up to me.

After dinner, I walked through the entire house, from the basement up to the second floor, casting a spell of protection. As I chanted, I used a water bottle to spritz a mix of consecrated water and Solomon's Seal infused in olive oil. The Solomon's Seal would help guard against Sebastian's return. It'd have to do until I could get to the herbalist and pick up actual plant roots.

I'd wanted to burn some Asafoetida as incense for another layer of protection, but the minute I removed the cap from the bottle, Rabbit started to gag.

It wasn't called Devil's Dung for nothing.

The Solomon's Seal was a first line of defense in the short term. After I put the demonstration with Guillaume behind me, I'd review my magical supplies and craft a spell to keep *any* demon from breaking into my home. I'd also learn the command needed to banish Sebastian if it came to that. If he returned, I needed to have the power to send him back into the Below. I'd never performed an exorcism but being prepared would bolster my confidence when the time came.

We went to bed early, Rabbit agreeing to sleep in the spare bedroom near mine without complaint. I was glad. He'd spent too many nights trying to fit on my small sofa. Before turning in, he checked with the network. There was nothing to report.

The phone Sebastian stole from me was still at his cabin. Whether he was with it or not, we couldn't know.

Sleep didn't come right away, and I kept my

bedroom door open. From the spare, I heard Rabbit's soft snore. It was comforting. I pulled the blankets up to my chin. While my mind ran through flashes of what had happened and what hell was to come, I curled into a ball. I needed to sleep.

Tomorrow would be here soon enough.

∞∞∞

I tossed and turned for most of the night. Rabbit seemed better in the morning, but his coloring was still off. His skin was sallow, and he moved as if his muscles ached. I noted he rolled his shoulders often, as if he were trying to shake off a heavy blanket. I made us both eggs while he scrolled through the messages on his phone, elbow on the counter, chin in the palm of his hand.

There was no new information from the Rabbits monitoring the quad in the Fringe's old compound. Things remained the same in the Walled Zone. The static continued, the pulses under it.

Rabbit messaged Templeton to tell him there wasn't an update. Templeton didn't reply, but

Rabbit confirmed he could see the message had been read on the Salesman's end. The battery on the phone Sebastian took from me had finally died. We could no longer track him even if he still carried the device.

My stolen phone was replaced by another one from the network. Rabbit worked his technological magic, entering the line of code so we could text each other. We agreed I'd leave it at home when it was time to go to the Congress building. The fact Guillaume had sensed the phone I'd carried in my purse when I was at the gala made me realize I wouldn't be able to conceal it from him.

Rabbit would drive me – we'd take my car. As a Rabbit he wouldn't be allowed on the property, but he planned to wait for me across the street. He took a moment to crack his neck, putting one of his big paws on his chin and turning his head from side to side. He laughed. He'd give the gate security something to fixate on while I was in the building.

Prior experience with Guillaume taught me I'd be tired when we completed the demonstration. Often, after our more intense sessions, I'd fall asleep immediately. I'd wake up later either on the floor where he'd left me or in his bed.

I preferred the floor.

A part of me held onto the hope the demonstration *would* only be a sample of how we did what we did. The elders would surely set limits. I needed to leave the building on my own two feet with my head held high. Loren understood. Hopefully his influence would buy me some mercy.

∞∞∞

Rabbit didn't talk during the drive across Matar to the Congress of Empire Witches. I was grateful. I didn't want to discuss what was about to happen. Mindless chatter would've sent me over the edge. Instead, he flipped through the few Empire radio stations, landing on one playing a sweet folk song. I sent a curious look in his direction and he shrugged, his eyes never leaving the windshield. He sang in a quiet tone. I closed my eyes and listened to his soothing voice, leaning my head against the window.

Less than a half hour later, Rabbit pulled up to the curb in front of the Congress building. Before I could even open the car door, a security guard stepped out from behind the gate, motioning for Rabbit to move.

"Yeah, big man," Rabbit muttered under his breath. He gave the guard the finger.

"Ignore him," I told Rabbit. "Okay, I'm going. Don't say anything to me. I can't handle a pep talk right now." I opened the door. I felt Rabbit's hand gliding from my shoulder and down my arm as I climbed out. His hand rested on the seat I'd vacated. I turned and offered a small smile. "Thanks."

"I'll be waiting for you across the street," he promised. His eyes glittered angrily as the security guard rapped the hood of my RAV4 with his knuckles and pointed down the street. "Fucking tool."

"Across the street," I repeated, ignoring the guard. I shut the door and stepped back as Rabbit pulled away. After giving the security guard my name, I was allowed to pass when he confirmed my 'appointment' on his roster.

Because I was going before the elders, I'd dressed conservatively in a long-sleeved navy sweater dress, its neckline resting at my collarbone. I'd loosely wrapped a paisley silk scarf around my neck, its colors swirling in shades of gold and brown, highlighted by a hue matching my dress. A camel-colored, vintage blazer served as an extra layer of warmth under my peacoat. The hemline of the fitted sweater dress landed below my knees, and I'd opted for low-heeled, knee-high leather boots in tan. Underneath it all, I wore a thick pair of tights. My hair was pulled into a tasteful French twist at the nape of my neck, secured with a dozen pins.

I passed through the wards and approached the blind being waiting to the side of the doors leading into the main hall. I transferred my purse to my other shoulder and pushed up the layers of sleeves on my right arm. I bared my wrist as her fingertips tickled over it. The black tattoo under my skin surfaced briefly, proving I was a witch.

Before the woman granted me access, I spoke. "Was it a demon the other night? The one who was looking for me?"

She ran a whitish tongue over the lips of her toothless grin. Sightless eyes peered into mine. "The demon came through there." She lifted an aged hand, stretching a crooked finger. I turned and noted an unmarked door in the wall near the entrance. No knob appeared on the surface facing us. I assumed it could only be opened from the other side.

Did this mean Sebastian door traveled into the building? I believed it was a possibility no matter what Congress elders thought. I turned back to the being. She held my hand in hers, keeping my wrist exposed. "Why didn't you tell anyone a demon breached the wards?"

"I was not asked," she answered. Her fingertips returned to my wrist. She stroked my skin, calling up the tattoo repeatedly. It was eerily soothing.

"But you told *me* he was here," I argued cautiously.

"He is a brother to my kind. He looked for you. He still seeks you," she crooned.

Behind me, I heard another witch approaching. "If he comes here again, you must tell someone. Okay? He's not supposed to be here."

"You are not like the other witches." The blind being smacked her lips, releasing her grasp on my hand. "You are the light."

"I'm what?" I wasn't sure I heard right. The hair on the back of my neck rose.

The witch waiting for me to move past the blind being coughed impatiently into his hand.

"What did you say?" I whispered.

The laughter erupting from her throat was drenched in phlegm as she dismissed me. "You may enter, witch."

∞∞∞

Loren waited on the other side of the doors. The revelation from the blind being shook me – something I certainly didn't need considering my reason for being at Congress. But I kept the information to myself. The demon was Sebastian. If the elders learned this, it would only make things worse. It was bad enough Guillaume knew. I blanched as Loren took my arm and began to lead me. Had Guillaume told anyone? Or was he keeping the information to himself?

"Let me check my coat," I started.

"There's no need," Loren replied. "Guillaume is requiring you to change your clothes. This way. Hurry."

"He's what?" I pulled my arm away. "What do you mean?"

"Lucie." Loren's normally shrewd eyes blinked rapidly. "I don't know what happened, but the elders were informed you gave up all control of today's demonstration. Is this true?"

I took a breath. "I gave up the right to choose the demonstration method. But I didn't agree to giving up 'all' control."

"But why? Why would you let Guillaume decide on how to demonstrate what you've accomplished?"

I didn't answer.

"Do I want to know?" He noted the tiny cut at the corner of my mouth.

I shook my head.

He reached for my arm again, the corners of his own mouth drooping. "Come. Let's get this over with."

∞∞∞

Before Loren left me in a private dressing room located deep in the bowels of the building, I asked if he'd seen Templeton. He had not.

The room was sparsely furnished, with a mostly empty wardrobe, a chair and vanity, and a full-length mirror. The dressing room was typically used by witches changing from their street attire into clothing designed for magical purposes. Or they might dress in costumes for certain rituals. They might not wear anything at all under their ceremonial robes.

The garment Guillaume wanted me to wear was similar to clothing I sometimes wore during sessions in France – a simple cotton shift with short sleeves. The hemline fell to mid-calf. Ornate embroidery covered it, containing magical symbols, including Guillaume's own personal sigil. The fabric and the embroidery were both white. When I pulled it over my head, I felt the magic he'd imbued into the material run over my skin. It was akin to having his hands roam my body. I resisted the shiver threatening to crawl down my spine. He was already exercising control to keep me off guard.

I'd removed my underclothes without a second thought. I knew what he'd do if I entered the room wearing my bra and underwear. He'd make me remove them in front of the elders. That was an additional humiliation I didn't need. I didn't bother putting my boots back on either. Barefoot, I waited, wrapping my arms around myself in the cool room. I looked into the mirror, smarting when I realized the material was thin enough to reveal the shadows of my areolas and a hint of the dark hair between my legs.

It would be wise to focus on the bright side. At least I wasn't naked.

Loren had also directed me to pull the pins from my hair. Guillaume wanted it loose. I sat at the vanity and undid the twist, placing the pins on the narrow surface. I combed my fingers through my hair, letting it fall over my shoulders.

Shortly after changing, a tap at the door alerted me to Loren's return. His gaze passed over the clothing I wore, noting the symbols in the embroidery. "He's not going to make this easy on you, is he?"

"I wouldn't expect anything less from him," I answered, taking his hand. We left the room and I let him lead me through several dim corridors. I became disoriented following the many turns we'd made in the winding hallways. I'd need to be guided back to the dressing room when this was all over.

As we approached a door at the end of a long hall, Loren stopped. "I'm sure you've never been in this part of the building. The rooms are used for certain magical activities and sometimes there are observers. On the other side of this door, you'll find a plain white room – walls, floor, and ceiling. I'm sorry, but it's not carpeted," he apologized. "Your feet are probably cold even now."

"I'm fine," I assured him, curling my toes. "What else do I need to know?"

"A table and a chair – maybe two – are the only furnishings. The floor is tiled. One of the walls is half glass. On the other side of it, nine elders will watch from a separate room. The seating is raised slightly, similar to a theater. That room will be dimmed as some elders want to keep their attendance to this demonstration private. But I will be in there supporting you."

He continued. "This separation between practitioners and elders is intentional so the magic happening in the room can be secured in a proper environment. Guillaume will put up his own wards. No one will enter the room while you two are working. But we will be able to see and hear everything."

As Loren reached for the doorknob, he glanced over his shoulder. A trio of witches approached – an older woman and two men. The men were not immediately familiar, but the woman was.

The Acton matriarch. Loren put his arm around my shoulders and guided me into the room, the other witches entering behind us.

Guillaume was already inside. He sat in one of the chairs at the table, browsing through a local newspaper. He didn't bother to look up. We all waited. One of the male witches behind me coughed into his fist. I turned, realizing he was the same man who'd stood behind me at the ritual of recognition. Dark-skinned with an impeccably groomed beard, he was younger than most of the elders I'd met – perhaps in his mid-40s. Nervous, he fidgeted as he avoided making eye contact with me.

My attention flitted to the other man. If forced to guess, he was probably in his late 50s. His graying blond hair was kept short to hide a retreating hairline. Well-dressed in a charcoal suit, his green eyes examined the symbols in the embroidery of my clothing. His lips flattened into a pink line. My instinct told me he struggled to understand them.

The Acton matriarch, dressed in an unremarkable black suit, ignored me. Amused, she waited for Guillaume to acknowledge us. She realized his game. What she didn't know is I understood it, too. Guillaume wanted to show me he didn't need to answer to Congress elders, which meant he was free to do what he wanted. The older woman assumed she was supporting his attempt.

I spent a year with Guillaume. Out of all the people in the room, I knew him the best.

If I disobeyed him, he'd punish me.

If I displayed weakness or fear, he'd punish me.

I gently removed Loren's arm from my shoulders and crossed the room. "Guillaume," I began, clasping my hands in front of me. "It's 1 o'clock. I know how you feel about tardiness. Are you ready to begin?"

He kept reading the paper, but he smiled, pursing his lips at the same time. He knew I was on to him. A moment later he lifted his eyes, peering at me over a set of reading glasses. "I always enjoy our sessions more when you are eager for them."

"I'm eager to complete the demonstration for *our* elders." I offered a thin smile in return. "After all, that's why we're here. To prove what we accomplished and to explain how it will serve *our* community."

He shook the paper once before folding it. Inhaling through his nose, he stood. "Then let's begin."

"A few things first," interrupted the Acton matriarch. "As we discussed, Guillaume, we want a clear explanation as to how you've accomplished what you've claimed. What we cannot see with our own eyes, you must prove through magic." The hostile woman adjusted her suit jacket and spared me a scornful look. "You need to prove your thinning witchline was in fact strengthened."

I didn't answer. Arguing with the woman was pointless. Let Guillaume deal with her.

Guillaume moved behind me and rested his hands on my shoulders. Resisting the urge to pull away, I refused to react to his firm touch. "If you will take your seats in the audience, I will cast my wards and we can begin."

"You may put up your wards after we leave. You will start your demonstration when I direct you to do so from the other side of the glass." She didn't wait for a response. "Gentlemen? Follow me." The woman abruptly turned and left the room.

Loren paused at the door before following the others. He didn't say anything to Guillaume but offered encouragement to me. "You'll do well, Lucie. I'll be on the other side of the glass watching. Michelle and I are proud of you. Remember that. I'll meet you right after you're finished in here." He turned away and exited, leaving me with a sudden lump in my throat. His kindness, though well-intentioned, rocked my confidence.

Guillaume sensed the change in my composure. His right hand pulled my hair aside and he bent closer to speak directly into my ear. "He's like a father to you, isn't he? A surrogate after your papa was taken from you as a child?"

I stilled. I never discussed my father's death. *Ever.*

"It must've been hard," he tsked. "But it wasn't your fault, Lucie. Not really." He released me, returning to the table where a briefcase sat by the newspaper. He opened it, pulling out two bottles of water and a few items he would use to set up his wards.

Guillaume's words chilled me. My heart knocked against my chest and my mouth grew dry. We'd *never* discussed anything significant about my parents. He only knew what I'd told him – they were both witches. They lived in

Matar. I had few memories of them. They died in separate accidents when I was very young. *Accidents.*

"May I have a drink of water?" I croaked.

He motioned absently to the bottles he'd placed on the table and I took one, turning the cap with a jittery hand. I sipped the water, silently telling myself to remain calm.

"Lucie, stand in the middle of the room and face the glass," Guillaume directed before I was ready. "Leave the water on the table."

Reluctantly, I set the bottle down and did as I was told. My throat still felt tight. To distract myself, I tried to see the men and women on the other side of the glass. A couple more bodies filed in as I watched. I couldn't see faces in the gloomy room, but it appeared eight elders were present. I could make out three men and one woman in the first row. I was fairly certain the woman was the Acton matriarch, and I knew Loren would be up front, too. I could see the shapes of four more elders in the row behind them. That meant one elder was missing from the group. So was Templeton. Despite his promise, I didn't believe he'd be allowed to join in observing us.

Guillaume moved around the room, raising his protective wards. I noted he chose a particularly challenging spell. The magic he cast was strong – overkill for what we'd be doing. His voice was low, and although Loren indicated they'd be able to hear what was said in the room, I doubted they could understand what he was saying.

It took longer than I anticipated, but he finally completed the task. He returned to the center of the room, standing at my side.

"Rest assured nothing can get in," he told me. "And nothing can get out."

I tried to see into the room beyond the glass as Guillaume addressed the elders. As he spoke, his hands formed several shapes and signs. He weaved a circle around us to help keep our magical work stable.

"The Congress asked Lucie and I to demonstrate how we achieved the goal of strengthening her thinning witchline. This is a problem for all the witchlines in the Empire, save for a few. The work we conducted in the year Lucie served as my student proved a witchline can in fact be strengthened. Lucie's theory of applying pain to produce an extreme level of energy to redirect back into her own witchline bore out." Guillaume paused, testing the invisible walls around us.

Movement in the back of the observation room caught my eye. The door opened, a slice of light coming into the room. Two people entered, the door closing quickly behind them. Both appeared to be men. They stood in the deep shadows instead of taking a seat. *Security?* I wondered. I squinted, studying the taller of the two. I could barely see the outline of his frame. His arms moved in the limited light, his hands appearing at his sides. I sucked in a breath. Was the man holding a top hat?

Guillaume heard the sharp intake of breath and sent a look of warning in my direction. I dropped my eyes to the floor. I didn't want him to know Templeton might be watching.

"As you all know, Lucie surrendered her option to choose the methods for today's demonstration. I have prepared several examples to educate – and perhaps even entertain some of you." Guillaume snapped his fingers and pointed to the floor.

Grinding my teeth, I knelt as gracefully as I could. I stared at the wall under the glass.

"Forehead on the floor, Lucie," he ordered.

I leaned forward, placing my palms on the cold floor. I lowered my face, touching my forehead to the tile. My breasts pressed against the hard surface. I kept my knees together.

"The obedience of a student is paramount." Guillaume circled me. "Cheek to the floor, Lucie."

These positions were familiar. I wondered if he planned on running through all of them. I turned my head, resting my cheek on the tile and closing my eyes. I waited.

I felt the sole of his boot press against the side of my head. He rested his foot on me as he continued. The humiliation of submitting to him in front of others was far worse than the uncomfortable position.

Guillaume continued. "First, we will open her witchline. As witches, you know how difficult this is to do. In fact, I'm sure most of you – if not all – have never been able to do it. Lucie and I work together to achieve this. I stabilize the environment around it and prevent it from closing when Lucie switches her focus. From there, Lucie feeds her witchline with her own energy after it's been raised to its limit. Doing this on her own, she'd need to split her effort between the two acts. Even if she were able to accomplish both the opening and the feeding, the lack of concentration needed to drive her energy into the witchline would prevent any significant benefit. It would be pointless."

My neck was starting to ache. I rolled a shoulder to relieve some tension. Guillaume increased the pressure of his foot against my cheek.

"Once the witchline is open and stable, we'll move to feeding it. Imagine a force-feeding. The raw power naturally flowing from witchline to witch is driven back." Guillaume's foot shifted against my cheek, and I could tell he was talking with his hands. "This requires a significant amount of strength behind the energy coming from the witch. This is why when Lucie applied to study with me, she outlined using pain as a motivator in her proposal. She understood pain would be the most effective. Lucie understands pleasure lacks the necessary power to drive energy back into a witchline."

"Unh," I grunted as his foot seesawed back and forth. I crammed my lips together when he abruptly stopped talking. He'd heard me.

Guillaume removed his foot and squatted. I felt a hand play with my hair. He wrapped a thick length around his fingers, pulling me upward as he stood. He kept me on my knees, however, holding me in place by my hair as he again addressed our audience. "I've been asked to keep demonstrations using physical pain to a minimum today. A shame. The more I apply, the better she responds. Lucie knows how to let her natural response to pain build before releasing it as energy at the precise moment. She's adept at recognizing the peak of the build on her own. The energy then pours out of her and she directs it into her witchline. She can tolerate a considerable amount of pain – more than I've seen young witches accept previously." He sighed. "But I agree. We should try to limit the use of physical pain."

Wary, I looked up at Guillaume.

"Too much physical pain and we won't be able to properly demonstrate other methods today." The glimmer in Guillaume's eyes was particularly cruel. "Pain expressed during intense emotional distress can be exceptionally productive if you tap the right source. We'll show how emotional pain can produce an increasing amount of energy as we progress from shame, to recollections of personal tragedy, and finally, to intense fear."

When I was his pupil, we touched on using emotional pain, but it was nowhere near as effective as physical pain. Because of this, we didn't use it often. What was Guillaume doing?

He released me. "Sit up straight, Lucie. Hands on thighs, palms up. Prepare yourself. We're going to begin."

I did as I was told, ignoring our audience and lowering my eyes. I slipped into the practice of centering myself through deep breathing, pulling in long breaths through my nose before letting them out through my mouth. I might be afraid of what Guillaume had planned, but I was also his best student and we did something remarkable together. We were going to prove it now. The elders would not be able to deny it.

"Earlier I cast a circle to support the use of impression magic. You'll be able to see a representation of Lucie's witchline," Guillaume explained. "You will see it prior to the feeding and then afterward. This should remove any doubts that have been voiced." His last comment was directed to the earlier remark made by the head of the Acton family.

I had to admit, impression magic was a brilliant idea and something he excelled at performing. He could be quite creative. Guillaume truly desired to prove our success. The opportunity to hurt me was simply a bonus.

Guillaume rose his own energy – I could sense it immediately. Commanding, confident, dynamic. The words of the spell he cast were complex, but his voice was sure. I nodded at his work. He'd produced a handful of blank canvases in the air around us. I could guess at what he'd planned. I'd open and push the witchline I could feel against a canvas. He'd keep it in place with his magic while he held it open. It would create a magical imprint of sorts. This would provide visual proof to the elders.

I remained on my knees and lifted my arms, threading my fingers together. Guillaume stood close behind me, his legs brushing against my shoulder blades. I leaned into him and he clasped my upraised hands, pulling them higher and forcing me to stretch. Our breathing synced and I felt my witchline running through me. I shut out everything else and put all my awareness into the vein of raw power feeding my magic. I could feel it entering my body and flowing through me. With Guillaume's supportive efforts, I easily opened a connection to it, reaching out to my witchline with the unique part of myself that made me Lucie, a witch nourished by the Bellerose witchline. Once I felt fully tapped into it, I envisioned gently guiding my witchline out of my body and against one of the magical canvases Guillaume had created.

"Good, good," he murmured, squeezing my hands. "Now let me."

Like all those times in France, I could sense Guillaume's influence on my witchline. As I relinquished control, he moved in to manage it. The handoff was seamless.

This wasn't the same as what I'd experienced with Templeton the day before. Templeton touched *inside* my witchline. Guillaume could only compel it to remain open while my attention went elsewhere. Guillaume's power remained *outside* of it.

As much as I wanted to turn toward the canvas to see what it looked like, I stayed committed to my effort, ever the dutiful student. I could hear Guillaume's controlled breathing as he stabilized his hold on my witchline. His energy filled the circle, then stilled. He released my hands. They dropped to my thighs.

Now the demonstration would begin.

Chapter 19

I startled when Guillaume suddenly bent and whispered into my ear. "The next time we are dancing, you will remain as my partner," he hissed. "You will not walk away from me again."

I flinched. Here it was, the punishment for rejecting him and taking Templeton's hand at the gala. An angry Guillaume would not hold back no matter what he told the elders. I waited, bees buzzing in my stomach. I knew the first attack would come from behind.

Delivering pain came naturally to Guillaume. He barely needed to think about the magic he laid across my back from shoulder to shoulder. I yelped as the first hot sting flitted across my skin. This method would leave no marks – Guillaume prized unblemished skin – but I would feel the imprint of each strike.

When you experience pain, your body produces endorphins to help you deal with it. At the same time, energy explodes out of your body. The level of pain dictated the amount of energy released. I'd learned to hold onto all the energy, letting it build until the precise moment when I could let it go and direct it in a focused channel toward my witchline. The witchline accepted it, growing stronger as it was forced to accept the energy I returned to it.

The second hit was much harder, lashing across my back in the same spot as the first. I cried out, rising up on my knees and balling my hands into fists. I gritted my teeth but pulled my energy close. It would not leave me until I was ready.

Guillaume dealt a series of fiery licks up and down my back. He didn't care if I screamed. In fact, he enjoyed the sound. The blows came faster, and I fell forward on my hands, my palms smacking the floor, my eyes screwing shut. The magical lashes sliced a horizontal pattern down the back of each thigh. He continued until I heard myself cry for him to stop. I shivered, my head hanging as I clung to the building energy so it wouldn't escape before I was ready to let it go.

But he stopped only to move his attack. Again, Guillaume knotted my hair in his hand. He yanked me backwards, keeping me on my knees, but exposing the front of my body to his abuse. The thrashing continued down my neck, over my breasts, and landed on my belly. The cotton shift I wore offered no protection. The magical emblems, along with Guillaume's sigil, flared into a deep red, blazing a trail throughout the embroidery.

Abruptly, he halted. I gasped for breath, my mouth hanging open, my eyes rolling up to him.

He calmly began again, attacking the top of my thighs. I spit out several broken words pleading for mercy.

But I held onto my energy.

Guillaume shoved me forward unexpectedly and I sprawled onto the floor, my chin hitting the tile. My head swimming, I struggled back onto my hands and knees. I didn't even care there were witnesses to my groveling. I wanted this to stop – he hadn't dialed back the amount of pain for the demonstration. Sweat dripped down my spine and also between my breasts. Drool leaked out of my mouth. I felt ill.

I crawled over to Guillaume, my fingertips

nervously bouncing on the top of his boots as I cowered. When I found the strength to lift my head, he delivered a final blow, slapping his magic across my face. My head whipped to the side, the crack sending a terrible vibration through my jaw. My hand smacked the floor as I toppled to the right, but I caught myself before falling. It hurt far less than the other strikes, but it marked the threshold of what I'd take. I'd reached the pinnacle.

Releasing the energy raging inside me, I drove it furiously against my own witchline, feeling the flow surge away from my body. The explosive energy flooded into the raw line of power feeding my magic as a natural witch. Muscles throughout my body convulsed, tightening and releasing rapidly as I forced everything I had into my witchline. The witchline reversed the course of its own current, now sucking hungrily on the energy I sacrificed up to it. I collapsed as the last of it left my body, quaking at Guillaume's feet.

As the final bit drained from me, I pushed myself wearily up from the floor. I lumbered into a resting position, still on my knees, but eventually straightening my aching shoulders and lifting my head. I couldn't stop my hands from shaking against my thighs. My eyes cut to the glass separating us from the elders. The two men who'd entered the observation room last remained by the door. I blinked, my vision blurry as I tried to see if the one still held what looked like a top hat.

"Another impression," Guillaume demanded. He assumed the same position as before and I sought out my pulsing witchline. He allowed his hold on it to slip and I pressed it into a second canvas. Again, we maneuvered through a tradeoff and he held it open.

"Excellent work." Guillaume rested his hand on top of my head. I longed to get past the burning sensation left on my skin from his aggression. My head felt like it was under water, and I struggled to listen to my tormentor as he described the impressions on the two canvases.

"Let's be done." My voice was barely audible.

Guillaume began to explain the next method we'd be demonstrating to the elders.

Emotional pain.

Guillaume paused to toss a clean handkerchief on the tile in front of me. "You have snot running out of your nose. It's disgusting. Clean yourself."

I grabbed the cloth and wiped my face, glowering at him. He brushed off my angry stare and instead concentrated on the canvases hanging in the air around us. The canvases displaying my witchline were splattered with vertical lines of red grouped closely together. The second canvas contained thicker rivulets – a stronger impression. It represented the fed witchline. Guillaume pointed out the achievement to the elders before waving a hand. The two canvases shifted to the back of our circle and several blank ones came forward.

He bent again, his voice low. "Pick a canvas and allow your mind to open freely to it. Once the connection is established, the images you see inside your mind will be projected onto the canvas. Do not attempt to shut down the connection. I will punish you if you do."

Nervously, I chose the canvas in the middle, unsure of what Guillaume planned. I felt him kneel behind me, his legs astride mine. He wrapped an arm around me, his hand sliding across my breasts. I lurched forward at the unwanted touch, and he pulled me back. "The elders will love this part of the show."

Guillaume's magic filled the circle and he spoke softly into my ear. He described some of the things we did when I was his student, calling up a selection of memories I'd buried when I left France. At first, I didn't understand what was happening, but soon I realized the magic he'd cast picked up on the imagery forming inevitably in my mind. It recreated those pictures on the canvases for all to see.

Me crawling up Guillaume's bed, wearing only the stockings he bought for me.

Me performing fellatio on him, my eyes open and glassy.

Me on top of him during sex, pitching forward, a curtain of hair hiding my face.

"Oh, my god." Horrified, I turned my head. Shame for what I'd done washed over me, followed by the humiliation of knowing everyone in that observation room could see. *Everyone.*

Guillaume snapped his fingers and the images melted off the canvases, dissolving in the air. He kissed my ear. "Does the truth hurt you, Lucie? Now everyone knows how much you enjoyed being my student. You cannot deny it."

"Stop it." I tried to pull away, but he held onto me.

"Oh, we're far from done." He grabbed me by the chin and forced me to look at the canvas. "Do not close your eyes or we will return to a second session of physical pain. Continue to hold onto your energy and do not release it until it's time."

Overwhelmed by what he'd done, I trembled and waited for the new emotional attack. Blinking furiously, I tried to hold back my tears.

"I learned some things about your childhood while you were gone all those months, Lucie. Things you've kept hidden from me." Guillaume laughed against my cheek, before rubbing his nose in my hair. "Let's see your papa."

Dread swept over me. I grew nauseous. "What are you doing?"

"Let's show them what you did."

What I did...

I began to frantically fight against him. "I don't want to see this. Please don't do this to me, Guillaume!"

The magic Guillaume created inside our circle became oppressive, stealing my breath and holding me still. His fingers and thumb dug into my cheeks as he made me watch the images flashing erratically across the suspended canvases. I tried to erase my thoughts, but

Guillaume had weakened me during the demonstration. He was a skilled torturer.

I swayed, lightheaded, staring in horror as the image of my father balancing precariously on top of a ladder angled against our two-story house appeared on a large canvas. It was winter, and he was hanging lights for the upcoming festival. The ladder slipped an inch here and there as he steadied himself, his palms pressing against the side of our house. Strings of lights and a bright orange extension cord hung in the air around his body. He stretched an arm to the right, looping the wires and cords over a series of durable hooks he'd drilled into our home below one of the eaves.

I watched as a 4-year-old Lucie, bundled up in her winter coat, came running around the corner of the stucco house. She clambered onto the bottom of the ladder, gripping the sides and jumping up to the next rung. "Daddy! I want to help!"

My father called out as the ladder slipped to the left. He made a grab for a large hook to his right. His lunge caused the ladder to shift again, catching his foot and causing him to lose his balance. Little Lucie fell backward, holding firmly onto the ladder, pulling it with her and out from under her father.

He didn't fall far. My father's arms slid through the wires, a random loop in the extension cord catching him around the neck. Suspended between the first and second floor, he flailed – his body twisting as his feet tried to find purchase against the prickly wall. The extension cord tightened around his neck, hanging him. His feet kicked uselessly, his tongue thrusting through his lips as he clawed at the cord with his hands. The child on the ground kept trying to lift a ladder that was far too heavy for her. She shrieked at the dying man, over and over and over.

"Daddy!"

My wail echoed through the room and the energy poured out of me as I watched the final images of my father's death bleed off the canvas. I didn't even care if the energy exploding out of me made it back into my witchline. Guillaume released me and I fell forward, sobbing into my hands.

I was allowed to grieve for a minute before Guillaume pulled me up yet again. This time his fingers dug into my upper arm. "Get control of yourself."

He stood directly in front of me, his back to the glass. He sneered as I fought to catch my breath. My face was wet and hot – my eyes burned. What he did was unforgivable. I hated him with all my heart.

I felt a sudden snap as Guillaume released his hold on my witchline. I gasped, shocked he'd cut the connection without warning. He'd never done anything that risky before. Hurriedly I called my witchline back to me, letting it slide back into its familiar position.

Guillaume waved a hand and all canvases disintegrated into puffs of smoke. He spent several minutes closing the original circle he'd cast. When he finished, he turned toward the elders. "As you can see, psychological pain is extremely effective. The energy pouring out of Lucie a moment ago was much more than what I bled from her during our first demonstration. Physical pain and shame are quite effective, but as we proved here, if you find the right psychological pain, it can exceed some of the worst physical pain inflicted. Every witch is different, of course, and the most appropriate method should be used to draw the greatest amount from the individual witch. Fortunately for us, there is much to work with when Lucie is the subject. Her willingness to explore the various types of pain with her body and her mind makes me believe she has a taste for it." Amused, he shook his head.

I gritted my teeth. There would come a day when I would repay Guillaume for what he'd done.

"I think there is one more method we can examine," Guillaume said.

His words made my flesh crawl. Guillaume wasn't ready to end the demonstration. My eyes darted to the glass. How much were the elders willing to let me endure?

"When Lucie was actively serving as my student, we experimented with other avenues outside of what we've demonstrated today. However, there was one direction I didn't explore to my satisfaction." He chuckled. "Perhaps I was too gentle with her."

The hot flavor of bile rose in the back of my throat. What could be worse than forcing me to relive my father's death? What other hell could he send me through to top how I made my father die?

He studied my red face as he continued to speak to the elders. "I've enjoyed an interesting visit to Matar. Yesterday I had the opportunity to witness some truly explosive energy produced by Lucie. I theorize we can achieve the same level of production today and direct it into her witchline. After careful consideration, I believe I can demonstrate an *extremely* effective method to drive a powerful flow of energy from a witch to her witchline."

Guillaume sent me one last terrifying smile before spinning and returning to the table where he'd set his briefcase earlier. He flicked the locks, reopening it. A length of rope and scarf appeared.

The directive came. "Stand, Lucie."

I looked straight ahead as Guillaume secured my wrists behind me with the rope. He braided it up my arms to my elbows, pulling them together, arching my back. Next, he rolled the scarf into a blindfold and tied it snugly around my head. Holding my upper arms in both his hands, he directed me to kneel again, lowering me to the floor.

I mentally talked myself into enduring this last foray into hell. I was so sick and tired of being made to kneel in front of others. After this, I wasn't going to kneel for anyone ever again.

"Don't move," he commanded. "If you do, it will hurt and I won't even need to touch you."

Sitting on my ankles, I listened to the rustling of his trousers as he walked back to the table. A moment later, I sensed his purposeful circling around me. The words he uttered were unfamiliar. He used a language I didn't know. I assumed he was casting another protective circle before we reopened my witchline.

Next, he addressed the elders. "The last method I'm going to employ is fear. Until Lucie pours the last drop of her energy into her witchline, I'm going to let one of her worst fears play with her."

My stomach cramped as his words assaulted me, my thoughts creating several frightening scenarios as I strained to hear what Guillaume was doing. I lifted my head and sniffed the air. He was burning Yew – dangerous to burn inside because of its poisonous properties, but not for natural-born witches.

Yew was associated with the dead and raising spirits.

"Guillaume?" Alarmed, I rose up on my knees. "Guillaume!" Oh, my god – what was he doing? The next words from his mouth shocked me.

"I do invocate and conjure thee, Sebastian St. Michel, demon; and being with power armed from the Spring of Dwelling, I do strongly command thee, in the vein of the Witch of Endor…" Guillaume's deep baritone filled the space.

"No!" I shouted, fighting against the ropes binding my arms. I needed to see – I needed to protect myself! I spit out the first word of power coming to mind as I struggled. *"Revelare!"*

The shock running through my body lifted me several inches off the ground before I crashed back down. I toppled over, landing on my side. My temple banged against the floor, the thud echoing in my ears.

But the half-spell I'd produced allowed the blindfold to loosen. It slipped down my face, the fabric resting in a band across my nose.

Using my left elbow, I raised up enough so I could see what Guillaume was doing. In horror, I realized I was surrounded by a line of soot. *Demon ash.* The air inside the circle sparked above me. The magic I'd let loose created a mini electrical storm.

On the other side of the room, Guillaume stood in front of a circle of salt. A spout of black smoke poured from the ground. The vile air churned as Guillaume continued the conjuring.

From my position on the ground, I looked to the elders. Although they were still shadowed, I could see some of the witches were now animated, standing and gesturing. My eyes roamed to the back of the tiny audience, searching for the man I believed to be Templeton. He was no longer there.

My attention flitted back to Guillaume and the frightening magic he performed. I watched as the smoke peeled away, revealing a crouching man in the middle of the circle. His head was lowered, his face hidden. His arms wrapped around his knees. He rocked back and forth on the balls of his feet, snarling. He was naked.

"I command you, demon, to come to this circle fully formed and bound to me and my orders," Guillaume intoned.

Sebastian writhed and moaned, his body shuddering as he was compelled to form inside Guillaume's circle. His body was slathered in sweat and the sound coming from deep inside him grew into a constant keening.

The crackling above ceased and I worked myself into a seated position, not once taking my eyes off the nightmare Guillaume was calling into the room. I shook as Guillaume finished the last line of his invocation.

Sebastian's head snapped up. Ignoring Guillaume, he set his sights on me, his eyes a fiery combination of black and red. He lunged forward, held back only by Guillaume's circle of salt. I recoiled, kicking my heels against the tile as I instinctively drew back.

Satisfied that Sebastian was properly conjured and contained, Guillaume turned to the anxious elders. He lifted a hand. "I assure you; this demon cannot leave the room." The vicious look he shot me next chilled my blood. "But I will release him from his circle."

Some of the elders were clearly voicing their objections on the other side of the glass. I could hear their muted protests. They were wise to worry.

Sebastian was beginning to take stock of his surroundings. His wild eyes roamed over the room excitedly. He rose, his muscles flexing, rippling underneath his skin. He scowled at the line of salt surrounding him, before fixing

Guillaume with an unwavering stare.

Guillaume was unaffected. "This demon was a Salesman. It appears he was not a good boy." He clicked his tongue. "But he has an interesting history with our dear Lucie. Apparently, they were lovers. It didn't end well." I watched as my tormenter pointed to Sebastian. "Obviously."

Sebastian seethed, a growl emanating from deep in his chest.

"I understand your frustration," Guillaume nodded. "She needs to be punished for what she's done to you."

"Guillaume," I began, shocked by the scene unfolding in the room. My witchline was closed – this was not part of *any* demonstration. "What are you doing? You can't do this." I looked to the elders for help. "He can't do this. You can't let him do this. This has nothing to do with our work in France!"

Guillaume ignored my cries. Instead, he returned to Sebastian's circle. "You can play with her but leave her alive and unblemished." With those last words, Guillaume swept his arm through the air and opened a doorway along the edge of the circle containing Sebastian. The salt blew away and Sebastian bounded out, landing at the edge of the demon ash circle where I was held hostage. His deranged smile shook me to my core. The fear spreading through my veins left me dizzy.

I pitched backward, my shoulder touching one of the invisible walls of my prison. The magic burned through the cotton fabric of my shift, coming in contact with my skin. I yelped, retreating in the opposite direction – but stilling immediately when Sebastian's hand grabbed my upper arm, steadying me.

The demon ash didn't keep him out.

"Shh," he breathed, lifting the loosened blindfold up and off my head. His lip curled as he glanced over his shoulder at Guillaume.

Bam! The room shook.

Sebastian frowned, his chin pointing toward the one door leading out of the room. It took me a minute to process what was happening. Then it hit me. Guillaume's wards were being attacked. *Bam!*

A massive amount of magic was smashing into the protective shield Guillaume raised before the demonstration began. *Bam!* Guillaume's focus switched from Sebastian to reinforcing his own wards. He grunted as he redirected his power, his arms opening wide as he chanted a counter spell.

"Lucie, hey. It's okay." Sebastian muttered under the noise. His shoulders twitched. "I can take you out of here."

My eyes cut back to Sebastian.

"I won't let that fucker hurt you anymore." Sebastian's gaze shifted to the witch who'd conjured him.

The declaration stunned me. I studied his profile. I witnessed a ripple of the man I once cared about crossing his face. "Sebastian?"

"I'm not bound to him like he thinks." Sebastian jerked his head back to me. He snickered.

"Why?" The word tumbled out of my mouth.

He leaned in intimately, his nose inches from mine. "It's a secret. I can tell you later, but first we need to get out of here." He didn't move a muscle, but he looked toward the door out of the corner of his eye.

In the moment, I honestly couldn't decide which was worse: Remaining at Guillaume's mercy or letting Sebastian 'rescue' me.

Sebastian wiped a length of the demon ash away. He grinned as if we were playing a mischievous trick on someone and not locked in the middle of utter madness.

With Sebastian's help, I rose to my feet. He pulled me from the circle of demon ash and paused to tug at the rope binding my arms behind my back. I surveyed the room while he worked at tearing the knots apart with his exaggerated strength. Guillaume continued his battle with the unseen force ripping repeatedly into his wards. In the observation room, Loren was pressed against the glass, his fist banging against the surface, his face a mask of horror. He realized I could see him and I saw him mouth a name.

Templeton.

Oh! It was Templeton slamming into Guillaume's wards. *Of course.*

As Sebastian worked through the knots, I homed in on Guillaume. With the circle of demon ash broken, I had my magic at my disposal. My fear of Sebastian was still present, but another emotion was overtaking it. *Fury.* I heard Sebastian laugh again.

"You're getting hot, Lucie." His finger skittered up my arm as the last knot released and my wrists were free. "Are you going to let him have it?"

"Yes." I raised my right hand, my palm facing Guillaume. With little effort, I brought up the hottest fire I could summon and let it fill my senses. The air around me charged. The hair on my arms lifted. I let the angry energy build, holding it back until I was sure Guillaume was absorbed in his spellcasting.

Then I let it rip.

"*Hiberent*," I hissed, blasting Guillaume with the fire power coursing through my body. He staggered, his concentration breaking, but he remained on his feet. A lesser witch wouldn't have withstood the attack, but it was still enough to disrupt him.

Templeton took advantage of the interruption and busted through the door. He threw up his arm to block the spell Guillaume directed at him. His colorless eyes clocked Sebastian.

"Leave before it's too late," I ordered, pushing Sebastian toward the door. "I need to make this stop."

Confusion swam across the demon's face. His shoulders twitched again, but he knew he couldn't win this one. He nodded. "Okay, Lucie. I'll go."

As Templeton lifted a hand in our direction, Sebastian's terrifying speed saved him. He crossed the room and door traveled out of the chaos as security rushed through the same door. I saw the armed witches shudder as the demon-Salesman passed through them and disappeared.

"Enough!" Acton yelled as she entered the room behind the guards. "We have seen enough. I order everyone to stand down!"

Templeton was at my side, wrapping an arm around my waist as his door travel energy grew quickly, rising around both of us. He pulled me to him.

Guillaume didn't miss a beat. "Lucie has disappointed me with her activities following her return to the Empire. She is cavorting with Salesmen, demons, and Rabbits. Her decisions following her study indicate she is reckless and not to be trusted. She should be returned to France for further training and discipline – what she achieved with her witchline cannot be lost. You've seen today what our work proves and how it can serve the Congress."

Speechless, I realized Guillaume had planned this all along.

Templeton's grip kept me from attacking my

former teacher. He lifted his right hand and a blast of frigid wind raged through the room. Papers from Guillaume's briefcase whipped into the air. A water bottle pelted the Acton matriarch in the back of the head, knocking her into a wall. As the power of the storm grew, the chairs and table flipped and spun in the mini tornado he'd created. Witches dropped to the floor to avoid being hit.

Templeton, the prophesied knight to my light, raced for the door, his hand gripping mine. My feet barely skimmed the floor as I was pulled through the air alongside him. Bright royal blue blinded me and together we door traveled out of the Congress of Empire Witches.

Chapter 20

Templeton took me to his penthouse in downtown Matar. This was the first time I'd been inside his personal space. We entered his city abode through a door leading into an elegant foyer. We'd left the Congress building rushing, but as we arrived, it was as if we'd simply stepped through a door.

He guided me forward by the elbow, walking us into a brightly lit open floor plan. A kitchen with its gray and white marble island was located to my left; a living room was to the right – complete with a low-backed, leather couch and two matching chairs in the same shade of walnut. The furniture sat around a short, square coffee table in front of an unlit fireplace. Bookshelves were built into the wall to the left of the mantel; an elaborate sound system covered the wall on the right. Beyond the living room furniture sat an upright piano, its finish a heavy, full-bodied black. An oblong dining table – which could easily sit eight – stood between the kitchen and the living space. Several newspapers sat folded on one end. All chairs were spaced evenly and neatly pushed under the table, their cushioned backs an inch from the table's edge.

The floors throughout the space were light hardwood, sporting an earth-toned rug here and there. The ceilings were easily 10 feet high. A wall of windows ran from the kitchen to the other end of the space, delivering a spectacular view of Matar's skyline. We had to be at least 50 stories above the city, but probably more.

The reality of where I was and what I'd experienced at the Congress started to sink in. Templeton dropped his hand from my arm and we stood catching our breaths. I realized he was staring at the cotton shift I wore, and I crossed my arms over my chest, mindful of the thin material.

"Lucie," he said, his voice rising. "You need to get this off. Now. Take it off."

"What do you mean?" I took a step backward as he reached for me.

"The embroidery. It's lighting up again."

Templeton pointed to the faint red coloring the symbols. As I watched, they grew brighter.

"Take it off now!" Templeton closed the space between us, grabbing the fabric around my hips and pulling upward. The shift slid past my shoulders and along my upraised arms. My hair tumbled back down over my bare shoulders as he removed the garment and balled it between his two hands. I covered my breasts with my left arm, dropping my right hand to cover the patch of hair between my legs.

Wordlessly Templeton turned and disappeared through the nearest door. I waited anxiously with only goosebumps clothing me. I glanced at the couch, but no blanket or decorative throw were to be found.

"Templeton?" I called. When no answer came, I checked on the other side of the door and found a modest office, but no Templeton. He'd door traveled out of the penthouse.

This was crazy. I was not going to stand around naked waiting for him to return. Off the same foyer we'd come through only minutes ago, there was a second wider hall. It was lined with several doors and I opened each one, peeking inside as I searched for a bedroom. I passed a coat closet, a powder room, and a utility room with washer and dryer before I found the penthouse's master bedroom. Two walk-in closets were near the bedroom door. One was completely empty; the other contained a limited selection of trousers, dress shirts, and suit coats. He had a surprising number of shoes. I noted he kept several top hats. I doubted any of them were approved by the Empire for door travel.

My fingers stroked the arm of one of the tailored shirts as I browsed through Templeton's clothing. The shirt would fit, but I judged it would be too snug across my bust and not as long as I'd like it to be. Pulling a pair of his trousers over my hips wasn't an appealing idea. Wearing his clothing was going to be awkward enough.

I left the closet behind and wandered farther. The master bedroom was laid out in an L-shape. I gaped at the large en suite bathroom, with its rainfall shower and separate tub set deep into the floor, before padding toward the bedroom proper. A king-size bed, with its solid headboard pressed against the far wall, filled the space. A lavender-gray duvet spread over it, with four matching pillows sitting in two fluffy piles perched on top. To the right of the bed was a nightstand. Under its lamp, a short stack of books waited. On the left side of the bed, an upholstered chair sat, its color a silvery pearl. A neutral rug spread out from beneath the bed, reaching under the furniture surrounding it.

Opposite the bed was a long, six-drawer dresser, its top devoid of any personal items or photos. A beautiful cherry wood, it matched the nightstand and headboard. A wide mirror was set into the wall above it. Floor-to-ceiling windows filled another wall. The heavy, champagne-colored drapes were mostly open, filling the room with afternoon light.

"Sorry, Templeton," I murmured. My face flushed with a guilty heat as I pulled open one of the top drawers. "I'm only doing this because I need something to wear."

I explored the contents of the dresser. Underwear, socks, and bright white undershirts filled the two top drawers. The middle drawers contained several extra blankets and flannel pajama bottoms. I touched a pair, my fingers skimming over the cozy material. I wondered if he slept in them or if he only wore them around the penthouse before bed. *Now is not the time to think about these things,* I thought. I gave my head a firm shake and pushed the drawer closed. The bottom drawers held a selection of tee shirts, running shorts, and sweatpants. *Jackpot.* I chose a green tee, its athletic logo faded, and slid it over my head before stepping into a pair of gray sweats. The pants were long, but the elastic at the bottom kept them from puddling past my ankles. I finished my outfit by grabbing a pair of plain white sport socks and pulling them over my feet. It didn't matter if they were too big – I needed something to wear. I rolled up the waistband of the sweatpants as I turned, stopping when I noticed Templeton standing quietly inside the door to his bedroom, watching me dress.

Blushing, I gestured toward the dresser as he came closer. "I needed to put something on. I'm sorry."

He appraised the outfit. A hint of a smile caused the corners of his mouth to briefly turn up. "Not exactly what I pictured you wearing the first time you visited my bedroom."

Those weren't the words I expected. I pulled at the shirt self-consciously, suddenly very aware I wasn't wearing a bra. "And what did you picture?"

Templeton raised an eyebrow but didn't elaborate. Instead, he bent, digging back into the bottom dresser drawer before handing me a hooded sweatshirt. "Another time."

I slipped the clothing on, zipping up the front and feeling a lot less exposed. Templeton held a hand out to me. "Let's get you some water."

I placed my hand in his and let him lead me out of his bedroom and into the kitchen. I leaned against the marble island as he filled a tall glass from one of the bottles he kept in his refrigerator. He handed it to me.

"Thank you," I said, taking a sip.

"Do you want to sit down?" He nodded to the dining table behind me.

"No, I don't need to sit," I told him. I tugged at my ear. Now that I was no longer at Guillaume's mercy, everything felt surreal. Had it really happened? I didn't know where to begin. I gazed at Templeton and shook my head. "I'm not even sure what to do now."

Templeton poured himself a glass of water, then stared at the bottle on the counter. I noted the spasm in his cheek. "I know he hurt you. I..." He cleared his throat. "I saw your body.

Your skin isn't marked, I know, but do you need help?"

"I'm okay," I answered, rolling my shoulders as I assessed the aftermath of Guillaume's efforts. "I'll ache, and I'm tired, but I'm okay. He was vicious, but I'll recover. I'll be sore for a few days."

Templeton refused to look up but nodded.

"It's the other things," I said, my voice cracking. Overcome with humiliation, I thought about what Templeton saw on those canvases. "Things I didn't want anyone to see. Things I didn't want anyone to know."

At that, he did raise his head. "I understand things are often more complex than they seem."

"Sometimes I just needed to feel pleasure." I swallowed the ball of shame in my throat. "It was a hard year in France. Sometimes I needed to feel..." I fidgeted with the cuff of the sweatshirt I wore.

"Today he exploited what you gave to him." Templeton replied. "It was cruel."

"It was Guillaume," I snorted. I thought about the other canvases, shuddering. "I don't know how he found out about..."

"What happened when you were a child was not your fault."

I nodded. "Yeah. Oh, god." I rubbed a hand across my forehead. "This is such a mess. I'll need to talk to Loren."

"I will speak with him." Templeton's tone was cold.

"No. No, you won't," I said. "This is for me to deal with. Loren has influence, but there was no way he could've stopped what happened today." I paused, reluctant to talk about Sebastian, but there was no avoiding it. "Guillaume, however, is going to be in a lot of trouble. Conjuring Sebastian as a demon inside the walls of Congress was a bad idea. I don't know what he thought he'd prove but –"

"He conjured Sebastian to hurt you. It had nothing to do with using your fear to feed your witchline."

Templeton was right – and I'd already realized what Guillaume had intended. But it was difficult to accept. Funny, the abuse in support of strengthening my witchline was something I was willing to tolerate. But unleashing a demon to 'play' with me for some sort of sick 'punishment'? I could not wrap my head around it. The level of Guillaume's arrogance astounded me. Thinking he could contain Sebastian after letting him out of the salt circle was insanity.

I thought about Sebastian's behavior in those strange moments. He freed me from the circle of demon ash. He untied my wrists. He told me he was going to get me out of there. I sucked my bottom lip into my mouth. I couldn't talk to Templeton about any of this. He wouldn't understand. *I* didn't understand.

"How could Sebastian get out of the room if Guillaume had him bound?" I asked instead. "I heard the invocation."

Templeton watched me with a sharp eye. "He's still a Salesman. After Guillaume released him from the conjuring circle, Sebastian bypassed the wards by door traveling out of there. The ones erected specifically to keep him inside the room were raised alongside the ones designed to keep everyone out."

Now it made sense. The wards were on the other side of the door. It was easier for Sebastian to get out than it was for Templeton to get in. I changed the subject. "How were you able to get me out of there? I don't understand. I'm not a Salesman – I can't door travel."

He knew I was purposely avoiding the Sebastian discussion, but he didn't call me on it. Instead, he explained how he door traveled with me. "Salesmen employed by the Empire carry all sorts of items. Plants and small animals can be transported. A new Salesman might be assigned an experienced Salesman to teach them the ropes. Jo Carter was tapped to train Emily so she'd get better control of her door traveling energy last year. They'd often travel together."

Templeton continued. "It's not a good practice to bring non-Salesmen with you when door traveling. The location needs to be foremost in your mind, and if you have someone with you, their thoughts can impact the destination. As such, the Empire does not permit Salesmen to door travel with a 'passenger.' The only time it's allowed is when one Salesman is training another, and the Salesman Court must approve their tandem traveling. I care little about the Empire's directives surrounding door travel, but I do agree it's risky to bring someone along who cannot door travel on their own."

"But I know you've door traveled with at least one other – Emily's mother." My voice faltered. It was Sebastian who held Emily's mom hostage in an effort to get his hands on the Crimson Stone. He didn't physically hurt the older woman, but it was a terrifying experience.

"Emily's mother is special." Templeton waved a hand dismissively. "But back to your earlier question. Yes, I can bring a non-Salesman with me when I door travel. It's dangerous and not something I'd do routinely. Today was different."

"Very different."

"It's also easier to door travel with someone who has magical abilities of their own – like you," Templeton said. "You have a higher vibration I can lock my door travel energy into and hold onto when crossing from door to door."

"Lucky for me." I took a drink of water. I couldn't imagine what would've happened if we were unable to escape.

"It's easy to hold onto your energy. It fits snugly against mine. It feels natural." Templeton shifted awkwardly.

I decided to spare us both any uncomfortable conversations for now. "What about your top hat? It's still at the Congress, isn't it?" He'd door traveled without it.

"A throw away," he replied. "If I get if back, fine. If not, no loss. I avoid wearing anything I'd rather not lose into the Congress building.

I wouldn't want to leave anything personal behind with semi-magical properties."

"Wise approach," I said. He was right. There would be witches who'd want to deconstruct any magic attached to the Salesman's power. "Alright, I guess we should get in touch with Rabbit and let him know what happened. Oh, crap! Rabbit's still sitting outside the Congress waiting for me. He drove me there today."

Templeton pulled out the network phone Rabbit had provided. He tapped a message. "I'll tell him you're here. We'll need to learn if there are updates from the Walled Zone. In the meantime, I'll door travel to your townhouse and pack you a suitcase so you can stay here."

He meant well – he really did. "No, Templeton. I can't stay."

A shadow crossed his face. "I have a spare bedroom. I won't disturb you."

"That's not why. It's not because I don't want to..." My voice trailed off and I motioned to the wall of windows. "You can't keep me locked away in a glass tower. I need to be in my own home – especially now. I need to deal with today's mess. I'll send a message to Loren. I want to talk to him as soon as I can."

"You're making it hard for me to protect you."

I set my glass down and circled the kitchen island, catching him off guard. Standing close, I brushed the front of his dress shirt with my fingertips and he stilled. "Right now, I need to protect myself. Hiding here only delays facing all these problems. You know it's true."

He touched my hair, pushing a few strands behind my ear. The tension he held around his mouth told me he was trying not to argue. "What are you planning to do?"

"I'm going to talk to Loren. I want to know what the fallout is from today. It's not going to be good, but honestly, now that the damn demonstration is over, I don't care what the elders think – or want." I shrugged. "And I'm going to set up a stronger level of protection at my home. I've let my guard down one too many times since I returned from France."

"I can help you with that." He was still stroking my hair. While I wanted to build on our intimacy, now was probably not the time.

"I'll accept your help." I gestured to the phone sitting on the island. "Has Rabbit replied? Can you text him and let him know I have a pair of old sneakers in the back of my car? Ask him to bring them up so I have shoes to wear. Then he can drive me home."

Templeton reluctantly reached for the device and sent the new message. He raised his eyes. "I'll meet you both there."

∞∞∞

Rabbit arrived 20 minutes after Templeton sent the first text. He handed me my shoes while eyeing my outfit. "Someone want to fill me in?"

"I'll tell you everything in the car," I said from one of the dining table's chairs while I pulled on the sneakers. "But in a nutshell, the demonstration turned into a real shitshow."

"You weren't expecting it to be easy," Rabbit replied. He squinted at Templeton. "I'm not working this out. How did Lucie come to be here?"

"I brought her here."

"You were at the Congress?" Rabbit asked.

"I was at the demonstration." Templeton didn't go into detail.

"How?"

Templeton stopped answering Rabbit's questions. The two men stared at each other.

"Rabbit, Guillaume took things too far. Way

too far," I told him. Rabbit returned his attention to me. "After driving me through physical and emotional hell, he conjured Sebastian in his demon form."

"He what?" Rabbit was incredulous. He gave his head a shake. "How did he...? I don't get it. I mean... He did what? But how could he?"

"That about sums up everyone's reaction." I lifted a hand, gesturing toward Templeton. "It just hit me. After Guillaume ran Sebastian off yesterday, he asked me who he was. I *gave* him Sebastian's name. That's how he was able to conjure him. He had his name."

Rabbit pulled off his knit cap, releasing his unruly curls. "The Congress let him do that?"

"No, the elders were as shocked as we were. I'm sure they couldn't believe it when he let Sebastian out of the circle," I said.

Rabbit whistled. "That's fucking insane."

"It was surreal." I rubbed my temples with my fingertips. "I need to get home. I'll tell you the rest in the car." I turned to Templeton. "Do you have a coat I can wear over these fancy threads?"

"I got it," Rabbit interjected before Templeton could answer. He took off his work coat and put it over my shoulders.

"Thanks, but what about you?" I shrugged into the coat.

"Yeah, I'll be fine," Rabbit scoffed. He hooked his thumb toward the door. "Let's get you home."

I paused, addressing Templeton. "You'll be there soon?"

Templeton's eyes had lightened when Rabbit gave me his coat. "Yes."

"Give us about 30 minutes," Rabbit said. "I'll text you when we get there. I'll get some Rabbits in the area in case there's anything going on at the house."

I followed Rabbit through the foyer to the penthouse door with Templeton on my heels.

Rabbit stepped out into the wide hall to call up the elevator.

I paused at the door, looking up. Templeton stood close. "Thanks for the clothes. You can have them back after I change."

He nodded, his face serious. "No hurry."

I fingered the neckline of the green tee shirt I'd borrowed. "But this shirt is so soft. I might have to keep it."

I slipped out before he could answer.

∞ ∞ ∞

"Do you ever use the Empire's messaging service?" I asked Rabbit as I buckled myself into the passenger seat.

Rabbit laughed. "No, why?"

"Can you break into it and send Loren Heatherworth a message for me? I want the message sent to his house."

"Don't want me to send a Rabbit to his doorstep?" Rabbit smirked as he dug his phone out of his pocket.

I cringed, embarrassed. "No."

Rabbit laughed, good-natured as ever. "And what's the message?"

"Tell him I'm fine. Ask him to please get my purse and the clothes I wore to Congress and bring them to my house. That I need to speak with him as soon as possible." I hesitated. "You know, he may not be home yet, but the last thing I want is to send a message to the Congress building. I don't know who will get it."

"Don't worry, I'll take care of it," Rabbit promised. He was still wearing the half-smile, half-scowl on his face. "We'll make sure he gets the message – and isn't terrified by some unpredictable Rabbit."

"Thanks. And sorry." I touched his arm.

He looked up from his texting, his thumbs still moving. "Are you honestly okay?"

"Yeah, I am. Tired and sore. Furious, but okay." I blew out a breath. "I never saw it coming. I was shocked."

Rabbit's eyes grew darker. "Did Sebastian touch you?"

I gazed out the windshield, thinking about what I wanted to tell him. "He tried to help me escape. Guillaume had tied my arms before the conjuring, but Sebastian freed me. He said he was going to help me get away from Guillaume. Then Templeton broke into the room. Before he could stop him, Sebastian door traveled out of there."

"So, he got away." Rabbit also turned to the windshield. He drummed his fingers on the steering wheel. "Does Templeton know about Sebastian freeing you?"

"No. He was trying to break into the room. He only saw Guillaume conjure Sebastian." I thought about it. "There was a separate observation room behind glass. The elders – and

Templeton – were in that space watching. I'm pretty sure Templeton left the room before Sebastian was let out of his circle. When Templeton finally got past Guillaume's wards, he saw Sebastian beside me, but he didn't know what had happened."

Rabbit started the car. "Sebastian 'helping' you can't be a good thing, Lucie."

I didn't answer. I didn't know what to say.

Chapter 21

As we drove back to my house, I told Rabbit what had happened during the demonstration. His face was unreadable. I skipped over the more explicit details of the hell Guillaume put me through, not wanting to revisit the experience either. At one point Rabbit's hand strayed over to mine and covered it.

Rabbit was blasé when I told him Templeton door traveled with me in tow. He shrugged it off, saying Templeton had 'a lot of power in him' and he was glad he was able to take me someplace safe.

We found a parking spot not far from my townhouse. I approached the front door cautiously, testing the wards. Nothing was amiss.

"Hopefully Templeton will be here soon," I said as we went inside. I kicked off my sneakers as I walked, stopping to wave a hand in front of the entrance leading into the living room. The gas insert inside the fireplace flamed to life. In the kitchen, I snapped my fingers and the lights switched on.

Rabbit paused, his eyes widening as I took off his coat and set it on a barstool. "You available for parties, too?"

"It's the witchline. This used to happen after sessions with Guillaume in France. It'll last for a day or two." I looked down at my outfit. If I could only climb into bed and go to sleep, I'd keep Templeton's clothes on. They smelled like him and it made me feel good.

"Was it something new for you? I mean, did the magic come about during your year in France?"

"No, I always had an affinity for fire magic and light work. But it'll be intense over the next couple of days." I stopped to consider the raw power running through me. "My witchline is a lot stronger. I'll be able to affect anything related to fire or electricity with hardly any effort for a while. I won't need to concentrate."

"Not too strange, I guess. You're 'the light' in the prophecy, after all." Rabbit pulled out his phone and sent a message. "I told Templeton we're here."

I froze, watching Rabbit as he continued to scroll through the latest round of messages.

Oh, of course.

"I'm going upstairs to change," I told him, feeling very different about myself and what I'd taken for granted when it came to my magic. "Help yourself to anything in the fridge."

∞∞∞

My body was sore, and I checked myself out in the mirror before throwing on a pair of jeans and a red sweater. Guillaume's magic hadn't left a mark. The aftermath of our session was invisible, as always. But I could still feel the lashes across my skin, the force behind the strikes. It wasn't only the burning sting I'd experienced, but the actual feeling of something beating relentlessly against my body.

Guillaume had a long reputation for delivering harsh punishment and it was no secret he employed pain as a tool when teaching his students. That was why I applied to study with him. I knew he had the power, the knowledge, and the willingness to explore more unconventional methods to achieve my goal.

But I underestimated his sadism.

And yet, it worked. We were successful. We proved it.

I did not regret the choice I made when I first started down this path to strengthen my witchline. But I was changing course after today. I was never going to allow Guillaume to touch me again.

∞∞∞

Downstairs, Rabbit spoke in low tones with Templeton. They straightened, ending their conversation abruptly when I stepped into the kitchen.

"No, please continue." Annoyed, I fired a black look at each man.

"I was telling Templeton the pulsing has significantly increased in beat and volume since this morning," Rabbit replied.

A small lie. I knew they were talking about me, but I'd let it slide. "The pulses are coming more frequently? Like a more upbeat tempo?"

"That's one way to describe it." Rabbit rolled his right wrist before absently rubbing it with his left hand. I saw Templeton's eyes dart toward the movement.

"You still have a team there?" I questioned.

"Down to two. One of my guys had to leave. His wife went into early labor." Rabbit's face split into a broad grin. "Twins. Everyone's okay, though."

"That's good," I replied. I glanced at the clock. It would take Rabbit and I several hours to get to the Fringe's old compound inside the Walled Zone. "The Rabbits who are still there, they'll let you know if anything changes in real time? They won't wait, right?"

"They know to contact me immediately. I want to know about every change," Rabbit said.

"And no Sebastian sightings there?"

"Right."

Templeton hadn't said anything during the exchange. I assumed Rabbit had already told him what was happening at the compound. I noted his eyes had lightened and he was studying Rabbit more closely. His lips pressed into a tense line as his gaze walked up and down our friend's body. I could sense his concern.

"It might be time to go into the Walled Zone ourselves," I admitted, watching Templeton.

"We should go first thing in the morning. We can bring the Crimson Stone and see if it reacts to anything."

That got Templeton's attention. "Will you wake it?"

"Maybe. I'm not promising anything," I told him. "But while we're there, if it looks like there's any trouble, we need you to grab the Stone and door travel to a safer place. We can't put it at risk."

"Are you going to try to open the doors?" Rabbit asked.

"I have no plans to open any door," I answered. "But I do want to see if the Stone reacts to the static and pulses."

Rabbit moved to one of the barstools. "Reconnaissance in the Walled Zone. Anyone else have déjà vu?"

The door knocker on my front door banged several times. Rabbit was back on his feet, in motion in a blink of an eye. Templeton pushed past me before I could stop him.

"Okay, this has got to stop," I muttered, hurrying after the two. I lifted my right hand. "*Offendiculum deambulatio!*"

Both Rabbit and Templeton stumbled to the

right before they reached the door.

"Knock it off," Templeton scowled at me as he caught himself. His other hand shot out and he grabbed Rabbit's arm, keeping him on his feet.

I strode by the two men. "Today's not the day to boss me around, Templeton."

Loren stood on the other side of the door, his face pinched. On the sidewalk beyond the steps leading up to my house, an unfamiliar Rabbit stood watching. His eyes gleamed black.

"Everything alright?" he called up to me.

I reached for Loren, pulling him inside. I waved a hand. "We're fine. Thanks."

The sidewalk Rabbit gave a nod before turning and crossing the street. I puffed out a breath into the cold air, watching a cloud form. *Guess the surveillance team is in place,* I thought.

Behind me, Loren cleared his throat. I closed the door and offered a grim smile. "You obviously got my message?"

The older witch lifted a paper bag. "Your purse and clothing are in here." He warily assessed Rabbit.

"Thank you," I said, reaching for the package Loren held. "May I take your coat?"

"I can't stay long," he answered. He nodded

to Templeton, his attention shifting again nervously toward Rabbit.

Rabbit's eyes glittered.

"Loren, this is Rabbit. Rabbit, this is Loren – a good friend of mine." I gestured between the two men.

Loren held out his hand. "Lucie has told me about you. I'm glad to know she has loyal friends surrounding her. It's nice to meet you."

Rabbit cocked his head to the side, his nose twitching, but he accepted Loren's handshake. "Likewise."

"What happened was inexcusable," Loren said as he turned to me. "Guillaume has lost favor with some of the Congress elders."

"What that group of incompetent witches allowed today proved the depth of depravity running rampant in the upper echelons of the witch community, Loren. You know as well as I do several witches in the room considered the demonstration sport. The more Lucie suffered, the greater their pleasure," Templeton spat.

I held up a hand. "We're not attacking Loren. He did everything he could."

"Templeton is right though," sighed Loren. "There were a few witches observing who enjoyed what you went through." He fixed Templeton with a knowing look. "However, Lucie had friends in the room, and you know as well as I do one of those elders is especially powerful."

"What's he talking about?" I turned from Loren to Templeton.

Templeton ignored me, choosing instead to smirk at Loren.

Loren continued to address Templeton. "I assume he's the reason you were given permission to join in the observation. However, your relationship with him won't save you. You'll be receiving a notification of your membership termination. You will no longer be a member of the Congress of Empire Witches. I'm sorry."

"What? Loren, why? This is ridiculous!" I threw my hands up in the air and started to storm away. I stopped, whirling around. "This is because he performed magic in the building, isn't it? They're getting him on a technicality."

Templeton didn't appear to be as upset as I felt. "I assume it's also because I broke into the demonstration, attacked Guillaume with a counter spell, called up a mini tornado, then door traveled out of the Congress building with Lucie on my arm."

The corners around Loren's beady eyes crinkled. "I particularly enjoyed seeing the Acton matriarch pelted with a water bottle."

"Wait, you're not upset?" I scanned Templeton's face.

"I will miss the library."

It still wasn't fair. "Can't he present his case?" I asked Loren. "I mean, forget me and the hell I endured – Guillaume conjured a demon! In the Congress building! Templeton was trying to put a stop to everything going down. There were clearly extenuating circumstances."

"Which is why Guillaume is being strongly encouraged to return to France. His actions will not go unaddressed," Loren promised. "He will be disciplined and warned against such reckless behavior in the future."

"But he won't lose his membership?"

"No, he will not." Loren shook his head. "He's a valuable teacher. The Congress does not want to lose him."

"Unbelievable." And yet, what did I expect? The elders were closing ranks, removing those who opposed their interests and keeping the ones who benefited them.

"The man you were seeing last fall," Loren

began. "The one without honor –"

Templeton interrupted. "You knew about Sebastian?"

"Only what Lucie told me over lunch," Loren replied to Templeton. He refocused on me. "He became a demon then?"

"Yes." I fidgeted with the neckline of my sweater.

"But he's not dead, is he?"

None of us replied to Loren as the words sunk in. I shook my head. "No, I guess he's not."

"Which explains why Guillaume couldn't exercise power over the binding." Loren waggled a finger in the air at no one in particular. "He assumed this Sebastian was dead. No, he's a very different type of demon. He either made a choice to become one, or he's paying a debt. Guillaume's conjuring and subsequent binding were more appropriate for a demon created upon death."

"Wait, how do you know Sebastian's not dead?" I asked.

"My line includes a handful of necromancers – not something that's commonly known. While I do not practice necromancy myself, in my limited experience in dealing with the dead

I've learned they lose the vibration they carried with them in life. Your demon still has his. In fact, it's agitating at an incredibly high frequency. I'm almost surprised you didn't sense it. It's quite noticeable."

My demon.

"Well, that might explain some of the things he told me," I began, stopping when I saw Templeton's eyes narrow.

"Guillaume told the Congress elders he first dealt with the demon here in your house. Is this true?" Loren asked.

"Unfortunately, yes. Sebastian broke in and held me hostage. Guillaume happened to show up at the right time. He chased him off." There was no need to tell Loren the whole story.

"My experience with demons is limited," Loren admitted. "But I can bring in a witch specializing in demonology who can help you banish him properly."

"That won't be necessary," Templeton cut in. "I can take care of this for Lucie."

Loren pulled a handkerchief from an inside coat pocket. He removed his eyeglasses and proceeded to wipe the lenses. "I have no doubt you can. But I am available for whatever help I might be able to provide."

It was time to change the subject. I didn't want to talk about Sebastian anymore. I needed more time to think about my recent experience with him. "Loren, I hope the Congress is satisfied now. I'm not willing to provide any more proof of how I strengthened my witchline. I have more than met any expectations the elders had."

"What we witnessed today certainly proves what is possible," Loren answered. "I cannot speak for what it means for the future." He glanced at Templeton, then back to me. "As I mentioned this past weekend, some families might take an interest in adding you to their branches. The potential benefit to their thinning witchlines would be appealing."

Rabbit remained quiet throughout the whole exchange, but he recognized immediately what Loren meant. He spoke, his voice low and dangerous. "Lucie isn't an animal to be bred."

Loren didn't shrink away. "No, she isn't. But I want her to understand the situation fully."

"One disaster at a time," I pleaded. "What you're referring to is not something I can deal with today."

"There's more, Lucie." Loren grimaced. "The Congress has suspended your membership pending an investigation surrounding your behavior since you returned from studying in France."

I barked out a laugh. "At this point, I'm not sure I care."

"You know how important membership is. While you're suspended, you lose many of your benefits. You cannot enter the building and the library is off-limits. Your case will be reviewed in three months. If the Congress decides to completely terminate your membership, your stipend will be cancelled."

"She doesn't need their pitiful stipend," Templeton butted in again. "I will take care of her."

"Oh, for god's sake." I slapped my forehead. "I am quite capable of taking care of myself. Who do you think has been doing it all these years? My house is paid for and unless the Congress is going to demand I return what they've already given to me, I'm more than fine."

"They'd never want to set the precedent," Loren said. "No, what you've been paid is yours to keep."

"I'm beyond disappointed in the elders," I said. "After working so hard, to be treated this way." My voice faltered.

"Me, too." Loren reached for me and I accepted his hug. I rested my cheek against his shoulder. He patted my back. "Do you want to come stay with us for a few days? Michelle would love having you near."

I gave Loren a squeeze before pulling away. "No, I'm good. I want to stay in my home. It's important for me to be in my own space. I do not want to hide."

Loren looked from Templeton to Rabbit. He frowned. "Perhaps a girlfriend can stay with you for a few days?"

"Perhaps," I replied. "I'll think about it."

"Well," Loren's gaze again slid back and forth between Rabbit and Templeton as he spoke to me. "Anything you need, you let me know."

"Thanks for everything you've already done. I'm sorry for this whole mess. I'm sure you've had fallout of your own to deal with," I added.

"Nothing an old witch like me can't handle. But I should be going." He inclined his head toward Templeton and Rabbit. "Gentlemen."

I opened the door for Loren and after he

stepped outside, I quickly joined him on the stoop closing the door behind me. "One more thing."

Loren gave me a curious look. "Yes?"

"You said I had a powerful friend in the room with the elders today."

"Yes."

"Can you tell me who it was?"

"No. Some elders prefer not to make their status known, Lucie. They have their reasons."

"Can you tell me this?" I asked. I pictured the elders filing into the observation room – how there were only eight, until the ninth one arrived with Templeton by his side. "Was that elder standing by Templeton during the demonstration today?"

Loren paused, his small eyes flashing. He nodded. "Yes."

∞∞∞

"Well, the fun continues," I said as I stepped back inside the house. The two men waited in the entryway while I was outside. I shooed them toward the kitchen. "You two have to stop hovering. You're making me nervous."

"I'm no fan of the CEW, but is your suspension serious enough to worry about?" Rabbit asked me.

"Could it get any worse?" I waved both hands at him. "Don't answer that. No, I'm mostly disappointed in the elders, and like Templeton said, not having access to things like the library will suck. But whatever. I wasn't always a member. I lived without the Congress before."

"Okay," he answered.

The three of us stood stupidly around the counter.

"I can spend the night here," Templeton spoke suddenly.

"I'll stay here tonight," Rabbit said at the same time.

"Actually, I was thinking about having Big Rabbit crash here. He has before," I said.

Both of them gawked at me.

"That was a joke." I shook my head. "No, I think I would like to be alone tonight." I motioned to Templeton. "But I'd like to take you up on your offer to help me strengthen my wards. I think mixing our magic might create an added layer of protection I can use right now."

Templeton wasn't happy with my decision to

spend the night alone, but he didn't argue. Instead, he agreed to help me with the additional spellcasting. Rabbit also made a point of telling me he'd have a contingent of Rabbits in the area if I needed any help. I was instructed to have my phone on me at all times.

We agreed to meet first thing at 7 o'clock in the morning. Rabbit would let us know if anything changed in the Walled Zone as soon as he heard anything.

Tomorrow we'd go see for ourselves if there was even a hint of the fifth and sixth directional doors opening.

∞∞∞

After Rabbit left, Templeton and I worked to add layers of protection to my home. I went over the wards I'd recently raised, confirming they were properly formed. Having a Magician working beside me was a new experience. While it was still Templeton, he wasn't holding anything back with me while we worked. He was focused, adept. The spells he cast were creative. The complexity would deter most.

We discussed the permissions of the spell,

finally settling on wording which would allow those I 'invited into my home' to enter. The beauty was in its simplicity. If you weren't invited, you wouldn't be able to pass through the wards. After some debate, however, we chose to leave the type of invitation ambiguous. For example, if Rabbit brought his crew with him, I didn't want to be required to stand at the front door inviting each person in one at a time. I didn't want entry to be dependent upon my being home either. The invitation, then, would consider the intent of the visitor as well as who I desired to bring inside my home. This made the spell more difficult as it needed to remain flexible and responsive to my visitor preferences.

But we accomplished what we set out to do. Templeton still wanted me to come stay with him – he believed I would be safer. Again, I thanked him and said no. To pacify him, I let him tell me the code used to get into his penthouse. The concierge already had my name on file, he said. I could go there at any time, no questions asked.

With the carefully crafted spells in place, Templeton said goodnight and I watched as he door traveled away through the pantry door. As the swirls of his energy dissipated into the air after he left, I realized how seriously he took his role in the prophecy. The Magician *was* my knight, protecting me in any way I would let him.

I had to wonder, though. Who needed me to be their light? And what exactly did that mean?

Chapter 22

With the extra protection spells in place, I was not as jumpy as I'd been the night before. The magic I'd performed with Templeton would keep out unwanted visitors. I was still horrified by what I'd experienced at Guillaume's hands, and I was angry at the Congress elders for letting him get away with it, but sleep would come fast. The day had left me exhausted.

I poured myself a big glass of wine and snagged *Empire Tales for Children* on my way upstairs. I'd read the next fairy tale before calling it a night.

In my bedroom, I changed into a pair of soft flannel pajama bottoms and the green tee shirt I'd lifted from Templeton. I'd sent him home with the sweatpants and sweatshirt I wore earlier. I didn't mention keeping the tee shirt. He'd figure it out when he looked inside the bag.

I shut off all the lights except for the lamp on my nightstand and climbed into bed with my glass and the book. Sitting cross-legged on my covers, I sipped at my wine. Only a week had passed since I'd returned to Matar. I shook my head. I'd left the Empire to grieve losing the man I thought Sebastian was and to figure out how to handle my complicated relationship with Templeton. I'd left to find the Lucie I used to be. The year I'd spent with Guillaume made me stronger in some ways, but terribly vulnerable in others. I'd learned that the hard way.

And now I was back in Matar, dealing with Templeton, Guillaume, and to my amazement, Sebastian.

Because he wasn't dead.

I held onto the hope Guillaume would return to France in the wake of his defeat. It was possible.

And then there was Templeton. I smiled into my wine glass. Tonight was so easy. The magic we worked together was effortless. Agreeing on what to do and how to do it raised some debate, but even that was enjoyable. We might struggle to get how we feel about each other right, but we intuitively knew how to combine our magic.

I didn't want to take it for granted.

The phone Rabbit gave to me was charging on the nightstand and I sensed the sudden heat it gave off. I checked the message. It was from my friend.

Everything good?

And then there was Rabbit, I thought. I could feel our relationship deepening. I took a big swig of wine. Rabbit was always looking out for me. It was his nature to take care of others. He solved problems and stayed loyal. And he *was* cute. I loved to tease him about his hair; those soft, black curls were irresistible.

He also had incredibly sexy arms. I swirled the wine in my glass before taking another swallow. I wasn't blind. Rabbit's masculinity was appealing. He turned more than a few heads when we spent happier times together last summer, but he never seemed to notice. I knew he had one or two 'friends' he kept company with from time to time. He never shared any details, of course, but there'd been a few mornings I'd guessed what he'd been up to the night before. He blushed adorably when I teased him.

I sighed. I wished he'd tell me what was wrong with him. The sickness I sensed when he was near was no simple bug as he'd claimed. I was torn between pushing him for an answer now and waiting until we got a handle on what was happening in the Walled Zone. I'd play it by ear.

All good, I texted back to him.

Okay. Get some rest. See you tomorrow.

See you then. I hit the 'send.'

Templeton had texted me before, but Sebastian stole that phone. I wondered if Templeton would be able to text me on this one, too. It was different from the electronic devices used outside of the Empire. Plus, Rabbit had put limitations on how I could use it. I understood. I wasn't supposed to have one, after all. But I'd like to be connected to Templeton.

I set both the phone and my wine on the nightstand before picking up the book of fairy tales. I opened it to the next story.

∞∞∞

The Blending

After the young girl finished dream-journeying into the Below, she stood by the sea. A huge, colorful bird flew overhead, dipping its wings to the right and the left, stroking the sky by soaring up and gliding down. It circled and landed in front of the child. The bird turned its head to the side, considering her.

"And what land in the Between is this?" asked the bird as it swished its multicolored tailfeathers.

"This is the Empire," the girl replied. "What is the Between?"

"This is the Between!" The bird spun around, flapping its wings. "I fly over all the places in the Between making sure the thin shadows go to the Below when they are born. Sometimes the wind blows very hard and I discover a new land. But it only happens when someone leaves a door open."

"Which door?" the girl asked. She thought of the North, East, West, South, the Above, and the Below doors. Surely they remained tightly closed?

"All of the doors," the bird crowed. "There are many, many doors. Don't leave them open – not even a crack! It gets too windy and I cannot find the thin shadows."

"I traveled to the Below and the thin shadows wanted the Light. I had none to give to them," she told the bird.

"The Light lives in the Between now. It ran away from the Darkness." The bird twisted its neck and

preened, burying its beak in its back feathers.

"Why did the Light run away?" The girl watched as the bird swung its head back around to face her.

"Because it was afraid the Darkness would make it forget it was the Light." The bird looked sad. "But the Darkness is the only way the Light can be the Light. The Darkness comes before the Light. It touches the Light. The Darkness keeps secrets and protects many truths. The Light reveals the many truths. The Light saw the many truths and became afraid."

"What about the One Truth?" The girl was puzzled. "The Beams of Light from Above said there is only One Truth and untruths."

The feathers covering the bird ruffled. "The One Truth is true. So are the many truths. The untruths are simply the many truths held upside down. If you hang from the Black Sky with your head touching the ground, you will see the untruths are truths."

The bird hopped from one leg to the other and the ground vibrated. "Just because something is an untruth here doesn't mean it's an untruth in another place. There are many truths."

"But the One Truth?" The girl prompted.

"Is true," the bird said again. "But it only lives

in the Above. There it must stay." The bird lowered its body to the ground and spread its wings. "Come with me and I will fly across the sea. From there you can see the Above, the Between, and the Below. From there you can see how they blend into one another with doors leading into the many imaginings and realities which make up everything."

The child made sure the pretty stones were still safely hidden in her pocket before climbing onto the back of the bird. The bird sprang up and they rose into the sky.

The girl looked down at the land growing smaller under them. She thought about the Light and the Darkness. The girl grew concerned when she considered the bird's story. If the Light ran away from the Darkness, wouldn't it simply disappear?

∞∞∞

I shut the book, running the last line of the fairy tale through my brain once more.

If the Light ran away from the Darkness, wouldn't it simply disappear?

There are witches who practice dark magic without a second thought. For them, it's simply yet another path to reach whatever it is they set out to do. There are those who wander into a gray area – the magic used isn't necessarily evil, but it's definitely dipping a toe in murky waters. I was no innocent. I'd swum in gray waters, but they're not something I'd dive into without careful planning and one hell of a good reason.

My fingers stroked the cover of the book of fairy tales. I was the light in the prophecy involving Templeton as the knight – the prophecy having nothing to do with the book on my lap. And yet, I found myself identifying more and more with the messages hidden in these tales. I didn't see myself as the child, but I did understand why the Light ran away from the Darkness. The Darkness wasn't only dangerous, it was easy to get lost in it.

The Light in the book of fairy tales – did it feel itself getting lost? Is that why it chose to disappear instead?

∞∞∞

I did fall asleep quickly, but it was a restless sleep. I dreamt of big, colorful birds pecking at my hair and slippery shadows crawling over my skin like large silverfish. I could hear their chanting: *Light, Light, Light!* Sebastian turned up, too, but he wasn't a demon. He was sitting in the glass atrium at his cabin drinking wine. He was relaxed, his feet propped up as he rested back against his Adirondack chair. His head rolled to the side and he looked at me through heavy-lidded eyes. He told me I glowed for him.

The dream morphed into the night in the library with Templeton. We kissed. I felt his tongue filling my mouth, his hand moving along my body possessively. When I pulled back, Templeton had become Guillaume. I jolted awake, anxiety creeping over my skin. It was only 3 o'clock in the morning.

I tried to go back to sleep.

Rabbit died in the next dream.

At 5 o'clock I gave up on a peaceful night's sleep. I showered off the nightmares before I dressed and went downstairs where I set a pot of coffee to brew. I popped two slices of bread into the toaster before picking up the book of fairy tales. There was one story left.

∞∞∞

The Ending

The colorful bird flew over the sea with the young girl on its back. They landed on a sloped hill overlooking the water. The girl climbed down, standing in the cool grass. "Where are we?"

"We're where we can see everything and everything can see us," the bird answered. "Look up and down."

The child obeyed and could see all the bright stars and moons and suns in the Above; all the lands and seas and mountains in the Between; and nothing but shadows and black in the Below. Every now and then she would hear a chorus of cries leaking out from the Below.

She noted a row of doors, hundreds of miles long, sitting atop the Between. "There are so many!"

"Each door leads to its own imagined place or reality. One door opens into your land in the Between. These doors blend into the Above. The Beams of Light from Above live there. It is a hard space for other creatures to endure. Most do not stay. Some get trapped," the bird finished.

"What happens when they get trapped?" asked the girl.

"They disappear into the bright white of the

Above. They cease to be."

This made the child sad. The Above sounded like a horrible place to live. The Below was a sad and frightening place as well. She was glad she lived in the Between.

"But what about the One Truth?"

"The One Truth lives in the Above."

"And the many truths?" she continued.

"Throughout all the realities and imaginings in the universe."

"And the untruths?"

The bird rose into the air, its beak pointed upward as it flapped its wings. "There are no untruths. There are many truths!"

"Why do you look for the thin shadows? Why must they go to the Below?" the child asked suddenly as the bird lowered to the ground.

"Because they want the Light, but they are not ready for it. Only when they are willing to live in the Light will they be able to leave the Below and find it."

"But where is the Light?"

The bird swept its feathered wing over her face. "The Light is in the Between, but it's hiding. Perhaps if you knew how to call it, the Light would return."

The child did not know how to call the Light, but her fingers touched the pretty stones in her pocket. She pulled them out and showed the bird – who agreed immediately: they were very special.

The Above, Between, and Below ebbed and flowed in the distance. "Can everyone see this place on which we stand?" she asked.

The bird nodded.

"Then this is where I shall hide the pretty stones." The girl dug a deep hole. She tore off a strip of cloth from her skirt's hem and wrapped the three pieces of stone in it. She gingerly placed them into the hole, returning the dirt to cover the cloth packet. She set a large, flat rock on top to mark the spot. The colorful bird plucked a handful of feathers from its shoulder and dropped them on top of the rock. The rich hues bled into the stone's surface: the reds, blues, oranges, and greens swirling and resembling a city skyline against the sunset.

"It seems we have come to the end," said the bird, lowering so the girl could climb onto its back.

The girl nodded, snuggling into the warmth of the feathers. "The pretty stones will be safe here, but what about the Light? Will it ever come back?"

"Only when it's no longer afraid of the Darkness," the bird replied as it spread its wings wide.

The bird hopped into the air, soaring up and diving down on a flight to return the girl to the Between. It would be there the young girl would wait to find the Light.

The end.

∞∞∞

I sipped my coffee and chewed a bite of toast. And there you have it. The book of fairy tales making everything as clear as mud.

Emily had found the Crimson Stone in an antique store in a city known for its artist community. The store was called *Common Vue* – the 'plain sight' the girl referred to in the first tale, *Three Pieces*. Emily had snuck into *Common Vue* to search for the Stone in the middle of the night. She was accosted by a corrupt justice of the Salesman Court who tried to take the Stone from her. Templeton arrived next and there was a struggle with this other man. The Stone slipped free. And that is how Emily came to be in possession of it.

The Crimson Stone is a powerful, magical gemstone that can be separated into three pieces. I believed it was the same set of stones as the 'pretty stones' in the book of fairy tales. And last year, I used it to close the fifth and six doors.

Afterward, I cast a spell and put the Crimson Stone to sleep. I gave it to Templeton since it belonged to his family – something we didn't know at the beginning of the journey. Well, none of us except for Templeton.

"Because he loves to keep secrets," I exhaled, once more opening the book of fairy tales to the last page. But what about the Light in the story? Did it ever come out of hiding? Did the Darkness find it?

At the end of the book, the 'pretty stones' were hidden. And then Emily found them. The Light, however, never came out of hiding. But was the Light something tangible – like the stones? Was the Light a person, like me?

It was weird to have these thoughts. I was already uncomfortable thinking of myself as part of the prophecy bringing us together:

> *A traveler is born.*
> *The knight protects the light.*
> *Their successor sets fire to the stone.*
> *A shadow is cast out.*

Not only was it unnerving, I didn't feel worthy to play a role in it, whatever the role of the light was supposed to be.

I read the final line of the last fairy tale again:

It would be there the young girl would wait to find the Light.

She would *wait* to *find* the Light.

A knock at the front of the house pulled me from my thoughts. Rabbit was early. Before opening the door, I peeked through the side window. A stranger stood on my stoop, holding a top hat. He smiled, but his eyes stayed mean. A Salesman? On the sidewalk below, I saw two male Rabbits appear, their bodies relaxed with their hands buried deep in coat pockets. But I knew better. They would spring into action at the first sign of trouble.

The Salesman looked over his shoulder, acknowledging the men. He turned back to the door between us.

"I have a message for a Lucie Bellerose," he called through the door.

It was early for this type of delivery, but it wasn't strange to have a message delivered by a Salesman. Some men and women were employed by the Empire in this capacity.

With the Rabbits watching over us from the sidewalk, I unlocked the door and pulled it open. "What is this about?" I asked.

"I have a message for you," he said, lowering his voice. "He wanted me to bring this to you." He reached inside his overcoat and pulled out an envelope. The Salesman glanced down at the sidewalk. One of the Rabbits had moved to the bottom stair.

"Who is it from? Why are you making a delivery at this hour?" I asked. Something was off.

"It's from Sebastian."

My gaze strayed to the closest Rabbit, then back to the man at my door. If he was making a delivery for Sebastian, he was not only a Salesman, but also connected to what was left of the Fringe. "What do you mean?"

The Salesman shook the envelope at me. "He wanted it delivered to you immediately. Here."

I saw my hand accepting it. "Where is he?"

"Dunno." The surly Salesman abruptly turned and descended the steps. He walked by the Rabbits as if they were not there.

"You okay?" The first Rabbit called up. The other one texted furiously behind him.

"Yeah." I realized I was holding the envelope

against my chest. I dropped my hand. "Yeah, I'm fine. It was a delivery. That's all. Thanks, guys."

He nodded, nudging his partner. The two reluctantly backed off, crossing the street and disappearing. I shut the door, locking it. I carried the envelope into the living room and sat on the sofa. It was sealed, and no writing appeared on the outside. I pushed my index finger under the flap.

A plain piece of folded paper was inside. I drew it out slowly. Opening it, I recognized the handwriting. Sebastian had scratched out a short note. He wrote:

Lucie,
Please come to me as soon as you get this message. I don't have much time left. I'm at the cabin.
Basha

I read and reread the message several times. What did he think I was going to do? What did he expect to happen? I checked the mantel clock. Templeton and Rabbit would arrive at any minute. I put the note back inside the envelope. Gritting my teeth, I made a decision I hoped I would not regret.

I took the envelope upstairs. After unlocking the spell I'd placed on my jewelry armoire, I placed Sebastian's message inside next to the tissues stained with his blood. I pushed the drawer closed and recast my spell.

There was no way I was going to the cabin. If he had little time left, maybe it meant he was going back into the Below. Maybe I wouldn't have to face him again.

I heard another knock on my front door.

∞∞∞

I let Rabbit in and we joined a waiting Templeton in the kitchen. No one could say these two ever ran late. Rabbit was always on time. Templeton was usually early.

Still swimming in guilt, I didn't look at either man as I poured cups of coffee for the three of us. Rabbit gave his update on the pulses coming from the compound in the Walled Zone. I snuck a peek at Templeton through my eyelashes when I slid the coffee cup toward him. He'd been listening closely to Rabbit, but now his attention swung to me. His pupils became pinpricks in his ice-blue irises and he scowled. *Dammit.* Did he suspect something?

I hastily turned away and handed Rabbit his coffee.

"So, a steady increase?" I rejoined the conversation.

"Barely an increase, but yeah. This was the report coming in about 15 minutes ago." Rabbit wrapped his chapped fingers around the coffee cup. He paused for a beat. "What was up with the early Salesman delivery?"

Living in a glass bubble was getting old.

"Let me guess, the camera is still pointed at my front door?" I avoided looking at Templeton, but I was aware of his continued scrutiny. Could he detect I was concealing something from them? Did he sense something was off?

"And I received a message from one of my crew. They texted me." Rabbit waited, a finger tapping the side of his cup.

"A letter was delivered. No big deal." I swallowed a gulp of hot coffee and coughed. I'd definitely crossed a line by withholding this from them. But I couldn't tell them. I didn't know how to explain my reluctance and I knew they certainly wouldn't understand.

Rabbit's nose twitched. "Okay. Okay, then." He turned to Templeton and shrugged. "Lucie and I are going to leave for the compound. It'll take us several hours to get there. We'll leave her car on a side road and hike in. That'll take us another 30 minutes. My guys know we're coming. Once we're there, I'll text you and you can door travel to us. You're bringing the Crimson Stone, right?"

Templeton gave a tiny nod. He resumed staring at me, coldness saturating his eyes. He was angry.

"We'll pick up something to eat on the way," Rabbit said to me. "Do you have hiking boots? There's snow on the ground there – probably half a foot. And bring your phone."

"Yeah. Let me throw on a sweatshirt, too. Then we can go." I ran my eyes over Templeton's clothes. He wore a soft blue dress shirt and black trousers. My gaze dropped to his feet. His leather shoes appeared to be freshly shined. I gestured at his clothing. "Are you going to –?"

"Text me immediately when you arrive at the compound, Rabbit." Templeton ignored me. "I don't need coordinates. I've traveled into those buildings enough over the past four months."

"Will do." Rabbit looked expectantly at me. "Grab your stuff so we can go."

I watched Templeton stalk toward the pantry door. "Templeton, wait."

His fingers hovered over the doorknob, but he didn't turn back around. "Yes?"

My mouth felt dry. "I'll see you there."

I felt, rather than saw, the sharp jerk of his shoulders before he door traveled out of my kitchen without saying another word.

Chapter 23

"What aren't you telling us?" Rabbit asked after we gassed up my RAV4 and hit the highway leading out of Matar. I was driving. Rabbit tapped a message into his phone while he waited for me to answer. When we were deep inside the Walled Zone, he'd take the wheel. He knew exactly where we were going.

The Walled Zone is to the west of Matar in the northern part of the Empire. It's mostly mountainous, and the weather tends to be brutal for a good portion of the year. The Fringe used the region to hide during some of the more fierce battles decades ago. It's remained sparsely populated. It's not the easiest place to live.

Sebastian's mammoth cabin was on the edge of the Walled Zone closest to Matar. We wouldn't be driving by it, of course, but it made my stomach turn to think we were close to where he wanted me to meet him. I squashed down the irrational thought that he'd know I was nearby.

I merged into traffic. Thankfully the roads were bare leaving the city and the sun was out. I hoped the weather stayed pleasant, but I knew it could change in a flash in a few hours.

I glided a hand back and forth over the steering wheel, hesitating. At least Rabbit waited to question me when it was only the two of us. "Why are you asking me that?"

"Lucie, quit stalling." His voice sounded tired.

I snuck a look at my friend, noticing the shadowy smudges under his eyes. Lack of sleep? Illness? "You're referring to the delivery I got this morning."

"You know I am."

"Right." I nodded, steeling myself. "Sebastian sent me a message. He's still at his cabin. He wanted me to go there."

Rabbit twisted his head back and forth, lifting his chin to the left, then to the right. I heard a crack. "Why didn't you tell us?"

"What would have it accomplished?" I asked.

He sighed. "You can't keep secrets from us. You're in danger. I know you're *conflicted* about

Sebastian. I don't know why you are, but I get that's the way it is. But don't keep me in the dark. It makes it harder for me. What you do or don't tell Templeton is your business, but if he's trying to help you, you should be honest with him, too. Enough with all these secrets."

"You should take your own advice." I fiddled with the radio. "You're not exactly the poster child for truthfulness these days. I can see that you're –"

"We're not talking about me."

"We should."

"Lucie, I'm shutting this down right now. Do you understand?" The abrupt hardness in his voice alarmed me, and I turned my head toward him. His eyes were solid black. He was furious.

"Rabbit," I began.

"Eyes on the fucking road or pull over and I'll drive!" He reached for the radio and jacked up the volume.

I let the blisteringly loud music fill the vehicle for a while. Rabbit alternated between texting and staring out the passenger door window. I tolerated the noise – and his silence – for as long as I could before shutting the radio off.

"I'm sorry," I said, watching the sunlight

bounce across the road. "I didn't tell you about the message because I don't know what to do about Sebastian. Sebastian is *my* problem because we were involved." I blew out a breath. "And I didn't want Templeton turning around and door traveling straight into Sebastian's cabin once he found out he was trying to contact me. You know he'd do something like that. I don't care how powerful Templeton is. We don't know what Sebastian is capable of doing now. We don't know the extent of his powers yet. I didn't want Templeton to run off into trouble without us."

Rabbit didn't answer.

"I left last fall because everything I had turned to shit. I needed time to get my head together and to come to terms with everything I'd *lost*. I came back months later and guess what? More shit. And I'm tired of it. I'm tired of everyone pulling at me and wanting something from me. I've hit my breaking point and frankly, I don't even know who I can trust anymore. Everyone wants something from me," I finished.

He snorted. It made me angry.

"Yeah. You know what? I'm counting you in that too, Rabbit. Only I haven't quite figured out what you think is going to happen between us." The heat rose quickly in my body along with a bellyful of rage. I couldn't seem to stop my temper from flaring and striking out.

Rabbit finally spoke, his tone bitter. "Don't flatter yourself."

"Tell me I'm wrong."

"What the hell happened to you, Lucie?"

I gripped the wheel, searching for the right words. "The man who broke my heart came back to life."

∞∞∞

We didn't speak for a long time. Once inside the Walled Zone, we pulled into a convenience store for gas and a bathroom break. I grabbed bottled water, a bag of pretzels, and a couple of day-old sandwiches, making sure one of them was vegetarian. Rabbit took the wheel and we ate as he drove us deeper into this lonely and rural part of the Empire. We became the only vehicle on the narrow road winding into the mountains. At times, snow blew heavily through the pass, making the trip even more treacherous.

I wanted to take back the things I'd said to Rabbit. The way I struck out at him was childish. It was mean. I was mad at him for not telling me he was sick, for not telling me what was wrong so I could help. Out of all my friends, Rabbit was the one person who gave of himself without asking for anything in return. He never expected anything from anyone. He showed up and took care of us. He deserved better.

The weight sitting on my chest made me miserable, but I didn't see how I could fix this now. I closed my eyes, my hands in my lap, and leaned my head against the seat. I'd make it up to him. I'd find a way to get him to tell me what was wrong, how he was sick, and then I'd help *him*. I suppressed a sniffle, my lip quivering like a child's.

I felt a hand cover mine and squeeze. Opening my watery eyes, I focused on the road beyond the windshield and nodded. I said nothing.

He'd already forgiven me.

∞∞∞

"Up ahead there's a side road where we can hide your car," Rabbit told me, breaking the silence. "The hike isn't bad. I'll text my guys to let them know we're coming in. Once we're in the compound, I'll text Templeton. We'll check the quad and see if we notice anything strange where the doors were located last year." He turned the car to the right and maneuvered the RAV4 off to the side. A frozen dirt road stretched into the woods and he backed into it. *In case we need to make a fast getaway*, I thought.

The weather had turned once we were inside the Walled Zone – the sun disappearing behind a ceiling of gray. A few flurries floated through the trees. Our breath puffed out into the cold air in front of us and we buttoned up our coats. I pulled up the hood on my sweatshirt, tucking my hair inside. Rabbit grabbed a canvas backpack from the back seat while I tugged on a pair of gloves. He texted our arrival to the Rabbits at the compound and got a thumbs up. Taking one last swig of water, I locked my car and we started our hike up the dirt road. The snow was a hard six inches under our feet. A steady crunch-crunch-crunch interrupted the stillness as we marched.

Twenty-five minutes later, we reached a high fence topped with razor wire. This was expected. I paused, craning my neck. A beat echoed from somewhere beyond the fence. "Can you hear that?"

"I don't hear anything," he replied. "But I can kind of feel something reverberating in my chest. I think it's the pulsing."

We picked our way along the perimeter of the compound for another 10 minutes until we reached the gate with its abandoned security guard booth. Once occupied by the Fringe, then the Empire guards, it now stood empty. The gate was left open and we entered the deserted compound.

The place was once owned by Ivanov Transport and the footprint of the physical plant included four large warehouses facing an empty quad. Several truck trailers remained parked on the opposite sides of the warehouses – one was destroyed in a firebomb attack. The burnt frame served as a grim reminder of the dreadful night we fought the Fringe.

Rabbit texted as we moved. "They're supposed to be in the first building. I told them we're outside now." His thumb slid on the screen again. "I just sent a message to Templeton, too. I don't know which building he's door traveling into, but I told him to meet us in the first building for a briefing as soon as he gets here."

"Then we'll go out into the quad together," I nodded.

"Yup." Rabbit studied his phone, his eyebrows pulling together. "My guys haven't replied."

"The pulsing is getting louder," I said. An uneasy feeling slithered over my skin. I shifted from side to side, warily taking in the emptiness around us. "Let's get inside the building."

"You feel it, too?" Rabbit asked, his hand grasping my elbow. "Move it."

"Is it paranoia?" I whispered as we scurried to one of the doors on the front of the first building.

"Maybe," he mumbled. "But something isn't right."

As we reached the door, a shrill squeal not unlike the sound of worn brake pads on a car pierced the air. The metallic sound crested over the endless pulsing. Rabbit pushed me inside the warehouse and shut the door behind us.

"What was that?" I breathed.

He shook his head. Unmoving, we waited. When the noise didn't repeat, he pulled on my arm again. "Let's find the others."

The warehouse was filled with discarded heavy equipment. Semitrucks, with their cabovers tilted forward and engines bared, created inky shadows over the floor. Rows of hollow truck trailers sat unused. The building was dimly lit – grimy windows, set near the ceiling, lined two walls. They did nothing to chase the gloom away. The floor was concrete and covered with dirt, oil stains, and in some places, dead bugs and animal droppings. There was no heat; the building was bone cold.

We kept to the wall and walked the length of the warehouse. Rabbit's last text to the two men we sought still hadn't been acknowledged. He messaged them yet again, lifting his chin and sniffing as he hit 'send.' He froze, his eyes swirling into a shiny black. He growled low.

The tiny hairs on the back of my neck rose, and I fought the nasty chill running through my body. "Rabbit?" My lips moved, but no sound came out.

He hurriedly sent another text before pocketing his phone. Motioning for me to stay behind him, we crept forward. As we blended deeper into the gloom, I thought of Templeton. I hoped like hell he was safe wherever he'd landed because something was definitely wrong. I concentrated on Rabbit's sturdy back. I was grateful I wasn't alone in this miserable place.

Ahead, a shaft of light cut through the murkiness and we headed for it. I assumed we'd find the other Rabbits there, but Rabbit stopped us before we rounded the corner of a canvas-covered trailer at the end of the row. We stood still, listening.

Nothing. No talking, no music, and no sound of computer hardware whirring in the background while the men worked.

Rabbit's nostrils flared, his lips pulling into a snarl. "Blood."

His head swiveled back and forth before he spied a scrap of two-by-four. He snagged it, wrapping a steady hand around one end. Rabbit lifted his other hand to his mouth, briefly touching his index finger to his lips and warning me to be quiet. "Stay," he mouthed.

I retreated into the blackness surrounding us, pressing my back against the warehouse wall. Rabbit edged forward; the two-by-four already lifted. He leaned into his next step, his neck straining so he could check around the corner. A second later his body jolted and he shrank backward. He gave himself a shake before swiftly launching himself forward again, this time disappearing around the end of the trailer.

Keep calm, I thought as my heart throbbed hard in my chest. The noise in my ears – the blood pumping through my veins – competed against the pulsing coming from the compound. Pulling off my gloves, I checked that my network phone was still safely deep inside my jacket pocket. It was. I shoved my gloves into the other pocket, looking up at the dusty shafts of light cascading down into the warehouse. Particles swirled in the pitiful rays. I studied them. The pieces of dust and lint raced through the air. I felt no draft. It was as if something big had blown through the warehouse and the churning dirt was part of the aftermath. I ditched my hiding spot, creeping around the corner after Rabbit.

The scene before me brought the stale sandwich I ate earlier back up into my throat. I smacked a hand over my mouth and swallowed. Across the short expanse, Rabbit registered my presence but said nothing as he inched toward the second dead Rabbit, leaning forward to check the body.

The first one he'd encountered had no head.

Blood was everywhere. Shallow pools dotted the floor. Up the wall, bright red splatters glistened, the jagged splashes painting everything. My eyes jumped from the headless body to a pair of legs kneeling on the floor two desks away. Something had ripped the two Rabbits apart. A steaming pile of entrails had been dragged across the floor, a swipe of crimson and wet black globs trailing after it.

"Oh, god!" I stumbled backwards and spun, the vomit surging out of my mouth. Bending over, my arms around my stomach, I retched three times, the wet sound pummeling the concrete under my feet. I gasped, my head swimming.

The metallic shrieking we'd heard outside returned – but now it sounded like it was coming from inside the warehouse. I whipped around, wiping my mouth with the back of my hand. Rabbit was on the move, his boots and jeans colored with the blood of his brethren. "Hide!" he gritted out.

I lurched around the corner and staggered along the wall, my hand bouncing over it for support as I fled. I passed two long, lonely trailers before checking behind me. Rabbit hadn't followed! I waited a beat before another piercing whine split the air. Pitching headlong toward the back of the nearest trailer, I fumbled in the semi-darkness. My hands darted back and forth, arms stretched outward searching for anything inside the trailer sturdy enough to grab onto so I could pull myself up and inside. My finger dragged across something sharp and I felt my skin tear. Wincing at the pain, I kept reaching.

An earsplitting cacophony of grating metal rattled the windows of the building.

My fingers found a large, steel eye hook secured in the bottom of the abandoned trailer floor. I wrapped my hand around it and attempted to haul myself up, lifting my foot and frantically seeking a toehold.

Before I could pull myself up into the trailer, an arm wrapped around my waist, dragging me backward. My yelp was silenced by a man's hand slapping over my mouth, his long fingers and thumb squeezing my jaw.

"Shh, shh, shh!" Sebastian hissed. I fought his grasp and bit his hand as hard as I could. Instead of releasing me, he gripped me even tighter and hugged me to him, overpowering me with his demon-enhanced strength. I struggled, instinctively raising the heat inside my body before I remembered it didn't matter. He was unaffected by my fire.

Sebastian held on, my back against his chest as he fumbled with the hood on my sweatshirt, pulling it down. The hand over my mouth remained. He breathed into my ear. "Be quiet. You don't want them to find you."

I stopped fighting, sucking air in through my nose in short bursts. He waited until I calmed, my body sagging into his. I reached up and tugged at his wrist. He dropped his hand from my mouth, turning me to face him. The red haze in his eyes permeated the orbs like a thickening fog.

Sebastian rubbed my arms up and down as if he were trying to warm me. Craning his neck, he peered over his shoulder. We listened for the same terrifying noise to return. His head suddenly swung back to me and he rested his forehead against mine. "They're here. You can't let them see you. Don't let them see how you can glow."

"Who?" I asked, keeping my voice hushed.

"The beautiful beasts," he murmured, unmoving.

The trembling in my belly blossomed and spread out over my limbs. "Is the fifth door open?"

"Yes." A hand moved up to cup my right cheek.

"Who opened it, Sebastian?" My voice was barely audible.

"It's Basha, Lucie." He brushed his lips over mine once.

No, please don't, I thought, flinching.

Another chirring vibrated through the warehouse. This time the horrible sound felt like it was filling my brain and I shivered. "Who opened it?" I repeated.

"They did." His right hand slid down my arm and he lifted my hand. Blood ran from the slice in my finger. He sniffed it before kissing my palm, his lips skimming over my skin to my wrist.

I wrenched my hand away. "Is the sixth door open, too?"

Sebastian's body stiffened. "Yes." Then. "I want you to come with me."

"Where?" I asked. The frenzied range of emotions flickering across Sebastian's face was dizzying: fury, fear, sorrow, confusion, desire.

"To the Below." He angled his head, leaning in to kiss me. I turned away and he nuzzled my cheek with his nose instead. He inhaled. "You need to come with me."

I pressed my palms against his chest and pushed firmly. "No."

He reared back as if I'd struck him. At the same time, a blinding light lit up the center of the warehouse. Sebastian bared his teeth, grabbing me by the wrist and forcing me to follow as he ran in the opposite direction. I didn't fight him. If the 'beautiful beasts' really were here, it seemed Sebastian was the lesser of two evils.

Again.

We burst out the other side of the warehouse and sprinted across the snow-covered lot. He unexpectedly changed course, dragging me behind him. The piercing screams swelled around us as we headed for the quad. I could see a shimmering rectangle of light standing in the middle.

The fifth door was open – at its feet, the black earth split in a wide gash.

The sixth door.

The doors to the Above and the Below were open.

The pulsing grew louder. I yanked free from Sebastian, covering my ears and working my jaw up and down to relieve the pressure in my head. Out of the corner of my eye, I caught a movement across the expanse. Templeton emerged from one of the warehouses. In his hand he held the Crimson Stone.

I knew what he carried because I could see the Stone glowing. Someone – *or something* – had awakened it.

Sebastian slid to a stop in the slick snow. "Oh, good. Pencil dick is here, too."

I checked over my shoulder. We hadn't been chased, but it wouldn't be long before whatever monsters were in the first warehouse came after us.

Templeton advanced steadily closer, focusing on Sebastian. I could see his energy rising around him – huge waves of royal blue swelling as he cast a spell. He held out the Stone and a line of fire shot along the ground from his feet toward the demon.

I expected Sebastian's demon speed to save him. Instead, he watched the fire race in his direction. As it reached him, he stepped forward, walking along the trail of fire like he was on a tightrope. His head lowered and he eyeballed Templeton as he shortened the distance between them with sure strides. He was impervious to the fire magic Templeton used against him.

The Crimson Stone grew brighter, turning the snow-white ground around Templeton into a fierce red. It pulsed, and Templeton was close enough now for me to hear him cast a second spell, smashing Sebastian with a punishing blast of energy. Sebastian's head snapped back as if struck, his body spinning. But he managed to remain on his feet.

The pounding in my chest sped up when I realized the Stone was *also pulsing* – and it was matching the pulsing thundering around us. Whatever caused this beating – *the fifth and sixth doors opening or the 'beautiful beasts'* – the Stone responded to it. It was aligning itself with it.

And it was attracting the 'beautiful beasts' Sebastian warned us about last fall. It was attracting the 'beautiful beasts' he told me were here now.

The screeching reached a fever pitch and I turned to see tall columns of light flooding out of the first warehouse. They were stretched thin, these beings – these light beams – extending from the miserable sky above, to the wretched ground of the quad. Horrified, I looked up and watched as a jagged opening appeared in one of the columns of light. The sharp sound of metal scraping against itself burst from the makeshift mouth.

If these 'beautiful beasts' came from the Above... *Oh.* My fingers dug through my hair and I pressed my fingertips into my skull. *The Beams of Light from Above* – the beings who sang to the little girl about the 'one truth' in the book of fairy tales.

I sucked in a mouthful of icy air. "How can this be?"

Behind me, Sebastian sprang to life and tackled Templeton, knocking him to the ground, one hand on his throat, the other wrapped around his wrist. He banged Templeton's hand against the hard-packed snow as he tried to force him to release the Stone. The two men wrestled – Magician and demon – as the Beams of Light drew near. Templeton managed to spit out another spell, flinging Sebastian through the air, his arms and legs flailing as he soared. He crashed to the ground, landing on his hands and knees, but leapt back to his feet in an instant. He charged, his left hand lifting and slamming down on Templeton's chest like a claw. Templeton didn't fall, but the blow rocked him.

More Beams of Light split open and filled the compound with their noise. The cruel sound tore into my eardrums.

Sebastian resorted to brute strength and delivered a series of punches to Templeton, nailing him in the face, chest, and stomach with lightning speed. Templeton, hindered by the need to hold onto the Crimson Stone, blocked the hits as he was able. He caught Sebastian by his jacket collar, violently twisting his body and throwing the demon to the ground. But Sebastian held onto Templeton, pulling him down with him. As Templeton thudded into the earth, the Stone, bright and pulsing, flipped out of his grip, striking the ground and bouncing.

I lifted my hand and called it to me without a second thought. *"Veni ad me!"* The Crimson Stone whizzed through the air and nestled in my palm like it had come home.

The Stone vibrated in my hand, its flames dancing wildly inside the gemstone. I held it with both hands, pulling it to my chest and cradling it. The fire magic pouring out of it and entering my body felt so good. It made my witchline sing.

The Beams of Light hovered on the edge of the quad, but when I brought the Stone to me, they shifted as one and glided purposefully in my direction. Perhaps they were drawn to the magical interaction.

"*Ignis defendat me,*" I chanted, pointing my right index finger, drawing a line of white-blue fire between us and the Beams. "*Fumus abscondere me.*" The flames rose fast and high. The second part of my spell took effect when the fire extinguished just as quickly, causing a thick batch of gray smoke to fill the quad. The smoke might allow us to somewhat see the Beams of Light, but hopefully they wouldn't be able to find us. I put the Stone to my lips. "*Sileo.*" Be still.

The flames inside the Stone disappeared immediately, its throbbing slowing, no longer matching the rhythm of the pulsing in the air around us.

The Beams ceased making their terrible noise at once. I pulled my sweatshirt up over my mouth and nose, stealing as swiftly as I could over the snowy ground. I searched for Templeton. I had no idea where Sebastian was either, but I could no longer hear the two men grunting and driving their fists into one another. My breath came in rapid pants as I cautiously hurried through the smoke. My mind raced ahead of me, and I wondered where Rabbit had disappeared to. Why didn't he follow me when he could? What if he didn't make it out of the warehouse? A sharp sob broke through my lips. What if he ended up like the other two Rabbits?

I had to find Templeton. We had to get to a warehouse and hide. Then I would text Rabbit. But what if Rabbit didn't answer? And if I couldn't find Templeton, I'd have to find Rabbit on my own. My body shook as my thoughts wildly bounced around my brain. *One step at a time*, I told myself. *Breathe.*

And then a Beam of Light was inches in front of me – its abrupt appearance catching me off guard, its high-pitched whine causing me to recoil. I threw up an arm, crying out as it let loose a branch of light from its column and touched my cheek. It was hot, a solar flare, the burning bright white of purity. I couldn't move as the pain consumed my body. I opened my mouth, but no sound came out.

Without warning, Sebastian crashed into me, rattling my teeth and breaking the Beam's control over me. I fell, crawling backward like a crab on my hands and feet, my ass dragging through the snow. I clutched the Stone in my hand. Sebastian spun around, standing between the terrifying Beam and me. He roared at the Beam of Light. His bellowing shook the ground under us.

The Beam responded by wrapping a slender tendril of light around his neck, lifting him higher and higher off the ground. His red eyes bugged out and rolled while his legs jerked. He choked, grasping at the bright noose strangling him, his mouth opening in a silent cry. I watched him dangle helplessly, his feet kicking... finding no purchase.

Rising from the ground, I lifted the Stone in both hands. *"Tenebris in lucem!"* I raged at the Beam of Light.

Darkness over light!

The Stone let loose with a brilliant flash and the Beam of Light shrieked, releasing its hold on Sebastian, dropping him to the ground and retreating into the dense smoke. Sebastian turned onto his side, coughing and gagging.

Blood trickled from a corner of his mouth and the scent of burning flesh assaulted my nose. He pushed himself up, his head hanging as he rested.

I drew back into a wall of smoke, watching his figure disappear as the gray built a screen between us. Turning, I sought the edge of the quad, leaving Sebastian behind.

Chapter 24

I risked sending out a wisp of my energy, seeking Templeton. A breath later, his magic connected with mine, drawing me to him.

He was battered. Sebastian had landed a fair number of punches and his nose was bleeding. His lower lip was swollen, and blood leaked out of his mouth and down his chin. There were cuts on his face. Like mine, his eyes leaked tears from the smoke.

We didn't speak. I shoved the Crimson Stone deep down inside the front pocket of my jeans before letting Templeton take my hand. We worked through the dense air to one side of the quad where it was easier to see. Hurrying along the wall of one of the warehouses, we found an unlocked door and stumbled inside.

"I lost Rabbit," I whispered, frantically digging into my jacket pocket for my phone. I texted

Rabbit, begging him to answer me. "His men were killed, and we were split up somehow. I don't know where he is!"

Templeton said nothing but kept a wary watch on the door. All the color was gone from his eyes, leaving only pinpricks for pupils in pure white. His breathing was labored.

I stared at my phone. "C'mon. C'mon, Rabbit." No response. "He's not answering me. We were in the first warehouse. We've got to go back!" My voice rose.

Templeton grabbed my arm and shook me hard. "Be quiet!"

I wriggled free. "We've got to find him!"

"*I* will go find him – after I get you the hell out of here," he wheezed.

Templeton was raising his door travel energy. I could see it. He was going to take me through the door behind me. "No! I'm not leaving him. You didn't see what they –"

Templeton's face was a mask of concentration. His familiar energy enveloped me and he reached out again. "I need to protect you."

"I'm not leaving Rabbit!" I ducked away from his grasp.

"Lucie!"

I threw the door open, wrenching myself from the waves of energy enabling his door travel and charged back outside into the smoky air, leaving Templeton to chase after me.

I had no idea where I was going, but with Templeton near, I took more risks. I reached out to Rabbit much like I would if I were sitting in my reading room and wanted to get a sense of a Tarot client's state of mind. I swept the compound in my mind's eye, trying to get a bead on my friend.

Templeton and I slowed before approaching the other side of the quad. We were near the first warehouse with Rabbit's slaughtered men inside.

"Careful," warned Templeton's voice from my right. "I can see your energy. The Beams might be drawn to it."

"This way." I motioned to a door leading into the warehouse. Once back inside, I turned slowly in a circle, getting my bearings. I pointed. "Back there. That's where we found Rabbit's men. They were torn apart, Templeton. Something – those Beams of Light – they ripped their bodies open." I turned my head, fighting the urge to heave. I doubted there was anything left in my stomach, but I wasn't going to risk it.

"Lucie, listen to me." Templeton's eyes scanned the space around us. "Whatever those light beings are, we are not prepared to fight them. The only thing we can do right now is leave."

"You would leave Rabbit? He means that little to you after everything he has done for me – for us? I can't believe you! You are the most selfish man I've ever met," I spat out.

Templeton's eyes were silver in the bleak warehouse. "My priority is you. Rabbit's priority is you. I will come back for him after I take you someplace safe. I have no intention of leaving him behind."

I refused to listen, choosing instead to go through the warehouse. "You have a choice," I told him. "You can help me find him or you can leave."

"I'm not leaving you."

"Then help me, dammit!" I set off down a row of heavy equipment. As desperately as I wanted to find Rabbit, I was scared I'd find something terrible. If he didn't get away... *Oh, god.*

We moved as covertly as possible. The Crimson Stone stayed quiet in my pocket. As we neared the back of the warehouse where the dead men lay, I hesitated. Bowing my head, I lifted a hand and motioned toward the shaft of light at the end of the row. "Can you go look?"

He guided me to the side, pressing on my shoulders so I'd sit on the bottom step leading up into a forklift. "Stay here."

I watched as he edged the rest of the way down the row and disappeared around the corner. My chest hurt from the hammering my heart was giving it. I checked my phone. Still nothing from Rabbit.

I knew it was only a minute or two, but it felt like Templeton was gone for much longer. When he returned, his mouth was pulled into a grim line. I feared what he would tell me.

"Rabbit isn't there with his men," he told me, holding out his hand. It was Rabbit's phone.

"Oh, fucking god." My fingers shook as I took the device from him. "Where?"

"On the floor. Near the scene, but not in it." Templeton tilted his head back, staring into the fading light above. The smoke from the quad had blocked what spare daylight was able to dribble into the warehouse through the filthy windows. "It's possible he dropped it and is looking for you in another building."

"So we go." I started to stand.

"Please." Templeton leaned his back against the forklift. I looked up. His eyes were closed and he rested his head against the wall of the cab. "Give me a minute."

I startled. Templeton never revealed weakness, but I could hear the strain in his voice. "Okay. I'm sorry."

He didn't reply and I sat back down, my hand shaking as I held Rabbit's phone. I shoved it into my pocket with the one he'd given me.

"Why were you with Sebastian?" Templeton's voice drifted down to me.

I lifted my chin and examined his face. His eyes remained shut. I wrapped my arms around myself. "He was in the warehouse. The Beams came in – I mean, I didn't see them, but it sounded like them. He called them 'beautiful beasts' and he told me we had to get away. And then we ran. We ended up on the quad and you were there."

"Do you love him?" The question was asked so softly I struggled to hear his words.

"I... No." I worried my lower lip, picturing Sebastian. "But I'm sorry for what he's become. I'm sorry for what we did to him even though he was not a good man. It's my fault he's a demon. I opened the sixth door."

"You still care about him." Templeton's chest heaved and he coughed unexpectedly. Fresh blood appeared on his lip.

"Yes." My voice was hushed. "I do." I hoisted myself to my feet. My body was exhausted, and I didn't know how much more I could take. I stood in front of Templeton, lifting my hands and placing them on the sides of his face. His eyelids slid open a fraction, the silvery-white barely visible through his black eyelashes. "But the person I want in my life is right here with me now." I stroked his jawline with my fingertip. "We just need to figure some things out when this is all over."

He gave a tiny nod, his hands wrapping around my wrists. He pulled my hands away from his face and hesitated when he saw the gash on my finger. "You're hurt."

"I cut my finger. I'm fine."

Templeton bent closer, squinting into my face. "You have a burn on your cheek."

"One of the Beams touched me. It was like having a hot poker pressing into my skin. I was paralyzed," I said. "Sebastian ended up fighting with the Beam and I got away."

"I see." Templeton released my wrists. I stepped back.

"The Beams of Light seem to move slowly. If we can avoid them, I think we'll have a chance. Let's find Rabbit and get out of here." I wiped a hand over my mouth. "I feel like he's not in this building."

"I don't think he is either," Templeton replied. He rolled his head back and forth on his neck and I was struck by how much the gesture reminded me of Rabbit.

"Alright, let's try the other warehouses. We'll find him. We have to. Then you can door travel us both out of here, right? Even if you have to take us one at a time, you can door travel with him, right?" I realized I'd unconsciously put my hand back into his.

"I can take him with me, but I will get you out of here first, you understand that?" Templeton squeezed my hand, allowing me to lead him through the shadowy rows.

"As long as you promise to take him too, that's fine." I pulled him behind me. We stopped at the door and listened. "I don't hear anything. You don't suppose they gave up and left?"

The look Templeton gave me was worth it. "Head for the second warehouse. It's the one I door traveled into. It's set up much like this building. If we don't see the Beams, I might have time to cast a finding spell over the compound."

"I can try to seek out his signature energy again," I replied. "But I'm not used to doing it over a long distance. The Stone might help."

"Use it as a last resort," Templeton directed. "The fifth and sixth doors are open."

"About that," I began. "Sebastian said the 'beautiful beasts' – the Beams – opened the fifth door. I'm not sure about the sixth door."

"I assume Sebastian had something to do with it."

"Maybe, he didn't say." My hand touched the pocket where the Crimson Stone was buried. "Why is the Stone awake? Did you manage to wake it?"

"It woke up on its own as soon as I arrived in the warehouse. The three pieces of the Stone have remained united since last year. The minute I door traveled into the compound, the Stone lit up." Templeton frowned. "I assume it's because it's connected to the doors."

"It automatically activated when Emily and I

saw the fifth door for the first time," I remembered. "That has to be it. But I'm not taking time to close the doors while Rabbit is missing and we have light monsters invading the compound."

"Or Sebastian roaming freely," Templeton said evenly.

"Right." I raised a shoulder. "Rabbit's the most important thing right now." I opened the door and we eased outside. The smoke was clearing; we'd have little cover.

Templeton motioned to the right and we headed for the next warehouse.

The Beams of Light were nowhere to be seen.

We found something much worse.

A massive dog-like beast raced across the quad chasing Sebastian. A second one rounded the corner of one of the warehouses, following the first. Sebastian's demon speed was the only thing saving him from being caught.

"What the hell?" I sputtered, stopping short. Templeton pulled me back into him and we pressed against the warehouse hoping we wouldn't be noticed. Terrified, I watched the scene unfold.

The monsters were like German Shepherds

on steroids. I'd never seen canines of this size. Enormous heads sat on muscular bodies covered with heavy, black fur. It was matted into hard bands lining their backs. They had to be at least six feet tall from the top of their heads to the ground they ran across. Their paws slammed into the snow as they charged after the demon. Sharp, blade-like claws protruded out of each one. Their jaws were wide, lips pulled back revealing sets of spiky teeth. Tall, pointed ears shot out of the top of their thick skulls. They were tailless and the putrid stench of the animals – a mix of old urine and wet fur – carried to our noses. Blood covered their faces and fur.

Most horrifying, though, were the empty eye sockets. Black holes tracked Sebastian as he fled.

The two caught up with him in the middle of the quad. Lips pulled back to reveal mouthfuls of jagged teeth, they herded him toward the spot where the fifth and sixth doors appeared.

"What are they?" I choked out. My hand floundered behind me to connect with Templeton.

"I don't know," he answered. His arm snaked around my shoulders, hugging me to him. "Don't move."

I sensed it before I saw it. The fear coursing through my body made my bones feel like liquid. I turned my head slowly to the left.

A third monster-dog had rounded the corner. In its mouth, a bloody Rabbit hung by an arm.

My Rabbit.

The beast dropped him to the ground where he crumpled in a sickening thump. The vicious animal growled, hunkering down and readying to pounce.

"No!" I screamed, ripping free of Templeton, my hand plunging into my jeans pocket and drawing the Crimson Stone out. I thrust my hand into the air and rose all the energy I could summon. I let the terror of what I witnessed flood my senses until I gagged. This time I cried out to my witchline for help instead of sacrificing my energy to feed it. I drew upon my witchline like I was starving.

The raw power flooding into me was overwhelming, and I stumbled headlong toward the gruesome scene. I was barely aware of Templeton hollering behind me. I felt a wave of his energy cascade over me. His first instinct was to protect me. *Always.* His spell wrapped around my body.

I pitched forward, gripping the Crimson Stone and pouring all my energy into it. I counted on Templeton's magic to keep me on my feet.

The explosion blasting out of my body was enormous, the crack in the air echoing across the compound. The sonic wave of fire blowing out from my core roared over the creature. It yelped as the power tore through its hulking form, knocking it backward. The beast twisted as it caught fire, scrambling to its legs and sprinting toward the center of the quad. Its mates forgot Sebastian, choosing instead to join in with a chorus of howls before diving into the wide tear in the ground and disappearing through the sixth door.

"Rabbit!" I shouted, running toward the unconscious man. His clothing, his face, his limp curly hair – everything was covered in blood. His eyes were shut. I didn't know where to start. My hands grazed over him, unsure of what to touch. "Rabbit! Rabbit wake up!"

Around us, shrieking filled the air.

The magic I'd performed attracted the Beams of Light.

They moved faster now, perhaps excited by the powerful blast of fire magic I wielded with the Stone. There had to be at least two dozen of them.

The Crimson Stone began to match the pulsing thundering in the air around us. My head swung back and forth, dizzied by the display. The Beams pulsed with the same rhythm.

Templeton's energy pulled away from me and he redirected it toward the Beams of Light. I saw the Beams shudder as he pushed it through them. I knew he was drawing on his extensive knowledge of magic, but as he told me in the warehouse, we were not prepared to fight them.

Reluctantly, I left Rabbit. It had to be the Crimson Stone drawing them in. I held it up in the air. I ran away from Rabbit and Templeton, heading for the middle of the quad.

Sebastian was engaged in his own hasty dance with several Beams. He managed to stay away from their dangerous tendrils, but he was running out of options.

"Sebastian!" I yelled. "How do we make them leave?"

His eyes darted back and forth searching for me. Sebastian's mouth hung open. His tangled hair was soaked with sweat – it dripped off his face. "They want the light, Lucie. They think it's theirs." He crouched, then jumped across the cavernous sixth door, dodging a Beam. His gaze strayed to the Crimson Stone.

"I don't know what that means!" I cried. Again, I drew from the well of energy inside me. I would pour it into the Stone. Maybe... Maybe a ball of fire. I was grasping at ideas. I'd throw a ball of light through the fifth door. I crouched, gripping the Stone with both hands. I flooded it with my energy.

I let the power build until the fire rolling over my skin centered on the energy growing in my hands. The ball of light I created was nothing like I'd ever produced. It spun faster, flames turning from orange and red to a blinding, white light. I stood, raising the ball above my head, extending my arms to the sky. Still clinging to the Crimson Stone, I balanced the glowing sphere in my hands. Fire coasted over my skin.

Around me, the Beams moved as one. Yes, they were coming for the light – *my light!* My body swayed with the force vibrating between my hands. "A little closer," I mumbled. I felt my hair starting to float around me. I could smell the acrid scent of something burning in the air.

I couldn't see how many Beams had crowded around me, but I needed to let go of the light. My eyes found the fifth door, the seven-foot-tall rectangle of light jutting up from the ground and towering over the sixth door. I arched my back, then thrust the blazing ball forward, the white-hot globe hurtling through the opening of the fifth door.

Around me, screeching from the Beams of Light rang out at painful decibels. Sebastian huddled on the ground by the sixth door rocking back and forth, his hands over his ears. He was screaming, too – the wailing pouring from his mouth unlike anything I'd ever heard.

Beams of Light zipped by me at amazing speeds. I dropped to my knees, covering my head as they passed. Each brush against me sent a violent shock through my body and into my spine. My body bucked like an abused marionette. When the pain stopped, I lifted my head, my attention landing on Sebastian.

He was no longer making that unearthly sound. Instead, he stared unblinking past me into the air above, his reddish eyes wide.

I turned.

In the air, Templeton's body convulsed, tendrils of the light wrapped around his torso. More strands streamed from the Beam of Light holding him, wrapping around his wrists and ankles, pulling his limbs back and forcing his body to arch like a human bow. His mouth was wide, light pouring out of it. I couldn't make out his eyes. Light burst out of each socket.

Weak lines of blue energy bled from his hands, dissipating before it hit the ground.

The Beam drained him of his power, of his life.

I climbed to my feet, lifting the Stone. "You can't do this!"

The Crimson Stone pulsed fiercely in my hand and I struck out at the Beam of Light, sending what was left of my energy against it.

But the Beam simply absorbed what I threw at it. In response to my attack, it lashed out with a thick coil from its column of light, striking me so hard I was blown back, falling and skidding across the ground. My hand smacked against the snow-covered surface, and I let go of the Crimson Stone.

Instantly, I rolled onto my hands and knees, crawling and chasing after it as it bounced toward the sixth door. The Stone smacked into one of the jagged rocks that pierced the earth's crust when the door to the Below was opened. The Stone broke into its three individual pieces, the light draining immediately from the gemstones.

I lunged forward, grasping the pieces and fumbling with the clasps used to hook them together. The fire inside the Crimson Stone was completely gone.

The Beam of Light holding Templeton prisoner passed over me. Templeton's limp body swung in the air. Light ravished his body. I could no longer make out his features.

"No!" Horrified, I watched as the Beam of Light glided by, silently crossing through the fifth door, disappearing with Templeton into the Above. "Oh, god, no!"

The fifth door pulsed, a blinding flash filling the quad before the door shimmered, a pearlescent shadow hanging in the air. It shrunk toward its own center. The rectangle gave one last hard pulse before dwindling to the size of a postage stamp and disappearing.

The relentless pulsing stopped.

The door to the Above had closed.

The anguish ripping through my body was unbearable. With shaking hands, I tried to reunite the pieces. "I can reopen it," I said aloud, my voice trembling. "I can do this. I can do it. I can put it back together."

But I didn't know the spell to reunite the three pieces to form the Crimson Stone. Templeton never revealed it.

The three pieces remained dull gemstones in my hand.

Sebastian watched my desperate attempts to reunite the pieces, his face no longer contorted in anger.

I burst into tears, covering my face with my arm. I sobbed into the crook of my elbow, gasping. Minutes passed before I raised my head.

I lifted my hand, the useless pieces now dormant. "I can't fix the Stone, Sebastian. I can't open the door when it's in pieces."

We stared at each other across the gaping hole in the ground.

"It doesn't matter. He's gone now." Sebastian's shoulders twitched.

"I won't let them have him!" I shouted.

Sebastian ran a hand over his head, fisting a lock of hair and pulling. His body shuddered. "I have to go. Time's running out. He'll send the dogs again."

I desperately looked around the dreary quad. Rabbit remained motionless on the ground. Horror bubbled up in my chest. "I need to get help."

Sebastian shook his head rapidly from side to side, a whimper escaping his lips. "I have to go. I can't stay." His eyes shot open, the red haze permeating them darkening. He stood, reaching out a hand over the sixth door, his palm up, his fingers stretching. His voice grew desperate. "Please come with me, Lucie. Please. I won't let anything hurt you down there."

I shook my head, momentarily dropping my gaze to the portal's opening at my feet. Faint echoes of *'Light-Light-Light'* floated up from the gash in the frozen earth. The stench leaking from the ground was unlike anything I knew. It was sickening – like standing in a room full of rotten meat. The smell stuck in the back of my throat.

Sebastian touched the air where the fifth door once stood. He peered down into the gaping hole of the sixth door, his chest swelling before a shuddering sigh escaped. He raised his head suddenly, his expression echoing the face of the man I'd fallen for not long ago.

"At least where they took him, there's light," he said quietly. Sebastian waved his hand over the sixth door. Even though I couldn't see it, I realized he was raising his own door travel energy. But I *could* sense it. The vibrations weren't the controlled door travel I'd come to know with Templeton, but Sebastian's were also strong.

"It's so dark down there." Sebastian's glassy eyes met mine. He touched the burn across his throat, his Adam's apple moving under his skin. His door travel energy connected with the portal at his feet. It caught him and pulled him through the sixth door, taking him silently into the Below. Seconds later the ground shook, heaving upward before flattening, groaning as it sealed the gap.

Both doors were now closed to me.

∞∞∞

Sitting on the ground, I cradled Rabbit's head in my arms. I pulled back an eyelid. His eye was a solid black with a whitish film covering it.

The dogs had mauled him. Blood leaked through slashes in his coat, and both legs were positioned at odd angles. I tried to wipe away the red oozing from his mouth with a glove.

I put my lips to the top of his head, kissing the wet curls. "Don't you leave me, too," I begged, my tears falling into the bloody mop of hair. "I need you."

With shaking hands, I used Rabbit's limp index finger to open his phone. Once past this layer of protection, I found the app connecting to the Rabbit network.

I texted:

It's Lucie. In Walled Zone. Fringe's compound. Attacked. Rabbit's dying. Please, someone help us.

I set the phone on the ground and lowered my body onto the snowy, blood-spattered muck next to Rabbit. I wrapped my arms around him, pulling him to me and raising the heat that lived in my body, trying to keep him warm.

As I held my dying friend, I stared out over the quad where the fifth and sixth doors no longer appeared. No sign of the portals remained.

And Templeton… The knight to my light…

He was gone.

Chapter 25

It was nearly two hours before a contingent of Rabbits swarmed the deserted compound. By then it was dusk and the air was freezing. My body shook with the cold while I kept pouring my remaining heat into Rabbit. I didn't dare attempt a spell. I was afraid I wouldn't be able to keep a steady stream of warmth going. He was still unconscious. I was on the edge of delirium. I'd spent the entire time talking to Rabbit, promising him he'd be okay.

The Rabbits who came to our rescue were not the men and women I knew to be part of Rabbit's crew. These Rabbits fought alongside us in the battle against the Fringe last fall. They were a hard, unsmiling lot. My sense was they resented helping a witch, but their loyalty to their own kind brought them to our aid.

They took Rabbit from me, rolling him onto a

board and covering him with blankets. When I tried to follow, one of the men pulled me back. I would be riding in a different van, he told me. Big Rabbit was coming from Matar and would meet us at a halfway point. My protests were met with stoic faces. They took Rabbit's phone from me.

But I kept the network phone Rabbit had given to me hidden in my jeans pocket.

No one answered my questions when I asked about Rabbit, if he was going to be okay. The van door shut behind me and I wrapped myself in a dirty blanket, sitting on the floor. Two Rabbits sat across from me texting. Occasionally they'd look up and scowl, but they wouldn't speak to me. I bore the silent ride, tears slipping down my dirty face, my heart howling in pain.

After passing me into a grim Big Rabbit's capable hands, we made the rest of the journey back to Matar in yet another van. My RAV4 would be picked up by some of his crew, Big Rabbit said. They would drive it back to the city for me.

During the last leg of the drive home, Big Rabbit explained to me that Rabbit was being taken to a cluster – a colony of Rabbits – and they would try to save him. But it was bad; his injuries were extensive. A non-Rabbit wouldn't have withstood such abuse at the jaws and claws of the dog-like monsters. Rabbit's biology was the only thing giving him a chance to survive. But I knew he was already weakened before he was attacked. I pressed Big Rabbit for answers and he admitted he knew Rabbit was sick. But he refused to tell me what was wrong.

Once home, Big Rabbit helped me up to my front door and inside the house. My legs failed in the entryway and he caught me, carrying me upstairs in his burly arms. In the bathroom, he stripped off my filthy clothes and put me in a hot shower.

I was only half-aware of the apologies and promises spilling from his lips saying that he wasn't looking at me. He put my hands on the wall and directed the water over my head. His tenderness brought on another wave of tears. While he waited, his back to me, I stood in the shower, my face lifted against the water. I rubbed my hands over my body and rinsed off the blood that had soaked through my clothing. The dark red swirled down the drain at my feet.

Rabbit's blood.

I was numb. The shock of what happened in

the compound was too much for me to bear.

Rabbit might die.

And Templeton was gone.

Oh, he was gone!

The thought stole the breath from my chest and I passed out in my bathtub, falling into the shower curtain. Big Rabbit caught me as I crashed.

When I awoke in my bed an hour later, Emily Swift sat at my side, her face blotchy from crying, her hand clutching mine. Big Rabbit sat in the chair, his tangle of loose curls quivering as he told her the little he knew about the hell I'd lived through. He told her Rabbit was in a bad way, and Templeton had been pulled through one of the doors and was probably dead.

At those words, I snatched my hand from Emily's, rolling over and burying my face into my pillow. I bawled until I was hoarse, Emily rubbing my back through the blankets and promising me it would be okay.

∞∞∞

The next few weeks were a blur. Emily stayed with me for the first three days, cooking meals I wouldn't eat and running quick errands by door traveling in and out of my home.

I'd told her about the Beams of Light and how they took Templeton through the fifth door. I sobbed as I described his suspended body, riddled with light, hanging in the air. I showed her the Crimson Stone. Together we tried to rejoin the pieces and bring the Stone to life, but we had no success. Without the Stone, I could not open the fifth door.

Emily, never one to wait for anyone and always willing to help, door traveled into the compound to see what she could find. The Salesman had some magical ability of her own and she'd used the Crimson Stone in the past. I handed the three pieces over to her, begging her to be careful and to return at the first sign of trouble. Then I sat quaking in my kitchen until she returned, her head hanging. The doors had not reappeared and the three pieces of the Crimson Stone remained silent even when she stood in the middle of the quad.

We studied the book of fairy tales, looking for a clue, but found nothing.

I reread what the colorful bird told the little girl about the Above:

"... It is a hard space for other creatures to endure. Most do not stay. Some get trapped," the bird finished.

"What happens when they get trapped?" asked the girl.

"They disappear into the bright white of the Above. They cease to be."

The passage tore me apart.

∞∞∞

Big Rabbit returned to tell us Rabbit was alive, but he was not out of the woods. He was in and out of consciousness. When he was awake, hallucinations came to him. Once he was convinced the monster dogs were in the room and had to be tied down while he screamed in terror, begging the others to help him.

Big Rabbit wouldn't tell us where Rabbit was being held. Locations of clusters were private. He promised to let us know if anything changed. I reluctantly showed him the network phone Rabbit had given to me. He took it, removing my connection to Rabbit and programming in a direct line to his own phone. Then he handed it back.

He told me not to tell anyone.

∞∞∞

At the end of the third day, my friend Anne Lace arrived. She traveled by train and Emily brought her from the station to my home. Anne, being Templeton's aunt, had come into the Empire to meet with her sister. She had the miserable job of telling the woman her son was missing. I thought I should join her, but Anne said it would be better if she went alone. Gavina Templeton was not known for her convivial personality during the best of times. Although Gavina knew her son well, and how no one could make him do something he did not want to do, Anne feared she'd blame me for the loss of her only child.

I understood.

I blamed myself for not being able to save Templeton. If I hadn't turned my back on him. If I hadn't been focused on Rabbit. If I hadn't dropped the Stone. If I hadn't been so weak.

If...if... if...

Anne also brought me a bracelet to wear on my left wrist. She told me it had been given to her during a bad time when she lost someone dear to her.

It was a silver charm bracelet. When I looked more closely, I saw the small charms consisted of a two-handled jar, a fly, a skull, a split heart, a headstone, and a top hat. Something tiny was carved on the top of the hat charm.

Hope.

I asked Anne to explain. It was Pandora's box, she told me. But this time, hope had been let out of the jar.

She told me there was hope.

Anne was not a natural witch, but she followed a path focusing on herbal magic. She brought me healing salve for the burn on my cheek. Over time the scar would fade. For now, it was a reminder of what I'd lost every time I looked into the mirror.

Anne was also familiar with the magical community in Matar. She knew about Templeton's powers – although I suspected she did not know he was a Magician. The three of us – Anne, Emily, and myself – discussed the problem with the Crimson Stone. Anne suggested we search

Templeton's private collection of books for the spell he used to unite the pieces.

The day after Emily returned to Kincaid, Anne and I drove out to Templeton's country home. Emily had visited there once before and described the extravagance I'd find. Still, I was not prepared for the lavish surroundings as I stepped inside the estate house. Anne simply shrugged. Templeton's grandfather had been extremely wealthy. Everything had been passed on to Templeton. His mother lived elsewhere.

At the estate I met Mr. Archie. He oversaw the day-to-day care of Templeton's estate and knew much more about me than I knew about him. The older man, dressed impeccably in a gray suit, brought us tea in a sunny sitting room. His face was pinched and I knew he expected bad news.

In the quiet room, I told him everything. I sensed his deep love for Templeton, and I didn't hold back. He deserved to know. When I'd finished, we sat without speaking as the reality of what had happened sunk in. Eventually Mr. Archie reached over and took both of my hands in his. He told me Templeton would not leave me unprotected for long, and I should not give up hope.

Unprotected.

He knew about the prophecy.

I couldn't speak around the lump in my throat. Anne took the lead, explaining the situation with the Crimson Stone. She asked for permission to access Templeton's private collection of books. We needed to find the spell that would reunite the three pieces. Then, if the Crimson Stone would not automatically awaken, we believed I could cast the counter spell to the one I'd used to put it asleep last fall. From there we could open the fifth door. We hoped.

It was a big ask even though the situation called for it. It was Templeton's most personal sanctuary we asked to enter.

Mr. Archie spent a moment warring with the need to keep Templeton's books on magic private and the chance that maybe, just maybe, we could find a way to reunite the pieces. Finally, he nodded. Rising, he led us through the large manor house to a wing locked behind a thick, wooden door. At the end of a long hall, we entered a room filled with floor-to-ceiling bookcases lining its walls. A standing desk stood in the middle of the room. Cupboards were built into one wall. Inside, I found labeled bottles with liquids and powders, as well as roots, bark, and minerals. A sound system was behind another door. I called up the last music played and the room was filled with avant-garde jazz.

What amazed me the most was how bright and cheery it was in the room. Flourishing green plants were tucked into corners and skylights above let in the natural light.

I caught a hint of Templeton's woodsy scent as I explored. I trailed my fingers over the spines of hundreds of books filling the shelves.

Mr. Archie left us to our search. I paused at the standing desk, my fingertips tracing over the paper sitting on its surface. Templeton's sweeping handwriting filled the sheet with notes. I skimmed it, smiling wistfully.

They were notes on how to strengthen the wards at my townhouse.

As I stood at the desk, I let a slip of my energy float out into the room. Within seconds, I felt a corresponding tug. The essence of Templeton's magic hung in the air and it pulled my attention to a thick book sitting on one of the shelves. The spine was blank. I removed it gently, opening the leather-bound book. Templeton's handwriting appeared on the pages. It was one of his personal books of spells.

Mr. Archie gave me his blessing and I took the book with me when I left. I'd promised I'd return it if it didn't yield the help we needed. Anne and I looked through it while still in Templeton's private library, but we hadn't found anything explicitly referring to uniting the Crimson Stone. Still, I would spend time with the book. Some of the language was ancient, and I'd need to find a resource to translate it.

Holding Templeton's treasure to my chest, I allowed myself to feel hopeful.

∞∞∞

Two days after visiting Templeton's estate home, I gave my name to the concierge in the building where Templeton's penthouse was located. After stepping from the elevator, I entered the code to gain access to his city home.

Inside, it was painfully quiet.

I walked to the living room first, browsing his bookshelves but found nothing to help me fix the Stone. Instead, I allowed myself the simple pleasure of reading the titles of the books he kept there. Each shelf focused on a different genre or topic: history, theology, jazz, science fiction, a selection of the classics, poetry, and thrillers.

I paused by the piano, lifting the fallboard and playing a note. The tone cut the silence in the empty penthouse, but it made me sad.

Next, I checked the tidy office he kept. I found nothing out of the ordinary.

I continued my search, ending in his master bedroom. The books on his nightstand were more fiction. My gaze swept across the bed and I brushed my fingers over his pillow. I resisted the urge to take it with me when I left.

But I did steal a bar of his birchwood-scented soap.

∞∞∞

Two weeks following the horror I'd survived, I pulled out the personal deck of Tarot cards Niccolò had created for me.

I flipped the cards face up and sought The Tower.

Sliding the vile image from the pile, I carried it to my kitchen sink. There, holding the card over the stainless-steel basin, I snapped my fingers and watched it catch fire. I held the card by a corner until the flames neared my fingertips, then I dropped it into the sink.

I opened the window to let out the burning stench.

∞∞∞

Four weeks passed since the nightmare on the quad. Big Rabbit stopped by to report that Rabbit was slowly on the mend. He wasn't talking, though, and he slept a lot. I asked Big Rabbit to tell him I missed him terribly.

Whenever I stood on my stoop, whether coming or going, I turned and looked toward the corner where the camera Rabbit had once hacked was located. I always waved. I didn't know if he ever saw me – or if the camera still delivered a screenshot of my front stoop whenever there was movement – but I hoped the images made it to him. My heart was even more empty without my Rabbit.

Years ago, a friend of mine lost the person she loved after a long illness. She said the worst part came in the weeks following the funeral because everyone eventually went home.

That's when the loneliness hit.

That's when she felt truly alone.

Weeks later after losing Templeton and Rabbit, I was starting to better understand what she meant.

∞∞∞

I let myself think about Sebastian, too.

I let myself grieve losing him. I allowed myself to think about the good times I had with him when I still knew him as Basha. I remembered the lovable parts of the cocky-but-charming man: The playful lover who made my skin glow when I wasn't looking, the one who teased me and pulled me out of the shell I'd built around myself after spending a long year suffering under Guillaume.

I still struggled to understand how he could be the Sebastian who led the Fringe – who was responsible for many deaths, who had done despicable things, who had pretended to be something he was not and used me to get to people I loved. I couldn't reconcile how he could be those two men. I couldn't understand how I didn't see the truth when we were together.

But I could sense the battle raging inside him. There was a sickness there. He was unhinged before he landed in the Below last fall. But he didn't die there like we'd assumed. No, somehow he was transformed into a new kind of monster. And his brain had been filled with horrors I didn't want to imagine. When I looked into those once confident eyes, I saw unbearable pain and fear. I saw confusion. The heart he broke inside me months ago has been broken again – but this time it breaks *for him,* not because *of him.*

I hadn't seen Sebastian since he begged me to go with him into the Below. I assumed he was still on the other side of the sixth door. Someone or something was keeping him there. I thought about what he'd said when crouching beside the ripped ground: *He'll send the dogs again.*

His words made my skin crawl.

I couldn't handle a repeat of what had happened. I didn't want him to return to me, but I didn't want him to keep suffering in the Below either.

Like the saying goes, it's complicated.

A part of me is grateful to him. He tried to help

me after Guillaume conjured him during the demonstration, and he certainly saved me from the Beam of Light, putting himself in harm's way.

Sebastian – *Basha* – continues to live in a secret part of my heart.

But I don't want to open it and feel the pain all over again.

∞∞∞

Loren visited to give me an update. He was happy to report that Guillaume returned to France, albeit reluctantly. My former teacher was furious at the Congress of Empire Witches for not forcing me to go with him for 'more training.' Apparently, my unknown friend in the elders advised Guillaume to discontinue all contact with his 'former student.' We'll see if Guillaume obeys. I'm not holding my breath.

However, Guillaume would be kept busy over the next few months with a new pupil. A prominent family requested permission for their only child – a son – to study with Guillaume to strengthen his witchline. They negotiated a short training period as a test.

Seems like no one was willing to commit to the year of hell I lived through at the end of his hands.

The Congress of Empire Witches now realizes Sebastian was the demon sneaking through the building on the night of the Witches Gala. Guillaume denied conjuring him during the event – which was the truth, of course. There is a part of me, though, that wonders why Sebastian chose to take such a risk. I have a troubling suspicion I wasn't the only reason why he was in the building that night, but I have put my concern aside. *For now.*

I couldn't tell Loren about what had happened in the Walled Zone. The fifth and sixth doors needed to be kept secret – this I still believed. But I did tell Loren there was a battle and that we lost. I told him Templeton was gone.

I managed not to cry, keeping my head high.

Loren saw right through me.

He told me the John Templeton he knew was uniquely powerful. He said I should never underestimate him.

∞∞∞

Seven weeks after Rabbit was hurt and Templeton was taken from me, Big Rabbit knocked on my door. He carried a sizable cardboard box held together with duct tape. He wore a huge smile and announced he had a special present for me.

He set the box down on the kitchen floor. I heard the meow before I saw the occupant.

A scrawny, orange cat popped out of the box. A mackerel tabby, his fur was striped with a small amount of white and he bore the classic 'M' pattern on his forehead. He turned, yowling at Big Rabbit before stalking over to me on four tall legs. He threaded himself around my ankles, a deep purr filling the air while he wrapped a lengthy tail around my calf. He rose on his hind legs, balancing himself with one white paw on my knee while another long-toed paw reached up toward me. He meowed, a set of gorgeous amber eyes sparkling as he worked his feline charm.

Big Rabbit ignored my protests of how I didn't have the energy to take on the responsibility of a cat. Big Rabbit said I was full of nonsense. This 'little fella' had been hanging out near a building where a crew of Rabbits were working in downtown Matar. Big Rabbit was planning on adopting him, but his girlfriend said no more. He already had five cats.

Besides, the 'little fella' needed love, he argued. As he squatted down by the skinny kitty to scratch the top of his head, Big Rabbit looked up and told me I had plenty of love to give.

Sometimes you have to jumpstart your heart again, he said.

I bit my lip and nodded.

∞∞∞

Nine weeks after I lost two men who meant so very much to me, I stood in the kitchen cutting up cold chicken for Flame, my naughty orange tabby cat. He meowed impatiently from the floor, thwapping me with his whip-like tail.

"The honeymoon is over, huh?" I asked, glancing down.

He thwapped my calf again. His coat was glossy and beautiful after a consistently healthy diet and a warm place to sleep. He'd bitched at me with murrs and meows when I was reluctant to let him out into my back yard. Eventually I caved. He'd disappear over my fence, but he always returned. I added a spell to my ward to alert me when he was at the door so he didn't have to wait outside in poor weather.

Behind me, the pantry door opened and I felt a touch of door travel energy float into the kitchen. Without thinking, I spun around, my foolish heart leaping hopefully in my chest.

Emily saw my face and instantly realized what happened. "Oh, Lucie. I'm sorry. I was going to send a message first, but I forgot."

"No. No, it's fine," I said breathlessly, waving the knife. We both looked at it and I set it down on the counter. Refocusing, I placed the plate of diced chicken on the floor next to Flame.

"Well, who is this handsome boy?" Emily asked, kneeling and running her hand over his back. Flame lifted his head and spared a sniff in Emily's direction, a headbutt to her hand, and a polite meow.

He went back to his dinner.

"This is Flame. See the reddish shape on the top of his head over the 'M'? It looks like a mini tongue of fire, doesn't it?" I explained. "Big Rabbit decided I needed a cat."

"Oh, my god. Did you know what a cat lady he is?" Emily laughed, standing. "Rabbit brought him by my house once and he almost turned himself inside out for my three furballs."

"Yeah, apparently his cat addiction hasn't gone over well with his girlfriend. Flame is now a part of the Bellerose household," I said.

"He's a lucky guy," Emily replied.

Flame gave us a butt flicker.

"I think that was intentional," Emily frowned.

"Trust me, it was. He's got an attitude," I told her.

"Cattitude," Emily corrected.

"Not that I'm unhappy to see you," I said. "But what brings you by?"

"The official invitation!" Emily announced. She pulled out a wedding invitation from the inside of her shoulder bag. "I stuck in the details of your hotel reservation and the rehearsal dinner."

I studied the envelope. My name was written in beautiful calligraphy. For a second I was reminded of Templeton's handwriting.

Emily must have caught something in my expression. "And, you never know. You might be bringing a date. He could be back by then."

Recently Emily began to talk about Templeton as if he were away on an extended journey. It made my heart twist. I wondered if this habit was a leftover defense mechanism from when she lost her Salesman father – *Templeton's mentor* – so many years ago.

"I mean, I was going to send an invitation to his house, but I wasn't sure of his address, you know? And I figured he'd just come with you anyway and..." She stopped abruptly, blinking rapidly and looking around my kitchen. "He'll be back by then. I know he will. He's Templeton."

I nodded. Flame rescued me by meowing loudly from the floor. I picked him up. Straightening, I supported his feet with my left hand and cradled him with my right arm. He rested a front paw on my breast, his claws extending and retracting. He rubbed the top of his head against my jaw.

Emily regained her composure. She pointed with her chin. "He's feeling you up."

I grinned. "He's a perv."

Flame purred happily.

I was reluctant to bring up Rabbit, but I knew he was supposed to escort Emily down the aisle and I hoped he'd be at the wedding. I desperately wanted to see him. We hadn't had any contact since the horror in the compound. "Have you heard from Rabbit? He's still walking you down the aisle, right?"

Emily shook her head. Her shoulders hopped up and down once. "I don't know. I haven't heard one word from him. But Big Rabbit is good about keeping in touch. He was kind of embarrassed, but he asked if he could walk me down the aisle if Rabbit wasn't well enough."

"You said yes?"

"I did. Big Rabbit and his girlfriend are coming to the wedding anyway. I'd be honored to have him escort me," she said.

"Rabbits. What would we do without them?" I asked softly.

Emily held my gaze for a minute. "Indeed." She put her top hat on her head. "Okay, I'd better get back home."

I set Flame down and we hugged. "I'll keep you posted," I told her. I didn't need to explain.

"He'll come back. Or we'll pry the door open and go get him." She put her hand on the pantry doorknob and started to raise her door travel energy. I couldn't see it, but I could feel it. "Easy peasy."

"Easy peasy." My smile was tight.

Emily winked and door traveled out of my kitchen through the former Pantry Express. I dropped my eyes to Flame. He was staring at the pantry door intently. "And that, my dear kitty, is the legendary Emily Swift. Falls ass-over-tincup into trouble at the drop of a top hat and still puts a nail into the coffin of the Fringe. And no one even knows the Fringe collapsed because of everything she'd risked." My shoulders sagged. "We all risked so much."

I left Flame to his chicken and retrieved Templeton's book of magic from the royal blue scarf I kept it wrapped in. I was still searching for a spell to reunite the pieces of the Crimson Stone, or even several spells I could stitch together and use. Much of the book was penned in an archaic language. I knew it would take me a long time to decipher it. Without access to the library at the Congress of Empire Witches, my progress was slow.

In my living room, I didn't bother to light the fireplace insert. The weather was turning warmer. The snow had melted. The world outside was coming back to life after a hard winter.

I curled up on the couch and opened Templeton's book. I traced his handwriting with my fingertip. Oh, how I missed him.

I missed the damn infuriating man who set me on fire, who made my skin glow.

I missed my knight.

Reaching inside my shirt, I pulled out the necklace I wore against my heart. I'd put the three pieces of the Crimson Stone on a thick silver chain. It was my way of watching over the Stone and keeping Templeton close to me. I ran my fingers over the gemstones.

"Someday I'll figure out how to put you back together," I whispered. "Then I'll wake you up. We'll open the fifth door. Then we'll go get him."

Flame stalked into the living room. He sat and spent a moment licking his paw and rubbing it over his face. He froze, mid-swipe. His beautiful cat eyes blinked once as he peered up at me. In a flash, he'd jumped up on the sofa and put his front paws on my thigh. I lowered my head and he bopped my forehead with his.

I scratched under his chin with my fingernails. "What do you think, buddy? Want to help me figure out how to get this damn thing working again?"

Flame meowed and lifted his right paw. His claws flexed in the air and he gently patted my cheek. He lowered his furry foot, tapping one of the pieces of the Crimson Stone with a pointed nail.

A tongue of fire appeared.

Startled, I leapt from the couch, dumping Flame from my lap and grabbing at the gemstones hanging from my necklace.

Flame hopped to the floor.

The other two pieces of the Crimson Stone lit up and began to hum. The three pieces started talking to one another, pulsing and eventually finding the same rhythm.

I gaped at Flame. He sat in the middle of my living room.

"How?" I breathed. "Flame, what have you done?"

Flame stood again on his four legs, spinning sweetly in a compact circle. Dumbfounded, I watched as the orange tabby cat's body twisted and his muscles rippled under the fur. He grew, raising up gracefully, shapeshifting from a handsome feline into a very pretty man with tousled strawberry-blond hair and striking amber eyes.

His tan body was lean, without an ounce of fat. His muscles flexed gently under his human skin. He rolled his shoulders, giving his young body a shake.

And he was naked. Completely and utterly naked.

His hands rested on his narrow hips, his fingers stretching like a cat flexing its claws. My eyes shot up to his upturned, almond-shaped ones.

Flame smiled broadly, white teeth gleaming behind a set of perfectly pink lips. He tossed his head proudly.

"Hello, Lucie."

Go to the Epilogue...

Epilogue

Sebastian paced back and forth in the dingy room, gritting his teeth as he balled his hands into fists. He whipped around, searching for something to destroy. Spying a cracked vase on the mantel, he grabbed it, throwing it across the room into the filthy wall where it shattered. The noise echoed through the dilapidated mansion.

"You sent the fucking dogs!" he screamed at his murky surroundings, his eyes automatically looking up toward the rotting ceiling. "The. Fucking. Dogs!" He kicked uselessly at a thin shadow as it raced by. He could hear it calling for the Light.

They never stopped calling. It drove him crazy. *Crazier.*

He froze, clenching and unclenching his fists before putting them against his temples. "I told you, she wouldn't come! I couldn't make her.

She wouldn't listen to me!"

Sebastian dropped his hands. His chest rose and fell as he stared unblinking into the blackness beyond the derelict room. "I did not fail. I didn't have enough time to convince her to come with me. You said she had to want to come. What the fuck did you expect me to do?"

His body spasmed as if an electrical current zipped through him. He stumbled over the ripped carpet.

"I said, I didn't have enough time!" He regained his footing, warily peering into his dismal surroundings. He hated the dark. Hated it.

Was afraid of it.

"Who's there?" Sebastian hissed, stalking through the room he once knew as his mother's parlor. "I know you're there."

A shape moved through the inkiness along the edge of the room.

"You." Sebastian's eyes glowed red. "I see you."

The shadow grew and swayed along a wall. Sebastian covered his ears and rocked back and forth, his eyes screwed shut.

"I don't give a fuck about the Beasties!" the demon roared suddenly, his eyes now wide and afraid. "Tell *him* I'm not staying here. We have a deal. If he wants me to keep my end, I can't stay in the Below. I *won't* stay."

Sebastian spun and left the lone Dancing Shadow behind. Outside the abandoned mansion, a disturbing replica of his family's confiscated estate house, he crept along the path leading away from the decrepit building he called his home in the Below. He was sneaking away to the portal door connecting directly to the Above.

The thin shadows, companions whether he wanted them or not, skated over the ground beside him. "Light-Light-Light!" they chanted.

"Yeah. Fucking light, light, light," Sebastian muttered. After a short hike, he stood in front of the sealed door. It was missing a door handle and made of a solid metal unfamiliar to anything he'd known before being thrown into this bleak world.

But he knew exactly where this door went. It led straight into the Above.

If he were able to get this door open, not only could he escape, he'd let the 'beautiful beasts' – the Beams of Light – into the Below.

Sebastian laughed, the sound bouncing through the vast blackness. And then there'd be real chaos in this lonely world. The Darkness could have all the light it wanted.

The Beams would wipe everything out. Everything in the Below would cease to be.

He let out a trembling breath. *"Everything,"* he murmured. "Everything would be gone."

Sebastian's voice caught in his throat and he bowed his head. His mind quieted when he closed his eyes. At this point he'd be willing to cease to be rather than spend eternity in such blackness. He missed sunshine. He missed light.

A shudder ran through his body and his eyes popped open. A thin shadow crawled up his leg. He gave it a shake and the shadow slipped off his body, disappearing into the gloom.

Sebastian swiped his tongue over his teeth, pausing and sucking thoughtfully. No, he couldn't give in that easily. He wouldn't quit. Who did they think they were fucking with anyway?

He had a witch he could make glow. She glowed for him. *For him.*

He'd make her understand. She just needed to bring her special light to the Below. That's what the Darkness wanted. That's all Sebastian agreed to do.

Then his end of the bargain would be fulfilled. He wouldn't have to live alone in the Below anymore, among the disintegrating walls of his old home with the stench of decay permeating the air.

And he wouldn't let anything hurt her while she was here. He'd take her with him when he left. He never agreed to leave her behind. He wouldn't abandon her in this wretched world like she'd left him – *was made to leave him.*

No, he wouldn't do that to Lucie.

He saw it in her bright blue eyes when she looked at him. She still cared.

And he heard what she yelled when she saved him from the Beam. The language she'd used might've been magic, but he'd understood the words.

Darkness over light.

It was the proof he needed to convince his jailer to let him go after Lucie again. She was willing to call upon the Darkness.

Sebastian's head rolled to the side. He squinted. The stupid Dancing Shadow had followed him, standing in the inky fog pervading the Below. He sneered at it.

"Go tell Asmodeus I'm not staying down here.

It's not over. I know I can convince her to come with me. Tell the Darkness if he lets me go, I'll get the Light to come back to the Below."

Coming in 2022!
Crossing the Witchline, by T.L. Brown

∞∞∞

Acknowledgements

My deepest thanks, as always, goes to my amazing alpha reader and husband, Gordon. What would I have done without you reading Lucie's story over and over, acting out difficult scenes, and talking for hours about character behavior? What would I do without your endless patience, love, and enthusiasm for my stories? Thank you for being *my patron*.

Another heartfelt thanks to Jill Elizabeth Arent Franclemont. Your willingness to jump from the crazy slapstick of Emily Swift into Lucie Bellerose's darker tale was very much appreciated. Thank you, my friend, for the beta reading, the feedback, the many Zoom meetings, and the support!

To authors and friends Jennifer Brasington-Crowley and Saffron Amatti: I'm such a big fan of both of you and your books. And you know how much I respect your experience and writing wisdom. Thank you for saying *'yes!'* when I asked if you would beta/ARC read for me. Thank you for the countless Instagram DMs and idea bouncing. Thank you for believing in me when I had doubts. *And thank you for putting up with shirtless men.* ☺

To my beautiful friends in the Instagram writing community: You are truly the best. Here's to great success for all of us!

And to my readers: YOU are making my dreams come true when you buy and read my books. As an independent, self-published author, reaching new audiences relies a lot on word-of-mouth. To those who tell others about my books, thank you. It means so much. *To those who take the time to review my book on Amazon and Goodreads – thank you, thank you, thank you!*

Find the Author Online

Website and Updates

Visit WriterTracyBrown.com to learn more about her books and to connect with the author in all of her social media channels.

Sign-up for the T.L. Brown Newsletter (sent randomly and occasionally).

Social Media

Instagram: @WriterTracyBrown

T.L. Brown on Goodreads:
www.Goodreads.com/TLBrown

Facebook.com/WriterTracyBrown

Other Books by the Author

The **Door to Door Paranormal Mystery Series** is a set of exciting, fast-paced mysteries by author T.L. Brown.

Door to Door (Book One)

Two worlds collide when Emily Swift turns 30 and her late father's journal lands on her doorstep...

Seventeen years after Emily Swift's father died, a door is opened to a new world, an Empire led by peculiar men and women called Salesmen – transporters of magical items. These Salesmen have the unique ability to travel from place to place, and even world to world, simply by stepping through the 'right' door.

Now that Emily is 30 it turns out that she can 'door travel' too, stumbling unplanned into kitchens, bathrooms, and alleyways as her connection to the Salesman Empire is revealed. Fueled by the cryptic notes and sketches in her father's journal, Emily discovers the real reason behind his death: he was targeted and assassinated by the Fringe, a terrorist group of rogue Salesmen.

After an attack that leaves an innocent woman dead, a rare book containing clues to the whereabouts of the Crimson Stone is missing. Emily is charged with getting it back. As she races through the Empire, she pursues John Templeton, the mysterious Salesman with extraordinary abilities, who seems to both help and undermine Emily at whim.

Join Emily in a fast-paced race to keep powerful magic out of violent, fanatical hands.

Through the Door (Book Two)

"The characters are like old friends, and the action-packed climax will have you on the edge of your seat. There's also a cliffhanger that'll have you desperate to read the last book in the series!"

- Saffron Amatti, author of the Lucas Rathbone Mysteries

"T.L. Brown's sequel to Door to Door, is a brilliant continuation of the Door to Door Mystery series. Magic, mayhem, complex characters, and an engaging storyline... *Through the Door* was unputdownable!"
- Shari T. Mitchell, author of the Marnie Reilly Mysteries

Relationships tested, friendships built, secrets revealed, sacrifices made...

Salesman Emily Swift is back – *and so is Templeton!* After learning about her supernatural abilities and finding the Crimson Stone, 30-year-old Emily Swift returns home to Kincaid to rebuild a normal life with her boyfriend. As she struggles to get a handle on her 'door traveling' energy, a strange warning squawks from her car radio: a rogue, terrorist group called the Fringe is still watching her.

Before she can figure out if the message is from a friend or foe, Emily's quirky mother, Lydia, goes missing – and resurfaces in the Empire! As Lydia travels from city to city in this peculiar world, a wake of chaos is created. Add the murder of a hated art critic and a kidnapping into the mix, and things go from bad to worse. The Fringe believes Emily knows where the magical Crimson Stone is hidden, and they'll stop at nothing to get their hands on it.

Friends Tara and Rabbit join Emily as they race against the Fringe to catch up with Emily's wandering mother. Will Emily's nemesis, the mysterious Templeton, join her in rescuing Lydia? What will it cost her? Is the price too high?

Doors Wide Open (Book 3)

"Brown is at her best in this high-stakes, fast-paced thriller starring the magical, mystical door traveling Salesman, Emily, her favorite nemesis Templeton, and my favorite woodland creature, Rabbit. Add in a sinister foe and an evil high priestess, not to mention a witch and book nerd…and you are in for a whirlwind adventure that keeps going until the last page is turned."
- Jennifer Brasington-Crowley, author of the Raven Song Series and the Stillwaters Series

"The fast paced, action packed and twisty storyline is the perfect ending to the trilogy. And, while it's challenging to do, Brown also com-

pletes believable and satisfying character arcs for her side characters we've come to know and love such as Tara, Rabbit, Templeton, and Jack."
- Brook Peterson, author of the Jericho Falls Cozy Mystery Series

Emily Swift: Reckless, unruly, unreliable... brave and big-hearted.

My name is Emily Swift and I'm a Salesman – one who's currently *persona non grata* with the Empire's leadership. I'm technically grounded, but I can still travel from place to place simply by stepping through a door. Any door.

I've been told I'm overconfident and take foolish risks. Allegedly, I'm unreliable. I've been accused of fibbing – okay, lying – and holding back the whole story if I think it's for the best. But here's the deal: I'm not the only one who's been less than truthful. I've been lied to, misled, attacked, held captive by a crazy terrorist, and even had to rescue my mother from kidnappers.

The Fringe – a rogue group of violent Salesmen – just murdered a friend and tampered with the North Door. I'm going to do whatever it takes to bring them down, and I'm counting on my friends for help.

I'm even taking a chance on Templeton... *Because this time I'm busting all the doors wide open.*

About the Author

Writer Tracy Brown lives in the beautiful Finger Lakes of New York State dreaming up epic stories and quirky characters who definitely make her life much more interesting. She believes magic still exists; you just need to look in the right places.

Tracy is the author of the Door to Door Paranormal Mystery Series, three books penned under the name T.L. Brown. She released the first book in the Bellerose Witchline Series, *A Thin Witchline Between Love & Hate*, in March 2022. Although this is a standalone dark fantasy series, the first installment picks up the tale following the last book in the Door to Door series (*Doors Wide Open*). Both series share some of Brown's most popular characters.

Tracy's married to one damn amazing man. Together they talk about music for hours, cook up fabulous meals, and raise clever chickens.

Made in the USA
Middletown, DE
18 April 2022